A CRIMSON COVENANT

NIGHTWALKERS OF CONCORD

AIMEE DONNELLAN

Editor: Quinton Li (https://www.quintonli.com/)

Cover artist: Katelyn McNeely (@tacticiankate.bsky.social)

Cover typography: Rachel Bowdler & Quinton Li

Chapter header art: Mawce Hanlin (@mawcehanlin.bsky.social)

Continuity Expert: Ty Donnellan

www.aimeedonnellan.com

ALSO BY AIMEE DONNELLAN

CATASTROPHE INCOMING

(Episodic novella series – fantasy adventure)

OUT NOW

The Chase Begins

The Collection Awakens

The Survivor Stands

The Labyrinth Beckons

COMING SOON

The Spirit Torments

and more!

IMAGE DESCRIPTION OF MAP OF ABORIA, EAST
(FOLLOWING PAGE)

A map showing part of a world, with part of a continent in the centre and northwest of the image. The far west is labelled Izirm, while on the other side of a mountain range the most prominent land mass in the image is labelled Kanin. Within Kanin there is the city of Orsun on the east coast, a place labelled Concord within a mountain valley some ways north, and a town called Ushonk on a road and river line northwest. The road appears to continue north, through a large forest and off the edge of the image, but looks as though it may end up crossing the mountain range into Izirm.

South of the main land mass depicted is a small land bridge area labelled as Skarn, and south of that is a continent edge showing more desert-type land. This is labelled as the Zhikadian Empire.

In the southeast part of the map is a large collection of islands of various size. These are labelled the Eastern Islands.

Beneath the image are some extended names:

- Theocracy of Izirm

- United Clans of Kanin

- City State of Skarn

- Zhikadian Empire

Aboria, East

Theocracy of Izirm
United clans of Kanin
City state of Skarn
Zhikadian Empire

Image Description of Map of Kanin
(Following Page)

A country map depicting a place of grasslands and occasional forest in the centre and south of the country, and a dense forest spanning dozens of miles across the north.

A large city called Orsun sits on the southeast coast, perched on a river that runs alongside a major road labelled the Grand Highway. The Grand Highway travels in a northwest direction and through a town labelled Ushonk, continuing up through a large forest and off the edge of the image.

A smaller road breaks off from the Grand Highway, leading to a series of towns. The central ones are Dressa, Khiz, Ziluuk and Barad. Further north is one called Abzah, and to the east within a circular mountain valley is Concord.

KANIN
ABZAH
ZILUUK
BARAD
USHONK
DRESSA
CONCORD
KHIZ
THE GRAND HIGHWAY
ORSUN

CONTENT WARNINGS

Depictions and descriptions of: violence, religious bigotry & zealotry, blood drinking, explicit scenes of a consensual sexual nature, very light BDSM, and a maimed body part (ear).

Themes of: death and grief, as well depression and anxiety.

Contains frequent coarse language.

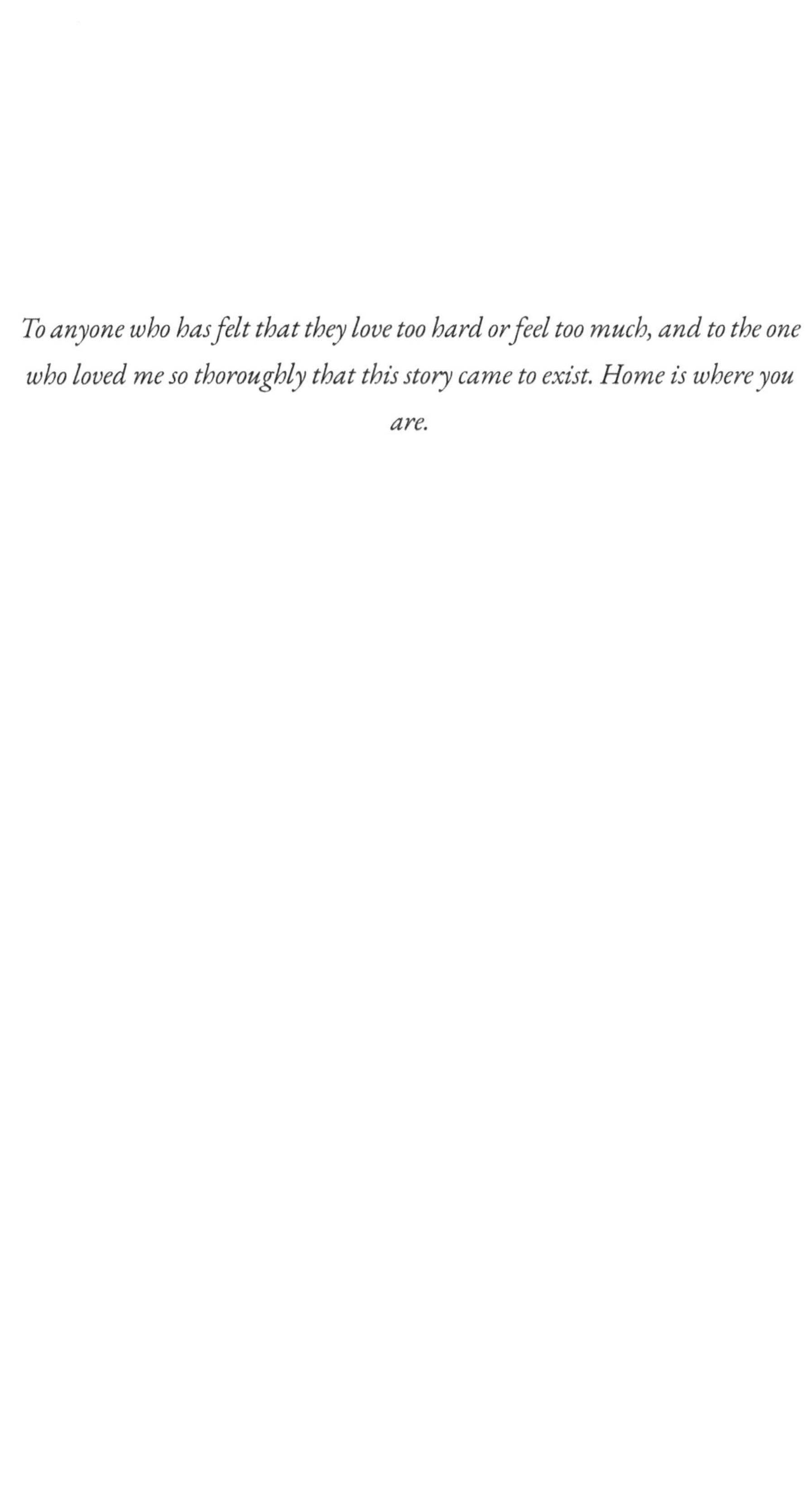

To anyone who has felt that they love too hard or feel too much, and to the one who loved me so thoroughly that this story came to exist. Home is where you are.

762 PF (Post Fall of the old Empire), 148 years after the end of the Dragon War

11th Day of the month of Thaw

CHAPTER 1
ARCHÉ

As the hunters close in, six against two, uncertainty creeps into Arché's heart with an unfamiliar thought. *We might not win this.*

At her side, her partner in arms is laughing. Laughing, like this isn't their fault the two of them are surrounded and backed into a wall.

"At least make it tricky for us!" Rohan shouts.

Arché growls under her breath. Her transformed claws twitch with temptation to smack Rohan instead of their assailants. It's not that they aren't *mostly* justified; fourteen years into their partnership they are a force to be reckoned with, Arché wielding a shield as offense and defense together while Rohan swings a maul with astounding power. But it is only if they don't make reckless decisions.

With a fight to salvage, Arché braces her shield in front of her and charges, knocking the closest hunter to the ground and giving her momentum to swing around and hit one of the others. It's all the opening Rohan needs to come in with their maul gripped in both hands, arcing in a wide circle and forcing everyone back. Their long braids fly around them, their dark eyes shining.

Rohan isn't just a force to be reckoned with. They are a force of nature. She is lucky to even exist in their periphery.

There are cheers from the side of the training yard, where the other lycan-vampire pairs sit watching. The training master quiets them with a wave of his hand.

With her fighting reputation on the line, even if she is the only one counting, Arché lets herself fall into the rhythm she and Rohan have cultivated so well. Back to back, twisting with each other, Arché blocking and Rohan landing punishing blows on the remaining four coming for them.

The hunters are regular lycans with years of experience out in the wild, volunteers interested in the unique challenge of battling the future leaders of the town of Concord. To combat the hunters' superior experience and bridge the gap of being outnumbered, the heir pairings have two advantages: the magical empowerment of the founding house bloodlines, and over a decade of training to be the perfect team.

Arché and Rohan are the only heir pairing with a majority of success, being from the bloodlines with the most combat relevant empowerments. The hunters' experience and higher numbers usually win—perhaps deliberate, to keep the heirs humble.

Rohan's family are physically stronger than all the other vampires, by considerable margin, and Arché's family heals faster than anyone. Hence, Rohan getting cocky tonight. But now, with their head out of their ass, they move together with synchronicity only possible with years of bespoke practice.

Rohan goes low. Arché goes high. The poor hunter tries to dodge both and ends up in the middle, taking the maul to the thigh and shield to the chin. He falls, and the others concede.

Cheers from the sidelines are led by Nikos, heir to the lycan Hunting Clan. Arché wishes he would have more sense than to cheer for her and Rohan over the hunters he'll one day be in charge of, but he beams at Arché without a care in the world.

To avoid betraying any further than the same casual friendship they've always had, Arché gives him only a small nod. No one knows they've been meeting secretly, or why, and it needs to stay that way.

"Alright, alright," the training master says with a shake of his head. "Very good. Let's move on to archery."

Arché and Rohan let out identical groans. They receive no pity, and have to line up with the other four heirs at the targets. Arché isn't awful at archery, but it's humbling to the extreme to be so mediocre at something when she is so gifted at close range fighting.

"Great work over there," Nikos says to Arché, when he ends up next to her.

"Thanks," Arché says without looking at him, as she continues to line up and overthink her shot.

An arrow goes wide, past the target and into the wall behind. Not Arché's arrow, but that of Nikos' partner, Lenora.

The heir to the vampire House of the Arcane, Lenora is of unremarkable height, strawberry hair, and quiet nature. Currently, she is staring at her wayward arrow with a glower that could wither a daisy.

"Whoops," Nikos chuckles, turning back to his partner in an instant. "What happened? Give it another try." He flicks his hand and an image of a smiling flower appears in the centre of the target, a simple illusion courtesy of Nikos' mundane magic. Lenora, despite herself, smiles at the sight of it.

There is something about him, this young man of blonde hair and similarly golden cheer, that can be hard to argue with. Lenora releases a breath and nods before notching another arrow.

Rohan, meanwhile, is missing arrows left and right, prompting Arché to turn her attention back to the pair she ought to be thinking on—her own. It's been getting harder, lately. Her mind would rather be anywhere else.

"So, drinks?" Rohan asks once the training master calls an end to the session, much to their relief.

"Drinks," Arché agrees.

Everyone has their little traditions. The healers, Aleka and Kirsa, heirs to the Hearth Clan and House of Clerics, tend to slip away to the library. Arché and Rohan have their ritual of drinks and peanut throwing competitions in their favourite tavern.

Nikos and Lenora always stay behind, and Arché waves to them in polite farewell as they prepare to continue their sparring alone. Nikos more recently explained that they use the time to work on Lenora's unique magic, which requires trial and error to train with no one able to teach her.

Arché knows little of magic, with only her mundane ability to briefly shape water, but had certainly felt silly for never considering how difficult it might be to receive magic no one else has.

Nikos returns Arché's wave enthusiastically, while Lenora gives a polite nod as she re-ties her ponytail.

Rohan whistles to hurry Arché up and she tries not to let it get under her skin as she follows them onto the street and towards the tavern.

She loves Rohan, as a best friend, as the only partner she has ever known and the best in battle she could hope for. So why, more and more, are they getting under her skin?

It's nothing significant. Nothing major. Nothing Rohan has actually done wrong. But small things they say hit anxieties in her chest in ways they shouldn't, in ways she can't explain without sounding absurd, and the more it happens and the less their jokes amuse her... the more she wants to retreat within herself and share nothing of her deepest feelings or desires.

She cannot shake the tiny part of her that screams: *Is this what I get, forever?*

Three years ago, the only romance Arché has ever attempted went awry. Going to Rohan for advice and comfort was the most natural thing in the world. Now, if she imagines something similar happening again... she hates that she'd likely keep it to herself. Like everything else she keeps locked away in her heart. Like the fears in the late hours of the morning when sleep should be taking her. Like fears of never being enough for the people that need her to be so much.

No one knows. And no one will—because she can't bring herself to admit to such an awful weakness—but confiding in Nikos about the Rohan stuff has let her *almost* hint at it. And then, you know, Rohan will do something wonderful like make her laugh until her belly aches, and she feels like the worst, most ungrateful friend in existence.

The tavern keeper has their table reserved, as always. They drink, and eat their peanuts, and for the thousandth time, Arché wonders what could be wrong with her, that she is nitpicking the best friend anyone could ask for.

They are on their third round of retrieving fallen peanuts from the floor when their names are called from the doorway.

"Arché Kalésen," a gangly teenage messenger calls. "Rohan Folkesen."

"Yes?" Arché asks, wincing at the picture of indignity they currently make. Two future leaders of the town, on their hands and knees on a sticky floor, scrambling for snacks.

"You're needed at the gate."

"What?" Arché asks in the same moment that Rohan asks, "Why?"

"I don't know. They just told me to fetch you, and the others, immediately."

Arché and Rohan glance at each other, then at the barkeep who remains an amused spectator to their antics.

"Go," the old man says. "I can clean up here."

They thank him and hurry off the moment they've grabbed their night packs and weapons. The messenger is already heading off down the street in the other direction, towards the training grounds.

Dawn is cresting, beginning to paint the sky. Rohan's eyes watch it with respectful caution. The vampires of Concord are not undead, like most vampires of the outside world. They are cursed mortals, passing on their vampiric nature to each new generation. Where sunlight burns traditional vampires, for the Concord vampires it is more a source of discomfort and fatigue.

As they walk, Arché nods to some of the daywalkers waking up, such as the bakers with the corner shop who serve Rohan's favourite chocolate twists. The bakers nod back, sharing smiles with Rohan.

Rohan tugs on their dark, braided beard. "What do you think we've been summoned for, anyway?"

"It's either a drill, or something really important."

"It better be, to interrupt our tournament."

Arché stifles a yawn. "Hopefully it's quick. My bed and I need to cuddle."

Rohan grins. "I'll serenade you if we're back late. One of my family lullabies."

Rohan has a singing voice not unlike a drunk, wailing demon. Or whatever Arché imagines such a thing to sound like. Fondness curls in her stomach, alongside worry that she might not be able to turn them down if they try to actually do it.

The front gates of Concord are not far. Perhaps a ten minute walk, if that. And how many times have Arché and Rohan made this walk, at this time of the morning? Countless since they were old enough to drink, with both of their homes being in this direction as well.

Summons aside, everything should feel ordinary. But something does not. The hair on the back of Arché's neck stand up and she finds herself glancing around every familiar street corner, at the faces they pass. Their town is large enough that not *every* person knows each other, but a majority at least.

Is Arché losing her mind, to think she's perhaps recognised two faces out of the last dozen they've passed?

"Rohan," Arché whispers.

"Yeah, I feel it too," they say, without looking at her. "Let's hurry up."

Hopefully their quickened pace looks like a brisk walk of two heirs on important business. Arché wonders if they are simply both tired and in some sort of peanut induced hysteria.

But then two hooded figures step into their path from the alley they're about to pass, cloaked in bright orange, with sun insignia across their robes. Not of Concord. Outsiders.

"Identify yourselves, now," Arché demands, with what she desperately prays is gravitas.

One of them answers by flinging a blade through the air and into her shoulder. It stings so much more than it should—silver, and their companion has conjured fire to their hand. Disbelief floods her body, mixing with adrenaline, and with that, the outsiders' intent is clear.

Rohan charges them with the maul drawn, while Arché howls and draws on the lycan essence within herself, letting her body shift. It's as natural as changing clothes or putting up her hair, but comes with a powerful itch that turns into an exhilarating burst of energy. Claws from her fingers and already bare feet, fur up her neck and arms, longer canine teeth, muscles tensing with new power. Still Arché, but enhanced. Enough wolf in her blood that she can harness some of it without the complete transformation of full moon nights.

Their attackers clearly knew of the nightwalkers' natures, but nature and skill are two worlds apart.

Arché charges the mage with her shield and knocks him to the ground while Rohan slams the maul into the body of the other. Fire blasts up from the ground and Arché keeps the shield positioned to take the brunt of it, though the wood may not last long.

"Why have you come here?" Arché demands. Her voice is a fraction deeper, shifted.

There is only a sneer, and more fire, so Arché knocks the mage out with one swing of the shield to their temple. In the same instance, a kneecap gives out under a maul, and the knife-flinger gets their lights knocked out by Rohan's fist.

It's an odd haze of moments as Arché and Rohan meet eyes and try to process the violence of what just happened. What they trained for, but never expected.

A scream comes from the next street over. Then another, further away, in a different direction. The soundscape of the city is changing from what it ought to be; crashes, smashes, and shouts are rising in every direction. Their home's safety and peace, compromised.

"We have to get to the gate," Rohan says, and Arché hates that they're right, that their summoning and *this* cannot be a coincidence. They'll be of the most use under their parents' direction.

They've barely turned a corner when they see more robed figures, hassling a pair of civilians. The moment they see Arché and Rohan, their attention shifts. It's another warrior and mage pair, and the heirs charge at once. The warrior dashes to meet them, while the mage puts one hand to a small mirror around her neck, the other hand kindling a bright yellow glow before she throws it at Rohan.

The magic strikes Rohan across the face and they scream like nothing Arché has ever heard.

Magical sunlight. Concentrated, designed to hurt. Like the silver, a direct and violent statement of intent.

While the next ball of light is gathered, Arché sidesteps the warrior and dives between Rohan and the magic. The light burns, but nowhere near agony. Arché may rise with the moon, but she has no quarrels with the sun.

"Fall back," Arché tells Rohan. She stands her ground against the warrior while the mage hurls more sunlight and she braces herself through it while Rohan makes a break for the alley behind them.

Arché curls her toes and their claws, waiting for the right moment, and whirls her leg around to slam into the warrior's helmet in a blow that sends them reeling back.

She follows Rohan into the alley, where they have sheathed their maul and begun climbing the side of the dress store to reach the roof.

"Are you alright?!" Arché calls up, as she puts her shield on her back and prepares to follow.

"Will be, just gotta—"

A streak of light shoots past Arché's head and Rohan cries out, losing their foothold and dangling from the roof, a good two storey drop.

A snarl sits in Arché's throat. She reaches for her most primal strength and uses it to propel herself to the roof in one hefty leap. Her clawed hands grab Rohan and hoist them over the edge, their solid frame no challenge at all.

"Thanks," Rohan gasps, and as they lift their head she gets a proper look at the scorched skin on their cheek.

Anger stirs in her chest, unfamiliar and unallowed. It's like an open flame near wine-soaked kindling—the wolf within her raking its claws on dirt waiting to break free. She follows her teachings and takes a deep breath before finding a distraction. In this case, their need to flee.

They race across the rooftops. Arché counts each leap and matches it to the thundering tempo of her heart.

"Who the fuck *are* these people?" Rohan asks as they run.

"I don't know, but—" Magic slams her in the back, absorbed by her breastplate but almost knocking her off balance. "We need to get down, now. Come on, the gate isn't far—"

And yet, her gaze tracks the streets below them and finds no obvious route. She can see too much. Robed figures all over, civilians being driven back into their homes, while anyone armed is battling in the streets.

Is anyone dead? Are... Are our people getting killed down there?

It's too big of an idea to fit. All they can do is scramble down to the junction she's spotted and make a break for it. They know the streets better than their pursuers, and after a couple of minutes, Arché looks behind and cannot see the pair from the roof.

"Good fucking stuff," Rohan says with breathless relief. "That hurt like a *bitch*."

Arché pats them on the shoulder. "I bet. You're doing great. Now—"

A figure steps into their path. Not just a warrior, but an imposition personified, nearly half of Arché's size again in height and weight. Their sword is an intimidating two-hander, glinting in the light of the rising sun.

"Stay behind me," Arché says.

"I thought I was doing great," Rohan says, and their breathing remains as shallow as the joke.

Stand together, says a voice from their training years ago, perhaps her mother. *Your partner is the future, as much as you are.*

Arché charges to meet the new adversary and brings her shield up to block his first blow. The impact sends shockwaves through her arm but she does not crumble. They trade blows, scraping off each other, until the greatsword finds purchase in her shoulder.

It's silver, just like the knives. Her blood races and sings, and her shield slams into her opponent over and over, any part of his body she can reach to try and throw him off. He staggers back, unable to meet her with the same speed.

"Drop the shield," someone from behind her commands.

Arché whirls around and sees Rohan struggling against the grip of another outsider. A dagger presses to their throat.

"I—"

Turning away was a mistake. The greatsword scrapes along the back of her armour and cuts her at her hip, making her cry out.

"I will, if you call him off," Arché says, hand touching her new wound and making herself wince.

The knife-bearer sneers. "Hardly. Our champion chooses his own battles."

Arché has no choice but to spin and meet the champion once more, leaving Rohan to fend for themself. Which, judging by the unfamiliar yelp that follows, is well within the other heir's means.

These enemies have no interest in being fair or reasonable. It's going to take everything Arché and Rohan have to win, but perhaps if they can take out the smaller one and fight the champion together...

"Arché—"

She spins at the sound of her name, at the cadence of which she has never heard before. The last syllable fades early as the knife slides across Rohan's throat and spills red like a waterfall.

CHAPTER 2
ARCHÉ

THE FLOW OF BLOOD feels as though it comes from Arché's own heart, pulling her insides from her and wrenching a howl from deep within her throat. Something shifts in her veins. Losing herself to her instincts would be the greatest possible transgression for a lycan of Concord, but this is the violence of distinctly mortal grief. A piece of her world, snuffed out. How is she supposed to stay in control?

She must. She must stay in control, and she must survive.

Survive, survive, survive. There will be time to grieve later, if she can survive.

Her ear pricks and Arché is able to twist just in time, the champion's greatsword hitting her leg instead of her neck. Her raging heart demands a battle, a chance to make them hurt as she hurts, but she needs to get away, except that would mean leaving Rohan.

She only needs a second. A second to see Rohan, to say goodbye. So she spins, lunges for Rohan's murderer, and throws him right into the champion. The moment he's in the air, she runs for Rohan's side.

Her best friend lies still on the cobbles. The pool of blood around them is such a final and vivid thing that she doesn't even look Rohan in the eyes. They are not there anymore, they will not be, and to see Rohan's eyes without that spark of life would be too much.

Her fingers close around the handle of Rohan's maul as she hears the outsiders coming for her. She whirls, releases, and watches the huge weapon soar right into the knife-wielder's knees. He drops, leaving Arché free to stare the champion in the face.

Cold eyes bore into her through the slit in the helmet, resolute and steady. He's barely taken a hit.

Arché runs. She cannot die, and she cannot win, so retreat is all that remains. She runs and runs, knowing no daywalker can catch her in her transformed state.

They had been headed for the gates, but now Rohan is dead and others are under attack. This is now a catastrophe of the highest order. Which means by town procedure... the cathedral is where everyone will gather.

Where her mother and brother will be, if they—

She shakes herself off that line of thought, before she can be lost to a spiral. Her family will be at the cathedral, safe and sound. They have to be.

Arché doubles back, taking new paths and getting the drop on another group of invaders with a shield charge that knocks them to the ground.

"The cathedral, come on!" she tells the terrified nightwalkers who had been backed into a corner, a pair of vampire blacksmiths by the looks of it. They hurry to follow her.

When she reaches the cathedral square, she stops dead. A sea of orange robes fill the space, surrounding the founder's pillar and blocking the path to the entrance. Her heart falters, stuttering with despair, before she steels herself. None of them have any visible weapons, and she has her shield.

"We're just going to push through," she says to the vampires with her. "Don't stop, just go. One, two, three!"

They run, bracing themselves for anything, but the moment they hit the crowd, it begins to part. The outsiders step back, leaving a clear path, none getting in their way. Relief rushes in to replace Arché's worry as she follows the vampires inside, but there is the lingering question of *Why? Why not attack? Why why why?*

The cathedral is packed with people. Thankfully, it is designed for just such a purpose, a gorgeous, expansive building of high ceilings and the usual eight shrines. The Trickster's ninth is hidden, of course, but Rohan found it years ago and showed Arché. The thought cuts deeper than expected and Arché takes another deep breath.

Steady. One thing at a time. If she is lucky, which may be asking too much at this point, then at the centre of all of this will be—

A tall, muscular woman stands in the middle of the seating aisles, talking to two of the other town leaders. Her dark hair is braided down her back and shaved on the sides, while scars cover her light brown skin where armour does not.

Kalé. Leader of the Warden Clan. Arché's mother.

"Kalé," Arché calls as she approaches the group. The other two are the heads of the Hearth Clan and House of Clerics, Aleka and Kirsa's parents respectively.

Kalé's head whips up and the hardened focus on her lined face shifts into relief. "Arché!"

She pulls Arché into a crushing hug which Arché wants to sink into more than anything, but if she does that, she is not sure she could leave it or stand on her own again. So Arché hugs back carefully, keeping her weight on her own feet.

"We feared the worst," Kalé says, voice soft.

"Andreas, is he—"

"He's here, and safe. Mira too."

"What is *happening*?"

Kalé pulls away and there is that shift again, from mother to Warden Commander. "They came to the gates first—Ulrich, can you fix her up, while I fill her in? Those damned silver weapons, look at you..." She shakes her head, focusing herself as the leader of the House of Clerics begins a prayer which sends warm healing magic along Arché's worst wounds. "They asked for a parley under their strange, unknown banner. Folke went to meet them." *Rohan's father.* "It... was a trick. They attacked at first opportunity, and clearly they already had people inside."

"Why? Do we know *why?*" Arché asks, and she hates how her voice catches in her throat.

"Not yet." Kalé's sharp, dark eyes travel over Arché again. "Where's Rohan?"

"They didn't make it," Arché says. Perhaps it is too blunt, or too hollow, or too something else altogether. But she has no gift for manipulating words away from truth, and they come out as they do.

Kalé's eyes flash with grief, double-edged as mother and commander. The prayer in Arché's ears finishes and immediately turns into a pained curse. The other leaders hurry to leave them alone, moving away to help other wounded.

Kalé swallows. "Arché, I'm so—"

"What can we do?" Arché interrupts. "What needs to be done? They're killing people out there. We can't stay in here forever. Can we win?"

"This is completely unprecedented," Kalé says. "The ferocity of the attacks, the mystery of their intent... and for the life of me I can't determine why they're letting us into the cathedral. Do they think they can burn it?

They'll never be able to get a fire inside we can't put out. But I... have a bad feeling. I think we're going to need help, from the outside."

"The outside?" Arché asks, incredulously. "No one even knows we exist, why would they—"

"Someone out there does."

Arché blinks. "Right. Alta." Her other parent, an energetic arcane researcher unsuited for town living who instead drops in for visits between ventures. "I don't think Alta alone can save us."

Kale stares at her for several moments, something dawning on her face unlike anything Arche has ever seen. "*Oh.*" A hand runs down her face, and her body shudders. When the hand falls, her mother's eyes are far away. "No, of course Alta can't, alone. But if a few heirs can escape—you need to get to Lenora and Nikos. Get out of here together. Then we'd have some hope."

Leave home? Now, of all times, when her people are in such a crisis? To go into the world of the daywalkers, where Arché has never been and would have to disguise her nature? Her first instinct is to scream *no*, to let her resistance to change get the better of her. But it's the only thing that makes sense, even if it is such a tremendous idea it barely fits in her head. They are outnumbered and on the backfoot. Their weaknesses have been anticipated and targeted with malice. Comfort is the last thing that matters.

"I—yeah. Of course." Arche runs the details of everything over in her head. "So Kirsa and Aleka will stay here to help the wounded?"

Kale nods. "Lenora and Nikos are unaccounted for."

"They'll be at the training yards—or at least, they would have been, when the attack started," Arche says, wincing at the uncertainty of their current location.

Lenora and Nikos will be an odd pair to be around on her own. But competency wise? A mage of questionable ability who always seems to be carting around a violin to the point of impracticality, and an incredibly proficient hunter. It's certainly better than nothing.

"I'll find them, wherever they are now," Arché promises. "Do you have a map of where Alta was headed?"

"I do, but I have something else I want to give you, too." Kalé reaches for the shield on her back and holds it out in the space between them.

The artefact of their house, dubbed Crescent Light, is forged of powerful, pale steel. It creates the perfect image of an almost half moon, and when activated a magical sheen fills in the rest of the space to create a full circle. Arché has seen it in action in the training yards, and has always known she is destined to inherit it, but imagining herself wielding it had brought up so many unpleasant anxieties that she'd stopped doing so. The artefacts are powerful enough that they cannot be wielded to their full power by just anyone. Crescent Light will only activate for the Warden clan's bloodline.

The metal reflects Arché's startled face, all wide eyes and tight jaw, as Kalé passes it over. At least her twisting stomach remains invisible.

"This should help," her mother says. "You're more than capable."

Words that would usually have Arché overjoyed, words which could have beaten back some of her worst worries on an ordinary day. But today? With everything riding on her shoulders, their people dying around them, and the future more uncertain than it has ever been?

Arché is in danger of losing a large quantity of peanuts and ale in an undignified manner.

"I—" Arché swallows her nausea as best she can. "Yeah. This will help." Once she can get her head around it. "I should go. Nikos and Lenora, we have no idea how much time they have, if they're okay…"

"She's the chosen Shadow, our attackers won't be prepared for that," Kalé reminds her.

"Right," Arché says, trying not to sound too dubious.

The reason Lenora is the only one with her magic is because it only crops up once every few generations, the Innate magic of pure shadow. But for someone supposedly *that* singular, Lenora has certainly never displayed any astounding feats of magic in front of Arché. But then, what would Arché know? Nikos hadn't been forthcoming on specifics about their private sessions. Arché would love to be utterly ignorant and incorrect on this point.

Arché hugs her mother goodbye and prays to any god who might listen that they will see each other again.

"They might be letting people in, but they're not letting anyone leave," Kalé tells her, as she leads Arché by hand towards a side section of the cathedral.

On the way, Arché spies a blacksmith she knows well who tentatively smiles at her from across the room. A friend with certain benefits, and sadly not one she has time to speak to. Meanwhile, Kale is scribbling on a page from the notebook she carries in her pocket at all times, harsh lines and odd curves and scrawled words.

"This door is small enough I don't think they've noticed it," Kalé says as they reach it. "I'll go out and distract them at the front."

"Alright," Arché says. "Be careful."

Kalé nods and pulls the top page from her notebook. "This is a rough map of where we sit in relation to the rest of Kanin, and the name of where Alta was headed. It'll help you reach the closest daywalker towns, where hopefully you can get a better map. It's the best I can give you for now."

While no genuine artist, Kale has succeeded in drawing a crude map that at least *seems* simple enough to follow. It's bizarre, knowing they reside within a country that has no idea they exist, in turn knowing so little about the rest of it. The United Clans of Kanin, not quite as united as they could be.

"Good luck," Kalé says, with one last fierce grip of Arché's arm, before she turns and heads for the front of the building.

Arché knows she must go, but there is someone else missing, someone she first needs to find—

"Arché!" Her brother Andreas, at seventeen, is already taller than she, but not by much. He runs to her and seizes her in a fierce hug. "Thank the gods."

He stops short as he pulls away, eyes fixed on the shield. A hand runs through his chin length hair.

"Where are you going with that?" he asks.

"I'm going to get Nikos and Lenora and we're going to get help from the outside," Arché says. His eyes light with idealistic fire, and she cups his face of irregular stubble with one hand. "So you need to hold the fort for me here, alright?"

Andreas exhales and glances back to his own partner, a familiar girl with cornrows who gives Arché a small wave. "Yeah, we've got this, don't we, Mira?"

Mira grins, her white teeth pointed and glistening. "Of course."

They are everything Arché had always wished she and Rohan could be, flourishing before her right as her own feelings of camaraderie had begun their slow withering. She has never held it against them, but it stings more than ever now.

Arché hugs Andreas with one arm and leaves the other open for Mira, beckoning her in, and she embraces them both, nuzzling Andreas on the side of his head and then Mira on her cheek.

"Look after each other," she tries to say, but she nearly chokes on the words and her chest well and truly feels as though it may collapse. She hides her face in Andreas' shoulder and takes a deep breath to try and get herself under control. "Don't do anything foolish."

"Not promising that," Andreas says immediately.

"Urgh." Arché releases him and swats his arm, forcing out a strange sort of laugh to trick her body into smiling. "See you... later."

It is impossible to say how much later. Weeks, certainly, if she is successful in her escape with the others. They've never been apart so long in her life. But they will endure.

Arché turns towards the side door before any other emotions spill from her. She has her hand on the brass handle, about to push, when Andreas speaks again from behind her.

"Wait, where's Rohan?"

Arché closes her eyes for a moment, her heart hammering against her ribs, her stomach about to wage a war. She prays he may forgive her one day, as he receives only the door closing behind her for an answer.

Now outside the cathedral, it is only moments before Kalé's voice can be heard from the front. It resonates with her natural charisma but is boosted by mundane magic so it echoes through the whole square.

"I demand an explanation for this attack. Who are you?"

Arché treads as lightly as possible, using the trees in the cathedral graveyard as the most sparse cover imaginable.

Another voice booms back from the intruders. Its volume must also be magical because the masculine tone is too soft otherwise. It turns Arché's blood to ice.

"I am the Prophet. And I do not believe you are in a position to make demands," it says, calm and confident. "Let us show her where things stand."

Arché presses on, but cannot resist looking back to find the owner of the voice and what he's talking about. There is movement in the crowd of outsiders, but they block her view. Arché climbs a roof at the back of the square while they are distracted so that she can see.

A figure with a high-collar and large staff watches as two outsiders dump something on the cathedral steps. It's too far to be able to see properly, but the blood-red armour, the artefact of the House of Sentinels, means there is only one person it could be.

Folke. Rohan's father. Unmoving. Burned beyond regular recognition.

Kalé stands resolute, and watches as two struggling prisoners are also brought next to the outsider's leader. From this distance, Arché can only recognise them from the picture they make as a pair, and by the unique spear on one of their backs. The artefact of the House of the Hunt.

Nikos' mothers. Alive, but in the hands of the enemy.

"I suggest you go back indoors, for now," the Prophet says to Kalé. "Unless you wish to turn yourself over."

Kalé growls, but otherwise says nothing, and turns her back on him to reenter the cathedral. Arché watches her mother vanish and also takes her leave, launching herself across the rooftops at top speed.

Concord is in chaos. Perhaps she is more noticeable up high but she cannot bring herself to walk the streets when the streets are now bathed in blood and bad memories. Their home was supposed to be safe. Protected. But how could they ever have prepared for something so intricately planned, so targeted? These people have known everything they needed to. There is less fighting now, less civilians, meaning either people are in their homes, at the cathedral or... well.

Closer to the training yards, Arché climbs down so as to disguise her destination for anyone who might have spied her from nearby streets.

There is no one in sight for now, letting her slip into the right street and make for the yards.

It's too quiet, and the entrance hall's door is ajar. When Arché steps inside, she nearly trips on a wide-eyed body she recognises like a gut punch—the archery instructor. Not someone she knew well, but a figure from almost every day of her life, if only in the background.

Who is this Prophet and his people? Who could do this, and why?

Further in, the wrecked reception holds several bodies from both sides, and Arché cannot bring herself to look at them. She moves through the doors and into the yards themselves, where she finds—

A huge dome of shadow. Darkness that defies the rising sun slowly spilling into the yard. And on its periphery, bodies. All robed in orange, without signs of what killed them. Arché kneels, checks for a pulse on the closest, and finds nothing.

No sign of Nikos and Lenora, except...

Lenora. The chosen of Shadow.

"Lenora?" Arché calls. "Are you... is that you?"

The dome flickers, then turns to wisps and dissipates, revealing two figures at its centre. Lenora, kneeling, her strawberry hair hanging over her face and her grey eyes shining through the gaps, shining with tears. Her hands are clenched in the shirt of the other figure, lying in front of her on the ground.

Nikos. The only one Arché had come anywhere near confiding in.

Nikos, now still, his shirt stained with crimson, his eyes staring up at the sky where he can no longer see the fading moon.

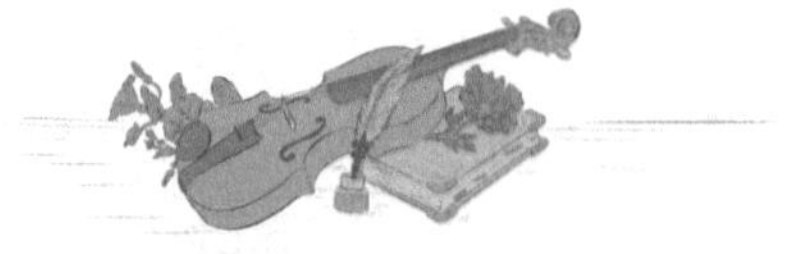

CHAPTER 3
LENORA

One hour earlier

Good practice is its own reward. Or at least, that's what Lenora's mother insists almost every day. At this point, Lenora has a complicated relationship with the word *practice*, because it has been used to describe continuous attempts to grasp a form of magic that will simply never be *hers*.

What a joke, to be the heir to the House of the Arcane, magic users who study the intricacies of magic from books and rituals and meticulous detail—and to be born the chosen of Shadow. To have magic running through her veins, ready to burst from her.

It doesn't feel special. It feels like a burden. But Innate magic is not something to be ignored, and so they train. Every day, after practice with the other heirs, she and Nikos train. And, finally, she is starting to get control over its intangible nature.

Heir training is over and the others are leaving. Arché and Rohan's laughter echoes loudly as they talk shit about something pertaining to peanuts, both insisting they are going to thrash the other. The healers both congratulate Lenora and Nikos on another good night's work and head off.

The scrutiny of others has Lenora hesitant to use her magic in the open, for fear of being even more of a letdown as a Shadow mage than as the Arcane heir, since she was never good at the latter before the shadow magic manifested. Around Nikos, at least, she is able to experiment in peace.

Lenora reaches for the shadow in the air around them, melding it with the essence within her and shaping it over her arm into a claw that covers her right hand. It is tangible, with some extra weight to it like a gauntlet, and she practices swiping it through the air.

"That was faster than last time," Nikos says, grinning at her. "Well done."

The smile is enough to make Lenora's heart flutter in her chest. It's moments like this where everything threatens to spill out of her, the *I love you* and *why don't you see?* But she keeps it held within, with *you're looking at someone else* and *things will never be the same if I tell.*

Nikos brings his spear to meet her claw. They find a slow rhythm, more of a dance than a fight, learning the steps and timing and testing the strength of the shadow claw.

It's slow enough that they can talk at the same time. They discuss the training at first, and Nikos swoons at how Arché had knocked one of the hunters flat on their rear with one shove of her shield.

Impressive, certainly, but the way his eyes sparkle as he speaks of it only drives agony into her chest as if it were his spear.

"Why don't you just *tell* her that?" Lenora asks, as if her heart wouldn't shrivel into a raisin if she ever had to watch Nikos and Arché like *that* together. She's no silver tongue, but can somewhat keep her true feelings hidden when needed.

"I did! But she never—" Nikos shakes his head, laughing in a wistful sort of way. "Enough about my romantic woes, Nora, what about you?"

Panic floods Lenora's entire being and she forces out a snort. "What woes? Didn't she finally start talking to you?"

Nikos bites his lip—a sign of reluctance in him, which is good. "I mean, yeah, but... she's got other things on her mind. We're just talking about... wolf stuff. It's not the right time."

Lenora has no idea what *that* means, but she'll take the chance to avoid his earlier question, so she gathers shadow behind him and slams him in the back, knocking him over and making him eat dirt. His spluttering laughter ignites giggles in her chest.

All this pining is ridiculous, on both of their accounts. Lenora is simply grateful that they have each other in any way, grateful she has someone who listens and sees her not as some Chosen or ill-omen like some of the House Leaders do.

They continue training until the first rays of sunlight are starting to creep across the horizon. Packing up is a relief, as exhaustion is quickly flooding in to replace her focused hold on the magic. It's been a long, productive day, and going to bed sounds glorious.

Lenora has just looped her arm through Nikos' for the walk home when there is a crash of wood, followed by loud shouts coming from the training yard entrance hall. The heirs are almost out the side exit, but after exchanging a glance with one another, they turn away and begin to move closer to the hall to investigate.

They make it five steps before the hall doors slam open. Strangers in orange robes and clothing, some armour clad and some wielding wands or staffs, stride in. Four total.

Nikos is rigid, his spear back in his hand in a moment. "What is this? Who are you?"

He is answered with a sneer and an arrow from the figure at the back, which sinks into his shoulder. Nikos growls and transforms on the spot, his teeth lengthening and claws growing, while fur covers his face and his ears shift into canine ones. Lenora resummons her shadow claw, and conjures small darts of shadow into her hand.

The heirs fight almost every day. Practice fighting, training for hunts or to defend Concord at any cost. And yet, some part of Lenora never believed it would come to that, while the rest of her whispered that if it did, it would be because of her being Chosen. That if Concord's fate came into question, the theory of the Shadow mages being heralds of coming disaster might actually be true. But that surely could not be what is happening now—

Nikos is locked in battle with a sword wielder who matches him for skill. The blade is silver, as are the arrows, which is beyond alarming. Lenora hurls her darts at the archer who is lining up another shot.

This is real. They're fighting an unknown force, who have offered no words or attempt at bargaining. Which leaves one thing.

We're fighting for our lives, she realises, perhaps too late.

Pure light curls around the staff of one of the mages. Lenora tries to leap out of the way as it launches towards her, but it catches her arm. The pain is debilitating, a burn that feels bone-deep, as if her blood is boiling around it. *Sunlight. The curse.*

She drops the darts and clutches her arm to her chest with a scream, and Nikos looks over with alarm. With him distracted, the warrior in front of him slashes their sword across his torso, making him howl. Leather armour cannot defend against such blatant strikes.

It's more frantic after that. Both of them hurt, both terrified. They back away as much as they can, trying to hold their own. The damned shadow claw won't even stay on her hand because Lenora's focus is too wrecked with how the burn on her arm stings. She knows she's right about the sunlight magic when Nikos takes several hits to much less effect.

"We need to run," Nikos hisses, grimacing as he takes another silvered arrow to the arm.

Lenora ducks another blast of magic and glances behind her to see if the entrance hall is a viable exit. A moment later, Nikos gasps her name as he pushes her over from the side.

She is halfway to the ground, twisting her head to see what had prompted such an action, when the silver sword runs Nikos through.

The world erupts into darkness as she screams.

By the time she becomes aware of anything at all, she can feel Nikos in front of her but not see him. Shadow surrounds them, shadow she doesn't recall even creating, her magic keeping them safe and contained from those outside. She peels away the top of the dome to let in enough light to let her see.

Nikos is still, and stained red. She has no idea what happened to their attackers, and doesn't care. All she knows is Nikos.

"No," she whispers. Disbelief renders her voice hollow, completely and utterly. "No. Come back."

But he doesn't. There is nothing. Nothing at all. Her ugly sobs are her only company, for gods only know how long.

"Lenora?"

She doesn't recognise the voice, not exactly. But something deep and instinctual inside her does, something that says *friend* while the rest of her is numb.

The rest of the shadow falls away. Bodies of their attackers litter the ground, no breath moving their chests, and she dully registers that she must have killed them. She cannot bring herself to care.

There is, however, the matter of the person standing in front of her.

Oh gods. Not you. Anyone but you.

It's such an awful thing to think. But her sense comes through next, and she sees Arché Kalésen for the heir, and ally, and friend she ought to be.

"Arché," she says. How absurd all her complicated feelings around the other woman feel now, when the reason for them lies dead between them.

"I'm so sorry," Arché says. She's as ragged as Lenora feels, blood covering her armour and grime all over her hands. She's transformed, half wolf and half woman, as familiar to Lenora as anything else.

She carries her mother's shield, Crescent Light. Her house's relic. That should mean something, something important, but inference is coming slowly, like her thoughts are trying to run through water.

"What—What's happening?" Lenora asks. "We didn't—they just came. Who were they?"

"Lenora, it's the whole town." Arché swallows. "We need to go. Now."

"What? Go where?" Lenora tries to think. Whole town. Emergency. "As in, to the cathedral?"

"No, I've been ordered to get you and—" Arché stops and purses her lips. "And get out. There's nothing we can do here, we need to get outside and get help."

The words come too quick, too unexpected. Lenora can only frown and try to get her head around them. She glances down at Nikos. Arché is strong enough to carry the body—gods, the body. The body.

Lenora breaks into a new round of sobs. It's all too much, and no matter how she tries, her brain can't grasp what it needs to, can't take everything in or make a single decision.

New noises come, ones she struggles to process.

"Lenora—oh gods," Arché says. "I'm sorry for this."

Lenora's view of the world turns sideways as Arché picks her up and flings her over her shoulder like a ragdoll. In the same moment, Arché begins sprinting for the side exit.

"Arché, no!" Lenora screams as Nikos gets further and further away. "Put me down, put me—"

More robed figures burst from the entrance hall and into the yard. Half a dozen. Far too many, and even the small glow in the hand of a mage is enough for Lenora to flinch in anticipation of another burn.

"We have to go, I'm sorry," Arché says again. Lenora hammers her fists against Arché's back and releases a scream wordless and awful as the only other protest left to her.

Lenora's backpack is near the side exit and Arché scoops it up on the way past with her free arm. The intruders are hot on their trail as they burst from the training yard, and Lenora finally sees Concord. Her shriek dies in her throat.

Smoke is rising to kiss the morning sky, drifting from the surrounding buildings. Shouts come from all around, and there is a body down the street, too far away to identify.

"The whole town," Lenora breathes, Arché's words from before finally hitting her.

Arché is too busy to answer, sprinting down the street at a pace only a partly transformed lycan could hope to match. Each powerful stride extends the gap between the heirs and their pursuers, and within half a minute, Lenora cannot see them at all.

Lenora fights Arché every inch of the way, screaming every kind of protest and promise of violence and declaration of hatred. She shouldn't, because it isn't fair, but *none of this* is fair, and maybe Lenora just wanted to lie down there and die with him, did Arché never consider that?

She's not sure if she says that part aloud. Arché never wavers, never answers, never slows. Not once does she retaliate in the way Lenora wishes for.

When they reach the river that runs through the western side of town, Arché finally comes to a stop, and Lenora is temporarily too exhausted to fight her any more.

"The river?" Lenora asks.

"It'll be harder to track us," Arché says. "No prints, less scent. Now, will you walk, or am I carrying you?"

Lenora runs her finger over the edge of Crescent Light where it rests on Arché's back. "You took me away from him."

Arché sighs and pulls Lenora off her shoulder, instead holding her at arm's length with her feet off the ground like she's a stray cat just pulled from the river. "We can't help him now, and he wouldn't want you to be hurt because of him."

The image of Nikos taking the blow intended for her flashes through Lenora's mind.

"You don't know the first thing about what he *wanted*," Lenora snarls, swinging a furious, petty kick at Arché's side. "You just—we just—you made me *leave him there*! We need to get him to Ulrich. Ulrich might be able to bring him *back*—"

Arché takes the attack with a stoic, resolute stature. Her face gives nothing away, and perhaps Arché has always been this shallow of a person, made only for simple laughter and nothing of substance, to never notice the doting manner of someone as wonderful as Nikos. Perhaps Lenora is a fool for expecting sympathy. But she'd certainly expected *something*.

"We don't know how long that takes or how it works," Arche says, slowly. "But they said the cost of resurrection is life for life. We don't know what that means, and Nikos isn't the only one who's dead. I'm sorry. We don't have time. We need to go."

Lenora screams at her. There are no words, only frustration, because of course she's right, of course there is no way it would be a simple thing. But she had to say it, had to be sure.

"We need to go," Arché says again. "I know it hurts, Lenora. But there's nothing we can do, except this. Getting out and getting help. If we get caught, it's for nothing. So are you going to help me save our home, or not?"

The sun spills over the horizon, over Arché's shoulder, and right into Lenora's eyes. She shies from it, and Arché turns herself so that her head blocks the rays from Lenora's face.

"I need help," Arché says. "Like it or not, we're all there is. Are you coming?"

Lenora bites her lip. Her protests feel so absurd, as if the sunlight has washed new clarity over her, sterilising her blinding fury. "Yeah. Guess there's nothing else to do."

She's still debating whether or not she can stomach adding the word 'sorry' into the mix when Arché gives a single nod and leaps into the river. Lenora follows, and they leave the town under its cover, trying to stick to the shadows that remain with the low angle of the rising sun. Some of the farmland is ablaze, and Lenora is doing her best to tune out the sounds coming from the town behind them.

Once they are outside the borders of the town and on the path to the mountains, Arché's wolf half fades as she comes back to her human form. Warm brown skin a few shades darker than Kalé's, dark eyes, and a short ponytail of dark hair pulled back. More handsome than beautiful—certainly nice to look at. At least, for people who are not Lenora. But then, Lenora's never paid attention to anyone who isn't Nikos, anyway.

Belatedly, Lenora wonders what has happened to her family. Everything has been such a haze. The twins are competent mages but young, and Disciplined mages are the weakest in an ambush because their magic usually requires preparation. But Lenora's mother once spoke of a failsafe spell enchanted into the very material of their family home, something she could activate in an emergency.

She'd never explained how it worked, but Lenora exhales with small relief at the thought that there is a high chance her family are safe in all of this—at the time of the attack, they should all have been home.

"Who are those people? The ones doing this?" Lenora eventually asks, as she glances back to the town which is getting smaller behind them every minute.

"We don't know," Arché says. "They're ruthless, in numbers we couldn't have imagined, and they had silver weapons and sun magic."

"They came here to kill us."

"It seems like it." Arché kicks at a rock in her path. "It seems so impossible that anyone could hate us this much *and* find us. We've never hurt anyone! But I heard their leader. He called himself the Prophet, whatever the fuck that's supposed to mean. He—" She pauses, her shoulders tense. "Folke is dead. And Eliana and Roxanni are prisoners."

Nikos' mothers. Always so busy with their work, always so glad to see Nikos and Lenora busy with their own. Good women. Kind women. Lenora's hand covers her mouth at the thought of them finding out about their only child's fate.

An unprecedented disaster for Concord. As that thought sinks in, Lenora is hit with the urge to vomit.

You're the chosen of Shadow, the council of leaders once said to her. *The first in centuries.* News that might have been exciting if someone hadn't added *and usually it means some kind of disaster is headed for Concord in this lifetime* before getting shushed.

She's never forgotten. The whispers never went away, that she is a herald of disaster. But that was only one of her problems; she's had enough worries to keep her busy without all that. Besides, if her magic were such a poor omen, surely the leaders would have made a plan?

Now it all seems like a sick joke. *Your fault. Your fault. You brought this, you brought this.*

"Oh, gods," Lenora says, clutching her stomach. She hasn't fed in hours and isn't convinced there is anything that could come up, but it sure feels like it.

"What?" Arché asks, frowning.

"It's all because of me."

"What is?"

"*This!*" Lenora gestures behind them. "The attack, Nikos, everything. They said a chosen of Shadow meant disaster was coming. We've always meant misfortune for Concord."

Arché blinks. "That's ridiculous."

"No, it's not!"

"Yes, it is," Arché says, looking at her with bewilderment. "I would go so far as to say *backwards*. If there's a correlation between chosen ones and disasters for Concord, then isn't that the magic coming to help the town? You're not the one to *blame*, you're the universe's attempt to give us a solution."

Lenora can only stare at her. Arché speaks as if it is so clear, and Lenora expects to feel infuriated or as though she's being spoken down to, but neither are true. There is something too earnest about Arché's face, about how she holds Lenora's eyes with her own.

"Yeah?" Lenora asks, voice awfully quiet.

Arché makes a face and brings her thumb up to pull on the edge of her bottom lip, brow creased in silent thought while she fidgets. "I mean—" She shrugs, all at once sheepish. "That's just how it looks to me. Especially now. We've gotten away. We're going to find help. You're literally going to save everyone. It supports my theory much better than, what, the council's?"

"Save everyone," Lenora echoes, hating how her voice almost squeaks. "Right. No pressure." She shifts her gaze to the mountains straight ahead and acts as though the thought doesn't make her want to run and cower in the upcoming cave until everything is over. Oh, to be able to sleep for months and let this horror and the world pass her by.

She won't. Can't. But for a moment she lets herself dream of it, before shaking her head back into sense.

Lenora certainly isn't, under any circumstances, going to allow *Arché Kalésen* of all people to comfort her on the worst day of her life.

CHAPTER 4
LENORA

LENORA HAS LIVED HER whole life in the valley that cradles Concord. It's a novelty to be on the border, to be entering the passage that takes them out of their hiding place, usually only used by the town's hunters.

Nikos must have walked this path many times, as the heir to the House of the Hunt. Lenora stares at the dirt beneath her feet as she walks, and considers how strange it is to almost feel closer to him now, walking in his footsteps.

Something flutters in her chest, like the feelings she'd get whenever he'd smile at her. It's something different, though. It feels like the last of her resolve, beating against her ribs, desperate to escape. Lenora presses a hand to her sternum and takes a deep breath. *My people need me,* she reminds herself. She must keep going, even if it's putting one foot in front of the other over and over. It's hard, with the sun beating down on her back, but summoning a parasol made of her shadow magic has done wonders for the struggles of walking in the morning sun.

Arché has continued to silently lead the way, but intermittently checks on Lenora over her shoulder. Lenora should feel grateful, but chooses to be bothered by it. Lenora knows how to *walk*.

The coolness of the mountain passage comes as a relief, and Lenora releases her shadow parasol back into the aether, glad for the chance to stop concentrating on maintaining its form for a while.

They walk for a few minutes before Arché comes to a stop and holds out an arm to prevent Lenora from continuing past her. When Lenora gives her a quizzical look, Arché puts her finger to her lips and nods in the direction they are heading. There is a turn in the passage ahead.

Lycans tend to have better hearing than vampires. Lenora shrugs to indicate she has no idea of what Arché is trying to convey.

"Several voices down there," Arché whispers. "We need to be *very* careful until we can tell who it is."

"There's a hunting group out at the moment, isn't there?" Lenora asks.

"Not if Eliana and Roxanni got taken prisoner, they must have been attacked on the way into the valley," Arché says. "But maybe a few got away."

They creep forward, silent as anything, until Lenora can make out the voices too. They are unfamiliar, and full of talk about the invasion and the unfailing leadership of the Prophet.

Fury and loathing bubbles inside her like nothing she has ever known, almost boiling over in an instant. These people talk of the murder of people they've never met and think it's admirable. There's no way to feel about it except—

"Hey," Arché murmurs, putting a hand on her arm.

Lenora snatches her arm back, bearing her teeth in a silent snarl at the unwanted touch. Arché holds her hands up immediately, apology all over her face, and Lenora realises how close to the bend she'd moved in her haze. Whoops.

"What's the plan?" Lenora asks. She doesn't want to be the one to ask: *are we fighting them? Killing them?* Those are not questions any person should ever have to ask, and yet... she's killed four already, and it might have been an accident, but no remorse settles in her heart.

"I—" Arché licks her lips, crossing her arms over her chest, the smallest Lenora has ever seen her. "If there *are* any survivors from the hunting party, they'll be ambushed and killed if these people are still here. They've made their position clear. It's against us. To a lethal point. I don't think we have any peaceful way to subdue them that wouldn't doom them to starvation. We're heirs of Concord. We have to act in the best interest of our people's safety."

"So... we need to kill them?" Lenora feels bad for how Arché winces at the words, but this is not a time for misunderstandings.

"If we leave them, and then find out they killed one of ours, would you be able to live with yourself?" Arché asks. It doesn't feel like a question just for Lenora. "I've never—I don't want to, but—"

The lycan heir shudders all through her body, but then squares her shoulders and lifts her chin.

"What I want doesn't matter," she says. "What's best for our people is what matters. This attack has changed everything, and... that's going to be an adjustment."

Lenora nods. "You're right. About all of it. I'm with you, ready when you are."

It sits about as wrongly in her stomach as everything else, the idea of becoming a killer, when being a vampire of Concord means coming from a culture of trying to avoid such a thing at all costs. But as much as

Lenora would never admit it outside of this moment, Arché is right about everything.

These people are an active danger. And the heirs of Concord must put their duty before all else.

"Okay," Arché whispers. She says it a few more times as she pulls her shield off her back and grips it with a shaking hand. "On my signal."

"What signal?"

"You won't miss it."

After a few moments, Crescent Light activates its empowered state, bright white magic filling in the rest of the moon shape so it resembles the full circle, and Arché breaks into a charge around the corner. She transforms with an almighty howl. *Oh.* Lenora follows on her heels and summons her shadow claw again.

The group of invaders—they must have a name, they must, but because they have not announced it so Lenora has no choice but to think of them as such—shout with alarm.

Arché meets the closest with her shield to their face, battering them off their feet and then slamming down into their torso. The cry is awful, and so is the satisfaction in Lenora's gut at hearing it. She might not relish the idea of *killing*, but people such as this surely deserve a little suffering.

Lenora reaches the next one. They're an archer, who has barely had time to grab the bow let alone notch an arrow, and Lenora lunges to slice them with her shadow claw, cutting deep.

There are four invaders total. One tries to charge Arché and gets thrown over her back, and on his reattempt he is shoved into a wall with a crack that echoes through the entire cavern.

"Huh," Arché says, looking astounded at her own feat. With a glance in Lenora's direction, the brief pride on her face turns to grim determination. "I'm sorry to suggest it, but... you should probably feed on one of them.

You'll need your strength. And if you're going to feed, and—well. You might as well drain one."

In usual times, a horrendous and sacrilegious suggestion, for Lenora to drain anyone. But these are not usual times, and their lives are forfeit already.

The archer in front of Lenora, already teetering on his feet, loses the rest of the colour in his pink face when her eyes flick back to him. "Oh gods, no. Everflame save me from—"

Lenora does not let him finish. It's too easy to seize his shoulders and dig her fangs into his neck. Blood usually comes from volunteering daywalkers, in a calm and civilised manner. Blood has never tasted sweeter than from the throat of an enemy, in an hour of violent vengeance and declared war.

She never usually takes a drop more than she ought to. It would be the pinnacle of shame, when the volunteer system is a foundational aspect of Concord's codependence between nightwalkers and daywalkers.

But this is not one of her people. Today is not a usual day. And this person made their choice.

Lenora overcomes the trained habit to stop and instead gives into the base instinct to continue drinking. The invader thrashes in her grasp, but less so with every second. The blood ignites the magical essence within her, within her bloodline, and it puts the strongest liquor or coffee to shame.

More. More. All of it, until she is on the ground leaning over a corpse, while her own body sings with life it has never known before. Her head feels as light as a feather.

Lenora looks up. Arché stands alone, the still forms of the other three invaders near her feet. She watches Lenora with curiosity.

"Wow," Lenora says, and her voice comes out almost giddy while her feet lift her up and down in small bounces. "This is... different."

"But okay? I figured… it would help," Arché says awkwardly. "We have a long journey ahead of us. I left this one alive—" She kicks the unconscious form of one of the invaders at her feet. "I figured we could tie him up and interrogate him, so we can try to find out what the fuck this is all about. And then you have someone to feed off tomorrow, too. I guess we'll need to figure out where you're going to get blood, after that."

The blood thing probably will be a problem, but Lenora simply can't process it as such in this moment. She's just relieved Arché is thinking everything through so well, because Lenora's brain is struggling to catch up to her fired up body, and overall it's a bit like an enthusiastic tap dance.

While Arché finds some manacles in one of the nearby bags and slaps them on their new captive, Lenora looks to the other people they defeated.

"You got all three of them on your own," Lenora says, impressed. "Just you, on your own—"

Something stops her dead. While every inch of her is still buzzing, a detail clicks, a crucial one so obvious she is horrified it took so long to notice.

Arché is alone. Fighting alone, just as Lenora is. No partner. No Rohan.

"Arché," Lenora says, voice quiet. "Where's Rohan?"

Arché pauses, her hands still on the manacles. She doesn't look up. "They didn't make it either."

Lenora recalls everything said and done between the training yards and here. Every awful thing she'd shouted. Her hands fly to her mouth. "Oh gods, Arché, holy shit, I'm so sorry—"

"You didn't know, Lenora," Arché says, standing and finally looking at her. Her face is still, her eyes resolute, and Lenora might just believe the projection of strength if the other woman's chest weren't shuddering. "Today is the worst case scenario. We don't need to talk about it. I don't want to talk about it. Sorry if you do."

Lenora is always on the side of *not* discussing uncomfortable topics. That being said, their best friends both being dead and leaving them to begin a journey filled with excessive violence is... one heck of a topic to avoid completely.

Arché kneels again, this time to run her fingers through blood that has gathered on one of the corpse's mouths. Before Lenora can ask what she's doing, Arché begins smearing the blood on the wall to form letters, dragging the body along with the other hand so it is close by.

Even then, the writing is a lengthy process, so Lenora busies herself by ransacking the camp for any useful supplies. There's water and dried food as well as a couple of bedrolls, but not even one bedroll will fit in Lenora's bag alongside the violin case.

When Arché is finished, the cave wall bears a warning to any who might come through, signed with rough attempts at the symbols of the Warden Clan and House of the Arcane—a half moon within a circle, mimicking Crescent Light, and a wand pointed at a cluster of stars.

"Good thinking," Lenora says. "The symbols are pretty good."

"Thanks," Arché says with an odd snort. "Are you alright? You're... bouncing."

Lenora stills the balls of her feet at once. "Oh. I've never drained anyone before. Obviously. I know my blood theory, but I never thought I'd go past the first stage of satiation. The second stage really *is* a high, like they said."

"Right," Arché says, thoughtfully. "Should we get moving? There's a cabin a few hours from here, if we can stay awake that long. The Hunt use it as a rest and supply point."

"Oh, we should take this bedroll, if we can fit it in your bag," Lenora says, shoving it into Arché's hands. "Mine doesn't have room."

Arché nods and manages to squeeze it into a small enough roll to get it into her backpack.

"You went out with the Hunt once or twice, right?" Lenora asks once they get moving. She remembers because Nikos had been so over the moon—no lycan pun intended—about Arché's attendance that it was all he talked about for two days each time. The thought doesn't hit her with as much bitterness or grief as it ought to. Mostly, Lenora is glad that the thing she knows best about Arché so far is her competence on multiple fronts.

As much as Lenora wishes she were stuck with *anyone else*, it's hard to pretend that anyone else would be better to have in this situation than Arché Kalésen. That thought, along with the energy boost from the blood, leads to an even better thought: *maybe we can do this.*

Once they're out of the mountain passage, Lenora is grateful for how the mountain's height blocks the sunlight from the east, but after several hours she has to summon her parasol again.

Arché carries their captive on her back, over her shield, as if it's nothing. She's unaffected by the sun in a way Lenora can't help but be envious of. Perhaps it's unavoidable that Lenora will always envy something Arché has, whether it's Nikos' affections or the easy daywalking capability or the ability to simply get on with things in the face of hardship.

Lenora is still walking. That's something. Nikos would be proud of her for that, at least.

The hunting cabin is unremarkable when they reach it. Plain wood, a single room, and a set of bunk beds against one wall with supply crates and a spare weapons rack on the others.

Arché dumps the captive in the corner and moves to stretch out on the bottom bunk bed.

"We'll need to take watches, in case he wakes up," she says. "And once we're out in the wilds on our own."

"Obviously," Lenora says. She knows *some* things. It's common knowledge that dangerous and sometimes magical creatures lurk in the shadows of remote places, alongside the usual mortal dangers like thieves or mercenaries. Just as it's unknown knowledge *why* such creatures exist in the first place, beyond general zooarcanology theories.

"Is it alright if I sleep first? I've done *so* much running today," Arché says. She begins unclasping her armour before Lenora can answer, her eyelids drooping.

"Oh. Sure. I'm still buzzed from the blood anyway," Lenora says. "I'd never be able to sleep."

"I thought so. Thanks." Arché's eyes flick to the undecorated back wall of the cabin. "We should leave a message here too. Could you work on that in the meantime? There are paints in my bag, little ones."

Lenora nods, and as Arché drifts off, it's easy to find the box of paint bottles and tiny brushes in Arché's backpack. Now that she thinks on it, she's seen Arché carving little figurines and objects in town meetings, seemingly just to keep her hands busy as she listens.

Selecting the yellow paint, Lenora gets to work replicating the message Arché wrote on the cave wall. It's uncomplicated: *Concord attacked and unsafe. Stay away, or return hidden.*

The tiny brush is so tedious that Lenora gives up on using it and sits down on the ground, summoning the arcane hand her family so often received for their mundane magic and dipping the hand's fingers in the paint before continuing the message.

That speeds the process up considerably without exhausting her arms, leaving her plenty of time to get out her sheet music notebook when she's finished. Several compositions sit incomplete, so she picks the one she's been working on the longest and plays around with some new ideas without the violin. Her musical ear and mind are sharp enough to compose at least partly on pure theory. She can see how it sounds later, and adjust from there.

After what must be a couple of hours, the captive begins to wake.

CHAPTER 5
ARCHÉ

ARCHÉ'S DREAMS ARE FITFUL. There is fire everywhere, and screaming, and blood on her hands she cannot wash off no matter what she does, and for the life of her she cannot locate Rohan—

"Arché," says a voice from somewhere else. "Arché, he's waking up. What did you want to do?"

The dream falls away and Arché cracks an eye open to see Lenora staring at her in earnest, eyes wide and lips still stained with blood. Blood of their enemies.

Their enemies.

Everything from the last twenty hours comes back to Arché in an onslaught of agonising memories, and Arché stretches so she has an excuse to turn her face away from Lenora and take in a large, trembling breath.

Rohan and Nikos dead. Others hurt, dead, or captive. Deaths, on Arché and Lenora's hands, by necessity.

"Not a dream, then," Arché murmurs. As if she could ever dream up anything as dismal as what has really happened. "Gods. Alright."

She smooths her hands over her face and last night's ponytail to try to collect herself and put on the face of the heir she needs to be. There'll be time to fix her hair once they are done with their captive.

"Should we talk to him together, then?" Arché asks, finally turning around to look at Lenora. "Or did you want to get some sleep?"

"Sleep," Lenora is quick to say. "You can talk to him. You'll do it better than me."

Arché can only lift an eyebrow at that, but she isn't in the mood for any sort of argument let alone one getting into anything like *that*. She simply lets Lenora crawl into the bed and grip the pillow as she falls asleep, leaving Arché with their unfortunate guest.

He's beginning to stir, and out of respect for Lenora's rest, Arché grabs him by the back of his collar and drags him out of the cabin, getting about ten feet's distance before releasing him against a nearby tree.

The impact wakes him fully. He twists, eyes snapping open as the manacles rattle with his movements, and then he goes still, fully registering his surroundings and the woman staring at him.

"Fuck," is all he says.

Arché squats right in front of him. "Tell me who the fuck you people are."

He lifts his chin in unwise defiance. "Why?"

"Because you attacked our town and killed our people," Arché says, wondering if perhaps she hit him too hard on the head in the skirmish. Or now, against the tree trunk. "Did you think we would let that stand?"

Of all the concerning aspects of this ordeal, the lack of remorse on this man's face might be one of the worst yet. He gives no answer.

"You don't want to make me repeat myself," Arché says, because she heard her mother say it to someone trying her patience once, and had marvelled at how good it sounded. "I asked you *who* the *fuck* you are."

"The Sunless Crusade," he says. There is a higher tilt of his chin, a glint of pride, which twists her stomach. "The Prophet received a vision about the town of nightwalkers, who need to be cleansed and brought back into the light."

"... what?" Arché stares at him. "I can walk in the sun. All the lycans can. Even the vampires, they just prefer not to. What's this about being cleansed?"

"It's what the Everflame wants. You shun the true light—"

"We worship the Everflame too," Arché says with utter bemusement. "They're in our cathedral, same as all the others. Nothing you're saying makes any sense."

The zealot—for that is what he is, Arché realises—frowns at her. "You can't worship the Everflame. It would be lunacy."

"Is lunacy really the word you're looking for when speaking with a werewolf?" Arché asks, almost laughing at his absurdity. "We *do* worship the Everflame. I swear, if this entire thing has happened because someone just *decided* there was something wrong with a town of people they had never spoken with—"

"You're trying to make me doubt, make me lose faith," the zealot says, eyes lighting with something powerful. "It won't work. I believe, absolutely. I have heard the Prophet's words. The Everflame themself told him."

Arché leans right into his personal space, until her face is an inch from his. "Bull. Shit. He must be lying."

"He speaks the *truth!*"

"People are *dead!*" Arché slams her palms against his chest, making his head hit the trunk behind him. He winces, but holds her gaze. "Your Prophet and his lies are the reason why. There aren't words for how fucked up this is."

"Their fire will cleanse you all, on the Solstice," he says.

"What? What does that mean?"

"The Prophet will take the nightwalkers to Cancium, the Holy City," he says, beginning to smile. "And there, the nightwalkers will be judged, and perish in holy fire."

Arché has always struggled with keeping strong emotions in check. It's a particularly difficult trait to have as a lycan, where controlling emotions while transformed is the most paramount tenet of her identity. There is no strict rule against losing oneself while in human form, but it still feels like weakness.

She stands and forces herself to stride around the circumference of the tree so she is not tempted by some currently strong urges to force meetings of head and tree until the latter is splattered with the contents of the former.

Such violent thoughts are unfamiliar and unwelcome. They are *not* who she is, or who she wishes to be. She cannot stoop to the level of these people, unless it is for the sake of someone's safety.

They clearly have no idea of the unique nature of the mortal vampires of Concord, that it is a magical curse and not undead atrocity that influences their natures.

The lack of distinction, just as with some lycans in the wider world being known to be dangerous due to a lack of control during the full moon, is exactly why Concord was founded in the first place. But in keeping itself secret, they have been attacked regardless, and now have no allies.

How absolutely, utterly unfair.

Arché stops in front of the zealot. This time when she gets down on his level, she takes his chin in her hand and doesn't bother trying to be gentle.

"I understand now," she murmurs. "And I see there is nothing left for you. Except nourishing one of the creatures you've sworn to hate. Let's call it penance, for your accomplice to multiple counts of murder."

For the first time, horror and fear cover the man's face as his eyes flick to the cabin, where Lenora sleeps.

"No," he says. "Not that. Just kill me."

Arché cannot help but feel grim satisfaction as she says, "No. The Life Giver would find that wasteful, I think. I'm more inclined towards the First Inventor, myself, or the Battle Maiden. But I've already beaten you in fair combat, and your pledge to a massacre of innocents revokes any requirement of mercy, I think—she and the Judge would agree. You know. Since you're so determined to bring gods into the lives of my people."

His face twists and he spits at her, but she shifts her head just quick enough for it to miss her cheek. "You mock me."

"I'm not actually in a laughing mood," Arché says, holding his face tighter until he winces. "I *pity* you. Because you're going to die soon, and meet your precious Everflame, and you're going to be told that you were wrong."

Defiance and doubt battle in his face. Arché shoves him away and they exchange no further words. Everything there is to be said has been uttered. Arché, despite never being the most devout, is confident in a way she suspects he is not—no god worth following would ever condemn her people the way he claims. With no inclination towards the Everflame in any meaningful way, Arché has faith that the nightwalkers who pray to the god of summer, fire and sun are as valued as anyone else.

How strange, to have more faith now than ever.

Arché drags the prisoner back inside and loops the manacles through a spear on the weapon rack to discourage an escape attempt. He's got the gaunt countenance of a doomed man, eyes flicking to the sleeping vampire every few moments.

With no pleasure to be found in watching him, Arché takes stock of the message Lenora wrote on the cabin wall. The colour isn't what Arché expected—bright yellow. A small, unexpected spark of endearment lights her chest for a moment, pulling a smile onto her lips. It will be interesting to see other sides to Lenora that are not just 'silent violinist'.

Guilt comes after that. There is something horrific about her looking forward to getting to know the vampire now at her side, when the last one died right in front of her. The vampire she was supposed to protect to the bitter end.

Arché cannot ignore how her wishes to not be stuck with Rohan for her whole life were answered in the last way she would have chosen. She knows it is not her doing, but with Rohan dead and Nikos with them as the only one who knew how Arché felt about them, her secret reservations are locked within her chest and more poisonous than ever because there is no outlet at all.

Her hands need to be busy, while she waits for Lenora to wake. Time to get a fresh block of wood from her bag, one slightly larger than her hand, and begin a fresh carving. Her mother is a strong presence in her mind at the moment, the beacon of leadership Concord needs now more than ever, the pinnacle of everything Arché needs to be, and the wife of the person whose help Arché is seeking.

The carving will make a good gift for Alta, when they reach their destination.

After a few hours, Arché wakes Lenora and suggests she feed and take watch again so that Arché can get in a bit more sleep before they leave, and their nocturnal schedule can be mostly maintained.

"Sure," Lenora mumbles against the pillow, without opening her eyes. "Give me a minute."

Arché waits for at least three minutes, but does not rush her. Lenora's breathing is slow and deliberate, reassuring Arché she has not fallen back asleep. Finally, Lenora gets out of bed and stretches before looking at their captive and licking her fang.

"Did you get everything we need?" she asks, voice groggy.

"Yeah," Arché says, as if a single word could encapsulate the horror of all she learned.

"Good. You nap, then."

Sleep takes Arché immediately, and when she wakes again to the beginnings of sunset coming through the window, there is nothing but the sweet sound of a violin. The music is beautiful but devastating, sweeping highs and slow lows, a melody that dances on the brink of too much and not enough. Arché wipes at the tears that spring to her eyes. No time for *that*.

She wanders out, to where Lenora is sitting against the same tree where Arché had interrogated their prisoner. Her eyes are closed, her fingers finding their way across the neck of the violin effortlessly.

"That's really good," Arché tells her.

Lenora's eyes snap open and the song cuts off. "Oh! Thanks." She chews on her lip and tilts her head. "I, uh, moved the body to one of the bushes a way off. I guess he'll work as fertiliser, after a while."

How easily they speak of these things now, when yesterday at sunset it would have been unthinkable. But times change, and so must they.

"Let's grab what we need, and go," Arché suggests.

The cabin has travel cloaks, a pouch of emergency coin, well stored food, and spare bows they can use to hunt game as they make their way through the grasslands to the closest daywalker town. It's called Barad and is a two night journey away if they continue northwest. And last but not least, there are spare shorts and shirts in various sizes, made of the elastic material the lycans use on full moon nights so that they can have clothing that does not tear when their body grows. Arché's own are back in her house, so she grabs a set that looks about right and shoves the garments into her backpack.

When it comes to the hunting bows, Arché takes one off the rack only to shake her head and hold it out. "On second thought, you're a better shot than me, if memory serves."

"Oh," Lenora says with a blink. "Yes, I think I am."

They set out, and it is a relief to feel the quiet comfort of the night set in around them. The above is a waxing crescent, and Arché watches it for a while as she walks, counting the days until it is next full and will fill her with its full power. She could use some more power, right now.

"So, what did he say?" Lenora asks.

Arché recaps the conversation as best she can. Lenora has much the same reaction as Arché—bewilderment, disbelief, and then fury. Except, unlike Arché, she does not hesitate to show it. It fills her up, informing every powerful gesture of her hands, lighting her eyes with a fire Arché has never seen. Arché didn't know such pale grey could *burn*.

"So all of this—" More gestures, as tears prick Lenora's eyes. "It's because some person claims the Everflame said we needed to be wiped out, cleansed, and all those people just *believed* him? Decided murder is fine, if someone says the Everflame *says so*?!"

She half shrieks the last part to the sky.

"I know," Arché says, shaking her head. "It's... senseless. Senseless bigotry."

"It is!" Lenora's hands are in her hair, clutching at the long waves. "What do we do, against people like that?"

"We keep doing what we've already done, if they're a threat," Arché says, trying to make it sound as reasonable as possible so she believes herself. "And we stick to the plan."

Lenora makes an odd noise in her throat. "I'm so—I kept wondering if there was any chance of us doubling back, to get Ulrich to Nikos and Rohan before it's been ten days..."

Stating the impossibility of such a thing now isn't necessary. It's obvious that Lenora knows. By the time they get Ulrich back to Concord, the spirits of Concord's dead will have long moved on.

"I never even asked you what the plan *is*," Lenora eventually says.

"You were a bit busy screaming at me to ask," Arché says, and she means it as a joke, but Lenora winces. "Sorry. You apologised. I was trying to—I'm—"

"We're both pretty bad at this, huh?" Lenora asks, with half a laugh.

"Bad at handling unprecedented tragedy and the pressure to fix a major disaster between two people? I suppose so," Arché says. "I'll be sure to tell Kalé it needs to be added to the itinerary for heir lessons in the future."

Lenora snorts. It's a sound Arché has never heard come from her, and is much higher and cuter than it has any right to be.

Anyway. Arché needs to focus on important things. "The plan is to head northwest and find Alta."

"Oh!" Lenora's eyes widen. "Right, your other parent."

"They're the only person we really know outside of Concord who is definitely an ally," Arché explains. "And because they're out and about in Kanin more often than not, they might know more people who can help. It's not... a lot. But it's not like Kalé and I had time to sit down and brainstorm it. It's the only thing we have."

"It's a lot better than nothing," Lenora says. "I don't know Alta very well. Didn't they get banned from town meetings, a while back? I remember my mother complaining about their attitude."

"About ten years ago, I think so, yes." Arché chuckles. "They came home ranting about *something*, but they certainly didn't care about being banned. Being in a room full of people who think they know better but don't is Alta's worst nightmare. It just made it easier for them to leave town for research projects."

Lenora is quiet for several moments, her eyes searching Arché's face for something. "Is it hard? Having them gone for so long at a time?"

The question takes Arché by surprise. "It was at first, when they'd been around for the first ten years of my life. But I realised they did it for me and Andreas, to not miss out on us growing up. But it was really hard for them. I know they love us, so whenever they're gone and I miss them... I think about how long they stayed, for us."

"They sound really interesting," Lenora says. "And I guess you've always had Kalé."

"Exactly. By the time Alta left, my brother and I didn't need more than Kalé could give."

They fall into a comfortable silence, walking through the grasslands in dusklight.

"You're... nice," Lenora says eventually, her voice quiet as she glances at Arché from under her lashes. "I... didn't know. I'm not supposed to like you."

A confused, anxious dance kicks up in Arché's chest. "What's that supposed to mean?" Arché asks it too fast, but she can't help it. The moment it seems as though she's done something wrong or upset someone, her entire body tends to hit a state of fight or flight, and any rational thoughts that *ought* to beat down the overreaction simply do not work.

Had Nikos told Lenora about Arché's worries? Has Lenora known all this time, how Arché is intolerant and ungrateful and unable to simply make peace with the difficulties of her position—

"I—nothing. Sorry."

"What did I do?" Arché asks, desperate for any answer that will quell the spiralling circles in her mind.

"Nothing, you didn't..." Lenora winces. "I'm sorry. Forget I said anything. It's silly. You're nice, and you're helping me a lot. Thank you."

Arché will certainly not forget Lenora has said this, and the thank you is simply too little too late. But it is not Lenora's fault that Arché cannot stop herself from overreacting. Lenora is under no obligation to like Arché, whatever the reason might be.

Now, if Arché can stop feeling betrayed by a dead man, in a few hours she might calm down.

CHAPTER 6
LENORA

Arché has gone quiet. The wrong kind of quiet. Lenora curses herself for letting her petty, unnecessary words out so carelessly. Of course Arché would want to know why Lenora is resolved not to like her, and it isn't going to be pleasant to hear.

But Lenora certainly can't tell her the *truth*.

Why can't Arché simply not care what Lenora thinks of her, so they can be mutually indifferent, for a sense of normalcy about this whole thing?

To make everything worse, the sun begins to stain the clouds with sunrise, and the only shade in sight is a singular tree which is *not* enough. Even so, a powerful yawn seizes Lenora and actually makes Arché chuckle.

"You first, then," the lycan says with a grin.

"That was already the plan," Lenora says, probably unhelpfully. "That tree isn't going to be much cover."

Arché slips out of her travelling cloak and tosses it over. "This should be big enough to cover you. Good job grabbing that bed roll, by the way, it'll make these days *much* easier."

Lenora can only imagine how absurd she looks, covered from head to toe with fabric, but there's only Arché to see it. As the sun begins to warm her through the dark cloak, Lenora can hear the soft scratching of Arché's chisel on wood. It's rhythmic enough that Lenora is able to fall asleep quickly.

A hand shakes her awake and Lenora stretches on instinct. It dislodges the cloak, causing midday sun to stream into Lenora's unprepared eyes.

"Urgh!" She hisses, turning her body and face to escape it. "Why is it so *bright*?"

Arché chuckles from where she sits nearby. "I do believe that's the point."

Lenora makes sure to give Arché her best unamused glower. "It's awful."

"It's the only reason anything grows."

"Still awful."

Ignoring Arché's chuckles, Lenora takes a moment to breathe in, then out. Getting up is always hard. She musters her strength and resolve and moves off the bedroll so it's free for Arché to use. Arché moves it so it's fully in the sun, letting her stretch out and bask in the warmth in a comfort Lenora could never enjoy.

It's difficult not to sigh at a ridiculous volume, but Lenora does her best and just thanks the gods that Arché didn't ask for her cloak back so Lenora can keep herself covered fully. The tree is free for her to sit at, and allows a decent vantage point over the land surrounding.

It's a slow afternoon. Lenora looks over her composition notebook again, but feels uninspired. Her throat begins to burn with a familiar thirst, and that is distraction enough. She's always known that her vampirism is the result of a curse, but it has never been more obvious than now, when her body demands more blood after using the excess for additional energy she didn't need the night before, instead of storing it for later.

Like the curse was designed to be an inconvenience more than anything else. There are precious little records on why *that* might be.

There are no more Crusaders to feed from. Animals, in a strange break from the usual rules of magic, do not work as a substitute. How in the world will Lenora be able to convince a daywalker to let her feed from them, without creating a panic or exposing herself unnecessarily?

She runs her mind in fruitless circles until Arché begins to stir with the coming dusk. The other woman smiles up at the stars before standing and stretching her body.

"Evening," Arché says.

"Evening," Lenora echoes. "We have a problem."

Arché's body tenses, and her eyes scan their surroundings on immediate instinct. When they seem to find nothing, they return to Lenora. "What sort of problem?"

"The needing blood problem."

Arché makes a face, and it remains twisted in thought even as she comes to sit with Lenora. "Yeah. I've been thinking about it. I know it's not done anymore, but... you'll have to take it from me."

"What?" Lenora doesn't mean to yelp the word, but whatever she'd been expecting Arché to say, it hadn't been that. "You?"

"I'm the only person who will be with you the whole time. I can consent to it. It won't endanger our safety or our objective. And my bloodline has the fastest bodily regeneration out of all the lycans. I'll replenish fast enough that it won't slow me down even with all the walking."

When Arché puts it that way, it seems so simple. Now that she's mentioned it, Lenora cannot recall seeing Arché or her mother or brother sporting any minor scrapes. She'd never questioned it, even with all the rigorous training.

"Our lessons say that lycan blood is a *lot* more potent," Lenora says slowly. "It's supposed to take us to the same stage that draining a regular person would."

"Makes sense, our blood has more magic," Arché says. "You having more energy doesn't seem like a bad outcome."

Lenora bites her lip. The idea of biting Arché is just so... bizarre. "You've never done this before, right?"

Arché actually laughs at that. "Given out unsanctioned lycan blood to a vampire? No, obviously not. But this is uncharted territory. It'll be okay. Just tell me what I need to do."

"Alright," Lenora says, a tiny chuckle escaping her as well. "Um. Turn around so you're facing away from me, then."

Arché does as she is bid. Lenora plants one hand on her shoulder and feels Arché tense under her touch. It makes sense; this is new and strange for them both.

Lenora's fangs meet the skin of Arché's neck but do not bite yet. "Yeah?" she whispers.

Arché actually shivers a little. "Yes."

"Hold still," Lenora tells her, sympathetic but grasping Arché's shoulder to ensure a wrong movement doesn't result in an injury.

The moment Lenora bites into Arché's neck, blood like no other rushes through her. It's hotter, richer, more *alive* somehow. And yet, the strangest thing is the noise that comes out of Arché.

It's halfway between a whimper and a moan, pained and high-pitched. Lenora cannot help but think that she'd expected Arché to be tougher than that. Still, there's nothing for it but continuing to drink until she's had enough, counting her usual ten seconds in a routine now second nature.

As Lenora lets go, Arché exhales for several long seconds.

"Are you alright?" Lenora asks her. She knows she shouldn't feel guilty for needing to feed, but having Arché react more audibly than any volunteer she's ever fed from has her off kilter. "The volunteers don't really talk about how it hurts."

"I'm fine," Arché says, without turning to look at Lenora, her fingers flexing where they rest on her knees. "It's a bite, of course it's going to hurt. I'm fine."

A giggle quite unlike any other leaves Lenora. "Okay. Good. Gods, they said it would be something else but..."

Lenora bounces to her feet and feels the urge to run in every possible direction. Arché turns, finally, a bit flushed in her cheeks and neck. Probably embarrassed about her poor pain tolerance. As if Lenora would judge her for that.

"I don't know what to *do* with this!" Lenora declares, rolling her body in the hopes it will settle some of the mania. "There's no one to fight, running seems silly—" She stops, and crosses her arms over her chest. "This is... weird and frustrating, actually. It's too *much*."

Arché stares at her for several seconds, and Lenora would pay good money to know what in the world she's thinking, because Arché's ears flush as dark as her cheeks.

"That sounds tricky, I'm sorry," Arché says, as she begins sorting out her backpack.

It's easier once they begin their night's travel. Lenora moves in dashes and half leaps until her body adjusts to the high, and the moment she does she cannot help glancing in Arché's direction and thinking of how tomorrow she'll get another taste.

Arché inquires after her wellbeing several times, to which Lenora assures her everything is fine.

Everything *is* fine, until Arché actually talks. Until Lenora is stuck thinking about how she wishes Nikos were here. To spar with to get the energy out, to feed from instead of Arché so that she could be closer to him than she'd ever been.

Which is a ridiculous, unhealthy wish because then she remembers he is dead. Remembers the emptiness of his eyes as he laid there in her arms. And then, all at once, her excess energy is the only thing that keeps her walking. Her best friend, her only true friend, closer to her than any member of her family… is gone. Taken.

Lenora will not cry in front of Arché. Will not break down, not be the one to crumble. Her pride could not bear it. She already needs far too much help from Arché, and if she needs anymore she won't be able to justify this dislike anymore.

With so few things left of home, that dislike is something Lenora is not ready to let go of.

So instead, Lenora plays her violin and lets it speak her melancholy and grief out into the world. Perhaps it will even help Arché with her own loss. Music almost feels like magic, in the ways it can touch people's hearts and soothe them. Gods know it has done Lenora more good than any kind of *real* magic.

There isn't much in the way of game as they walk, but Lenora spies one rabbit and manages to get in a good shot to score them some meat.

"I don't know how to prepare it," Lenora says sheepishly as she brings it back to Arché. How absurd, that she'd never asked her partner to show her one of his most essential skills. She'd never thought she'd need it.

"That's alright," Arché assures her, taking the rabbit. "Nikos taught me."

Lenora bites her tongue and does everything in her power not to scream up at the stars because *of course he fucking did.*

It's hard to say if Arché's tendency to laugh at Lenora's behaviour is making the entire situation better or worse. The most obvious one being how Lenora hisses at the sun when woken up for her watch. On one hand, it's aggravating. On the other hand, Arché has a nice laugh. Lenora tries very hard to dislike the laugh, and fails, so she has to take issue with its existence instead of its manner.

"You're not going to win this battle," Arché says. "The sun isn't going away."

"Doesn't mean I have to like it."

"Well, there's some rabbit cooked for you, when you're ready."

"Give me a minute."

So far, Arché hasn't questioned how long it takes Lenora to get up to begin her evening. It's a thing so much easier to hide at home, in the privacy of her own room. Without tragedy, without the pressure of someone's watch for survival, at home this battle would take much longer. Here, she has to push herself in different ways. She is needed. She cannot stay on the ground, here in the middle of nowhere.

I can do this. I am strong enough to get up and face the night ahead.

Once Lenora is up and Arché is stretched out in the sun, Lenora finds herself caught by how the warm light compliments the hues of gold and brown in Arché's skin and hair. Their nocturnal hours mean that she's never seen Arché like this before. It suits her.

Seeing a fraction of what Nikos had seen in Arché Kalésen is *not* how Lenora wants to start her day.

Instead, she plays her violin, and when the sunset comes, she serenades it and appreciates being able to see it properly after years of sleeping in and battling with getting out of bed.

When Arché wakes, she offers her neck to Lenora as if the previous bite had been no problem at all. So Lenora feeds, and Arché still makes an absurd noise, but then they're able to get on with their night. As they walk, Arché shows Lenora a crude map and how they might reach the nearest daywalker town sometime during the next night.

It's almost an easy rhythm. Sleep, grumble, take watch with the violin, feed from Arché, get walking.

Lenora will *not* compliment Arché, but the way she is continuing to offer her blood even with how it's clearly agony... well, it says a lot about her commitment to their current collaboration.

Besides, Lenora tried to suggest that if Arché stopped squirming, it wouldn't hurt so much, and that had only made Arché laugh in a bizarre manner. So at this point, Arché needs to make the process easier on *herself*.

"You don't seem to be adjusting to the blood," Arché observes.

Lenora, who has been charging ahead because she feels like she might burst at the seams and wishes they had the time to spar, shrugs in an exaggerated manner.

"It'll be fine," Lenora says. Arché seems about as sceptical as Lenora has been about Arché's wellbeing post-bites.

They're doing a marvelous job of this working together and trusting each other thing, that's for sure.

"So, this daywalker town... you think we'll hit it around midnight? Will a daywalker town have anything open at midnight?" Lenora asks a while later, peering at the map again. She runs her tongue over her fangs, trying to remind herself that she'll need to be careful about keeping her mouth more closed to hide her nature, as most daywalkers only know of undead vampires and would fear her with sound, if misplaced, reason.

"Everyone likes to stay up late to drink," Arché says. "So, hopefully a tavern or an inn. Somewhere we can stay. Concord had places open on all sorts of different shifts."

Sure enough, the night is at its deepest when they make out the shape of civilisation in the distance. It's quiet as they draw closer, the town gates open with no one but a sleepy guard at the entrance.

It's *so* quiet that Lenora is unnerved, and steps closer to Arché on instinct as they walk. Without knowing how many visits this town—Arché said it is called Barad—gets or at what time, it is hard to say if their arrival is out of place.

"Just stay calm, and be polite," Arché says under her breath. "Like nothing's wrong, because nothing is wrong."

Sure enough, the guard nods at them as they reach the gate. His armour has inflections of green and decorative antlers on the pauldrons. It rings a bell in Lenora's memory. *The Stag Battalion*. Kanin's law enforcement, community-run after training in the capital, Orsun.

"You two visiting?" he asks. "Been here before?"

Arché shakes her head, giving him an easy smile. "No, we haven't. Is there somewhere with rooms to stay in?"

"The Firelight Inn," he says, eagerly, darting into the road so that he can point down it. Lenora imagines she also might be excited for someone to talk to if she were to work a shift when she'd rather be asleep. "Just follow the main road, cross the square, and it'll be up on your right."

"Thank you," Arché tells him.

He beams, and Lenora wonders if he's older than nineteen. The smile then turns into a yawn, which he smothers with a sheepish grin before he moves back to his post.

"Have a good night!" he calls as they make their way into town.

Once out of earshot, Lenora tries to turn her muddled feelings into words. "I don't know what I expected... but that wasn't it."

"We can't let our guard down just because one tired boy was nice," Arché says, without looking away from the street ahead of them. The place is pleasant enough, with houses similar enough to Concord, and yet there are tiny details missing or different that scream out. The quiet of the night. The closed curtains. The way almost every single home has a hook holding a basket of flowers on the front door.

"I *know* that, I was just—" Lenora clicks her tongue with irritation. "Nevermind."

At that, Arché finally glances her way, discomfort washed over her features. "Sorry. I overexplain. A lot. Worse if I'm worried. Drove Rohan up the wall. I don't think you're not clever enough to not know anything, I'm just *always* thinking *but what if they just happened to not think about it this one time and then everything goes wrong because I didn't check?*"

"Oh." Lenora tilts her head, taken aback by the way Arché's arms have crossed over her chest, how her shoulders have locked. "It's... okay. That's good to know. I'll try to make sure I don't take it personally."

Arché exhales. "Thanks, Lenora."

How the fuck did this turn into Lenora comforting Arché? Lenora regretting being grouchy? What's this about Arché Kalésen having strange issues with communication and a heaviness in her frame while talking about it? Why couldn't Arché just be some annoying, hyper-competent figure that Lenora can reasonably be bothered by?

Thankfully, they reach the Firelight Inn before Lenora needs to say anything more or find the answer to any of *those* questions. It's a cozy building with two floors and lights shining from within, though mainly from the ground floor. As they walk in, it consists of a dozen tables, and a bar on the left near a staircase that leads to the second storey.

It is empty but for the barkeep and a sole figure drinking in the far right corner. Arché begins striding up to the bar, and Lenora follows, realising she's not practiced speaking without her fangs and really ought to stay silent until she's got it sorted.

Thankfully Arché has no such concerns.

"Hi there," she says to the barkeep, with a smile that seems to come to her face so effortlessly. "Would we be able to get a room to stay in, and some food?"

"Of course." He's a man of elven blood, his ears pointed and hair bright green where it is cut around his chin. "We've got a vegetable stew, a chicken stew, and some other cuts of meat as well as seasonal fruits and nuts."

"I'd love the chicken stew, and some of those fruits," Arché says. "Would you happen to have a rare steak, for my friend?"

Lenora tries to hide her surprise at the suggestion. While animal blood has no sustenance value for the vampires of Concord, it still tastes quite pleasant, almost like an odd equivalent to sweets. Clearly, Rohan had enjoyed their share of indulgence in such a way.

"Absolutely," the elf says, smiling in Lenora's direction. "For that and a... twin room? Double?"

"A twin room, please."

"We'll put it at two golden pieces altogether, and that can include a plate each in the morning as well."

Arché hands over the coins. It's perhaps a bit more expensive than Concord, but then Concord's businesses never relied on travellers, so Lenora is unsure how it would compare. Economics have never been a strong interest of hers.

The barkeep smiles again, this time in a polite way with his mouth closed. Lenora carefully mimics it, and while it feels awkward, at least her fangs are still hidden.

Arché and Lenora settle themselves in the opposite corner table to the one already occupied, and wait. Lenora should not be so alarmed at finding herself directly opposite Arché, looking her right in the face for longer than a few moments, but there has been so much walking and so little of... this.

It's disarming. There is a gentleness in Arché's eyes that Lenora does not wish to know yet cannot shy from because it is the only safe thing for miles. Seeing how wonderful Arché might be hurts in an odd myriad of ways, with grief for Nikos and his ridiculous crush and shame over her own resentment. It mixes in her stomach like an alcoholic punch that makes her feel deeply nauseous.

"We're okay," Arché says, quietly. "I'm sure we're not the strangest travellers to pass through."

"I know," Lenora murmurs. "I guess it's just hitting me that we're really not at home anymore. And we're only here because—"

She can't finish. She doesn't need to. Arché nods.

"I know."

Of course she does. They're in this together, and as much as Lenora may not like it, Arché understands all but the deepest, most secret parts of Lenora's grievances.

They share their meal in comfortable, companionable silence before going to their room upstairs and falling into a bed each on either side of the room.

"Real bed," Lenora mumbles into the pillows. "So good."

"Yeah," Arché says, nuzzling her face against the soft sheets.

It's a different thing, to slip away to sleep in a place of relative safety, not having to worry about keeping watch. But this time, perhaps because the sleep is deeper, dreams come.

Lenora's dreams are never kind. This is no exception. She is lost in shadow, hearing her mother's voice telling her to simply try again, try harder, and she'll have a breakthrough. But a breakthrough of what? She can't see, not a thing, until Nikos' voice calls to her and she runs to try and find him. Runs blindly into the dark, reaching for him… and never finding him.

She wakes in a sweat, tears streaming down her cheeks, and she furiously wipes at her eyes and breathes deep before her body can cave into real sobs. If it does, she is not sure she would ever get up again. She has to keep going and stay strong, or all is lost.

CHAPTER 7
ARCHÉ

ARCHÉ HAS A PROBLEM. A deeply inconvenient, mortifying problem. Volunteering to help sustain Lenora had been the easiest thing in the world—their home was founded on vampires and lycans supporting each other in any way possible, and Arché is truly the only option that makes sense.

Having never been bitten before, there had been no way to anticipate how her body would react to it.

Apparently, something deep within Arché *loves* being bitten in a rather specific way.

The first time? She'd hoped it was the shock that brought such a ridiculous noise out of her, but then the blood just wouldn't leave her cheeks, and despite the pain all Arché could think about was the rush it sent through her. The second time? There was no way to deny it. It absolutely does not help that Lenora then runs around complaining about having pent up energy, as Arché can only think about how she would seek out Sierra, a delightfully strong blonde blacksmith, her friend with benefits she'd not had time to say goodbye to back at the cathedral.

Thinking about Lenora blowing off steam in the same way is unhelpful, and deeply inappropriate, like all the rest of it. Neither of them are in the place for that sort of thing.

Thankfully, Lenora, by some miracle, seems to be reading Arché's embarrassing noises as ones purely of pain. It's an unexpected safety net, but a useful one for now.

Their wakeup in the tavern room is pleasantly slow, as they are up early by nightwalker standards, still in the mid afternoon, if Arché is gauging it correctly from the partial light coming through the curtains. (How odd, to have light coming through the curtains, when in Concord the nightwalker houses are fitted with ones thick enough to keep every house as dark as needed.)

"Do you want to feed now?" Arché asks as she pushes herself into a sitting position. Might as well get the ordeal over with.

"I guess I should," Lenora says, biting her lip and crossing the room to stand in front of her. "Okay. Stay sitting like that."

"Oh you're—" Arché swallows as Lenora begins to bend at the waist to lean into her neck. It's a different kind of space invasion, and it sets Arché's heart into a higher pace when Lenora's fangs are nowhere near her skin yet. *Get it together.* "Alright."

"Are you still sure this is okay?" Lenora asks.

"Yes," Arché says, voice firm. "You need it."

Lenora's hand lands on her shoulder while the other gently pushes Arché's neck to the side to make room for her mouth. The manhandling involved continues to catch Arché by surprise.

It's the moment right before the bite that seems to hit almost as hard as the bite itself. The feeling of Lenora's breath hot on her neck, the anticipation of knowing the sharp pain is coming... it's unparalleled.

Until Lenora's teeth actually sink in. Arché cannot stop the whimper that is ripped from her, as the pain, the pure sensation, shoots through her body. Her toes curl on the floor. It's exquisite and absurd and Arché cannot fight it to save herself. A shiver runs up her spine and she jerks with the force of it—

Lenora pauses her feeding to growl in the back of her throat, grabbing Arché's shoulders more firmly and holding her in place. "Stay still, or I'm going to take a chunk out of your neck," she hisses.

Arché hates that Lenora's growl, her commanding tone and rough hands, do nothing to calm her. Quite the opposite. Something deep and primal urges Arché to reach for Lenora's hips to anchor her in return, or perhaps see how it feels to pull Lenora against her and—

No. Arché clenches her fists atop her knees and rides out the agonising final few seconds. As soon as Lenora is finished, Arché dips her head so that Lenora cannot see how affected she is by the whole thing. It is harder to hide her ragged breathing, however.

"Arché?" Lenora asks, immediately back to calm pleasantness. "Are you okay?"

When she's not biting into Arché's neck or frowning at seemingly un-related comments, Lenora can be quite pleasant. Especially in these quiet moments right after. The check-ins are sweet, and Arché would appreciate them under any other circumstances.

"I'm good," Arché lies.

"Okay. Thank you."

"Of course."

Arché moves to her backpack at once, seeking her carving tools, anything to give her a reason to look anywhere but Lenora. This whole thing is ridiculous. Arché has never been beholden to these particular primal urges before, the ones that quicken her blood and send heat rushing straight down.

The whole thing is completely inappropriate. Lenora has not asked to be the object of such unsolicited desires, and is as lost in grief as Arché herself. Neither of them are in the place to be doing such things, it's simply that physical urges are naturally stronger in lycan bloodlines.

But it would *certainly* help if Lenora didn't keep glancing back her way and licking the tips of her fangs.

"What?" Arché says. She's doing a poor job of retrieving her equipment. The partially carved Kalé figurine rests in her hand, but nothing else.

"Sorry," Lenora says, now biting her lip. "I keep thinking about having more. Of your blood. I guess because it's stronger, it's almost like food with the perfect amount of salt. I just want more."

"Right," Arché says, intelligently, while pretending she isn't imagining what would happen if she allowed Lenora more, right now.

What a ludicrous situation. Arché will listen to none of that, and to all of her training about remaining in control, as all lycans of Concord must. Anything else is unthinkable. In the meantime, all she has to do is fill her mind with images of Sierra and what she and Arché had gotten up to. Arché had enjoyed being involved with someone as strong as her, someone who could hold her down, but she's always been curious about other dynamics—

And her mind has returned to Lenora. Without permission. Again.

"I'm going for a walk," Arché announces. "I'll look for supplies. Like a tent." Her carving hits the bed as Arché gently throws it onto the covers.

"Oh! Are you sure it's safe?" Lenora asks, with clear surprise.

Arché fixes her with a look that conveys how obviously she can take care of herself, and Lenora relaxes and gives her a small smile before returning her attention to the sheet music she's spread in front of her at the room's working desk.

Getting downstairs and into the open air has never felt so good. There's no crime in being horny, of course, but with the current state of things the entire thing feels so *wrong*. So much is at stake. And Lenora couldn't be more uninterested or indifferent.

Arché doesn't actually want to have sex with Lenora, or anyone. Arché wants to get moving, to be a day closer to Alta, to a solution that might save their people. Her body just needs to get on the same page as the rest of herself.

Thinking on her mother's teachings, and those of Eliana and Christos, Arché finds a tree near the village square and sits under it, letting herself fall into the deeper meditation techniques taught to the lycans from a young age. Stopping and listening to everything around you. Clearing of the mind, calming of the body, reharmonising the two. Regaining control.

This is something she can do, something she has trained for. Staying in control. Always.

When Arché opens her eyes again, feeling more herself, a small part of her shrinks at the sight of several pairs of daywalker eyes regarding her with various flavours of curiosity.

It takes everything she has to ignore it and move to some of the local stores to inquire about dried food, a one-man tent to ease Lenora's daytime sleeping, and extra water flasks.

She is able to return to Lenora with a sense of victory, and Lenora's eyes spark with relief the moment Arché returns to their room.

"You're back," the other woman says.

"Tent," Arché says, dumping it on the ground unceremoniously. "No more unfriendly sunshine for you."

Lenora's entire face lights up with so much excitement it is dazzling. "Oh, thank the gods. And... you. Thank... you."

It seems difficult for her to get the words out. Which is odd, because while Arché may have never given her an undue amount of thought in the past, spoiled or ungrateful are certainly never qualities that shone out from Lenora previously.

Arché just shrugs and decides not to overthink it. "You're welcome."

Once the sun is down and they've had another meal downstairs, they head out of town and along the daywalker road to the next town. It's three nights to Ziluuk, and within two hours the walk has been so uneventful that Arché cannot avoid something that has been lurking in the corners of her mind.

"What you said the other day," Arché says, "about how you aren't supposed to like me. What did you mean, because I'm trying not to let myself stew in it... but I am."

Lenora might shrug her shoulders, but Arché does not miss how tense she is just from it being brought up. "You're a good person, that's all."

"Am I?" Arché asks. "Great. I'm trying my best. You're... a great person, also."

Lenora laughs, which is bizarre enough, but the smile that comes next might be the only proper one Arché has seen since their escape. It makes Arché almost trip over her own feet.

"Not that I'm trying to beat your compliment," Arché hurries to add. "It just seemed like a better word for you—which isn't to say that you're not a good person. Uh."

"I can see why he liked you," Lenora says, as she shakes her head with exasperation which is not unkind. She pulls out the map, which she has begun to keep instead of Arché, and examines it while murmuring numbers to herself.

"Right, well, I'm glad someone else likes me, but it doesn't really answer my question," Arché says. "Was it your violin teacher? Your dad?" She's never had a conversation with Lenora's antisocial father, but one never knows these things.

Lenora sighs. "No. Him." She pauses, as if that should mean something. "Nikos."

"Oh!" There is a tug at Arché's heart, of comradery and grief. "Right. Well, yes, I would hope we all liked each other, mostly. At least those of us that talked. Obviously you and I... didn't... much."

Grey eyes blink at her. When Lenora does not answer, more words tumble their way out of Arché's mouth.

"Wait a second, this makes even less sense now," Arché continues. "Why would Nikos thinking I'm okay mean that you were supposed to like me, and now, what, you're changing your mind?"

"You really have no idea, do you?" Lenora's disbelief is obvious, and hopefully so is Arché's bewilderment.

"Clearly not," Arché says. "Could you *please* start making sense now?"

"It doesn't matter now," Lenora mutters, her face jerking away so that Arché can no longer see it. "He's—you know. It doesn't matter."

"It clearly does, to you, which means it matters for us."

"There is no *us*," Lenora snaps.

Arché recoils from the tone, her heart instantly hardening until it is as heavy as an anvil. And yet, despite the complex rejection surging through her, she cannot help but bite back. "Bullshit," Arché says. "We are alone in an unfamiliar land with only each other. We've both lost people, and have others to save. We're both heirs of our bloodlines. We are helping each other. There is a we. There is an *us*, whether you like it or not."

Lenora stops walking, the motion of it causing her loose hair to fall into her face. Her arms cross over her chest as it trembles while her feet kick at the dirt road. Arché comes to a halt and waits.

When Lenora glances up, just for a moment, Arché tries to ensure her face is empty of anything but earnest questioning. Lenora's lips purse as she holds Arché's gaze for one second, then two, then three.

"... it's not you," Lenora eventually says. "It's me. I... got a silly idea in my head about you and decided you must be awful. You didn't do anything. You didn't do anything at all. I just... need to let go of this idea. Because you're right. We're in this together. This is us."

The weight in Arché's chest gives way, and Arché is able to release a heavy breath.

"Okay," Arché says, quietly. "Thank you for explaining. I always worry too much about whether I've done something to bother someone, without knowing. When you said that... well."

Arché spreads her hands in a sheepish, helpless gesture.

"Oh." Lenora's eyes widen. "Shit. I'm really sorry."

Arché isn't quite sure why she does it, but she sticks out her right hand into the space between them. "Friends? Or, at least... to being... a team."

Lenora makes a noise that sounds half like a hiccup and half like a laugh. She takes Arché's hand and shakes it. "Friends could be... nice."

The moment lasts too long. The two of them, standing in the middle of the desolate road in the midnight air, hands and gazes locked. It feels exposed. Arché's never been too averted from eye contact, but she is not sure she has held it this long with *anyone*.

And then it's over. And they walk in comfortable silence until the sun starts to rise.

The new tent makes all the difference for sleeping during the day. Lenora glares much less upon being woken for her watch, and even Arché has to admit that it is a relief to have some of the daylight blocked out. While not quite as peaceful as the sleep in the inn room, it's a significant upgrade from their previous outdoor arrangement.

"I was thinking we could try your wrist instead of your neck," Lenora says to Arché as they pack up the tent. "Maybe it won't hurt so much."

Arché, once again, sends a quick prayer to whichever god is helping her out by sustaining Lenora's belief that Arché's responses to the bites are from intense pain. Without knowing anything about Lenora's romantic or sexual history, Arché certainly doesn't want to make her uncomfortable on a matter that can mean wildly different things to different people.

"Sure," Arché says, and it all seems perfectly logical until Lenora is sitting next to her on the cool grass, cradling Arché's hand in gentle fingers. The fingertips of her left hand are callused, in stark contrast to those of the right hand she used to shake Arché's own yesterday. It makes perfect sense, as her left hand is where her fingers press violin strings against the neck of the instrument. What makes less sense is why Arché's mind has to race through noticing this detail now of all damned times.

"You'll still need to try and be still," Lenora says, as she lowers her mouth to the sensitive skin of Arché's wrist. Her breath is so *warm*.

In hindsight, this idea is not perfectly logical. As Lenora sinks her teeth in, her eyes flick up and find Arché's, and of all the things Arché could have attempted to prepare for to endure this bite, that is *not* one of them.

There is only one thing for it. Arché squeezes her own eyes shut as the delicious sting shoots through her arm, hoping that the way her face twists continues to resemble pain. Gripping her knee helps ground her through the sensations and reactions she is so beholden to.

When it is over, Arché opens her eyes to see Lenora wiping her mouth on the back of her hand. A filthy, unbidden part of Arché's mind conjures an entirely different context for such an image, and Arché has to swallow as another wave of heat shoots down her body like an aftershock.

"You wriggled *worse*," Lenora says.

Her exasperation and its matching frown is so stern that it saves Arché from herself and throws her into something else entirely—laughter. Lenora's eyebrows only knit closer together.

"I'm sorry," Arché says, before any further scolding comes her way. "I don't mean to."

"Laughing isn't a good way to show me you're taking this seriously," Lenora retorts, crossing her arms over her chest.

"Your cross face is just..." Arché gestures vaguely, and under the scowl that comes her way a moment later, she lacks the bravery to elaborate any further.

Lenora rolls her eyes when no true answer comes and lets out a huff which pushes an errand strand of hair out of her face. "We should stick with the neck. I have better control of you that way."

Arché's useless brain immediately imagines Lenora in *full control*, such as pushing Arché onto her back with irritation and leaning over her to get the perfect angle for a bite—and this is certainly not the time for *that* line of thought. In fact, never is a better time. Never, ever, ever.

Hopefully the cough Arché forces out as she stands comes across as something other than the avoidance tactic it definitely is. She mumbles something about getting her backpack ready for their night's journey, and thankfully Lenora asks no questions.

Arché is content to eat some of their dried food as they walk, and she gets the pleasure of listening to Lenora's violin as they make their way along. One doesn't need to know much about music to appreciate someone who plays from the heart, and there are no falters in the melody, no stutters or slips. Lenora is talented, and has plainly worked hard to become so. There is an elegance to her movements, not just the slide of the bow over the neck but how the strides her feet take change while she's playing the instrument. She half glides, half dances, letting the music carry her forward to keep up with Arché.

"I'm so glad you bring that everywhere with you," Arché says. "That you had it with you, when we had to leave so fast."

Lenora glances up, and her playing slows but does not stop. "Me too. You're the one who made sure to grab my bag on the way out. Thank you, for grabbing it."

Arché shrugs. "I knew it was important."

"My mother always said it was silly, taking it everywhere," Lenora says, making a face. "But sometimes I wanted it at weird times, you know?"

"Nothing is silly, if you care about it," Arché tells her in a firm tone that makes her blink in surprise. "Alta always told us that. They're adamant about following and indulging passions. If the months away on research and exploring didn't make that obvious."

Lenora smiles, her head tilting as she mulls it over. "They sound great. I wish I knew them better."

"You'll see them again soon enough."

"That's true!" Lenora glances around the landscape, the endless seas of grass and sky around and above them. "It'll be nice to see a friendly face out here. It's so... odd, being away from home."

"I know. It seems so ridiculous to have to be so careful around the daywalkers when they've been so kind so far, but if there are any more of the Crusade out here, it'll only take one person..." Arché shakes her head. "I hate this."

"Do you... think Concord is alright?"

"No, I don't think it is," Arché says. "There's no way that Rohan and Nikos were the only ones we lost—" Pain flashes across Lenora's face at the mention of Nikos, and Arché feels guilt but continues. "However... our people are strong. They look out for one another. That Crusader I interrogated said the nightwalkers are being taken to Cancium to be judged. So that means they must be alive, for the most part, for now. And if our mothers are with them—"

"Mine won't be," Lenora blurts out. "She has a spell, something she set up a long time ago she could activate to lock down our house and keep everything inside it safe. My family might all be inside, with whoever else they could get in, in time."

This whole time, Arché has pictured Lenora's straight-backed, intense mother at the head of the nightwalkers, stepping up with High Cleric Ulrich to bolster the vampires of Concord in their time of need. And she's actually been in *Concord*? Hiding in some sort of safehouse spell?

"At least they're safe," Arché says, instead of several of her other racing thoughts. It feels unfair to judge, to think of it as an abandonment of the duty of leading a house, when Arché cannot presume to know all the reasons behind the creation of such a spell.

But it sits wrong. Especially alongside the comments of Lenora's mother belittling Lenora's passion for her violin, it sits wrong, and a small dislike for the woman creeps into Arché's heart.

"At least Kalé will be with the others. They'll need her," Lenora says. "You said Folke was killed, that Eliana was captured. What about Christos and Ulrich?"

"The Hearthfather and the High Cleric were both at the cathedral, so they'll be with the prisoners, I suppose," Arché says. "Four out of six. That's not... a worst case scenario."

"Thank you, for saving me," Lenora says, abruptly. Her eyes drop to the ground, her toe jabbing at a stone in the dirt and flicking it down the road ahead of them. "Without you, I would have..."

She doesn't finish the sentence. She doesn't need to. Arché remembers her words all too clearly: *maybe I wanted to lie down there and die with him!*

Words of grief, to be sure, but there had been something else to the words. A hopelessness Arché could not understand, one she has seen colouring Lenora's edges, its weight holding her down when it has her in its clutches. Without those words, Arché worries she may never have noticed it.

"I've got you," Arché says, meaning the past and present and future all at once. "That's what matters."

Lenora looks up, eyes wide and shining with something unreadable. "Yeah. I guess you do. How many of them did you have to get through? To get to me?"

Arché makes a face at having to think back to the attack at all. "A few. I avoided the ones I could. They had some kind of champion, who had a sword bigger than *you*. I could handle the others, but not them. I had to run. I just ran."

"It's hard to imagine anyone making you run away," Lenora says. "You're our best."

The description takes Arché aback. She's never thought of herself as the best at anything. "I—well. I don't know about that, but I certainly couldn't take him."

Lenora seems annoyed on her behalf, only to brighten a moment later. "Well, at least we fight well together," she says, seeming surprised by her own words. "I hadn't thought about it... but we do. So maybe if we see the champion again, we'll take them down."

A grin comes to Arché's lips. "I'd like that."

The stretches of silence on their journey are becoming more and more comfortable all the time. Now, if their eyes happen to meet in the same moment, more often than not they'll exchange a smile. Arché has to wonder how Lenora feels about that with her irrational dislike she refuses to expand on, but she's clearly doing a great job of battling it, so Arché won't complain.

About an hour further down the road, the faint and distant light of campfire appears, and once they're closer, distressed shouts pierce the night's quiet. Arché breaks into a run without a second thought, and hears Lenora follow.

"Back!" a voice shouts, from behind a stick lit with flame and swinging wildly in the faces of dark, otherworldly beasts making violent snaps with toothy maws. "Get out of here! Leave!"

The beasts shy from the light, but there are three, circling, trying to find an opening.

Arché and Lenora meet each other's eyes, exchange wordless understanding, and charge.

CHAPTER 8
ARCHÉ

IT IS ONE THING to know that creatures of magical, dangerous influence roam the world's wild. It is another thing to actually come face to face with some. Arché's excursions with the Concord Hunt had not been nearly so eventful.

These creatures are somewhere in shape between a hound and a bear, covered in shadow. And when one turns and meets Arché's eyes as she charges into the fray, she is shocked to see nothing but void. No sign of life, or a soul.

They are empty. Corrupted, by something, beyond repair.

Arché activates Crescent Light and slams it into the face of the closest beast. It snarls, and one of its companions turns to advance on her also. Good. The more the merrier, and the less their previous victim needs to deal with.

They're fast. So is she. Their jaws snap but only meet her shield.

There is a yelp from nearby, as Lenora leaps onto the back of the third creature and plunges a claw of pure shadow into its back. It whines and shakes her off, and Arché dashes to be the wall between Lenora and the danger. Let them all come. She can take them.

One of the beasts makes a dive around Arché, going straight for Lenora's neck. Arché slams her shield down on its back. Lenora jumps to her feet and swipes at one of the others as they are advanced on from all sides.

Arché shifts so that she and Lenora are back to back, like how she would fight with Rohan. They have not practiced this. Perhaps they need to. Lenora and Nikos had their own method of fighting, constantly swapping in and out of who is in front and who is behind. That won't work here. Arché and Lenora both do things in close quarters—even if Crescent Light gives Arché some flexibility, she cares little for it in a real fight.

"Try to turn when I do," Arché says. "I'll turn if there's an opening for you to strike, and you turn if you need me to block for you."

"I—" Lenora presses against the side of Arché's back, and Arché brings the shield around to let a beast's head collide with it as it tries to bite Lenora. "Okay. Okay."

It is slow and imperfect. But it's a start. When Arché sees one of the creatures about to lunge and leave itself exposed, she lurches and lets Lenora come around to sink her shadow claw into its belly, while its teeth sink into the back of Arché's forearm.

With a roar of pain, Arché brings her shield back around and watches as the sharp blow turns the beast to dust.

"What the fuck?" Arché asks.

There is little time to dwell on the question, of course. But with one down, the remaining two are easier, especially when a flaming branch comes down to whack one of them square on the head right when it is about to get a mouthful of Lenora's free hand.

Claw. Slam. Branch, again. The second one turns to dust.

And, when Lenora's claw gets in a brutal tear across its throat, the final one dissolves just like the rest. The moment it is gone, the branch drops and the person wielding it falls to the ground, breathing heavily.

"Thank you," they gasp. "*Fuck.*"

A feminine figure with brown skin and dark hair, they wear loose trousers and a cloth tunic in some of the brightest colours Arché has seen all in one garment. It is tied across the chest rather than sewn for shape.

"Your arms," Lenora says, with concern. "Are you okay?"

The stranger winces as they examine the deep scratches dripping with scarlet. "Well. Other than this, I'm peachy. But I'd be a dead woman if it weren't for you. Thanks."

Lenora's eyes linger on the blood, as Rohan often did if Arche got a bad cut, but as expected of a well-nourished vampire of Concord, she is in complete control and unmoved.

"Thank goodness we were close by," Arché says, horrified at the thought of the alternative.

"I've got a basic medical kit in my bag, just in the tent," the stranger tells Lenora. "Grab it for me? I don't want to. Bleed on things." The flow isn't fast enough for immediate concern, but there are drips from multiple places.

"Here," Lenora says, sitting nearby and beginning to go through it.

"Are either of you any good at this sort of thing?" their new acquaintance asks. Lenora shakes her head, but Arché had plenty of experience stitching up Rohan after they found some new terrible idea to act on.

"I'm not bad," Arché says.

"I'll take it." The stranger holds out her arms and smiles. "I'm Leahi, by the way."

"I'm Arché, and this is Lenora," Arché says, smiling back. "Alright, bear with me." It is a simple enough process, to use the sterilising poultice with a gentle touch and wind bandages around the worst of the sections.

"You two are travelling late," Leahi observes, as Arché works.

"Oh, I guess we are," Lenora says, and Arché tries not to cringe at the questionable attempt to feign ignorance about something deeply obvious.

"Lenora's skin is so sensitive to the sun she might as well be allergic," Arché tells Leahi with a snort. "We found travelling by night works better, with how far we have to go each day. Meanwhile, you're travelling alone."

"The roads are usually safe," Leahi grumbles. "I just got unlucky. I'm not helpless, I actually stopped a handful of them on my own, but there were just too many. I ran out of magic, so all I had was the branch."

"You're a mage?" Lenora asks, eyes lighting up.

Leahi nods. "That's why I'm usually fine on my own. Innate magic. Like yours?" When Lenora nods, Leahi smiles at her. "Haven't met anyone with shadow magic. But then, I haven't met anyone with sonic magic either. Look at us."

"*Sonic* magic?" Arché asks. "Like, sound?"

Leahi twists her body to show an ornate wooden flute tucked into the folds of her tunic. "That's the one. Woodwind instrument makes for a good focus, in my case." She glances at Lenora with an eye so immediately discerning that Arché blinks at her changeable manner. "Didn't see a focus on you."

"Oh," Lenora says, all at once looking embarrassed. "Uh. I had to learn to go without. I couldn't work out how to channel my magic into anything. I don't know if my magic just clings to me in weird ways or if I was just rubbish at the technique but... I'm self-focused, I guess."

Even Arché knows how practically unheard of that is, for an Innate mage. How had she never noticed it about Lenora before? Training together all that time, never seeing her with a crystal or staff like Kirsa wielding her holy magic with an amulet to the pantheon or Lenora's mother weaving her Disciplined magic creations with a delicate wand of gnarled wood. Gods, Arché needs to learn to pay better attention to details which have further implications. Half-noticing things does no one any good.

"Why *did* they let you do it that way?" Arché asks. "It's dangerous, isn't it? For Innate mages to not have a focus?"

Lenora curls her arms around her knees, tucking her chin on top of them. "I think they just got tired of trying to teach me something that people usually get in the first month of training. After six months, they stopped trying and told me that I could train with Nikos and figure it out my own way."

Arché swallows a growl, and Leahi lets loose a colourful torrent of curse words.

"What the *fuck*?!" Leahi asks, horrified. "Do you want me to punch them? Or explode their eardrums? I owe you now, it's the least I can do."

Lenora laughs, any weight in her eyes gone in a moment. "Thanks, but it's fine."

"It's not," Arché says darkly. "I think your mother and I need to have words."

Lenora shakes her head with an exasperated expression. "I think we have bigger problems than my mother right now, Arché. Let's focus."

"I *am* focused. I'm just also making notes, for later."

Leahi's brown eyes flick between them with curiosity, but her eyelids keep drooping. "Gods, I want to stay up and chat, but I'm smashed. Are you two going on this way? Could I tag along? Safety in numbers, and all that. I'm headed to meet a friend in Khiz."

Arché and Lenora exchange glances, then shrugs.

"We *are* travelling by night, but if you can make that work for you," Arché says, "no problem."

"Sure," Leahi says, nodding. "Just... lemme take a quick nap. I'll be right with you."

She gets herself settled in her tent, leaving Lenora and Arché sitting by the remains of the campfire. Far too late, Arché becomes aware of the bite wound on Lenora's arm, and the several she acquired herself.

"You're hurt," Arché says, shuffling closer and making an assumption that Leahi won't mind if they borrow some of her poultice. "Let me help."

"Your arm is covered in blood, and you want to help me first?" Lenora scoffs.

"I'm fine." Arché glances at the arm in question, which is finally beginning to sting in the night air. "I mean. Unless you... want some."

Lenora's head tilts, confused for a moment before understanding dawns. Her gaze flicks to Leahi's tent opening; there is no movement in the fabric, and no sound from within other than soft snoring. When she looks back, her eyes are alight with a new spark.

"I suppose so," she says, reaching for Arché's bloody left forearm.

It's almost like the wrist bite, in the way that something in Arché's chest kicks up just with the way Lenora's hands gently support the arm but this time with her fingertips on the sensitive underside. Her mouth descends to the wounds on the top of the arm, and Arché shivers as her tongue licks across the gashes. It's painful and strange, but that is such an apt descriptor for so many of her interactions with Lenora at this point that Arché can only take odd comfort in it. Besides, at least the wounds are being cleaned this way.

When Lenora is done, she lifts her head to give Arché a red stained smile, with starry eyes from the rush of the lycan blood's power.

"Thank you," Arché says, as if she is not going to be thinking about the feeling of Lenora's tongue on her skin. Not at all, not ever.

Lenora giggles in that way she never does except after intaking Arché's blood. "Thanks yourself."

"Your turn," Arché says.

Lenora sits quite well as Arché applies poultice and bandages to her large scratch. Arché tries to be as gentle as possible, dabbing gingerly and doing the bandage as slow as anything and consistently checking Lenora's face for signs of distress.

"Arché," Lenora says, with an eyebrow up and a smile on the corner of her lips, "I'm not made of glass. Just do it."

"Not wanting to hurt you is not the same as thinking you can't handle it," Arché replies, but she does speed up all the same. One quick tie and tuck, and Lenora is all sorted. "There."

Arché works on her carving while Leahi naps, and Lenora elects to take inventory of their current supplies, food and money. They have enough to get by, but a few more catches of game to get some better meals in would go a long way.

"Alright, I'm up!" comes a voice from the tent after some time. Leahi's head pokes out and she grins. "Huh. You two *are* as good looking as I remember."

Lenora shakes her head while Arché simply chuckles, her ego now pleasantly boosted for a moment.

The road is different after that. Leahi is upbeat, upfront, and full of jokes and casual flirtations, but her presence pops a bubble Arché had not even realised existed. The intimacy of a secret. The identities Arché and Lenora now hold to their chests, the loss they share and understand at their core, the daunting mission ahead of them.

Lenora is even more quiet than usual.

"So, where are you two from that has such questionable magic training practices?" Leahi asks as they walk.

"Nowhere important," Arché lies. "There are questionable people everywhere."

"I suppose." Leahi is plainly underwhelmed by the answer, but doesn't push it. "I'm from the Eastern Islands. This is my first time in Kanin by myself. Been on enough of the trade ships, but we only usually dock in Orsun for a day or so. I'm meeting a friend who used to visit us, and we're going to go to the Festival of Flame back in the capital. So long as I don't die on the road."

There will be no Festival of Flame in Concord this year. Arché tries not to let the thought weigh her down, and she forces a smile at Leahi instead.

"We can probably get you to your friend in one piece, at least," she says.

"Can't ask for more than that," Leahi answers. "I appreciate you letting me tag along."

Further into the walk, Lenora gets out her violin to play, and Leahi's eyes light up with new passion as she grabs her flute.

"No magic, just music, I promise," she says, before joining in Lenora's song.

Some of the tension in Lenora's face melts away and the two play through the night, filling the air with music that bridges the divide which had felt so apparent.

At the risk of falling into the exact trap they had been trying to be wary of, Leahi does seem to be a safe sort of daywalker. Being from the Eastern Islands, the completely opposite direction to Izirm, the chances of her being involved with anyone in the Crusade are almost zero. The islands trade mostly with Kanin and the city-state of Skarn, because everywhere else is simply too far to be worth the journey. Unfortunately, that's about all of Arché's knowledge of the islands summed up, as that's all the global geography lessons back home had covered on them.

When the first rays of light begin to seep into the sky, they slow and begin setting up camp. Leahi doesn't question the watch order suggested which places her in the middle of Arché and Lenora, and proceeds otherwise normally until Arché wakes Leahi up and goes to settle herself down.

She and Lenora are sleeping at the same time. In the same, small tent. With someone else on watch.

While Arché tries to get as much space as possible between herself and Lenora as she lies down, there is not much to be had. Lenora's brow is creased in sleep, and she immediately rolls over to press against Arché's side. The crease eases slightly.

Having a sleeping Lenora pressed against her arm was hardly part of Arché's plan, but the sight of her curled up like this tugs at Arché's heart, a nameless but almost tangible thing, like a scent on a breeze.

Lenora's actual scent is a mix of blood and lavender. The latter comes from a small bottle of oil she's carried for as long as Arché can remember, and the main reason Arché knows this is because Rohan had been allergic. They'd avoided sitting near Lenora if she'd applied the perfume recently, or Rohan would start scratching incessantly. Truly, who in the world had ever heard of a lavender allergy, anyway?

It's a lovely smell, now that Arché can safely appreciate it. With it filling her nostrils, Arché finds sleep easily.

Dusk welcomes her as always, and Arché rises quickly, finding Leahi doing the same.

"You know it was a rough night when I've slept all day," their new acquaintance says with a grin. "I'm sure I'll adjust okay."

"Your arms doing alright?" Arché asks.

Leahi flexes them, wincing slightly, and shrugs. "Could be worse. It is what it is."

Arché's eyes shift to Lenora, who is giving a small wave of greeting from where she is sitting with her notebook. Awful realisation dawns on Arché as Leahi begins packing up her tent. The lack of privacy means feeding Lenora is a serious complication without compromising their identities.

They need some sort of excuse to go off on their own, out of her line of sight. But what?

Only one thing comes to mind which will absolutely, certainly work. Arché takes a deep breath, curses the situation and herself for not having anything better, and strides up to Lenora.

"Evening," Lenora says, as Arché nods and leans over almost double to whisper in her ear.

"You need to feed, and we need to do it away from her," she says, quiet as possible. "You'll need to look like I'm seducing you away into the woods. If you're not sure how to do that, maybe try thinking about how good my blood tastes. She needs to think we're going off to do... you know. Stuff."

Perfectly on cue, as Arché pulls back, Lenora blushes a perfect pink. "Oh. Right."

Arché takes her hand, and pulls her up and towards some taller hills a short walk away.

"Feel free to take your time," Arché says to Leahi. "We'll be back."

Leahi looks between them, her face taking a journey from confusion to bafflement. "What? *Now*? You have to do that *right now*?"

Arché, without a clever comeback, glances at Lenora. The vampire is biting her lip and looking at Arché with a hunger that lights Arché's body on fire in an instant, which is unfair, because it shouldn't work like that when Arché *knows* Lenora is faking.

Leahi, however, throws her hands up in resignation. "Alright, alright. I'm just the tagalong, don't let me get in the way."

Arché is relieved that she doesn't seem irritated so much as just genuinely bewildered by their life choices and sense of prioritisation, which is entirely fair under the circumstances. Their positions would be identical in the reverse.

They walk until they are certainly out of earshot, their hands still clasped in the small space between them. Lenora's slender palm fits nicely against Arché's own, smooth against Arché's calluses—a thought Arché curses herself for a moment later.

"Did it work?" Lenora asks.

"As well as it could have," Arché says. "I'm *so* sorry. I should have realised before now, that we would need some sort of plan..."

Lenora lifts an eyebrow. "It's fine. It doesn't matter what she thinks."

It's absolutely true, and yet Arché had not expected the response.

"Fair enough." Why does she wish that Lenora were more bothered or affected in some way by all this? Is it because Arché's neck feels hot even as they discuss the unimportance of what is not even happening? Is it because of what images might be running through Leahi's head? Images of Arché and Lenora, entangled in a way that has nothing to do with blood drinking?

The lack of trees means all they can do is have Arché sit at the base of one of the small hills and let Lenora kneel in front of her. There is something about the way the dying sunlight frames Lenora's face with a soft glow that compliments her strawberry hair so perfectly.

Arché wonders, with a jolt not unlike being hit over the head with a blunt weapon, how she never realised how utterly beautiful Lenora is.

"Hold still," Lenora says as she grips Arché's shoulder. Her voice is just stern enough to turn Arché's brain fuzzy even before the fangs touch her neck.

This entire biting situation is getting absurd. As Lenora drinks and the glorious pain shoots through Arché's system, she is not completely convinced that sneaking off to have sex would feel better than this. Still, she cannot keep her hands from sitting on Lenora's waist and grip it firmly through the ordeal—the ordeal of trying to pretend it's not glorious, that this isn't fast becoming the most precarious of slopes.

Lenora withdraws, her gaze dropping to the hands on her hips. Arché withdraws in an instant and mutters an apology while Lenora similarly lets go of Arché's shoulders.

"You okay?" she asks. When Arché nods, Lenora's eyebrows crease with new thoughtfulness. "How do people usually look, after sex?"

Arché forgets how to think. "Um. What?"

"Did you sleep with Maggie? I'm sorry, I've been assuming this whole time you've got, you know, experience with this kind of thing. I don't, that's why I'm asking. It needs to look convincing, right?"

"No, I nearly did and then I broke it off," Arché says. "But I do. Have experience. Sierra... taught me a lot of things. The blacksmith on the north side. We weren't dating, just... friends having fun."

"*Oh*, right," Lenora says.

"Are you—have you just not done any of that because you didn't feel like it, or because you aren't into sex at all?" Arché asks. She cannot help herself. A part of her is screaming to know just how much of her most physical fantasies are entirely impossible.

Lenora frowns. "I'm not sure. I'm definitely a lot less interested than most people. But I've been interested... a bit. With one person. I think I need the emotional side to be there, to be interested in that sort of thing."

Arché wonders if Lenora and Nikos had been involved, and Arché had simply been too preoccupied to notice. Nikos would surely have mentioned it, wouldn't he? They hadn't discussed him nearly as much as they'd discussed Arché. He hadn't seemed to mind, but by the gods Arché needs to get better at asking other people about themselves more.

"Good to know," Arché says, as she gets to her feet. "I'm flexible. On the emotional part. Not with all of it. I only like women."

"*What?!*" Lenora squeaks. "Really?"

Arché outright jumps at the suddenness of the sound. "Yes? I thought everyone knew. Rohan and I made jokes about my lesbianism about three times a day. Surely people were around for that."

"Well, some of us definitely weren't," Lenora says, her voice still entirely the incorrect pitch.

"Okay, well, to answer your previous question, sometimes after sex, people are bouncy and happy, sometimes they're chilled out and happy. You're usually bouncy with the blood power, so if you can get rid of that bizarre look on your face and go back to that, we'll be fine."

"Bouncy and happy," Lenora says, voice sounding strained. "Right. I can do that, I just... excuse me for a second."

She turns around and shrieks at the top of her lungs into the open air. It lasts precisely two seconds and is followed by silence punctuated by echoes of the shrill noise. Arché is unsure if the echoes are physical or simply bouncing around the corners of her skull.

Lenora turns around, a smile plastered on her face. "I'm bouncy, I'm happy, I've been doing sexy things with you, because that's what we do. Me and you. Yep. This is fine."

It would be convincing to anyone who didn't know that the sickly sweet tone of voice is *not* how Lenora speaks. The word disturbed doesn't quite cover how Arché feels about the whole thing.

"Lenora, respectfully, why the fuck do you care who I'm attracted to?" Arché asks.

"I don't," Lenora says in that same fake tone. "You can be attracted or not attracted to anyone you like, and it should have nothing to do with me."

"Obviously, and yet for some reason that doesn't seem like the case."

Lenora takes her by the hand and even fixes Arché's undershirt collar to cover the bite location better. "Come on. We need to get back."

Despite a thousand questions—or rather, two or three questions repeating a thousand times over each—racing through Arché's mind, she lets Lenora lead the way for now.

"Sorted?" Leahi asks upon their return. She's packed up both tents and has everything ready to go, and is writing in a small notebook she tucks in her bag. Where confusion had been before, an amused smugness sits on her face now. "That was *quite* the scream."

The nightwalkers look at each other, and Lenora turns scarlet.

"*Oh*," she says, covering her face with her hand immediately.

To maintain the pretense, Arché quickly does her best to look extraordinarily pleased with herself, as the supposed reason for said scream coming from Lenora.

"All sorted," Arché says, and Leahi snorts.

But it is *not* all sorted, and as soon as she and Lenora have a moment alone, they'll be having a talk about what the fuck that was all about.

CHAPTER 9
LENORA

Women. Arché Kalésen only likes women.

Crucial information, which if she had known early enough could have changed Lenora's life, that somehow she and Nikos managed to miss for fifteen years. Information Lenora now spends the better part of two nights stewing over, as they continue their journey to the town of Ziliuk. There is nothing to be done, of course. As far as problems go, this one could hardly become *more* irrelevant, but if it is so irrelevant then why does Lenora feel so enraged every time it crosses her mind?

Possibility is always the cruelest of tormentors. Lost possibility, somehow, is the worst of all.

All the while, this new sexual pretense continues to disguise the feedings. Lenora has no problem with it. It is simply odd, like pretending to laugh at a joke she doesn't understand. But then, that's often been her experience with people discussing sexual matters in any context, so it's not completely unfamiliar territory.

Arché certainly doesn't seem comfortable with the whole thing, and despite everything that has happened and literally made Lenora scream at the universe, Lenora isn't going to criticise any way she goes about making sacrifices for Lenora's wellbeing.

If only there was a way to make it less painful. Arché might be tough, but she sure can't keep quiet during the feedings to save herself.

Leahi's presence is a mixed bag. It's saving Lenora from a conversation she *really* doesn't want to have about Nikos, and having another musician to play along with is a special treat and comforting in a way she could never have expected. But there is a constant warning in Lenora's head, blaring *outsider, outsider we cannot trust* over and over.

The strangeness of the world outside Concord, the unknown nature of the daywalkers in it, makes it impossible to feel truly safe. Even with Arché by her side.

Lenora's wakings are still agony, every time Leahi rouses her for the final watch. She knows she must get up, but the new variable of the warmth of Arché's body next to hers makes it even more difficult than usual.

A lack of motivation and resolve ought to feel like an absence within her. But it isn't. It never has been. Every evening, it is a weight on her chest, keeping her down. Every evening, she fights the battle to rise despite it. Hopefully that counts for something.

"This is such a strange time to come into town," Leahi says as the trio arrive in Ziliuk a few hours before dawn.

The town is silent, almost as if asleep alongside its inhabitants. With unremarkable farms on the outskirts, the thing Lenora notices is the detail of the carved decorations of the doorways in the houses inside the town walls. For some reason, it's only the door and window frames, and Lenora nudges Arché to ensure she, a woodcarver, notices the detailing.

"Oh, wow," Arché says, and moves a little closer to have a look as they make their way through. "I'd love to do this when I get my own house, one day."

The tavern is similar, but more grand, with a round wooden sign hanging above the doorframe and reading *The Sunchant Inn* with the most gorgeous spiralling sun carved above the words. It's a beautiful work of art, and yet the depiction of the sun sends a chill down Lenora's spine. After the attack of the Sunless Crusade and the brazen iconography on their garish clothing, Lenora is not sure she'll ever be able to look at stylised suns the same way again.

The inside of the tavern is empty but for a bartender with her head buried in a book bearing a half-naked couple on the cover.

"Hiya," Leahi greets, striding forward. "Got any rooms free?"

The barkeep sets the book aside and blinks her large eyes at Leahi's abrupt entrance. She's small in stature, so much so that the top of her head would be level with Lenora's waist, and her ears are pointed similarly to an elf's while her hair is soft purple. A gnome. Elves aren't the only ones with bloodlines influenced by fey.

"Just the one room," she says, running a hand through her green curls. "Is that okay? Might be a bit tight for three."

"Oh, they're cozy, we'll be fine," Leahi says with a grin back at Arché and Lenora. She hands over some money. "Baths?"

"Down in the basement, I can put some towels down there," the barkeep says.

"Thanks," Leahi tells her, giving her a little wink as she takes the room key, which results in a powerful blush.

How some people just *do* that sort of thing and get the right responses from others, Lenora has no idea. Can it be learned? Is it just instinct?

"I'll probably wash in the morning," Leahi says as they make their way towards the rooms around the back of the tavern floor. "You two do as you like."

"I want a bath," Lenora says at once, and Arché nods in agreement.

The stairs down to the basement are creaky, and the ceiling is low, but the still water looks so inviting that none of that matters. By unspoken agreement, both women turn away from each other and disrobe so that they can enter, never again turning around.

"Gods, finally," Lenora says, taking more joy in scrubbing her underarms than she would have ever expected.

"*Such* a relief," Arché agrees.

Despite having never been naked in someone else's presence in her adulthood, Lenora is not uncomfortable. There is a trust that Arché will not turn around without a good reason and a calm in knowing that it would not be a disaster if she did. Regardless of what else is going on, Arché has never come across as judgemental in any way.

It is quiet but for the splashes of the water, and a few flying streams dance in Lenora's periphery. Arché, playing with her mundane magic. Lenora wants to strike up conversation instead, as having privacy away from Leahi is a rare gift, something they should make use of, but no words seem like the right ones. Lenora has caught Arché regarding her with persistent confusion a few times on the journey here, and Lenora simply isn't ready to explain her outrageous reaction to learning about Arché's sexuality.

But with each day that passes, withholding any truth from Arché feels more and more wrong. So in the absence of truth, Lenora will at least try to avoid lies, but it means she cannot even make small talk about the success of their journey so far, because she would have to lie about having hope of their luck continuing. She simply does not possess such optimism.

The towels are soft, and Lenora wraps herself up with a content sigh, and turns a little too quickly. Arché's bare back is on display, droplets of water sliding down the ridges of the muscles, along the line of her shoulder blade. Then the towel catches them, as it is wrapped around, but new drops fall from the slicked back hair on her neck and down her spine.

Lenora has never understood why some people get so ridiculous around people with pronounced muscles. She still doesn't, really, but seeing Arché like this brings her closer to getting it, in a theoretical way. It's strength, and symmetry, and the artistry of lines more detailed than just simple, soft skin. That has a sort of sense to it.

When they reach the room, it has two single beds and Leahi is already snoring away in one of them.

"Ah. The squish," Arché says, and in any other situation Lenora might have laughed at the juxtaposition of her serious tone and the unserious word. "She thinks we're sleeping together, so…"

Lenora bites her lip. For all the various complications in their relationship, Lenora has been quite enjoying the luxury of basking in Arché's body heat the last few nights in the hours that Leahi is on watch.

"Sharing will be okay," Lenora says, hoping Arché doesn't come up with some noble, tough option like sleeping on the floor.

Arché's eyes hold hers for a moment, a mystery cloaked in comforting dark brown. "Sure. I'm not scared of your pointy elbows."

Lenora frowns at that, but Arché grins in such a way that it's difficult to stay annoyed. Even with the recent revelation, Lenora must admit that this resolve against liking Arché Kalésen is simply not going to work. Arché has done nothing to earn her ire, and done *everything* in her power to make Lenora's life easier since their escape from Concord. To pretend otherwise is simply bordering on cruel.

Even so, stripping down to their underlayers and awkwardly getting into bed together is a different level of conscious closeness that Lenora immediately regrets agreeing to. Their limbs bump and poke until they find a viable position on their sides, with Lenora facing the wall an inch from her nose, and Arché behind her.

Lenora tries not to be so rigid. But she's never been this close to anyone, since... well, ever. Arché's warmth, previously a pleasant indulgence, now overwhelms her on all sides due to their difference in size and decreased space.

"Lenora," Arché whispers, against her ear. "This was your idea. Are you okay?"

"I will be, just... gimme a second." Lenora takes a deep breath and wills her body to relax, to calm. It takes time, but they have plenty of that, and Arché says nothing else.

Slowly and steadily, Lenora's body relaxes against Arché's.

"Well done," Arché says, with so much genuine warmth and pride that it hits Lenora like a sledgehammer.

Or rather, like a slam into an almost shattered window. It makes contact, the tiny bit of praise, and it's the way no one but Nikos has ever said anything that implied they were proud of her. It's how no one has ever held her like this, not ever, and she never realised how starved she'd been for touch until now. It's that nothing has felt safe since Concord. But now, for a fleeting moment, she feels protected.

Lenora cracks down the middle. Tears come in a torrent as every bit of grief, doubt and hopelessness pour out of her.

"Everything is just... too much. And they're all in danger," Lenora sobs. "I have to stop myself from thinking about them, or I know I just won't be able to keep it together."

"I know," Arché says, "I know." She holds Lenora tighter, her arms so strong and solid that they are Lenora's only anchor to the world. "But we're going to help them. We're here, and we can do it."

"All my life, no one has thought I could do anything," Lenora whispers. "Except Nikos. And he was taken, right when I needed to believe in myself. I miss him *so* much."

"I know."

Lenora's heart feels like a void, growing and growing and threatening to swallow everything else whole just to fill the emptiness. And all at once, the secret of her feelings feels so incredibly pointless.

"I loved him," she says, eyes still fixed on the planks of wood making up the wall.

"Of course you did."

Lenora twists so that she is on her back, staring up at Arché's strong jaw before the other woman's head tilts to match her gaze. "No," Lenora murmurs. "I was... *in* love with him."

She's never voiced it before. Relationships between heirs are not technically forbidden, but they might as well be. There is a rule against the merging of the bloodlines to preserve the magic in the founding houses, and an expectation of heirs having children to maintain the town's governmental structure. So she and Nikos could never have been together forever anyway. It had never just been about his crush on Arché. Everything had been against them.

"... oh," Arché says. "Did he know?"

Lenora shakes her head. "He had feelings for someone else. Between that and... you know, heir stuff. It was never going to be a good idea."

"Did he? He never seemed like the type to keep things close to his chest," Arché says. Her face is twisted in genuine confusion, and Lenora cannot help how an odd, near hysterical laugh escapes her throat.

Arché well and truly never had any idea.

"He said it seemed like you had too many things on your mind," Lenora breathes. "I think he was worried that giving you another thing to think about would be a burden."

"Why would hearing about him having a crush be a burden—" Arché trails off when Lenora fixes her with a sceptical eyebrow. "You said that you and he didn't know I only liked women, why would you care about that unless—oh *fuck*."

"Yeah."

"And the whole time, you were in love with—"

"Yeah."

It's strange, having a conversation like this, whispers in the dark with faces only inches from each other. And yet, with every word released into the open, the void within Lenora shrinks ever so slightly.

The journey Arché's face is going through forces another small laugh from Lenora.

"You had to listen to him talking about me?" Arché asks, and when Lenora nods, the lycan groans and buries her face in the pillow above Lenora's head. "I am so, so sorry."

"Yep, it pretty much sucked. And now it turns out, it was a waste of everyone's time."

"I couldn't for the *life* of me work out why my sexuality could have any bearing on you," Arché says, with a chuckle. "Gods, that's so unlucky."

How odd is it that now Lenora mourns Nikos specifically for never being able to see how he reacts to that particular piece of news? In the great context it means so little, but imagining how he would have *laughed* at himself creates an image that aches.

"I miss him so much," Lenora says, rolling back towards the wall as a new wave of sobs takes her. She mourns what could have been, what likely never would have been, and everything else. She mourns her best friend and only love. She mourns the sanctuary of their partnership, and the life raft it had been in her most trying hours.

Arché holds her all the while, and sniffles from behind Lenora make her think that she is not the only one crying now.

"They'd be glad they're missed," Arché eventually says. "But they wouldn't want us to fall down and stay down. They'd believe in us. I know it."

Lenora swallows. "That's why I don't want to get it wrong."

"We won't," comes the answer, but it is a second too late, a fraction too hesitant.

Naturally, even Arché has doubts about Lenora's capabilities. It's not something Lenora can hold against her, but it's the only thing Lenora needs to fall into tears that keep her throat thick and eyes wet until she loses consciousness.

Returning to the waking world brings sore eyes, a deep thirst in her throat, and the same warm arms which had broken Lenora's walls so thoroughly. It is slow and comfortable and Lenora touches her fingers to the grain of the wooden wall as the words exchanged before sleep play over in her mind.

Through it all, sharing laughter alongside tears isn't something she'd expected. But life is unexpected, in that way.

As Arché wakes, sometime later, the lycan yawns and stretches her entire body. It makes for an odd experience on Lenora's end, and she can only think how jealous Nikos would be of her current position. It wrenches a sound from her which is half laugh and half sob.

"Evening," Arché says. It is the most gentle Lenora has ever heard her speak, like someone tipping a toe in water to test the temperature. "Well. Almost."

"Evening, almost," Lenora echoes. She rolls onto her back like she had when they'd been talking before, giving Arché a shy smile before she can convince herself out of being polite. "Thanks. For this morning."

Arché nods slowly, her gaze intense and unfathomable. "We're in this together. All of it." Her head shifts to check over her shoulder. "Leahi's out. We could get you fed."

"Yes please."

Arché hurries to grab a sock and put it on the doorknob outside before sliding back into bed with Lenora. "That should work."

It's a different position, but easy enough to leverage. Lenora only has to press herself against Arché, and she finds she fits perfectly against her chest, with an angle to tilt her chin up and sink her fangs into exposed neck.

Arché shudders, her fingers gripping the back of Lenora's undershirt as she groans. Were it not impossible, Lenora would whisper a sorry, a thank you, anything. But all she can do is take what she needs, and quickly.

Upon having her fill, Lenora lets her head rest against Arché's chest for a moment. A quiet thumping sound is alarming until Lenora realises it is Arché's heart racing not far from her ear. Adrenaline can be a powerful thing.

Lenora's head spins from the lycan magic and her fingers trace over the line of Arché's bicep with absent fascination. "You're so good to me," she murmurs into Arché's shirt.

Arché says nothing. Her heart takes a while to calm, but once Lenora is sure that she's okay, they are able to get on with business.

By the time Leahi knocks, they are the picture of normalcy with Lenora doing some wake-up stretches and Arché doing some one-handed push-ups.

"You can come in," Arché calls.

"Just checking," Leahi says, walking in holding the sock that was placed on the doorknob.

"Ah. Thanks. Just throw it to Lenora."

Leahi does as she is bid, and sits on her bed to watch Arché's exercise routine with admiration that definitely seems to be only partially related to the physical fitness involved. Typical.

"Lucky girl," Leahi remarks with a grin.

"... which one of us?" Arché asks, barely out of breath.

Leahi's eyes flick between the two of them, several times, and then she shrugs. "Both."

Arché makes a noise which is half a laugh and half something else, but Lenora could not begin to decipher it. If it is something to do with Leahi insinuating things about finding them both attractive, Lenora is not particularly interested anyway.

Their next stop is Khiz—Leahi's meeting place with her friend, and one of the last places before Abzah, the town where Alta is supposed to be.

By the time they have an early evening breakfast and head out to, sunset is halfway through. With a full belly as well as her thirst sated, it is even easier to enjoy Leahi's company. It takes Lenora a couple of hours to realise that the woman has the brazen laugh of Rohan, the bright vivacity of Nikos, and a passionate fire all her own.

Perhaps Lenora is only seeing what she is desperately missing. But where initially Leahi had come close to rubbing her not quite right, Lenora now sees her in a better light. So when the daywalker gets out her flute again, Lenora throws herself into a duet with much more enthusiasm than before.

Where Lenora moves lightly on her toes, Leahi's movements are much more peculiar, in a way that can only be measured and deliberate. Right as she goes to breathe into the flute, she grounds her weight with a dig of her heels and bending of the knees.

"Breath control," Leahi explains when Lenora inquires about it. "This is my focus, remember? Sonic magic has its advantages for music, but it also means that literally any note I play could backfire if I slip up."

Arché makes a face of horror, and Lenora can't blame her. Having to keep one's art so controlled sounds like a burden. And as for one's magic... Lenora has always known in theory that Innate mages are supposed to be eternally battling for self-control, and yet... it has never quite been the case for her.

While Lenora has never cared *much* for being like everyone else, continuously finding out that something about herself is unlike anyone she knows is getting tiring.

"Anyway, that's a me problem and I've got it down," Leahi assures her. "Let's play."

With the high of the lycan blood, it is easier to get carried away in the joy of the music, of the two instruments singing out into the night, with Arché's enthusiastic clapping in time serving as impromptu percussion.

It's at the height of the joy that the guilt hits. It pierces her like an arrow to the chest, making her feel like the monster the Crusaders believe her to be. How can she dance and smile like this when her people are locked up and being taken to their deaths? When Nikos is already dead? How dare she?

"Lenora," comes a voice from next to her.

She's stopped mid-dance, her violin hanging at her side, barely in her grasp. Arché holds her shoulders, searching her face for something, and Lenora cannot take those eyes. Not the worry in them, not the safety they try to promise. It's a trap; the last time Lenora believed them, she'd broken, and her composure is still cracked for it. It's not Arché's fault, but Lenora cannot afford such a mistake again.

She tries to speak, but cannot find the right words. Instead, she shrugs off Arché's hands.

"What is it?"

"This, all of this," Lenora says. "I shouldn't be having *fun*. What the fuck is wrong with me?"

"I—nothing, nothing's wrong with you," Arché says, brow creasing. "I mean, things are—" She falters. "Things are messed up."

"And we're walking down the road, completely fine, dancing around. How is that fair? What would they think, if they saw us, seeming like we don't care what they're going through?"

Arché bites her lip. Her shoulders are losing height with every second that passes. "I suppose I just... thought as long as we were moving in the right direction, that's what matters. But you're right. It feels wrong."

A sharp note from the nearby flute jolts them both into looking at Leahi.

"Look, I don't like asking about people's business," she says. "But you two are freaking me out. What's going on that has you two acting like you can't enjoy yourselves for five minutes?"

"You wouldn't understand," Arché says.

"That tends to happen when someone has no explanation, yes," Leahi retorts.

Lenora puts her violin away and takes a deep breath, letting the night air flow through her and pretending it is ice, freezing her into something remotely composed. "It doesn't concern you."

"I don't know, I'm pretty fucking concerned—"

Arché shushes them both abruptly, her head snapping towards the road ahead of them. Sure enough, when Lenora follows her gaze, she can just begin to make out a shape travelling towards them.

"Everyone be quiet and act normal," Arché says, before Lenora and Leahi can say another word.

But Leahi opens her mouth again. "What do you mean act normal? Normal people are allowed to have arguments—"

"Just come over here and walk until they've passed," Arché says, sounding somewhere between attempted civility and begging.

Leahi stares at her, follows her glance up the road, and squints into the darkness. "Oh! How the fuck could you see that—"

Despite muttering confused questions, Leahi moves into line with Lenora, who has begun walking with her arms wrapped around herself. Arché strides forward, overtaking them easily.

The person driving the cart is a figure with a grey beard falling long over his chest, most of his face obscured by his hood.

Lenora wonders how much he heard, how much he saw. If their voices carried, if he is wondering what the three of them are doing on the road at this time, and on foot.

"Evening," he says, with a tired nod. His head tilts as if about to ask a question, but his eyes flick over Arché a second time. "Safe travels."

"You as well," Arché says.

They pass, and continue on in silence until the sound of his horse and cart is all but faded. Arché's body finally relaxes in front of them.

Leahi makes a noise with her tongue. "So... do you two want to explain what all that was about, before? Now that we're done being jumpy at the sight of an old man in a cart."

"We can't explain, Leahi, I'm sorry," Arché replies, before Lenora can lose her temper.

"A lot of people say can't when they mean won't," Leahi mutters. "So which is it?"

There is a small pause. "A bit of both."

"Maybe I can help—" Leahi tries to say.

"You can't," Lenora tells her, without turning around. "This whole thing is something we have to do on our own. No one can help."

"We appreciate the offer," Arché says to Leahi. "Really. It's just... complicated beyond belief. And trust me when I say it's the last thing you'd want to get involved in."

Leahi lets out a long breath that turns into a whistle. "Well, you sure are presuming a *lot* about what I would want without actually having a clue. So maybe you're right. Maybe I shouldn't be involved."

The bitterness is potent. Lenora can't blame her. But it's better that they don't get tangled up with a daywalker, no matter how well meaning or powerful.

Leahi might walk with them in the night now, but she is not beholden to it as they are. Not burdened by it. It is Lenora and Arché, alone. A thought that once would have been one of Lenora's worst nightmares, and is now simple fact.

Part of Lenora still wishes Arché would leave her alone forever. But more and more, she knows it is only because Arché is making everything more complicated. Complicated, because Lenora is now having moments of being so grateful for her presence that it almost takes her breath from her lungs, or even worse, has her wanting to cling to Arché and never let go.

Mortifying. Time to keep walking and never be honest ever again.

CHAPTER 10
ARCHÉ

Guilt is an old, poisonous friend. More and more since her teenage years, Arché has felt its claws dig into her, stirring up a panic that can be quelled only by resolution. Reassurance. Proof, of some kind, that Arché is not a horrible person who has upset someone else or done something to lose their love.

And then, as soon as that resolution comes, everything is calm. And Arché is left wondering why in the world she had felt as though everything was crashing down, when it had been something so small.

But the next time always came.

Lenora pointing out that they were busy having fun while their people suffered had ignited one such claw of guilt to pierce Arché's chest. And then, before it could be resolved because Arché can't exactly get her mother's reassurance at the moment, Leahi's angry huffs at being excluded add another wound.

So they walk, three women in three different, unpleasant silences. And Arché tries to act as though her heart is not trying to drag her body to the ground with its sudden weight, because there is nothing either of her companions would be able to do about it.

She crosses her arms over her chest, as if that will support the rest of her, locking everything and trying to take deep breaths to calm herself. It isn't enough. For every bit of calm the breaths provide, a single thought about her people or Leahi next to her ignites everything back up.

It seems like some cosmic joke, that the fate of Concord lies with the two most fragile heirs. Lenora, with those fraying edges, that deep melancholy that holds her, and... Arché. Who needs only a small change in someone's voice or body to kick her into a state of painful anxiety.

Failure is not an option. And yet, in moments such as this, it is hard to imagine how in the world success could be a possibility.

No words are exchanged as the trio makes camp, and Arché waits until Leahi and Lenora are asleep before the cavern in her chest empties in a torrent of tears and ugly, silent sobs. Her eyes sting, and yet the release of the pressure is such a relief that she embraces it wholeheartedly. She lets herself feel all of it. The grief for Rohan, and their father, a man who had always graced her with approval and warmth. Grief for Nikos, who had always been the best of them. The one who *should* have been the saviour of Concord. He wouldn't have let anything get in his way.

Arché cries for her mother and brother and Mira, hoping desperately that they are alive and unhurt, praying she has not been clapping and laughing in ignorance of them actually being dead, agonising over the fact that she has no way to know.

Last comes the guilt. The guilt around Rohan. Knowing that she was not the friend they deserved, and not knowing whether to feel worse for the fact that they died not knowing it.

Then, like clouds at the end of a storm, things begin to clear. Her body slowly rights itself, finding its balance now that she's let out everything that was in the way.

The deep breaths work now. Arché gets out her carving and begins work on the finishing embellishments of her tiny Kalé. The daylight washes over her. Things go on, and so will she.

When she wakes Leahi for her watch, the daywalker is reserved and brisk, which is fair. Arché crawls into the tent where Lenora sleeps and finds unexpected relief at how Lenora still subconsciously rolls into her. The warmth and softness is a comfort Arché hadn't dared hope for.

The scent of lavender lulls Arché to sleep.

Few words are exchanged as they wake, with Arché and Lenora walking away from camp hand-in-hand to keep up the deception, with Leahi continuing to refrain from commenting. There are some trees dotting the grasslands now, allowing them a little more privacy.

"Are you okay?" Arché asks Lenora, as they come to a stop against one of the trees.

Lenora regards her with eyes so large and grey they're almost like tiny moons, searching Arché's face for something. "No. But I think it would be worse, if I was. There's nothing okay about any of this."

"No, there's not," Arché says. "And trust me, I'm really good at being hard on myself and I was, all of last night. But I also think... there's only so much we can do. Forcing ourselves to be miserable this whole time doesn't take any burden away from the others. I think as long as we're doing the *most* that we can, for them, we need to be kind to ourselves. Or we'll never make it."

"That... makes sense," Lenora says. "I was thinking about Nikos and... he'd be *so* pissed if he knew I wasn't being kind to myself." Her hand brushes a stray hair from Arché's bun away from her cheek, and Arché catches a breath before it can hitch in her throat. "He was a lot better at looking after me than I am. I know that's—"

"We can't control how hard we find things, but we can control what we do next," Arché says. "I know it isn't the same but... maybe we can help each other, when our minds are being difficult. We're not alone, unless we choose to be. We have each other."

"Yeah," Lenora says, tilting her head, her voice even softer than the fingertips lingering near Arché's ear. "You're right. *Of course* you're right—" It's odd, the way she says that part, but it turns into a strange laugh that batters away any possible worry on Arché's end. Then, Lenora smiles, something small and hopeful, like a candle in the deep dark of the night. "Thanks, Arché."

Why does Arché's chest feel strange again? Can she not get a *break*? There is no anxiety, no guilt, so why is her heart doing cartwheels—

Lenora moves into Arché's space and bites into her neck, and the suddenness of the pain stops Arché's brain in an instant, flooding her with the usual mix of pain and pleasure that continues to feel so dangerously good.

Time is strange. Usually these bites stretch out in glorious agony, but this time it rolls like a wave, with Arché hyper aware of the scent of lavender and sweat on Lenora's skin, and the tickle of her long hair against Arché's cheek, the proximity just as intense as the bite itself.

And then it's over. Lenora pulls back, but not very far, and for a second they are sharing each other's breath. Arché's heart hammers against her ribs so violently it makes her jerk upright, creating more space between them even as Arché accidentally looks at Lenora's lips and finds herself appreciating the shape of them, how the top forms a perfect bow.

Those lips stretch into a grin. "Are you alright?" Lenora asks.

"Yes, always," Arché says, probably too fast, so she grabs Lenora's hand and pulls her away from the tree, back towards camp. Away from that dangerous moment, away from the urges to pull Lenora into a crushing hug and utter promises to protect her no matter what comes at them.

This is blood loss and endorphins, Arché tells herself with exasperation. *Have a modicum of sense, please.*

When they get back to camp, Lenora bounces around as she packs her things. Leahi watches them, her expression no longer reserved but instead blatantly curious. Arché lifts an eyebrow at her, to inquire if everything is alright, and gets a near identical eyebrow in return.

So, Arché moves to pack up her bag, and Leahi comes to sit next to her.

"On a totally different angle to last night," Leahi says slowly. "Are you two, like, all good?"

Arché blinks. She tries to determine what in the world Leahi could be talking about, but comes up entirely short. "What?"

Leahi's voice is quiet enough that Lenora cannot hear, as she leans in a bit closer. "Look, I know it's none of my business, but... whenever you two go off, she always comes back skipping. But you're always quiet. And, I don't know, off? I might be just making shit up, but I swear, I'm seeing it every time. So, are you two... *okay?*"

It takes a few seconds to click that this inquiry is about their supposed sex life.

"*Oh,*" Arché says. "No, it's—we're—fine. Good. It works for me." She feels herself blush just saying it, but she needs to be convincing. "Trust me."

Leahi grins sheepishly. "Okay. Just checking."

It's all fine, until the next evening, Arché is hyper-aware of Leahi's eyes on her as they return from their private dalliance. The moment she gets a chance, Leahi checks in with Arché again, and once again Arché assures her of her general wellbeing.

This time, however, it does not go unnoticed.

"What was that about?" Lenora asks, as soon as they get walking. "You and Leahi."

"Oh." Arché curses how her cheeks burn, and lets her gait slow so that they fall further behind Leahi and her ears. "Well. She thinks we're, you know. She's worried about why you're always skipping and I'm... not."

"You do get... pretty weird, afterwards. Not the bouncy, happy stuff you told me to do."

This is an area of great danger. "Well, I never got lessons on how to act like I was having great sex when really I was serving as sustenance. Gods, there's so many good jokes I could make about that—"

"Why are you talking about jokes right now? Maybe Leahi's right," Lenora says, with a frown that is somehow adorable and intimidating in equal measure. "Maybe you're not okay, and you're not telling me."

"I'm fine," Arché says, rolling her eyes. "Seriously. Everyone can stop worrying about me."

The conversation is left there, but Arché can practically hear Lenora's discontent as they continue to walk. So, like a perfectly reasonable and well-balanced person, Arché strides ahead to catch up with Leahi and ask her questions about the Eastern Islands as a way of distracting herself.

Thankfully, once one gets Leahi talking about her home, there is little that will slow her down.

Of course, once the day comes and their watches pass, all too soon it is a new evening and Arché must march away with Lenora once again.

This time, something is off before they're anywhere near the bite. Lenora's face is blank enough to be eerie, yet also rigid. It's baffling, and Arché tries not to let it unsettle her, but before she can come to any kind of peace about it, Lenora manhandles her into position and bites into her neck.

It's fast. Not rough, but clinical, and this time Arché's whimper is of a different and genuine pain as confusion drowns out everything else. It doesn't feel good.

When it's done, Lenora wipes her mouth and steps away, clasping her hands behind her back.

"Ready when you are," she says, as if they've finished some sort of meeting.

"Yeah," Arché replies, on instinct. Everything feels off, her entire body shaken to the point of fog seeping into her mind, and she has to force her feet to move.

Lenora takes her hand partway through the walk, but the hold is wooden, and she says nothing at all.

Arché had always been so dismissive of how Lenora would check in with her after every bite. It had seemed so silly, and yet now her mind screams at how she had missed its necessity. The bites are so intense for Arché that Lenora's check-ins have essentially served as aftercare, and now without it, Arché is *not* okay. She feels wrong. Used. Dismissed.

Arché's head continues to swim as they make it back to camp, and it is a relief to leave Lenora's side but a struggle to latch onto the next task, her routine becoming a haze.

"Arché?" Leahi again, her hand on Arché's arm. "Okay, you can tell me to fuck off, but now I'm *actually* worried."

"I'm fine," Arché says, and silly inspiration hits her. "I just, uh, couldn't get it up."

"Oh!" Leahi's eyes widen. "You know, you can get things to help with—"

Arché can't keep in the genuine laughter that seizes her at Leahi's earnest reaction. "Leahi, sorry, that was a bad joke." She lets herself sigh, just a little.

"Lenora and I… things are tricky, I guess, right now. But we'll get through it. I'm sorry that it's awkward, for you to be on the periphery."

"Right." Leahi makes a face. "Sorry for, you know, the meddling. I just always want to help fix things, if they seem like they need it."

"You mean well," Arché agrees. "Thank you." The gratitude is real. It's soothing, to her confused body and heart, to have someone checking in on her. It would simply be more ideal if it were Lenora.

The rest of the night is the most silent yet. Even Leahi doesn't try to make up for the absence of conversation, except with some playing of her flute. It could almost be comfortable, if not for Arché feeling as though Lenora is avoiding looking at her.

Luckily, sleep has that miraculous tendency to refresh everything, and it washes away the taint of last night's bite to leave room for worry about how the next will go.

Arché's heart leaps into her throat the moment Lenora takes her hand, and her stomach twists with dread. She's not sure if she'll be able to keep it together, if it goes the same way.

"Was that last one better?" Lenora asks, once they're away and alone.

Arché frowns. "What?"

"The bite. Was it better that way? I thought it would be, but then you didn't… I can't tell what's going on in your head. Ever."

"No, it wasn't," Arché says, crossing her arms and biting her lip at the mere memory. "It was… not nice, actually. Please don't… do it like that again."

Lenora's face falls. "I'm so sorry. I thought it might make it… easier, for you."

"Easier, how?"

"Well. I realised—at least, I think—why you make the noises you do."

Arché's face gets so hot she fears combustion, and yet would welcome it. "Gods, Lenora, fuck, I'm so sorry, I really can't help it—"

"I know, it's okay," Lenora assures her, planting her hands on Arché's shoulders. "It just happens, right? I was just worried the whole thing made you uncomfortable. It seemed like it."

"Oh!" Arché releases a long breath. "No, not nearly as much as the idea that I was making *you* uncomfortable. At first I didn't know if you had any experience with that kind of thing, then you told me you didn't, and it's not *you*, it's just... me."

"And physical urges are stronger in lycans, I know," Lenora finishes. "The things Nikos got up to with some of those hunters..." She makes a face, and Arché is hit with a vague memory of Nikos sneaking away from the hunter camp with another lycan guy their age.

In retrospect, she has a fresh understanding of why he'd looked so mortified at her noticing him doing so. When he'd later explained in earnest that it was only sex, she'd politely replied that it was none of her business and didn't understand why he was telling her anything. Now, she understands why he'd gone so quiet.

"I'm really glad you understand," Arché says honestly. "It's easy for these things to get confused."

"Definitely. But you don't need to hide anything, Arché."

Arché nods. It feels vulnerable, having to admit to how the last time had felt, and then to the nature of her experience in these moments. Despite the uncomfortable exposure, the truth and understanding between them comes as stark relief.

"Okay," Arché murmurs, as she tilts her head to present her neck. "Just... not like last night, alright?"

"Not like last night," Lenora says, her voice a whispering promise so soft it soothes all the wounds of the previous feeding. "Never. I'll look after you, Arché."

Her hand slides up Arché's neck, as if sealing the promise with touch, and Arché tries to hold in a shiver and find the breath that has vanished from her lungs. Without a bite, she cannot justify such reactions, and she will have no acceptable explanation for either of them.

"Ready?"

"Ready."

Lenora bites. For the first time, Arché does not restrain the moan that wrenches from her throat. It feels wrong, and *wonderful.* The urge to grab Lenora and pull her closer is so strong, and even more forbidden now, so Arché reaches behind herself to grab at the rough bark of the tree. When her human fingers don't get the grip she wants, she channels her lycan essence just enough that her hands become claws that sink into the wood.

And then, before she knows it, it's over. Arché takes deep, slow breaths and lets her claws retract and shift back.

"Better?" Lenora asks, licking her lips clean. "It seemed... better."

"Uh huh," Arché says, trying not to let it come out high-pitched. "Better."

It is, compared to the previous time, but anything would be. This matter of not holding back at all is a bit much, and Arché is feeling that keeping herself restrained is the better move. Otherwise, the rest of her might start getting... ideas.

Still, this time, when they walk back to camp hand in hand, it feels like the easiest thing in the world.

Leahi beams when she sees them. "Good."

"Huh?" Lenora asks.

"Don't worry," Arché says, giving her hand a squeeze before releasing it. "Come on. You said we're likely to make it to the next town tonight. Khiz, right? Real beds, waiting for us."

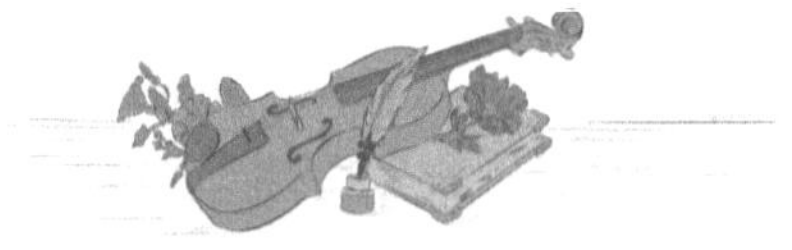

CHAPTER II
LENORA

Bodies are strange, being so at the mercy of bizarre sensations and urges. In another life, Lenora might have been compelled to study it, as some form of academic. The relationship between mind and body has always been fascinating. In this life, the strangest of events around her are defined by such oddities.

Lenora and her ancestors are forever cursed to be dependent on blood, always a little thirsty. Meanwhile, some people, vampires and lycans and regular mortals alike, can be overwhelmed by physical urges for pleasure that make it incredibly difficult to resist. Food. Alcohol. Endorphins from exercise. Drugs. Sex.

With twin siblings on the cusp of adulthood, Lenora had barely gone a day without hearing a joke about sex. With limited interest in such things herself, she'd tired of it quickly. It had been a relief that Nikos had only ever mentioned his own adventures in passing, as she'd not wanted to hear about it even without her pining for him in the equation.

Arché and Rohan had often been throwing around crude jokes. Which may have played a part in Lenora's less than enthused feelings on Arché as a person, pre-Crusade.

But now, the last thing Lenora can do is judge Arché for her reaction to Lenora's bites. She can hardly be expected to keep that part of herself repressed. Perhaps if they come to a town large enough to have a brothel, Arché could blow off some steam there. That can apparently be healthy, if the individual is comfortable with such things. Based on the description of her relationship with Sierra... Arché might be.

Khiz has nothing that looks like a brothel, though admittedly Lenora would have no idea what to look for. The tavern is at least easy to locate, a large place named the Blue Axe, with enough rooms that Arché and Lenora are able to get one to themselves.

"Twin or double?" the bartender asks.

Arché glances at Leahi, who is busy counting out coins, then back to the bartender. "Double, please."

Right. Their deception. It's weird, to be pretending to have sex to hide bites that are making Arché sort of want to have sex. Weird only due to Lenora's absolute indifference on the matter. But if it's keeping their secret, and Arché is okay, that's all that matters. Lenora isn't a prude; Leahi can think whatever she wants.

"I'm crashing *now*," Leahi tells them as soon as she's paid for both rooms. There are shadows under her eyes which speak to her struggle with the nightwalking schedule, and Lenora finds herself admiring how the daywalker has pushed through without complaint. Or questions about Lenora's sunlight allergy.

The double room is simple and pleasant, with the double bed against the back wall as well as a small wardrobe on the right and a desk on the left.

Arché is quiet tonight, but has always given Lenora a smile if their eyes meet. It's a relief, as after revealing to Lenora how poorly she'd handled the attempt at a detached bite, she'd been worried Arché would hold such an error against her. It would be justified, with how unfair it was to Arché, who has done nothing but give Lenora whatever she needs. But instead she is just... the same Arché.

"Are you okay?" Arché asks.

"Yeah," Lenora says, giving her a smile. "Just... thinking I'm lucky that I'm on this journey with you. And not someone else."

Arché makes a baffled face at that. "Huh?"

"You're nice, that's all." Lenora's explanation is not proving adequate and she sighs. "Nevermind."

Arché still seems uncertain, but opts for preparing for bed instead of asking questions. Once they're both in the bed, Arché shuffles to the opposite edge, as if touching Lenora will make her break out in a rash.

"We shared a smaller bed than this before," Lenora reminds her. Sure, it had been a disaster for Lenora's composure, but why is Arché so concerned? Unless she hated having Lenora cry on her, which is possible but doesn't feel right.

"Out of necessity," Arché replies. "This is... different necessity. I don't know."

"I mean... you're warm. I'm not going to complain," Lenora says, trying not to sound too eager because she has no reasonable explanation for how much she enjoys sleeping closer together.

"Well, I want space," Arché says, rolling to face away from Lenora and curling her body into a ball beneath the blanket.

It might be disappointing, but is probably for the best. Lenora settles in on her side, relishing the softness of the mattress and the silky feeling of the bedding, both balms for her well-torn body. She can only imagine how exhausted she would be if not being fueled by lycan blood the whole way.

By the gods. Leahi. A regular mortal, with only Innate magic setting her body apart as far as they know. No wonder she's been so exhausted by every dawn! She's been trying to keep up with two magically enhanced people without even knowing it.

She voices this to Arché, who groans, and they agree to check in on Leahi when they wake before they part ways now that Leahi is where she wants to be.

Lenora falls asleep with ease at the thought of leaving Leahi and their deception behind in Khiz when they wake. It's been exhausting.

The sound of intermittent slaps and thuds wakes her. She leans over the bed to see Arché doing push ups with claps on the floor next to the bed.

"Evening," Lenora says, with bewilderment.

"Evening," Arché replies, as if there is nothing bizarre about the intensity of her evening workout. "Good sleep?"

"Yeah, you?"

"Decent. Can't complain."

There is something soothing about the rhythm of the claps that has Lenora falling back into the pillows and slipping into a comfortable doze. It's a nice change to take things slower and simply enjoy the fleeting comfort of the bed.

The road beckons, as it always does, with an imagined chorus of her people's voices crying her name and pleading with her to hurry. But amidst them all, of all people, is Arché's mother Kalé. Her strong gaze, her unwavering voice that is seldom argued with.

Pace yourself, Lenora can imagine her saying. *It's a long road ahead. You'll need your strength.*

As far as strength goes, Lenora takes it from Kalé's daughter in the most literal, physical way. Arché's blood is as sweet as ever, and Lenora is sure to murmur thanks and check in on her companion. It is a commitment she will not neglect.

Arché is ever quick to get on with things, despite the flush in her cheeks and neck. Lenora is relieved that they have such clear communication and priorities, to not be such silly people as to turn it into a problem, no matter how odd it is for Lenora to know she is causing such feelings in another person.

A knock at the door is followed by Leahi's voice.

"Breakfast, lovebirds?" she calls. "My treat still, before you get going."

"Sounds good!" Lenora replies. "Be down in a minute."

It's an unfortunate thing, to not realise you're going to miss someone until you're saying goodbye to them. Lenora settles herself across a downstairs booth from Leahi and returns her large smile, considering how refreshing it had been to meet someone who knows her simply as Lenora.

Not an heir. Not a chosen one. Just Lenora. It's utterly new, and precious.

"So, onward with your mysterious, difficult mission?" Leahi asks once they've all ordered some food.

"That's the one," Arché says. "Wish us luck."

"All the luck I can. It seems tough, and I know I slowed you down so... I appreciate it. You letting me come along." Leahi makes a face. "And you saving my life. All of it."

"I'm sorry we didn't slow down more for you," Lenora says. "We didn't realise we were probably hard to keep up with."

Leahi snorts at that. "Yeah, just a bit! Talk about a workout, I've never thought I was slow or unfit, but you two are something else, almost like—"

The door of the inn slams open. Two figures walk in, a pair dressed in bright orange with high collars and symbols of a blazing sun across their chests.

Crusaders. The blood in Lenora's veins boils at the sight of them, her entire body going rigid.

Several of the local patrons, busy having their dinner, spare a few glances for the new arrivals and lift an eyebrow or two before going back to their conversations. How strange, to think they are not seeing the world in red, as Lenora is.

The Crusader pair survey the room, land on Lenora's table, and begin making their way over. Before Lenora can determine whether to panic or leap at their throats, Arché's hand finds hers under the table, holding it tight.

"Breathe," Arché says, low and soft. "We don't know what they know, yet."

Leahi's eyes flick between both of them, and then the approaching Crusaders, trying to put together a puzzle she doesn't have all the pieces for.

"Hey there," the taller of the Crusaders says, a human man with sandy hair and a pair of shortswords on his hips. He comes too close, leaning on their table with the palm of his hand.

Extremely within biting distance. It would be so easy for Lenora to take a chunk out of him, to see the fear in his eyes like the zealot outside the cabin as she'd finished him off. She shouldn't like it, shouldn't want it, but the loathing and fury burn so hot in her chest. She cannot bear it, and vindication is all she has left.

That, and Arché's hand on hers. Keeping her grounded. Reminding her of what is at stake if they act too rashly.

"You lot seem like you've been on the road. Seen any weird stragglers? Runaways?" the Crusader asks.

A snort escapes Arché. "Stragglers? What? Make sense, please, before our br—food arrives."

"Rabid werewolf town had some people escape our roundup," he replies. "Danger to the general public, you know. Trying to do our part."

"Uh huh," Arché says, with disbelief and disinterest so potent it almost convinces *Lenora*. "We weren't around during the last full moon. We haven't seen anything, sorry."

Leahi's eyes fall to Arché's right shoulder, the one facing Lenora and out of sight of the Crusaders. The shoulder that bears the tattoo of Kalé's transformed paw print with a symbolic border representing the six houses of Concord. Lenora's mouth goes dry as Leahi meets her eyes with new questions burning in them.

Of course, that is when their food is delivered by the barkeep, who awkwardly slips past the Crusaders to put down the plates before hurrying off before they can even say thank you.

The talkative Crusader makes an impatient, annoyed noise. "Well, there's a pair of them, and they could rip innocent farmers limb from limb." His eyes run over them as a group, especially Arché and her arm muscles—thankfully, not the tattoo out of his sight. "You look pretty capable. Want to earn some extra gold? The Sunless Crusade would reward you for their capture. Or, you know, if taking them alive is too difficult... that's just how it goes sometimes, right?"

He grins and jiggles a pouch on his hip in what he must think is an enticing manner.

Lenora pokes at her food and forces herself to put a piece of steak into her mouth so that she can focus solely on chewing it. She could not swallow if she tried, with her stomach in an uproar, but it gives her something to think about that isn't committing murder in the middle of a daywalker establishment. As pleasant as it would be to drain him until he is empty, empty of words and bile and hate and every last drop of blood.

Arché sighs, as if bored, but her hand is clutching Lenora's so hard it is starting to hurt. "No thanks. We're already on a job. All booked up."

"Fair enough. Travel safe, then."

With that, the Crusader and his fellow go to sit at the bar and order drinks. Lenora holds the morsel of meat in her mouth, unable to swallow but loathe to put it back on the plate.

"Thank the gods I left the shield upstairs," Arché says under her breath, her eyes still half watching their enemies across the room. "Gods, I—"

"Ow," Lenora says, when the grip on her hand finally becomes too much to bear.

Arché releases her at once, wrapping her hand over her stomach as she stares at her plate like it will provide her some kind of relief or answer.

"What the fuck is going on?" Leahi whispers from across the table. "What's the Sunless Crusade?"

"I can't—" Arché goes to stand, but Lenora grabs her by the forearm. "Lenora, I need to—"

"You can't, your tattoo, they'll see it," Lenora says quickly. "We can go, but we need to move, you know, together. We'll go upstairs til they leave, yeah?"

Arché freezes, and stands while rotating her body to keep her right side facing away from the Crusaders. The stairs are on the opposite side of the room, meaning Arché will have to be facing exactly the wrong way to cross it. So Lenora takes her right hand and half-latches onto her arm, as if they are the couple they keep claiming to be, Lenora's head and hair completely covering the tattoo site.

"Can I help?" Leahi asks.

"Talk to me, distract me, please," Arché says, and Lenora is horrified to realise that she's never heard Arché beg before.

Leahi jumps to the task, falling into place on Arché's left and launching into a story about how she and her brother had stolen their cousin's canoe to win a bet and ended up stranded on a tiny island until they were rescued by their tiny, unimpressed, terrifying grandmother.

It forces a few weak chuckles from Arché, while Lenora walks in silence. The world is tinted red, but it's different now. The moment she'd registered that Arché needed more help than she did, her own feelings fell away into almost nothing.

There will be time for Lenora to feel all of this. But Arché needs her. That's more important.

They cross the room, and get up the stairs and into Arché and Lenora's room. The moment they get the door locked, Arché falls into the desk chair and leans over her knees, gasping in a breath that shakes her whole body.

"Arché," Lenora says, dropping to her knees next to her, hand still on her arm.

"I'm sorry, I couldn't—" Arché shakes her head. "When things are that bad and they *smile*, I don't know what's wrong with me but I just feel like I'm going to..."

She doesn't finish explaining. Lenora desperately wishes to know what word she is holding back, wants to understand so she knows how to help, but nothing comes except heavy breaths.

"Who *are* those people?" Leahi asks. "The Sunless Crusade? What the fuck kind of name is that?"

"They're murderers," Lenora says, the word biting with the fury she is trying to keep in check. "And liars."

"Zealots are the ones who name themselves things like that," Arché elaborates, quietly, her head still down. "They think they're doing the Everflame's work. They're not."

Leahi's hands rest on her hips while her head tilts, brows creased with focus. "They mentioned a town. And two runaways."

All at once, the truth is demanding to be spoken before Leahi's trust in them evaporates. Lenora squeezes Arché's knee so that Arché's wet eyes glance in her direction. They stare at each other for several seconds, exchanging a wordless question, before both nodding.

Arché sighs and lifts her chin to look at Leahi properly.

"Yes," she says, "and the only thing they got right is how little they care if any of us die. There's no such thing as a rabid werewolf, for fuck's sakes. All we are is a bit different and they decided to attack us for it."

"So... you're both werewolves?" Leahi asks. There is no fear, only intrigue, her eyes alight with curiosity's fire.

"I am," Arché says. "Lenora... not quite." She lifts an eyebrow at Lenora in equal question and invitation. Where Lenora expected to feel nerves, there is only a soft excitement in her chest. With a giggle, Lenora lets herself smile wide enough to show off her pointed fangs. Leahi's jaw drops.

"Woah! That's so—" Leahi stops. "Wait, don't vampires tend to hurt people, though? Like, by nature?"

"The lycans and vampires taught each other different aspects of control, centuries ago," Lenora explains. "We do need to feed, but we can do it safely. With consent."

"Though we did need a cover story for why we had to keep running off every morning," Arché says, managing a small grin at Leahi.

"Right," Leahi laughs. "Gods, and all the questions I was asking—" Her cackle stops short. "Your town was attacked, you said? I'm so sorry, here I am just—that sounds really fucked up. And now they're walking around telling lies about you and trying to hire people to hunt you?"

"Pretty much," Lenora says. While a part of her still wants to go downstairs and tear the Crusaders limb from limb, it is quieter now. The validation of Leahi's horror, and understanding, serves as a balm that is calming her scarlet vision. "We're the only two who got away. As far as we know."

"They're taking our people to Cancium," Arché continues. Her right hand comes to rest on top of Lenora's own, where it sits on Arché's right forearm. "We don't know how, exactly, we just need to work out how to stop it. But that's what I meant, when I said you don't want to get involved. It's awful, and dangerous."

"Yeah, but how the fuck am I supposed to just get on with my month knowing this is happening?" Leahi begins to pace, snapping her fingers with such a rhythm it creates a small loop of echoes, just surreal enough to have Lenora realise it is her magic manifesting in a small way. "Where are you headed now? I could ask around, in the meantime. If they're transporting what, dozens? Hundreds of people? They won't be able to do it without someone seeing *something*. I'm good at talking to people. Let's find out where they are."

"Even asking around might be dangerous," Arché tells her.

"So is walking down the road," Leahi retorts, and there is no possible rebuttal to that, given how they met her. "I owe you a lot more than a few songs and paid rooms. I'll do what I can."

"We're headed to Abzah, it's a bit of a northern detour, but if they're headed for Cancium I guess we'd be coming south and needing to keep moving west," Lenora says, leaning on Arché's arm as she thinks it over. The warmth is more comforting than ever.

"Alright. I'm not sure where I'll be by then. I'll leave a message here, if I leave. But I guess that makes this goodbye, for now."

They both stand, and Leahi grabs Arché in a tight hug, which Arché is quick to return. Lenora gets a turn next, and in the seconds before the contact Lenora is sure it will feel wrong and uncomfortable. But Leahi is somehow soft and solid at once. It's the first proper hug Lenora's had since Nikos, and she doesn't mean to cling but is sure she does, her body shuddering with the shock at the comfort the single embrace provides.

"Are you going to be okay?" Leahi asks.

"I think so," Lenora murmurs.

"We'll be fine," Arché says, with a lot of confidence for someone who had been shaking from head to toe a few minutes before. "The one thing they had right is that we're powerful, and to them, dangerous."

Leahi nods and slowly releases Lenora, who pulls her arms back to her sides and tries desperately to look normal about the whole touch-starved thing that hopefully isn't painfully obvious to everyone else.

"Then I'll see you down the road," she says. "Don't you dare get killed."

With that, she leaves, a mist of mixed feelings sifting through the room in her wake. Arché sits back in the chair, her elbow hitting the desk as her face drops into her hand. Lenora plays the conversation back in her head and finds her arms wrapping around herself.

"Powerful and dangerous," Lenora repeats, Arché's words somehow the most absurd part of the whole thing. "Yeah, right."

"Objectively, we are," Arché says.

"Well, it never feels like it," Lenora mutters. She sits on the floor with her bag and begins repacking it. "We have training, and natural advantage. Those are tools. They're not... *us*."

Arché does not reply. When over ten seconds pass and no words are exchanged, Lenora glances up to see Arché staring at the wall, unmoving.

"Arché?"

"Sorry," Arché says, coming back to herself with a wince. "You're right. We're... we need to be more than our tools, to pull this off."

"Are you okay? After... all that?" Lenora asks.

"I should be asking you that," Arché says, standing abruptly. "I'm so sorry, I was supposed to be helping you, and then I just... started unravelling."

"You did so well talking to them, I couldn't even *speak*," Lenora is quick to say. "They've hurt both of us, Arché, we're allowed to be upset at the same time."

"Sometimes things take an extra minute or so to hit me, but then when they do..." Arché exhales long and slow. "That could have been really bad. Not losing control is our entire thing." Her hand runs up her arm, over her tattoo.

All the werewolf talk reminds Lenora of something important.

"Arché, when's the next full moon?"

CHAPTER 12
ARCHÉ

To be a lycan asked when the full moon is, and not have an answer, is mortifying.

Arché opens her mouth, realises she is lost in the daywalking world in more ways than one, and closes it again. She can only groan into her hands.

"Fuck, I didn't even—the lunar dial in the town square, I've never needed to give it a second thought. I haven't been counting the nights."

"This is the fourteenth night we've been out of Concord, together, including the first when we escaped," Lenora says.

Arché blinks. Without letting herself be distracted by questions of how and why Lenora knows that so easily, she thinks back as hard as she can. The last full moon was practically in another life. A life before the attack. A life when their best friends still drew breath.

"Uh, alright then, so... soon," she guesses. "A few days? I suppose we can take a look once we get outside. I can usually feel it coming, once we're on the cusp."

"How would you normally spend those nights?" Lenora asks. While technically only one night is the true peak of the full moon, the night where the green stars come out, the peak and the nights either side of it are considered the three full moon nights to anyone from Concord.

A smile tugs at Arché's lips. "My family and I liked to go out into the fields and wrestle all night. Or we'd just run, for hours on end, racing the length of the valley. Sometimes Rohan would come to wrestle. They never could keep up when I was transformed fully."

Lenora nods, genuine interest lighting her eyes. It's good to see the stress and hatred falling away to make room. "Okay. Well, you let me know what you'd like me to do. I can be... as involved or not involved as you like. I can try to run with you, but I'm not much of a wrestler."

It's a sweet offer. And yet, it hits Arché like a hammer to the face, because it is the *reasons* behind the offer that catch her off guard. Lenora is saying this because they will be alone. Arché will be away from every other lycan she's ever known. Arché will be the *only* lycan for miles when the full moon comes.

She'll... what? Release a howl to the sky and hear nothing but her own echo, instead of dozens of other howls in a gorgeous dusk chorus? The thought is so wrong that her stomach turns.

"Arché?" Lenora asks. It's the second time in only a few minutes that she's had to pull Arché from her own thoughts. How embarrassing.

"Sorry," Arché says again, and gods she is tired of how much she needs that word. "I'll have a think. I hadn't thought about being away from them. But your ideas are... really nice. Thanks."

"I know it won't be the same."

"At least hopefully all the others are together." Arché lifts her chin, in the hope of giving the illusion of bravery. "They need each other more than I need them, right now."

An odd grin comes to Lenora's face. "Wait, those Crusaders will have three nights of fully transformed lycans as captives. That's going to be a nightmare."

"Good," Arché says, mirroring the grin. "Now *that's* a happy thought."

They agree it is better to wait for the zealots downstairs to either leave or get considerably drunk before trying to leave the inn, just in case, and spend some time looking over the map so they can be sure of their course. From Khiz, they have only road left between them and Abzah, the last place Alta was headed.

They're almost there.

An hour later, they gather their things and creep down the stairs to see if the coast is clear to make their exit.

They make it halfway down when one of the Crusaders turns the corner at the bottom of the staircase and begins staggering up the stairs as the reek of alcohol assaults Arché's nose.

Fuck. As Arché's heart skips a beat before launching into a panicked drum roll, Lenora's hands take Arché's left forearm in a vice grip from where she's a few steps higher on the stairs. There's room for the Crusader to pass, but not comfortably. Moving back to the top to avoid him might look suspicious.

Arché's tattoo is covered by her travel cloak, but she is acutely aware of how it would only take a small shift for him to get a glimpse. And Crescent Light is on her back, too large to cover with any practicality. A beacon of affiliation with the moon, obscured only by her back to the wall.

They all but hold their breath as he comes closer, one slow step at a time. It's the one who tried to hire them, the one who spouted so many lies.

He is almost in line with Arché when his gaze flicks to Crescent Light. When he turns his head curiously, the stench of ale worsens. He stops where he is, his height equal to Arché's. So close to her, and it is a difficult thing to not ram his head into a wall.

They cannot risk violence here. There is far too much to lose. But he's an inch from Arché's face.

"Your shield… it's a moon," he says slowly.

"Yes," Arché says, unable to respond with anything better. She can't claim it's a religious symbol, because the god of the moon is the Winter Wolf, the least helpful thing she could bring up. "I… like curves."

The Crusader blinks. As absurd as the whole thing is, the haze of alcohol is working its charms, because there is a tug at the corner of his mouth. He chuckles to himself, just once, and continues up the stairs.

He reaches the top. They stay still, probably longer than they should, too paranoid to budge. Once he is gone from their sight, turning at the top, Arché finally exhales.

"Gods," Lenora murmurs. "That was too close."

"Let's get moving, before he thinks about it any longer," Arché agrees.

They hurry downstairs and are relieved to see the other Crusader so drunk that he is embracing a table, allowing them the chance to get some food from the bar to take on the road.

Even just stepping outside and looking at the nearly full moon sends a tingle down Arché's spine. The magic in her bones anticipates the change and the rush of power it will bring. It's easy to walk at a brisk pace out of town to ensure there are no unwanted Crusade tails.

It's fourteen days to Abzah, at least by the conventional road and regular walking pace. But it is a twisting road, and with the full moon coming they plot a shortcut through the grassland in between. If they're running at their supernatural speeds, it may well cut several days.

It's unlikely anyone has forgotten Arché's energetic parent, if they have encountered them, so the only danger is if Alta has moved on without giving any word or trail. Little point worrying about that now, as it'll only result in an unhelpful spiral, so Arché pushes the possibility aside.

After three nights of simple travel, companionable silence, and small talk, they finally reach the first of the nights where the moon will reach for what lies in Arché's blood and bring it alive.

Even from the moment Arché wakes, she feels like she's on fire. It's not painful. It is pure power. Pure life. She could run for miles, right now, before the transformation is even upon her.

"You okay?" Lenora asks, when she catches Arché bouncing on her heels.

Arché nods, a little manic, with a grin that seems to convince the vampire. They pack up camp, ensure Lenora gets in a quick feed before she has to bite through fur, and Arché changes into her stretchy garments.

Then, the moonrise is almost upon them. Getting bitten while hypersensitive to everything going on in her body sure is an experience, but the anticipation of the transformation overrides everything else tonight.

They wander into the long grass. Arché shivers as she looks up at the moon beginning to peek through the dusk sky, and digs her toes into the dirt. A few moments later she falls to her knees, hitting the ground and splaying her fingers across it.

Everyone has their own way of taking the transformation. Arché likes to close her eyes to better feel the soil around her fingers and toes, soaking in the moonlight and listening to the world all around. Letting herself tune into it. The world is a strange place, wild and magical and impossible to predict—but when Arché transforms, she feels like she belongs. She feels her heart beat alongside it, something more visceral than a mere sound.

Her body rolls. Her fingers turn to claws, and her limbs grow fur, and she gasps through her human mouth before it shifts into a muzzle. Not a full wolf, like a beast, but a fully transformed lycan. Bipedal, but able to move on four legs where needed. Muscle and power and speed in ways beasts could only fear.

Arché tilts her head back. With her first transformed breath, she howls to the moon with everything her lungs can give. She howls first for the joy of it, then for the power, and third for the family who should be here and are not. That one hurts, as it pulls at her heart, but all she can do is stand and stretch.

She is still Arché. She still has her own heart, and most of her mind. Her instincts are simply in charge now, instead of her higher cognition.

There is a familiar smell nearby. Friend. Lenora.

Arché rushes to her, sniffing her with new intensity before nuzzling into her shoulder. Lenora giggles and pats Arché on her furry head. It feels fantastic, and Arché's foot scratches into the dirt.

"Wow," Lenora says. "I've never watched it before. Not really. How are you doing?"

"Good." Speech is trickier, transformed. Simply because it's harder to form people words without a people mouth. Words also come to mind a bit more slowly. But that's alright. "Run?"

Lenora grins. "Sure."

They take off northward as previously agreed, at an impossible speed. They keep it up for an hour before Lenora tires.

"I'll walk fast, and you can just run circles around me," Lenora suggests.

Arché is perfectly happy with that. She could run and fight and leap, but there is nothing to fight, so running is what there is. She runs circles around Lenora for hours.

Finally, as the first light of the coming sunrise begins to lighten the sky, her body begins to tire. Lenora takes charge on setting up camp while Arché gingerly searches a backpack with her claws seeking dried meat to chew on.

They sit, and Arché munches on her findings. Lenora smells nice and Arché leans into it, resting her head on Lenora's shoulder and earning a hand stroking over the back of her head.

It feels so wonderful that Arché releases a deep sigh and nuzzles closer. Her head ends up in Lenora's lap, and a comfort true and deep begins to sink into Arché's bones. Safe. For this moment, this feels warm and safe.

The power of the moon slips away, seeping out of her bit by bit, and she flexes her legs as the fur disappears and her face flattens into its usual shape.

Lenora's hand stills on Arché's head. When she speaks, her voice is soft and gentle. "How was that?"

"Good," Arché murmurs, sitting up slowly and stretching her arms above her head and then behind her back. As far as full moons without her family could have gone, it went well. "It would be better if you could keep—"

A new idea flashes through Arché's mind. It would be deeply frowned upon in Concord, but they are not *in* Concord, and it is only a step further than they have already gone. There's no reason it shouldn't work.

"You could take more," Arché says. "More blood. So you can keep up."

"Uh, no," Lenora says, blinking at her. "Anymore and you'd be in danger, *you'd* be too weak to go fast. You know, blood loss?"

Arché shakes her head, fast. "All the lycans heal *much* faster fully transformed. So my family... even more so. I'd be back in top form within... two hours? And then we could cover a *lot* of ground."

Intrigue swims over Lenora's features. "Hmm. That is... an idea. If you're *sure* about the regeneration. This would be the worst time to get it wrong."

"I know," Arché assures her. "Trust me. I'm sure."

"I'll think about it. Let me sleep on it."

"Sure. Can we switch watches? I'm ready to pass out from all the running." Arché is relieved when Lenora nods immediately, and she practically dives into the tent bed roll.

Arché swears she only blinks before Lenora is waking her up. A deep and dreamless sleep is a blessing, though, and Arché is able to jump up and busy her hands with the finishing touches of the carving of Kalé. If she can get it painted in time, it will make a fine gift for Alta.

As the afternoon rolls on and brings the evening ever closer, Arché's leg begins to bounce vigorously. It is half excitement, half tense anticipation. What a messy, complicated thing to feel melancholy mixed with the usual exhilaration.

Lenora pokes her head out of the tent just early enough to scowl at the remaining rays of sunlight. Arché cannot smother her chuckle, and there is a growl of annoyance from inside the tent.

"Good evening," Arché says, to the tent.

"Yep. Soon. When the sun is gone."

Fondness kindles in Arché's chest, warm as a winter hearth. Is the scowl still on Lenora's face? She'd trade so many things to be able to see it.

"Let's give it a try," Lenora announces, when she emerges from the tent at least five minutes later. "The longer feed. If you're still sure."

Arché nods. "Definitely." Despite the agreement, Lenora still carries concern in her tense shoulders. "I'll push you off if it gets too much."

"Okay, good." Lenora's shoulders relax and she comes to sit next to Arché on the log. "Now?"

"It's now or never."

The bite comes as hard as all the others. Arché clutches the back of Lenora's shirt, practically drunk on the sensation of the moon's building power and adrenaline of the bite. They reach the point where Lenora would normally stop, and there is a pause, so Arché pulls her a little closer.

Lenora drinks, and Arché's head begins to spin. It's like battle, the blood that remains pounding in her head and body due to the loss of the rest, rushing through her as if trying to make up the difference. A little more. A little longer. Lenora pauses again and Arché takes the chance to gently push her away.

"That's enough, right?" Arché asks.

Lenora's pupils are blown so wide the grey is almost invisible. She licks her lips and fangs, slow enough to almost distract Arché entirely from what is happening.

"Woah," Lenora murmurs.

"How does it feel?" Arché cannot hold back a grin of curiosity.

Lenora grins back in an instant. "Like I could run for days. Are you okay?"

"Light-headed, but that'll pass once I transform. On that note—" Arché stands and walks into the grass, falling to her knees again and letting the moonlight wash over her all over again.

Above her, a green band of stars shines through the sky, only ever present on the peak night of the full moon. For some reason, the daywalkers in Concord never see them. Does that mean people out here can't see them either? It's something she's meant to ask Alta about, since oddities of the world are their favourite topic, but Arché has forgotten over and over.

She gives herself to the world. Her howl rips through her as the lycan takes over, separate from its people but sworn to their protection. Her spinning head rights itself, though some weakness lingers in her limbs. It will soon pass. Her blood knows few limits.

"Ready to run?" Lenora asks from beside her.

Arché's large mouth grins again, the shape entirely different. "Let's go."

They pick their course and run. Races, sprints, the odd circle. Within an hour, the weakness from the blood loss is entirely gone. It is pure expression of their magical natures, of the latent power they usually keep in check, running wild. Lycan and vampire, as empowered as possible, running alongside each other, unstoppable allies.

They might be dozens, or hundreds, of miles from Concord, but they *are* Concord. They are what their town was made to be, the alliance of its foundation given form.

By the time the night comes to a close, they collapse against each other on bedrolls without a tent. Lenora smells nice again and Arché curls into her while Lenora's hand runs over her fur.

Next thing she knows, she's human again and being woken by Lenora for her watch. She has no memory of changing back, or Lenora leaving her side to put the tent up, but she bids Lenora a good sleep and gets out her whittling knife.

It feels so wrong, to be sitting and working on a little figurine when the nightwalkers of Concord have no doubt been having a horrendous time at the hands of the Crusade. Arché knows reasonably that they could not travel without rests or watches, that going without either would be wildly dangerous. There is so much time *waiting* when they could be travelling. But one wrong step, and their people's only hope is crushed when they are. Arché has always known she was important, in the way all the heirs are, but it is wholly different to think of protecting herself as a way of saving everyone else.

All there is now is to trust the process. Walk, sleep, carve, get bitten, then back to walking. It is getting them there, one day at a time. Each day she is away from her mother, she carves more of her likeness into the wood in her hands, pouring every bit of love and worry and hope into the wood. They just need to keep going until they reach Alta.

This is all to reach Alta. It's been several years since they've seen each other, and with everything that has been happening, the idea of getting one of Alta's enthusiastic hugs soothes Arché's troubled heart.

Alta is a genius. The first to come up with outlandish ideas and solutions, the one who thinks of a thousand obscure things before lunch. If anyone can fix this mess, they might be able to, or at least know someone who can.

The thought keeps her cheery through Lenora's usual grumbling at the sun as she wakes and begins packing up the tent, and Lenora is plainly relieved to sit facing away from the final light of the day as they prepare for another deeper bite.

Arché groans this time, and Lenora makes her own odd noise against Arché's skin, sending Arché's spinning head into a true tangle of endorphins and absurd fantasies simmering under her skin and about to boil over.

Their eyes meet as Lenora pulls back, both of them short of breath from the ordeal. Something crosses Lenora's face, something brand new, and before Arché knows what is happening, Lenora's lips are on hers.

Lenora. Lenora's lips. Lenora kissing Arché.

It might have been different, in another moment. But with the world spinning and the moon bleeding power into her veins, there is no fighting the instincts she has been battling for dozens of nights. Her hands seize Lenora by the shoulders as she kisses her back, rough and hungry as if she needs to devour her in turn.

It takes several seconds for sense to come back to her. It comes like a slap to the back of the head, and Arché lets go of Lenora like she's an open flame, sending Lenora falling back onto her heels. They sit, similarly dazed, staring at each other and yet only half seeing.

"Huh," Lenora murmurs.

Whatever Arché might have expected from anything resembling this situation, it is not this. With her heart in her throat, she searches Lenora's face for something, anything, that could explain what just happened. Anything to give her hope about *why* it happened, without Lenora asking her first, without Arché asking *her* before grabbing her.

But whatever Arché wants to see... it is not there. And she didn't expect to see it, but that doesn't stop it from hurting so much more than a bite ever could.

There is no time to discuss it; the moon is upon them. So Arché scrambles to her feet so that she might move away, her pulse pounding in her ears as she tries to find herself before she changes. She barely makes it to a clear spot in the grass and slides on her knees as she comes down to the grass, the shift hitting her almost on impact.

As it rolls over her, the howl she lets out is not for her family. It is not for anything but the turmoil in her chest. She releases it to the sky, desperate to be rid of everything that confuses and hurts, hoping that when morning comes it does not return with everything else human.

After comes quiet. The stillness of the night punctuated by the rustle of the grass and the whispers of the wind, and then Lenora's soft footsteps.

"Ready?" Lenora asks. She is smiling as if nothing happened at all.

Arché knows that is wrong. But she cannot have this conversation while this version of herself. So they run as if it is the night before. Each stride is another towards Alta, towards family, and it is enough to drive Arché forward. There's no real antics tonight, just pure sprinting for hours, crossing the sort of ground no daywalkers could dream of.

When the first hints of sun begin to taint the night sky and they stop to make camp, Arché collapses to the ground and lets Lenora handle the tent again.

Everything is fine, until Arché remembers that it isn't. It takes Lenora sitting next to her and putting a hand on her head for Arché to remember the hurt that had come before the transformation.

It is so visceral in this form that Arché immediately flinches away from Lenora's hand.

"No," Arché says, before shuffling further away to her own spot.

Lenora's face twists with baffled rejection. She started this, and should have expected something like this, but they can't talk about it until human Arché is back. Wolf Arché needs space to feel the sorrow and conflict of it all vibrating her bones, space to curl up and nap.

Human Arché wakes with a blanket over her body. When her head jerks up as she feels a small nudge wake her, all she sees is Lenora's back disappearing into the tent.

There is a pang of guilt before the anger comes back.

Lenora kissed Arché without consent. But Arché, similarly, escalated it far more than Lenora may have wanted. What a mess of a situation. Arché could scream with frustration at why Lenora couldn't just *ask* so that Arché could politely decline and keep everything simple. (As if it could ever, ever be that.)

And yet, even as the initial wronged party, Arché cannot stop thinking about how *hurt* Lenora had looked when she pulled away. They have to discuss it, and Arché plays a thousand possible versions of the conversation through her head over the hours that pass.

The moment Lenora emerges from the tent, Arché's pulse quickens tenfold with deep anxiety. Everything she practiced turns into a fog.

"Hey," Lenora says from behind Arché, her hands shoved into her dress pockets and her shoulders low. "I'm really, really sorry. I didn't—I shouldn't have done that."

"No, you shouldn't," Arché agrees, voice flat as she turns around, and Lenora winces. "But I shouldn't have done what I did, either. I'm sorry, for that."

Lenora shakes her head. "It's... you don't need to. You were just—" She awkwardly gestures, and Arché nods, relieved that they understand each other on *that* point at least.

But there is one more thing. The burning question. The answer Arché could not find, and will not rest until she acquires.

"Why did you do it?" Arché asks, too fast, before she loses her nerve.

Lenora swallows and her gaze drops to the dirt as her foot scuffs it. "I don't know. I wasn't really thinking, to be honest, I just—"

"Well, you shouldn't kiss people if you don't mean it," Arché says. It comes out harsh, flat, and Lenora looks up so abruptly it is as if she has been slapped.

It is necessary. Half self-preservation, and half one last desperate attempt at trying to get Lenora to come back with justified retaliation. This would all be different, if Lenora said she *did* mean it. Arché has no right to want that to be the case, but it comes unbidden, forbidden, relentless. A realisation in reverse, a punch to Arché's gut as she's hit with a longing that has nothing to do with sex and everything to do with Lenora. Lenora's eyes of liquid moonlight, the way she crinkles her nose when she's annoyed, the way she laughs like she's still learning how.

Oh. Oh *fuck*.

"Right," Lenora says, biting her lip. "Yeah. I'm sorry. I'm so sorry, Arché. Are we... okay?"

And with that, the truth Arché had known is confirmed. Her newly aching heart takes the blow with bravery and she does everything possible to keep it off her face.

Why now? Why *them*? Why this?

"Of course we're okay," Arché says, honestly. "Apology accepted. I just wanted to make sure you knew. I fucked up too. Let's just forget it ever happened."

As if Arché *ever* will. She will only be able to push it aside, like she has with Rohan's death, with the last embrace with her mother and the truth she never told her brother. All the things she must not think on or it'll be too much.

"Forget it happened," Lenora echoes, swallowing. "Okay."

Arché has spent much of recent years wondering how it is possible to get so many simple things wrong. There is no way she'll be able to step into her mother's shoes one day without everyone being disappointed. She wasn't strong enough to appreciate Rohan *or* save them. And now, she has fallen for someone who cannot and does not want her, someone in love with a dead man.

Somehow that just *completely* fits the mess that is Arché's life. The one she is so desperately trying to hold together so that no one else can see the cracks.

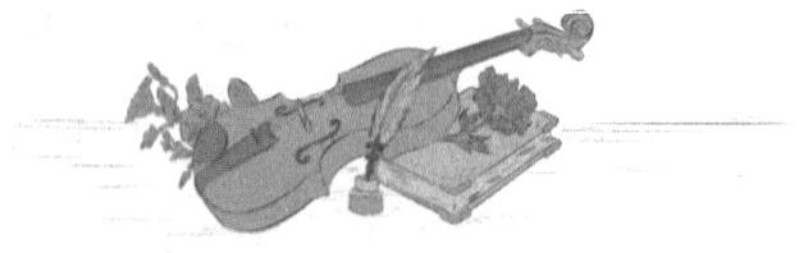

CHAPTER 13
LENORA

LENORA HAD NEVER KISSED anyone before all this. There had been no plan. Pure impulse became thoughtless action, and Arché had suffered the consequences of that mistake. Poor Arché, with her reactions to being bitten, being kissed so immediately after. Of course she'd grabbed Lenora the way she did.

It had certainly been an experience. All the times Lenora wondered about such things, it had always been Nikos. Nikos' arms, Nikos' lips. How bizarre the world is, that she has experienced what he had been dreaming of. But not in the right way, not in a way any of them wished for.

She won't easily forget the pain shining in Arché's eyes. *You shouldn't kiss people if you don't mean it.*

Hurting Arché is the last thing Lenora wants to do. Such a line of thought would be absurd to many past versions of herself, but it is pure truth. Arché is selfless and resilient in the extreme. That selflessness goes all the way to a near fault; she clearly suffers discomfort of several kinds for Lenora's sake, and there is little Lenora can do but be grateful.

But this? Lenora can work to do everything possible to repay her for every kindness.

The last night of travel to Abzah is quiet. Arché finishes painting the carving she's been working on since their journey started, a marvellous rendering of her mother. The ever indomitable Kalé, standing strong with a sword sheathed on her back.

"That's amazing," Lenora says, feeling honoured that Arché has even given it to her to hold and admire. "Gods, you've put so much work into this."

"I figured Alta would like it, since they go so long without seeing her," Arché says. "And... carving it felt like she was closer."

Lenora nods and hands the figurine back over for Arché to wrap up in cloth. "Are you worried about her?"

Arché makes a face. "Yes and no. In a fair fight, she can more than handle herself. But that's the problem with these people... they don't fight fair. And she might have had to lay down arms to save some of the others. Fighting isn't always the best option."

"Leaders put their people first," Lenora says, directly quoting Kalé from one of the heir training sessions. "She never did seem like the type to say anything she didn't mean."

"No, never," Arché chuckles. The weight in her eyes betrays her true feelings.

Lenora wants nothing more than to launch herself forward and hug Arché tight as anything. She rocks back and forth on her heels, pushing the urge back. She's invaded Arché's space without consent enough already; she will not do so again. Sure, she could *ask*, but that might just make Arché *more* uncomfortable.

It occurs to Lenora that other than a farewell from Leahi, she hasn't been hugged by anyone since Nikos. Before that, she can't remember the last time anyone aside from him touched her in such a way. What a wonderful, wonderful moment to realise how physically isolated she has been from most of her world all her life. Right as the only bright spot left in her world wants space from her.

She wants to reassure Arché. But this revelation, alongside Lenora's constant battle with optimism and hope not leaving room for much else, steals any words that might have been the right ones.

"Lenora? Are you okay?" Arché asks. Her head tilts, eyes soft and concerned.

"Just worried about everyone," Lenora says. It's not really a lie. It's just a very, very small part of the more complicated truth.

They reach Abzah perhaps an hour past midnight.

It might be the most peculiar, astounding place Lenora has ever seen. Vines, branches and moss grow around the buildings as though they have every business being there, and everything else seems to be adjusted around it—flower pots nestled into curves of branches, designs painted across the vines, signs hung off whatever is most conveniently located.

"This is *amazing*," Lenora breathes, and Arché nods, looking around with similar wonder.

"Sure is the sort of place Alta would like," Arché says. "I just hope they didn't find somewhere else to be, in the meantime."

"Is that likely?"

"Once they ended up three towns over from where they originally meant to be, because they heard about a book that *might* be there. We had no idea why they weren't getting our letters," Arché says with a fond shake of her head. "Their point of focus is... highly variable."

Lenora can only giggle at the visuals that conjures as they head into the tavern, a place with vines curled around the door and a sign bearing the name The Primal Pour carved into a particularly thick vine overhead. As they step inside, a large man covered in fur greets them with a wave.

"Hi there! You're out late," he says, all cheer. "How can I help?"

Arché begins sorting out a room and food, and Lenora has every intention of assisting before she spies a black cat creeping around the other side of the bar. She kneels and extends her hand to try and entice it over.

There is sound that starts repeating, and it takes several seconds for Lenora to realise it's her name.

"Huh?" she asks.

Arché coughs. "Double or twin room?"

"I'm fine with anything," Lenora says, without looking away from the cat and only half processing the question. Beds are beds, after all. The cat comes over to rub itself against her hand and her heart swells with delight.

The cat stays long enough to brush past her legs and hips before wandering off, and Lenora returns to Arché with new satisfaction teeming through her.

"An arcane researcher," Arché is saying to the barkeep. "They talk real fast, get distracted by random stuff easily—"

"Oh!" He nods his head vigorously. "They look like you? Longer hair?"

"Yes, they do, a good bit," Arché says, her face lighting up.

"Thought you looked familiar," he says with a chuckle. "Yeah, they came through, said they were headed to the ruin out of town. Red-scaled girl with them?"

"What, like, a dragonblood or wildblood?" Arché asks, eyebrows up.

"I'd guess dragonblood, but I wouldn't bet much on it. Seemed like an intern type." The man shrugs. "Ruin is six hours up the north road, the weird shit on your left. Can't miss it."

"Weird shit is not very specific," Lenora says.

He grins, unbothered by the minor critique. "It's a bunch of weird, broken buildings and plants that are even wilder than the ones here. I don't know how else to describe it. You'll see what I mean."

They can do little but take his word for it and get settled in a booth with food.

"I'm excited to meet Alta properly," Lenora says.

Arché chases a potato around her plate with her fork. There is a tension to her that Lenora cannot place, a bounce to her leg under the table that sends vibrations through the floor to Lenora's foot. "I hope you like them. They can be a bit much for some people. I've never understood it, though."

"They helped raise you, I'm sure I'll think they're great," Lenora says with a smile. Surely anyone who contributed to Arché being who she is is someone worth knowing.

Arché blinks, then smiles. "I—thank you. I didn't know you thought so highly of me."

"I do," Lenora says honestly, sipping at the glass of wine she is nursing. "I had you wrong, because of something that had nothing to do with you. I'd be the first to tell myself that." Arché does not answer immediately, still seeming surprised by the whole thing. "What did you think of me? Before all this?"

Arché hesitates, wine glass at her mouth, pursing her lips around the rim. "I... honestly didn't think of you much at all. I always thought your situation seemed tricky, having different magic to your family. But you always seemed alright, with Nikos. I was so wrapped up in my own things, and we never talked, so I just didn't..."

How strange, to exist in someone's periphery for so long, when their presence loomed like a shadow. And now, for them to be someone so essential—

That's what Arché is. Essential. In the most unexpected way. It is the last thing Lenora would have chosen, and yet the best thing that could have happened after it all started falling apart. This is real friendship. The only thing Lenora has to compare it to is what she had with Nikos, but even then, Nikos had been devoted to so many things it had been impossible to get the full attention she wanted so desperately. He was torn between his training, the Hunt, his mothers, the volunteer work he did around Concord... he cared for Lenora deeply, but could so rarely slow to give her most of himself. Only when she *really* needed it.

How strange that Arché feels so different. The heir to the Warden Clan is torn between similar things; their mission, her family, and the fight ahead of them. And yet her focus is singular, all-consuming in the moment and then switching when needed. When she is there for Lenora, she gives Lenora everything, with a loyalty in her eyes fierce enough to often catch Lenora off guard.

"I'm sorry, that must sound so fucking rude," Arché hurries to add, when Lenora spends several moments staring at her and not speaking.

"No, no, it's honest," Lenora says. "Thanks. What about now?"

"Now?"

"What do you think of me now?"

Arché's leg stills under the table as her lips part in soft surprise. Her eyes hold Lenora's, full of *something* but tricky as ever to read. "I—I think that I see you. And I wonder how the fuck I didn't, before."

"You *see* me?" Lenora has no idea what that is supposed to mean. She's asking about Arché's thoughts, not her eyes.

"I see how you try," Arché says. "How hard you've tried since *forever* because the world weighs on you and you work *so* hard to move anyway. And now, you're... learning to have fun? It seems so, anyway. You have a really great smile, and I'm starting to see it more, and everything might be beyond fucked up but I can't help but be glad."

The words hit like a blow to the chest, the succinct insight unexpectedly sharp. So much of her life has been working and struggling and so often not achieving what she wanted or how she wanted it. Trying to grasp her family's Disciplined magic and failing so miserably. Trying to control and work her shadow magic with no teacher. Desperately pining after Nikos instead of considering anyone else around her.

This has been different. No expectations of her usual life. Just the road, just walking with Arché and playing music with Leahi and simply existing without the shackles of someone else's expectations. There have been moments of joy, between the horrors, purer than anything that came before.

"You notice... a lot," Lenora exhales. "Damn. But yeah, the timing is... weird."

"I suppose if we waited for everything to have good timing, some things would never happen," Arché says, with a small sigh. "We can't control what we feel, or when we feel it."

There's an odd earnestness to Arché's words, something that sees the words sink deeper into Lenora's heart, untying a knot that had tangled up within her. A knot of guilt, unravelling because Arché is right. Feeling guilt over experiencing joy, over unconscious feelings that happen without intention, is absurd.

"I'm so glad we're friends now," Lenora says. "You're... great."

Arché smiles, and it seems a bit tight, but it reaches her eyes and that's what matters. "Me too."

They sleep the day away in a double bed where Lenora manages to work up the courage to ask Arché if they can sleep close to one another. To her relief, Arché agrees, and Lenora is able to let the warm safety of Arché lull her into a peace that lets her sleep. No fleeting joy or new companionship will fix the things that run through her brain, the emptiness and hopelessness that always try to drag her down... but in Arché's arms she feels anchored.

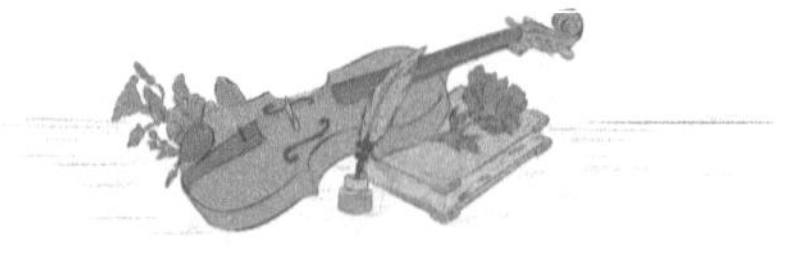

CHAPTER 14

LENORA

THE RUINS ARE AS easy to find as promised, at the end of one night's walk. A mess of broken walls and columns, vines covering the ground and stretching over cracked marble as if trying to fill in some of the gaps in the architecture. Not that flora can be *that* sentient, as far as Lenora knows. Moss covers the ground thicker and thicker the further in they venture. Following it, hopefully to a central point, brings them to a staircase that disappears down into the depths of the earth.

"Do you think this is it?" Lenora asks.

Arché makes an ambiguous noise. "I don't know what else could be."

The whole entryway is shrouded in darkness, but there is a faint glow from within, dim even to their eyes. Arché makes her way down first and Lenora sticks to her heels. The stairs bring them into an underground passage, the flicker of flames coming from around a corner, further in.

A figure steps into the end of the passage and there is a loud click. A crossbow.

"Identify yourself," calls a voice.

"Friends," Arché replies. "Looking for Alta."

A pause. A wave of a hand. Hanging lanterns along the length of the passage light with flame, bringing colour and warmth to the space.

"Arché?"

The crossbow lowers. Its wielder is a short, haphazard individual in their forties—human in appearance with dark hair tied in a bun at the back of their head, strands escaping all over the place. Their robes are stained with ink and hanging open over a plain shirt and trousers. Their boots have a healthy coat of dirt across the toes and sides.

Now, looking at them properly, Lenora's memory can place them as Alta, the strange spouse of the Warden Clan leader. The one who had been banned from council meetings, though Lenora's mother had never explained why.

"Hey, Alta," Arché says, stepping forward.

The crossbow hits the floor. The bolt triggers and Lenora yelps as it goes flying, but thankfully it misses everyone present and hits a far wall.

Alta and Arché embrace fiercely, with laughter on Alta's part and utter silence on Arché's. Lenora feels wrong watching it, seeing how Arché's body shakes as her arms clutch Alta for dear life.

"Gods, I missed you," Arché murmurs.

As they pull away, Alta's eyes roam Arché's face with fascination and a love that shines so brightly it hurts Lenora to witness.

"Oh, look at you, my girl," they say, smiling with awe. "You look more like Kalé every day. But—and I don't mean to seem unhappy to see you, because that's not it at all—*what* are you doing here?"

"Uh, it's... a long story," Arché says, biting her lip and glancing at Lenora. "And almost none of it is good."

Alta blinks at Lenora with even deeper bafflement. "Lenora?"

"You have a good memory," Lenora says, surprised.

"It's certainly been noted, but you're the only chosen Shadow in several generations. There's no merit to knowing who you are," Alta says, snorting. "The real question is why you of all people are here with my daughter."

"Well—"

"Wait." Alta holds up a hand and looks between them again. Their gaze is so deep, so intense, that Lenora cannot hold it. "Gods. It happened, didn't it? The disaster. Something terrible. Just as warned."

Nausea seizes Lenora's gut and squeezes it. "What?" she manages to say.

"I told them," Alta says, shaking their head furiously. "I fucking *told* her—they brush me off, ban me, and now look at—" They look up sharply, breaking from their own ramble. "Come. Tell me everything. My assistant is further in doing some etchings, we have some time to speak before she returns."

A few twists and turns deeper into the structure and they are in a simple indoor camp, with a firepit, cooking pot, and a pair of tents.

"Sit, I have some leftovers," Alta says. Bowls filled with stew are promptly thrust into their hands. "Now talk, and eat."

Arché does the talking. She recounts it with a stiff, wooden voice which cracks only at the mention of Rohan's fall and having to leave everyone behind as they made their escape. Alta's face remains composed as they listen, but their body betrays their sorrow, their shoulders low and the high energy seeping from them the longer Arché speaks.

"You made it here," Alta says, with a small smile of pride. "Well done."

"Thank you," Arché replies. "It hasn't been easy."

"Of course not, they don't teach you a damn thing about the rest of the world. It's madness."

Lenora cannot keep quiet any longer. She has toiled in silence, unable to stomach a single mouthful of stew and instead playing with the spoon as she waited for a chance to ask the question burning in her soul.

"The attack," Lenora interrupts. "It's because of me, isn't it? You said there was warning, but the warning was *me*, chosen Shadows mean disaster."

"No," Alta says, and they actually leap to their feet before repeating themselves with twice the volume. "Fucking—*no*. This is exactly what I wanted to avoid, you getting some sort of *complex* because they're looking at it completely backward. If there's a flood and you happen to find a raft, you don't start blaming the flood on the raft! You think *thank fuck I have this raft*!"

Lenora stares at them. "What?"

"I said it made no sense for it to be your fault," Arché says, a strange half-smile curling her lips. "If we get a special powerful mage right before disaster strikes, then that's *good*. Not misfortune."

Alta laughs outright. "I knew you got my brain! That's my girl."

Arché flushes, shifting uncomfortably at the praise. "Thank you."

The whole thing sits so wrong that Lenora has to take a breath and stop herself from losing her temper or composure. She wraps her arms around herself before forcing out her next words.

"Except I'm not some super powerful mage. I'm just... unique, and... floundering."

Alta flaps their hand. "Well, that's not your fault, you don't even have your full power."

"My *what*?!"

"We'll get to that," Alta says. "It's the only idea I've had since you filled me in and I'm really hoping I'll get a less risky one. *Anyway*!" They clap their hands together loud enough to make Lenora jump in her seat. "This confusion with the chosen Shadow and impending doom, it's exactly what I was trying to tell them all. They have a gift put in their laps with a warning label saying *you'll need this later, trust me* and do they do anything about the disaster they've been told to expect? No? They called you bad luck and moved on. Then I point it out and tell them to take the sticks out of their asses and use them to build something constructive, and get banned from council meetings for life."

Arché and Lenora glance at each other and fall into horrendous laughter. They shouldn't. Not when it is the doom of their people being discussed. But the seriousness with which Alta explains why they had been banned, after all this time... is too much to not be moved by.

Alta lets them get it out of their systems, cracking a small smile. Behind it, though, is something quietly pained.

"Folke, Rohan, and Nikos," they murmur. "Ulrich told me he thought he could—but not *three*—"

Before Lenora can ask what in the world that means, Arche's head twitches.

"I think your assistant is coming back," Arché says, and sure enough footsteps precede a new face.

A young woman appears from a back exit, something leading further into the structure, that Lenora hadn't even noticed with how much Alta had kept her attention. Alta's assistant is a young woman around Arché and Lenora's age, with a short blonde pixie cut and scarlet scales across her cheeks and one side of her neck. One tooth sticks out over her bottom lip, long and pointed, standing out from the others as she gives them an uncertain smile.

"Oh! Hi?"

"Raavi, this is my daughter," Alta says with a grin. "And a friend, Lenora. They've come a long way, and they need my help."

Raavi's eyes flick to Arché and widen. "Wow. Arché, hi, I've heard so much about you!"

"And I'm so glad someone is keeping them company out here," Arché says with a genuine smile. "I worry about them talking to themself for too long."

Raavi nods. "Absolutely. None of this was *planned*, but I'm doing my doctorate at the University of Orsun, and we crossed paths and got talking because they saw my textbook. Next thing you know, we're here!"

Orsun is the capital of Kanin, the country they're in, but Lenora knows little else about it. The ignorance that seems so obvious to condemn now, that she'd never questioned. Concord was their world, until it was ripped away.

"Home's in trouble," Alta says to Raavi, solemn again. "They've come here because they're not sure where else to go." Their eyes flick back to the nightwalkers. "At least, I'm guessing."

"Yeah," Lenora says. "It was your wife's idea."

Alta nods multiple times. "She knows she can count on me when it matters. If only there were a simple solution to all this."

"That sounds worrying," Raavi says, her eyebrows creasing together. "I'll help in any way I can, but... what kind of trouble?"

"Uh..." Arché makes a face and looks between Alta and Raavi with uncertainty. "Alta, you said you had an idea about... Lenora's magic."

"Yeah, I did," Alta says, looking like they regret ever mentioning it. "Uh. Shit. Well, home has been selective with their history teachings, for a start. Your, er, predecessor left home and never returned, in their time. They were following a traitor, to bring them back to see justice, but... neither of them were ever seen again. Their last rumoured location is an estate four night's travel from here. That's the whole reason I first came up this way, I wanted to see if I could find anything that might help you out—finding *this* place just happened by accident on the way. When I couldn't get into the estate, I decided to pursue this instead."

"What do you mean, you couldn't get in?" Lenora asks.

"Well... there's a huge dome of shadow around the whole place. Giant, impenetrable barrier. Nothing is getting in or out, not even light. The records say others looking for Vali, the chosen, tried to get in too. I thought that with my natural knack for thinking outside the box and my general arcane expertise, I'd be able to get in where they couldn't, but... no luck. I've been operating under the assumption that the *next* chosen might be able to succeed where everyone else failed."

All eyes turn to Lenora, Raavi's confused ones a second behind.

"Right," Lenora says, because she loves pressure to succeed at impossible tasks the same way she loves eating nails. "I mean... I guess I can try."

"Obviously that's all you can do," Alta says. "But my guess is that some of the power is stuck there, unable to return to whatever source distributes to the next heir. I don't know what else could be powering the barrier, and no offense intended, but the report I've heard about your abilities aren't as overwhelming as the ones that came before. It won't be a coincidence."

Lenora presses her lips together so she does not vocally disagree. She is perfectly capable of being a magical disappointment in multiple areas, of that she is sure.

"Why don't we all get some rest," Arché suggests, glancing in Lenora's direction. "Then we can make a plan."

"Oh, so you're on the nocturnal schedule too," Raavi says with interest, stopping to scribble something in a notebook she pulls from a belt on her hip. "Wild! I've adjusted well, I think." Alta immediately agrees, making the girl beam.

"Do you take watches here?" Arché asks Alta.

"No, but I do need to refresh the alert spell the two of you set off on the staircase," Alta says. "Do you have tents? That looks like one in your bag."

"We've got a tent."

"Good. I'd hope so."

Lenora looks at Arché, realising the implications of not having to sleep in watches and having the tent to share between them. Arché's body heat, hers to enjoy, so long as Arché is still comfortable with that. "No watches!"

Arché smiles at her. "That'll be a nice change."

"Don't let me keep you from your rest," Alta says, before pausing and hurrying to kiss Arché on the cheek and pull her into another hug. "I'm very glad to see you. We'll talk more tomorrow."

"Definitely." Arché gives them one more big squeeze. "Sleep well."

There is an odd sense of calm that comes with zipping their tent for privacy from Raavi. Lenora releases a breath. The tightness in her chest begins to ease.

"All this time," Lenora says, shaking her head. "Alta was banned because they tried to stick up for me. And then went out on a mission to find more things to help me? That's... the strangest thing."

Arché stretches her arms out above her head. "I never thought to question *why*. It just seemed so... easy to believe it was for something ridiculous, I never even asked. I was, what, ten? I simply didn't have any interest in Concord politics yet."

"I had someone in my corner," Lenora says quietly. "I didn't even know."

Arché tilts her head, searching Lenora's face. "Well, Alta is always in the corner of common sense, even if it isn't obvious to other people at the time. So, that tells us a lot about what everyone *else* was doing."

It could be bias talking, but Lenora finds herself nodding. Now that she's met Alta properly, it's completely believable.

They both pull off their outer layers and curl up on their bedrolls, facing each other in the small space.

"We made it," Arché murmurs. "It seemed so far away."

"And now we're far away from everyone else," Lenora says, shaking her head. "And Alta wants me to break through some magic no one else has been able to touch?"

"Their logic makes sense. I bet it will work."

Lenora's frustration bubbles within her and she swallows words that will not help. Words like *I thought we would have more* and *how could this be the only plan we have* and *why does this have to be so hard?* Sometimes she thinks Arché must know, must understand, but she's *Arché*. Daughter of Kalé. She clearly doesn't hold the same concerns in the same way.

Which, in all honesty, is something to be grateful for. One of them needs to keep it together, and it almost certainly isn't going to be Lenora.

"We should sleep," Arché says, while keeping her eyes open and on Lenora.

"Yeah." Lenora is in no hurry to close her eyes either. There is too much comfort to be found in Arché's brown eyes for Lenora to want to move into another moment yet. "So... sleeping in a tent *inside* is new."

Arché grins. "I used to do it with Andreas. We'd have pretend camping trips in our bedroom, back when we shared one."

"Cute!"

It is easy to talk more of Arché's childhood and brother, until they decide their time is better spent sleeping.

CHAPTER 15
ARCHÉ

HAVING THEIR TENT WORKS out in their favour, given that they need to be able to feed Lenora without giving certain things away to Raavi instantly. Arché does her best to be quiet, but it is as challenging as ever. Worse, actually, which is absurd because it ought to get *easier* to resist, it ought to affect her less. But it is the opposite.

The fantasies in her head, wildly inappropriate as they are, end when the bite stops and are slammed closed like a box filled with deadly poison. It cannot be left open.

Breakfast comes as a relief. Raavi is chirpy and talkative, asking questions about 'home' with good-natured curiosity that Arché does her best to sidestep.

"Your Shadow magic sounds fascinating too," Raavi says to Lenora. "Do you know its source? Innate magic sources are so fascinating—"

"No, it's a point of debate, actually," Lenora says. "If anyone has a good theory, it's probably Alta."

Alta pops their head out from behind a pillar. "Oh, I have *several*, but none with any legs to stand on. That's the problem with this magic, no one is documenting anything because the superstition has made them all *incompetent.*" They release a heavy sigh, which turns into a smile as they look at Lenora. "Maybe when all this is over, you and I can fix that. I'm sure the next person to get the magic would appreciate it."

Lenora blinks. "Oh. Sure."

"Great! Now we just have to get to the 'when this is all over' part." Alta comes to sit in the breakfast circle. "We'll give you new supplies, but we have work to do here—I'd been planning on trying to find a way to harness this magic to help Concord's farms, but I might be able to turn it into something more... immediately useful for offense. We'll work on it while you head to the estate, see if we can get it done by the time you get back."

Raavi apparently hasn't received this information prior, because she immediately sets down her plate and begins scribbling in her notebook.

"So we're on our own again," Arché says.

Alta sighs. "Sorry, kid."

"I suppose it's better than you lying and saying you can magically fix everything."

"We're blatantly outnumbered," Alta reminds them, as if it were possible for them to forget. "To form any true opposition we need to increase our power. Having Crescent Light is something, but hardly enough. Lenora is the one with the most potential to increase in the immediate timeframe."

Lenora fidgets next to Arché. "No pressure."

"No, quite a lot, actually," Alta says, making a face. "I'm sorry, Lenora. I know it's not fair. But it's the reality."

When Lenora says nothing, her gaze on the fire, Arché reaches for her hand to give it a squeeze. It seems like the correct thing to do. Lenora gives a hint of a smile in her direction.

Before they know it, they are supplied and out at the top of the steps as the sun falls below the horizon. Time to say goodbye, even if it is a brief one. Arché's entire being protests, insisting on the unfairness of leaving Alta so soon when all she wants to do is hold them tight.

Alta clutches her with a death grip as they farewell. At least the sentiment is shared.

"I hate the idea of sending my little girl off to her doom," Alta says. "I don't know what the fuck is in there."

Arché hits them in the shoulder, shaking her head with disbelief. "Alta! Please, some optimism. You know, *don't worry, I know you two will sort it all out no problem.*"

"Don't worry, I know you two will sort it all out no problem," Alta echoes, a proud grin taking over their face.

"Exactly. We've got this."

"Fuck, I hope we've got this."

It falls from Arché's lips when they've been on the road for no more than five minutes, as she looks back at the ruin. A *very* strange giggle leaves Lenora, making Arché bring her gaze back to her companion.

"What happened to optimism?" Lenora asks.

"Well, you know, this whole situation... it's such bullshit," Arché says, throwing her hands up with exasperation. "Two heirs with no idea what they're doing, teaming up with a spouse of a house leader, and that's all we've got. Against an entire *cult*. To rescue hundreds of people."

"Well, when you put it like that..." Any trace of a smile fades from Lenora's face. "You've never—not like that."

Her arms wrap around her torso. The shadows she had been playing with across her fingers melt away into nothing. Her eyes are focused on Arché, wide abysses of grey. Falling, falling, falling.

What was that Arché had been thinking about everything weighing Lenora down? She can practically see despair trying to crush her. Surrender crackles like lightning in the air, ready to strike Lenora as her resilience balances on a knife edge.

"But that's our advantage," Arché is quick to say. "They have no idea how strong we are. They have no idea how far we've come, or what we'll do to save the others. They think they're backed by the Everflame but we know they're wrong. We'll work out the details as they come."

Lenora nods slowly, teeth biting down onto her lip. "And if I can't get through the barrier?"

"You'll be able to," Arché says. "I'm sure of it."

"How? How are you sure?" Lenora's voice trembles with the loaded question, with another moment where Arché knows it's one wrong word and the damage done cannot be taken back.

"Because Alta trusts the magic, and I trust you," Arché says. "I've seen your magic, and what you can do. The dome Alta described sounds exactly like the dome I found you in, just bigger."

"The dome you found me in?"

"With Nikos."

"... oh."

"You can do this. We can do this."

Lenora nods, then does it a second and third time until she gives Arché another smile. It is so rife with gratitude that Arché feels a strange weight take up within her chest.

She can't show her own doubt. Because her belief is the only thing keeping Lenora afloat. What a damning, unfair thing. But then, Lenora never asked to be the chosen Shadow, never asked for her mind to be so much crueler to her than it is supposed to be. Arché can shoulder the burden if it evens things out, if it means together they keep walking. She's strong enough.

They are far enough north now, that watches don't feel necessary. The Crusade will be taking routes on or close to the highway and common beasts are no threat to them. So, they curl up in the tent together.

"I just feel safe here," Lenora whispers as she curls against Arché's chest. She glances up at Arché, who feels her heart skip a full beat. "Like it's just us, in this tent, and nothing else is anywhere because they're not *here*."

"Yeah," Arché says, running a hand down Lenora's back with a featherlight touch, and feeling her body shift in response. "Just us."

"I know it's silly, with everything that—"

"It's not silly." *I feel it too. More than you know.*

"Oh." Lenora smiles again. "Good." With that, she closes her eyes and doesn't speak another word.

Arché feels Lenora's heart calm and slow with her breathing, and once the other woman is asleep, she lets herself take a moment to savour how it feels to hold her when she cannot be caught doing so. How it feels? Like everything she's ever wanted and everything she's never thought to want, all at once.

In short: it's getting worse, and Arché is helpless to stop it. It's a silly heartache in the face of much more serious mortal peril, at least, and as long as she takes these little moments she can bear it. These moments to savour what she cannot have, and doubt their chances of success when Lenora cannot see it and spiral.

All is well. Lycans keep everything under control. They must. And so that is what Arché will do.

Waking up to a content, snuggly Lenora is something that Arché could certainly get used to, but absolutely must *not* get used to. Arché fights to think the most dry, complicated thoughts about woodworking techniques possible in order to keep her thoughts from the vampire in her arms.

"Can we stay a bit longer? Before we get up?" Lenora asks. "I hate getting up."

"Of course," Arché says. As Lenora smiles in response, Arché has to wonder if Lenora has realised how often those words are Arché's answer to her questions.

Perhaps it is better if she does not, actually.

"I'm thirsty," Lenora says, voice soft and low as her eyes meet Arché's. There is something new in them, something that stirs desire deep in Arché's belly. It might only be a want for blood, but when they are lying like this, there is a part of her convinced it could be something else. Utter delusion. "May I?"

Arché nods and Lenora leans into the crook of her neck, biting almost immediately. They've only been this close a few times, doing a bite lying down, and Arché can't help how she grabs Lenora's waist because there is nothing else to hold on to. The curve of it fits perfectly in her hand and this might be what torture truly is because it is pain and bliss and wanting.

As Lenora pulls back, she wipes at her mouth with the back of her hand. "I'm always amazed at how good you taste," she murmurs.

Arché stares. Her hands still rest on Lenora's waist even as her eyes search the other woman's face for any sign that she has any clue what she is saying. But there is nothing. Lenora is oblivious and it's agony.

Blood burns in Arché's face and ears, and everywhere else much lower. She lets go of Lenora and jerks away, displacing Lenora back onto her bedroll as she hurries out of the tent. Fresh air has never been so necessary. Gods, this whole thing is so humiliating.

"Arché? Are you okay?" Lenora asks, following immediately. She takes another look at Arché and this time her eyes widen and her hands come to cover her mouth. Even so, Arché hears the giggle she tries to stifle. "Oh. I'm sorry."

"It's fine," Arché says. It isn't. She wants to mean it, desperately so, but the laughter makes it so much worse.

Lenora's head tilts. "I—it doesn't seem like it. I'm sorry I laughed, I just don't always know what to do when *this* happens."

"It'll pass," Arché says, which is true at least. "I should get changed." She ducks back into the tent and pulls on her shirt, but Lenora's hand comes to rest on her arm.

"Arché," Lenora breathes. "Is there anything I can do to help?"

"No, there isn't."

Lenora bites her lip as Arché looks back at her, which is distracting enough in itself, but the look in her eyes is something else entirely, something soft and earnest. "I just... I'd do *anything* if it would help you, Arché."

Arché's mind stops functioning in favour of flying into some truly absurd, graphic situations that belong only in smutty books like the kind Rohan used to read. It takes several moments for her to come back to the present.

"Anything is a dangerous word, Lenora," Arché manages to say. Her voice actually trembles with the force of the desire and exasperation and exhaustion battling inside her. "You shouldn't throw it around like that, you can't just—you can't just say that to people."

Lenora frowns. "Well, I'm not. I'm saying it to you. And I mean it, anything—"

"No, you don't," Arché snaps. "Not anything. Not the things I'm thinking right now. That's not what you mean." She forces herself to step back, and runs a hand over her eyes, forcing a breath out. "I'm sorry. You're trying to help, and I'm just—I'm sorry. There is nothing you'd be willing to do that could help me. We just need to get on with it."

"Okay," Lenora says, crossing her arms over her chest. "I mean, I guess you're right. 'Anything' might mean something I'm not willing to do, but... I know you'd never make me do something I didn't want to, Arché."

"Right." Arché curses how much faith Lenora has in her, when it does not feel deserved. "I suppose that makes sense."

All the same, as they finish the rest of their routine for packing up camp, Arché knows she will be cursed with remembering those words from Lenora's lips in her wildest, filthiest fantasies. Fantasies she must keep absolutely, extremely close to her chest.

It must be easier, being like Lenora, not feeling this sort of attraction or almost never at least. It must be so much more simple than every part of Arché's body screaming for things it simply cannot have.

Once they get walking, Lenora is quiet and Arché is relieved. The weather turns to torrential rain in the second half of the night and Lenora conjures an umbrella made of shadow to keep herself dry. She tries to expand it, but it keeps snapping back to its original shape.

Lenora growls with frustration. "Sorry," she says, to a soggy Arché walking alongside.

"It's fine," Arché says with complete honesty. "I like the rain." The nightwalkers don't tend to get ill in the same ways daywalkers do, with much less vulnerability to exposure to the cold and wet and the simple sickness it brings.

Besides, the rhythmic sensation of the drops hitting Arché's head and shoulders is soothing, and the wet ground gives way under her toes just enough for it to squelch. It's a sensory delight.

Their next camp sees them hanging up Arché's sodden clothes and Lenora's stockings at the front of the tent to drip dry, while they lie down and listen to the rain battering the tent walls above them.

The sound of it is close to music to Arché's ears and Lenora's words from the night before begin to make more sense. The rest of the world feels far away, thousands of raindrops between them and anyone else. The only world is this tent and the friend shivering in her arms.

"Are we okay?" Lenora asks after a while. She does not elaborate, even when Arché does not answer right away.

"Of course," Arché says, like always. "We're in this together, no matter what. And when we get you this magic, those assholes will be so afraid of you."

"They already are—"

"For the right reasons, this time."

"Okay. Sounds good."

After two more nights of travel, they reach their destination a few hours before dawn. It is an unmistakable thing. A small sphere of darkness had covered Lenora and Nikos back in the training yards; this dome nearly buries the sky. It blocks out the stars, the forest, everything ahead of them, with only the curve of the sphere betraying its form against the world around it.

"You're up," Arché says.

Lenora nods and steps forward, her hand extended towards the barrier.

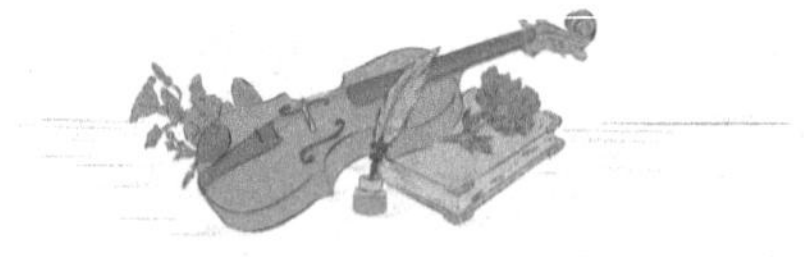

CHAPTER 16
LENORA

Even before Lenora touches the barrier, she is recognised. Seen. Blood rushes through her ears, buzzes through her body, and the shadows within reach for the barrier.

The shadow coats her hand right as it makes contact, and the dome's darkness is as cold as the rest of her magic. At her touch it parts for her, around her, forming a doorway like a split in a waterfall.

Lenora looks back and offers her other hand to Arché, who takes it so as to be able to follow her inside. As soon as they are through the barrier, the entryway closes and leaves them in pitch darkness. No stars, no moon, nothing but the faintest shapes that would be nothing at all for daywalkers.

"Those supplies from Alta. Did I see a torch?" Lenora asks.

Arché fumbles in her bag, but a few moments later is able to strike a small flame onto a cloth-wrapped torch. It isn't much, but nightwalker eyesight can do a lot with only a little light.

Ahead of them is a two-storeyed manor. Its distinguished design is now hampered by disrepair; scratches and chips marr the finish of most edges, in such a number that immediately raises questions.

"So, absolutely nothing bad happened here," Arché says, her voice weak even as it tries to joke. Lenora is beginning to suspect her attempts at humour in the face of adversity are more for Lenora's comfort than anything else. It's appreciated.

The light is enough to make out movement coming around the house. It is slow and irregular, so much so that Lenora might have struggled to marry it with any theory at all if not for an awful, clattering croak.

"What is that—oh gods," Arché says, as a skeleton comes into the radius of the light. "No, no, absolutely the fuck not—"

With a growl, Arché shifts and leaps forward to knock the skeleton to the ground. Crescent Light is sheathed on her back, with Arché's clawed hands slamming into the ribcage of the animated, rotted frame of the corpse. The crack of bones echoes through the encompassing darkness. It might have been satisfying if not for the sounds of more rattling nearby.

"Arché, there's more," Lenora says. "We should get inside."

Arché's head snaps up to Lenora, then to the darkness to the right of the manor, where sure enough half a dozen more skeletons are making their way closer. Luckily, they are slow on their flimsy ankles.

"Inside," Arché agrees.

The front door might once have been impressive, with its ornate frame and double doors and brass knocker, but now it is half torn apart. Convenient for squeezing through, but not for stopping the skeletons from following.

Lenora reaches for her shadow magic and finds it easier to seize than ever. A flick of her wrist sends it to the doorway, while a slide from her other hand smoothes it into a wall that blocks the entire passage.

"*That* works," Arché says, her grin showing off her large canine teeth before she shifts back to her human self.

The inside of the house has suffered from general battering, but not as much as the outside. Some of the walls are marred, with the odd bone fragment on the wooden floorboards.

"What exactly are we looking for?" Arché asks.

"Alta just said I'd be able to get in, not what we had to do," Lenora says, making a face. "I don't even think they knew. We had no idea what would be inside. But... some part of the last chosen Shadow must be here. I guess I'll... know it when I see it? Hopefully?"

She wishes she sounded more sure. Arché almost never wavers, always knows how to manage herself and her skills, and the last thing Lenora wants to be is a liability. If it is the two of them against everyone, they need to be a dynamic team. Lenora must be able to hold her own.

"Of course you will," Arché says, and when Arché says it, Lenora is *so* close to believing.

There are stairs leading up and several doors at the end of the entry corridor, *and* doors to their immediate left and right. Lenora almost suggests splitting up to cover ground before realising how unsafe that would be. Their only time limit is in weeks, in hundreds of miles travelled, a scope far outside of this. A few more minutes per room are worth taking to be safe.

Through the left door is a living area, with bookshelves covered in dust and a fireplace still stocked with fuel once half burned. A spare wood basket sits next to it, untouched.

A window in the lounge smashes as a rotting hand reaches through. Lenora suppresses a scream, and a squeak comes out instead. She summons her shadow claw, the effort making her head swim due to maintaining the wall at the same time, and slices the claw through the corpse's arm.

The claw falls away a moment later and Lenora staggers back into a musty chair, clutching her forehead and doing everything she can to keep her focus on the wall.

"Shit," Arché mutters. She hurries to grab furniture from around the room to barricade the windows, then tears up some of the floorboards to get extra bits to jam into place. Lenora can only marvel at how she does it all with her bare hands. There's knowing that the lycans are capable of incredible feats of strength, and then there is seeing Arché who has trained her entire life to maximise that advantage.

The scrambling noises fade as Arché jams one last piece of floorboard behind a cabinet.

"Nice," Lenora says, forcing herself to stand and clutching her head.

They explore the room across the hall, a bedroom where the neglect burns colder than the stale air.

"This whole place is so wrong," Lenora says. "Undead things outside, this whole house feeling... off. What *happened* here?"

"The corpses had a sort of shadow to them," Arché points out. "Is that... a thing your magic can do? Reanimate corpses?"

Lenora turns to look at her, horrified. "No! I don't know! Do you think I've ever tried?!"

"No, I just—" Arché rubs her temples. "Sorry. I didn't think that through, I forgot you don't have records."

"No, and I don't plan on trying it out," Lenora says, and if it were anyone but Arché she might have snapped a little at the sheer implication. It has her hackles up as if she is feline where Arché is canine. "My magic has always felt more linked to cold than life or death. Like the absence of light, and what it brings. Maybe the last chosen Shadow could take life instead of heat. I don't know. We might not all work the same."

"That makes sense. Sorry."

Something thumps above them, then turns to faint scrambling. Lenora's eyes follow the direction of the movement to the fireplace in the lounge, currently visible through the doorway.

"Arché, I think they're trying to get in through the chimney," Lenora says, with horror. "I can't block that off too—"

"No, it's alright, we'll..." Arché pauses and traces her eyes over the ceiling to the fireplace. A bizarre grin stretches her lips. "Huh. They want to come down the chimney? Fine."

She dashes to the bookshelf, grabs a tome, and murmurs an apology to the Scholar before ripping the pages out and throwing them into the fireplace along with two new pieces of wood.

"Light it up," she tells Lenora, nodding at the torch in her hand.

Lenora finds herself laughing at the absurdity of it, but she doesn't have a better idea. As she presses the flame to the torn book pages, Arché runs from the room and returns half a minute later with a bottle of whiskey.

"Back up," Arché says, and as soon as Lenora does, Arché takes a swig of the whiskey before throwing it into the fire. The flames flare as the glass breaks.

"That should slow them down," Arché says, with a grin so wolfish it catches Lenora off guard.

Neither of them have had much cause to smile since the start of their journey, reunions with Alta aside. Despite the danger and uncertainty of the current situation, it's nice to see how Arché's face transforms when it is jovial, when it takes pride in something. Why has Lenora not seen it more on their travels? The two together make Arché so striking, so handsome and beautiful, that Lenora can only stare.

"Are you okay?" Arché asks.

Lenora blinks. "Yeah! Fine."

A skeleton falls down the chimney and into the roaring fire. It screeches with its remnant of a voice, and the sound is awful, but then it goes still. The shadows slip from its form, and the bones fall into the kindling.

"You know, I really had no idea if that would work," Arché says. "Never had to deal with shadow infused skeletons."

"Fire is destruction," Lenora says. "Even some magic recognises that."

Another skeleton lands in the fire, and this time Arché actually cackles at the noise it makes as its essence disintegrates. "We should... probably move before that stops working," she says, with one last giggle. "Come on, there was another room I wanted to look at."

They come into what is either a library or a study. The walls are lined from floor to ceiling with shelves of books, and the ones directly behind the central desk stand out. More clumsily bound, as if done by someone who only half knew how to do so, and matching with consecutive numbers on the spines.

Lenora hurries to study them, finding them to be journals, while Arché searches the rest of the room. They form a lengthy biography,

"Alta said the last heir left home searching for a traitor," Lenora says. "These are signed *Hilvar*. They must be our traitor. Oh. They're from the Warden Clan, Arché."

Arché stiffens. "Oh. That's unfortunate. Why do I have *no memory* of the Council saying anything about a traitor when they were covering our significant history?" Arché comes to peer at the book over Lenora's shoulder. "The immigration of daywalking citizens, the change from lycan to daywalker feeding volunteers, the opening up of younger siblings to partnerships with people not from the founding houses, all of that..."

"But no Hilvar," Lenora murmurs, eyes fixed on the signature. "I guess they just didn't think we needed to know."

"You needed to know," Arché says, a fierce look coming onto her face. "If it had something to do with the last chosen Shadow, you need to know. And it was my clan that had the traitor, I'd have liked to know too."

"They don't even know what happened."

Arché huffs and slicks back strands of hair escaping from her bun. "They still could have told you—gods, I wish I'd realised how bullshit your entire situation has been since your magic manifested. I don't know how I missed it—"

"I didn't talk about it, Arché," Lenora tells her, closing the book with a sigh and putting it back on the shelf. "I already felt like I was getting everything wrong. If I admitted it, that was even worse. Only Nikos knew, really."

Arché stares at her for a moment with some kind of deep astonishment, one that Lenora can't make sense of. Lenora's not really made it a secret that things were awful and she was struggling through. Not to Arché, not since they started.

"I'm so glad you had Nikos," Arché says a moment later, her expression shifting to a warm smile. "Between helping you and listening to me, I'm amazed he had time to get anything done."

"I was so *jealous* of you two hanging out, but I never wanted to hear about it." Lenora smiles to herself at how trivial it all seems now when it had been world-shattering at the time. "Knowing what I know now... I haven't even asked why you finally wanted to hang out with him."

The smile falls from Arché's face. "Oh. You know. He was just... understanding."

"I know," Lenora says, waiting for elaboration.

"I— could I tell you about it later? Not... now."

Lenora had never imagined it to be anything as cryptic as Arché's hesitation now suggests. So naturally, concern and curiosity tug at her with poor sense of priority. Arché is right that now is not the time to be getting into all of that, with a skeletal incursion just outside.

Another skeleton lands in the fireplace, but this time they don't have line of sight. Lenora is not sure what it says about her that she is willing to take the risk of not checking on it in favour of putting a hand on Arché's arm.

"Sure," she says, looking up at Arché. "And you don't have to tell me if you don't want to."

Arché swallows and looks sorely tempted to take the out. Lenora had said it because it felt like the right thing to do but gods now does she almost regret it.

"We should get moving," Arché says, instead of committing to either course of action.

As they make their way through the rest of the downstairs rooms, Lenora tries not to stew in her thoughts and fails terribly. The idea of Arché having a secret shouldn't bother her so much. But it feels deeply, awfully wrong. Arché knows practically everything there is to know about Lenora, now. Can they not be confidantes for each other, in the midst of all this? Do they not both need it? Would it not be more equal, make them a more effective pair in the face of every possible adversity?

"Time to go upstairs?" Arché asks when they come back to the corridor. The other rooms have yielded nothing.

Glass smashes and boards go flying as two sets of skeleton arms break the lounge's window barricade. A single skeleton hobbles out of the fireplace, tripping over the bones of its predecessors.

"Time to head upstairs," Lenora agrees, and they begin scaling the steps. With one yank, she pulls the shadow wall at the front door forward, so that it blocks off the foot of the stairs to buy them more time against the onslaught.

Arché takes the stairs two at a time with ease. Lenora expects failure when she tries to mimic her, but with her hands braced against the narrow walls her body surprises her. Blood rushes through her, accelerating when the skeletons rattle against the shadow wall. Adrenaline and fear work wonders.

"Shit," Arché says as she skids to a halt at the top of the staircase. "Uh, Lenora?"

Shadow tendrils. Wrapped around the door ahead of them, blocking the way. Or rather, blocking the way to anyone but her. Lenora slides around Arché to land her hand on the wood. With the same pulse as when they'd reached the dome outside, the tendrils withdraw within seconds.

"This has to be the place," Arché says as she wrenches the door open. "Everything here responds to you."

"It better be in here, or we're going to have to—"

They come into what must have once been a decadent master bedroom, the size of three tavern rooms put together. On the opposite end of the room, two figures are locked in place. Statues? Shadow encases them, the many tendrils spreading from their location across the walls and floors, only now retracting from the door but not going far. One of the figures is masculine, a greatsword in his hands, while the other figure is androgynous with pointed ears of elven blood, the sword of their opponent plunged through their abdomen.

"No way," Lenora says softly.

"What am I looking at, Lenora?" Arché asks. "They can't be... real. Can they?"

They shouldn't be. Of course they shouldn't be. Every piece of logic points away from it, but there is something about the figures that locks Lenora's chest with a vice grip. Her feet bring her forward, step by step, half in a daze as she stares at the face of the person captured in their moment of impalement. Their face is twisted with pain and their arm flung out to the side. Upon closer inspection, their extended hand is the focal point of shadow in the room.

"Vali," Lenora breathes.

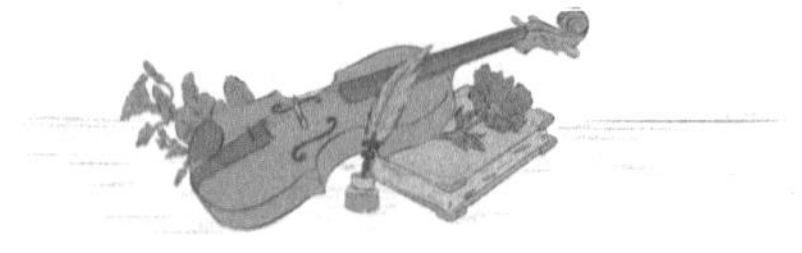

CHAPTER 17
LENORA

WHILE LENORA STARES AT Vali and has a small crisis of history, personal distress and disbelief, Arché gets to work barricading the door with the bed and vanity. Downstairs, the shadow barrier is beginning to fail, each whack from the bony hands resonating in the back of Lenora's mind where she maintains her connection to the shadow she's formed.

"Alright," Arché says as she comes to stand next to Lenora. "Whatever this is, it must be what we're looking for, right?"

Lenora tears her gaze away. Theories run wild in her head, but only lead her to one place. "I think we need to sever the tendrils. To release this."

Arché nods and pulls out Crescent Light, murmuring to it so it pulses and fills itself in with magic to form a full circle shape. She begins making large swings down and across, again and again, severing the tendrils around her. Lenora almost follows suit with a shadow claw, even if it would be a strain with the barrier, but then kneels instead. Like with the other magic at the door she finds connection and it snaps like a coil, reeling back towards Vali.

"Huh," Arché says, eyebrows up, impressed. "So. What do you think these two are?"

"Vali and Hilvar," Lenora says, finding herself certain of it. "I don't know how, but they seem frozen. None of this really makes sense, unless it's all coming from Vali."

"But it's been over a hundred years, how could—gods, as if I would know what magic is usual, here," Arché mutters with a shake of her head. "The shadow is going *back* to them. What does that mean?"

Lenora points to Vali, where each tendril has returned and pulled away some of the shadow covering them and Hilvar. "It's unfreezing them."

The shadow barrier downstairs turns back into nothing, and the clatter of skeletons up the stairs reaches the door barricade all too fast as Arché and Lenora are stuck watching the shadows doing their work.

"Wait, but Vali has a sword through them," Arché says. "If they're still alive, we might not be able to save—"

She stops short as the shadow melts from the top half of Hilvar, revealing the wolf print tattoo on his right upper arm, identical to hers in all but the detail of the paw.

"Warden Clan," Arché murmurs to herself. Horror flashes across her face, and she launches herself forward and seizes Hilvar from behind, by the arms, restraining him as the shadows finish melting away.

Vali falls off Hilvar's sword. They hit the ground and Lenora runs to them, her heart panging at the sight of the blood staining their shirt.

"Vali," she says. "I'm sorry, we can't—we don't have any magic that can—"

She cannot help but choke on the words. How many times has she wished to have advice from a past chosen? To have someone, anyone, understand what no one else can?

Vali's hand comes to touch her face, and something in her chest catches as their lips begin to form a word… only for the hand to drop and the last breath to leave their body.

"No!" Lenora clutches their shirt, battling the hopelessness that is digging its claws into her ferociously. "Please—"

She gasps as the shadows rush from Vali and into her. Every inch, every vein, every breath is consumed by magic so potent it ought to suffocate. But it is familiar, like plunging into the freezing waters of Concord's river. The wrong person might panic or drown, but not Lenora. The magic knows her, perhaps better than she knows herself, and she shudders as it infuses itself within her existing magic.

After having squeezed her eyes shut from the force of it, Lenora opens her eyes and takes in a new, gasping breath. Dusty air never tasted so good. Soft light pours through the windows, the faint shine of the moon and stars, no longer obscured by the dome. Behind them, a horrendous clatter announces the deanimation of the skeletons as Vali's magic no longer maintains them. The magic is now Lenora's, and no dead bones will walk under her control, even if now she realises it may have had nothing to do with life and may simply have been the shadows physically wrapping around the skeletons to manually move them. A feat impossible before, far beyond the focus and reach she possessed. It doesn't sound so difficult, now.

"Lenora," Arché says. Her brow is creased with worry, even as she continues to hold Hilvar, whose eyes are locked on Lenora with an unreadable expression.

"I have it," Lenora says, with breathless relief. "All of it." It will take time to even know what that means, but it feels a lot more like hope than anything did even a few minutes ago.

"Can I go now?" Hilvar asks. He sounds so bored and unfeeling that Lenora can only stare at him.

"I don't know what Concord was like when you left it, uncle," Arché growls, "but I wasn't raised as heir to our clan to let traitors walk away. Especially after *murdering* a chosen Shadow."

"Uncle?" He tries the word on his tongue and makes a face. "How long were we stuck like that?"

"A century at least. So, great great great uncle, maybe. But a traitor first."

"A century," he echoes, shaking his head. "So they'd all think I'm dead. You could just let me go. I don't want to fight family, but I will."

"Lenora, grab the sword from him—" Arché tries to say, but Hilvar's teeth lengthen at the same time his claws rake up Arché's arm. Her hold on him breaks as she yelps, and with a howl her partial transformation comes in just as fast as his, in time to stop his sword swing with the newly long claws of her free hand.

It's a battle of lycans, locked together. Sword versus shield, traitor versus heir. Hilvar looks as though he was frozen in his mid-thirties, meaning he has an extra decade of Warden Clan training over Arché.

Lenora has seen Arché fight, but not like this. Not this speed, not this ferocity, not even against the zealots they had killed on their way out of the valley. Those people were blundering compared to Hilvar. The match up is terrifyingly even, instinct for instinct, blow for blow.

He swings with the sword, with such power it makes Lenora flinch, but Arché brings the shield up just in time and uses it to push him back. Her leg tries to sweep him entirely but he's already planted himself and turns to use his shoulder to take advantage of her ungrounded stance. Arché falls back, but her extended leg whips around with the momentum to tuck under her body and catch the rest of her body in a crouch. The shield comes up again when the sword swings down like an executioner's axe. Arche drives herself up, against the force of him trying to keep her down, barely budging as she gives the contest of strength everything she has.

But it isn't all Arché has. Arché has Lenora.

Reaching for her magic had never exactly been difficult, but it had required such focus to ensure it formed anything close to what she wished and did not go rogue in any way that could harm someone. Now, as Lenora taps into it, it flows as easily as water. Shadow claws come to her hands in mere moments just in time for her to rake one across Hilvar's back.

He growls and whirls around, his claw coming only inches from her face. Lenora brings up a wall to protect herself but is only halfway done when Crescent Light slams into his upper body. He wavers but does not fall.

Lenora is ready when he comes back to try again. Arché is a considerable obstacle, but he shifts around her and the shield with expert footwork and a perfectly timed dodge. When Arché dives for him, he feints and she stumbles past.

"I killed one shadow rat today," Hilvar spits at Lenora. "Looks like I'll need to kill another."

"No," Lenora says. The word comes so easily, so calmly.

"No? You think you're stronger?"

Lenora shakes her head as she brings her claws up to meet his sword when he tries to bring it down on her. "No," she says, nearly buckling under the force of him, the power in her claws the only thing slowing his momentum. "But I'm not alone."

Crescent Light slams him in the back. He shrieks as the light burns.

It's like a song changing key. Arché and Lenora fall on him in unison, in rhythm so perfect it's as if they had been training with each other for a decade instead of with their fallen friends. Arché is quicker than she has any right to be, moving around Hilvar to block any attempts to hit Lenora. No matter where he turns, Arché has followed him or slipped around the other way, catching the blade on Crescent Light's edge. Lenora slips through the cracks and slashes with her claws. Or, if she needs to leap back, hurls the jagged claws through the air as tiny, brutal projectiles and then forms a new claw.

Creating new shadow, more shadow at a whim, comes so easily now.

Their harmony is a thing of beauty, but it's a lot of hits for Arché to take, even from behind the shield. Lenora can hear her grunts getting a little more laboured each time, can see her knees bending deeper under the force of Hilvar's strikes. And he's learning.

He's from the Warden Clan, the lycan fighters of Concord, of *course* he's learning. Raw skill has gotten them this far, and yet here it isn't enough. He's near impossible to predict as he begins to learn their tells and instincts—they are on the defensive too soon, and will never win that way.

Why had Lenora never tried to learn strategy? How had she been so focused on her magic, the damned magic, that it never occurred to her to study different types of fighters beyond the basics or what was right in front of her?

There is always some new way to be a failure, even now, when she wields more power than she ever has—but there is no time to be a failure. No breathing room. They must be victorious here or all is lost. If the power is what Lenora has, then that is what she must use.

Using unpracticed, unmastered magic is only taboo for Disciplined users like her mother or her siblings. But it's heavily discouraged for Innate mages who lack control, as the consequences can affect more than just the mage themself. Lenora will simply have to continue to shun expectations and go on instinct.

Once Arché blocks another blow for her, Lenora throws herself backward, to get as much distance between herself and Hilvar. Then, with the precious few seconds she has, she reaches for the shadow inside her and spreads it across the floor underneath Arché and Hilvar. It coats the wood like dark oil, and Lenora grins to herself.

At least, until Arché glances down at it. Hilvar takes advantage of the distraction and sweeps her feet from under her, and Arché fails to catch her balance on the new surface. As she falls, Hilvar brings the sword into her side. When he lifts the blade, all Lenora can see is the red of Arché's blood.

Arché's blood. Arché's howl, as she has never heard it before. The world flashes crimson with Lenora's fury, and she screams, her hands reaching out and bringing the shadow up Hilvar's legs to encase him. Her emotion spike turns the shadow edges sharp, however, and impale Hilvar through his right calf and left thigh.

He is stuck, though still armed, and Lenora is tempted to drain him and take away every bit of power he possesses. But considering him for another moment, she is overwhelmed with disgust. No traitor blood will pass her lips.

Arché uses Crescent Light to smack the sword from Hilvar's hand and he screams furiously, a litany of threats and pleas falling from his lips as he tries everything to get the freedom almost in his reach. Because Arché is still clutching her side with a bloody hand, Lenora hears none of the words. They will get him nowhere, anyway.

Lenora stalks closer and Arché drops the shield to pick up Hilvar's sword instead, testing its weight in her hand with a look of distaste.

"I don't like swords," Arché says through gritted teeth. "But I like traitors even less."

With him locked by Lenora's shadows, the blade runs through him in echo of his murder of Vali, withdrawing so the blood can pour from his chest in a slow spill. One act vile, the other fitting vengeance at the hand of one of his own clan. And yet, despite all of that, Lenora cannot quite get used to watching the light leave someone's eyes and knowing she has played a part, killing hand or helping one.

But then Arché drops. And Lenora forgets Hilvar even exists. She falls to her knees next to her companion, her only friend, her only anything.

"Arché," she chokes out. "Are you—what do you need me to—"

"Help me keep pressure on it," Arché murmurs. "I heal quickly, we just need to get through the next few minutes."

Lenora blinks with new inspiration, something she wishes she'd thought of for Vali but perhaps she needed their power for this, for it to come to her so easily. She pushes Arché's hand off the wound and crafts a mask of shadow over the wound in its entirety, making it impossible for any blood to escape.

Arché stares at the strange sight when Lenora's hand lifts to reveal it. "Huh. That's... genius."

Lenora's fingers are bloody and she sucks them clean with a pleased hum. The praise brings a flush to her cheeks, but she does her best to ignore it.

"I'm so sorry," Arché says. "About Vali. I can only imagine what that would have meant, if they—"

"They didn't," Lenora interrupts, with a small sigh. "I nearly drove myself to terrible things so many times thinking of if things had been different, my whole life. If I wasn't the chosen Shadow. If Nikos and I hadn't been heirs, maybe I would have told him how I felt and he would have *seen* me. If he had ever looked at me the way I wanted him to, the way he looked at you..."

She can only shake her head.

"Sometimes the only way to move forward is to know you can't change anything behind you," she continues. "Sometimes you just have to take the next step. And the next. Sometimes that's the only thing that helps me—"

Get out of bed in the evening.

Those words do not come out. They will not, even though Lenora knows she is hardly the only one in the world with depression. It's just one more thing about herself she wishes to be rid of. It would be nice if there were not so many of those things.

Arché's eyes are soft. They drink in every word uttered, and the silence that came instead of the words left unsaid. Her hand comes up to cup Lenora's cheek. Strong. Large. Callused. So gentle that Lenora goes absolutely still, unsure of what to do.

"You carry it so well," Arché murmurs. "I didn't see it for so long. Never guessed. I'm sorry."

Her thumb brushes across Lenora's cheekbone and Lenora presses into her palm on instinct, fighting tears trying to spring to her eyes.

"It wasn't your job," Lenora says.

Arché brushes stray strands of hair behind Lenora's ear. "It is now." Her hand drops and Lenora misses it the moment it is gone.

Lenora exhales, heavy and slow, her chest full of nameless emotion. She lets her head drop onto Arché's upper torso, letting the odd weight of everything wash over her as she tries to make sense of it.

"Partners?" she asks without lifting her head. What other question is there now? What are they to each other now, if not the thing they thought they'd lost forever, only to find it in the wake of destruction?

Arché's hand comes to rest on the back of Lenora's head while the other curls around her waist. "Partners."

It is impossible to say how long they stay there. Lenora holds the magic on Arché's wound steady, but it is a small occupation of her brain while the rest basks in the warmth and steadiness that is Arché Kalésen.

CHAPTER 18
ARCHÉ

Leaving Vali and Hilvar where they are is not an option. Thanks to the shadow bandage, Arché is able to get moving again after five minutes of lying with Lenora on the floor of Hilvar's bedroom, especially with Lenora maintaining the bandage over the next hour.

They've never had to build a pyre before, but it is mutually agreed that they will rest easier with Hilvar's body burned. The world's magic is too strange to risk him being able to come back somehow.

They give him no rites. No words. Just a torch to the wood, his body inside wrapped in a dank curtain.

Vali, however, they wrap in the softest blanket left in the house. Lenora whispers words to the Winter Wolf, the god of death and cold and shadow. They bury Vali under a patch of wildflowers in the manor's garden, and discuss how one day perhaps they'll be able to return and bring Vali home to Concord.

"I suppose we'll have to do this for Nikos and Rohan, at some point," Lenora says, staring at the flower patch.

"... yes, I suppose so," Arché says. Rohan is the last thing she wants to think of, right now. "Do we want to sleep in the manor? Or the tent?"

The sun is just about upon them, and Lenora winces at the sky.

"Tent," Lenora says after a few seconds of deliberation.

Once they're set up, Lenora insists on Arché lying back and letting her examine the wound. Arché is not inclined to argue with a bossy Lenora and really should not feel so warm about the way she frowns while demanding that Arché let her look after her.

It's that sort of thinking that is going to ruin Arché. It needs to stop. But how can she, when Lenora's array of facial expressions each elicit some different sort of fondness in Arché's chest?

The wound is still vivid on Arché's skin, but almost closed. No more blood is coming out.

"It'll be nearly gone by morning," Arché says with a grin. "Thank you."

"I'm so glad you're okay," Lenora murmurs.

They rest with the first taste of victory under their tongues.

Arché wakes with new inspiration. Her plans lie inside the manor, so she works on trying to extract herself from Lenora's hold without waking the vampire, but Lenora rolls and snuggles further into her. It tugs on Arché's heartstrings far more than it ought to. She can picture how Lenora had pressed her face into Arché's hand back in the manor; the memory is blurred around the edges from the blood loss at the time, but Lenora burns bright at the centre of it.

She burns bright at the centre of Arché's entire world. Like the sun Lenora so despises, she has become the light and warmth Arché looks for in every waking moment. While sleeping, she is so beautiful, almost free of worry if not for how her fingers clutch at whatever part of Arché or the blanket they can reach.

There is merit in admiring and loving something simply for the sake of doing so, and Arché wishes she were so enlightened. As it is, with every breath she considers her feelings for Lenora, another needle of pain impales her heart, as she knows Lenora will never share these feelings.

Besides, the magic of the founding bloodlines means that heirs cannot be life partners because children are a necessity but not ones who could potentially wield more than one artefact at a time. It's one of the reasons Lenora never told Nikos of her feelings, and Arché and Lenora would fare no better together.

Even so, Arché cannot stop herself from brushing an eyelash from Lenora's cheek and murmuring a quick 'be back soon' as if Lenora can hear her.

Hilvar's journals are Arché's inspiration, his records of what went wrong in Concord and the rest of his books which must still hold historical value. Alta will surely jump for joy upon being presented with them.

There's an old cart in what might have been a caretaker's shed, so Arché wheels it to the front door and begins making trips with armfuls of books.

By the time Lenora emerges from the tent, Arché is loading the last lot and feeling deeply accomplished.

"What are you—" Lenora rubs at her eyes and stifles a yawn. "Oh. For Alta?"

Arché grins and dusts off her palms. "It'll slow us down a bit on the way back, but I should be able to pull it."

Something odd flickers across Lenora's face, lifting her eyebrows before making its way down to curl her lips at one edge.

"Maybe you don't need to," she says. "My magic feels *so* much stronger. Let me try something."

She sits in the dust in front of the cart handles, and begins to weave threads of shadow from thin air. Even compared to the night before when she'd created the barrier for the front door, Arché can see how much more quickly the magic springs to answer her commands. The threads twist into a dark cylinder with extensions to attach to the handles, and Arché is bemused until around the cylinder the magic forms a large, solid wheel.

"*Oh*," Arché says.

Lenora stands, moves to the side, and reaches her hand forward to twist it in a circular motion. The wheel rolls forward one rotation, bringing the cart with it. Lenora squeaks with delight, her hand covering her mouth as she bounces on her toes.

"Will you be able to do that the whole way?" Arché asks.

"Probably not, but... at least then I'm pulling my share of the weight," Lenora says. "We can take turns, yeah?"

A shared weight. Their near effortless partnership, bringing mirrored smiles to their mouths and making for a simple start to their journey.

They alternate hours, with whoever is not exerting themself to pull the cart merely walking alongside, the pace slow enough that it allows for a sort of rest.

Four nights of travel. Four nights of enduring the bites through even deeper struggle. Four nights of collapsing into the tent with Lenora, both of them much more exhausted than usual. There is no specific moment that hits Arché, but she swears each night her heart is more violent in her chest as she falls asleep with Lenora curled up into her. It beats against her ribs, screaming protest at her inaction, refusing to listen to every perfectly good rebuttal her brain supplies it. By the third night, it hurts in a physical way. It shouldn't. Such a thing should be absurd. But it's so much that holding it in is becoming more and more impossible. How can she keep walking alongside Lenora, falling asleep next to her, and not pull her close and whisper every promise in the world?

Several hours before dawn on the fourth night, the ruins come into view, dark outlines against the sky which is a few shades lighter. The stars are barely visible through the thick clouds, and the smallest of rumbles have sounded above them. They have barely parked the cart outside the ruin staircase before Alta comes barrelling up them into the open air.

"Oh, thank the gods," the academic says before pulling Arché into a crushing hug. "And your training. All that training, gods, I will kiss Kalé like you won't *believe* when I see her next—wait." They pull back and stare at the cart, their jaw dropping. "Books?"

"From the manor," Arché says. "Journals, from the betrayer. And other books he had."

"And the chosen?" Alta asks, looking to Lenora.

Lenora smiles and waves a hand to disperse the shadow wheel on the cart. "I have Vali's magic. You were right. It was stuck there."

"I knew it, I just knew it!" Alta cackles. "What happened?"

The two nightwalkers explain how they had found the old members of Concord frozen in the final moment of their battle, and how Vali had fallen while Hilvar put up a fight.

Alta nods with quiet approval. "You did so well." They pull both Arché and Lenora into a tight hug, one arm each. "And you brought me all this. Amazing. I'm so, so proud of you both."

The words seize Arché by the throat and choke it with overwhelming emotion. Hearing them will never stop hitting her like a hammer, after craving something like it for so long. But while Alta's pride is a glorious thing, it is not a replacement for what Arché really needs: Kalé, saying the same thing. Having that pride shine in her, in the one she must succeed without being a failure.

"Thanks," Arché murmurs to Alta.

Lenora ducks behind her hair the moment they are released, muttering a thank you and hurrying inside with her bag, saying something about being tired.

It strikes a chord of concern in Arché, and she stares after her. The first lot of raindrops of the coming storm begin to fall on Arché's shoulders.

"Arché?" Alta glances down the stairs. "Is she alright? Did I do something wrong?" Oh, how similar they can be, sometimes. Alta's hands twist in front of them, brow furrowed with immediate worry.

"It probably wasn't you," Arché says. "I don't know. She's had a lot going on. Since, uh, forever. I never realised, until recently."

"Yeah, bit of a shit deal, being the chosen Shadow without the full power," Alta agrees, looking slightly reassured but not entirely. "She's doing well."

"She's amazing," Arché says, staring after where Lenora disappeared, voice soft as she speaks words she hasn't managed to say to Lenora's face.

Alta's eyebrow lifts and their eyes spark with something. "Oh?"

Arché wishes it were possible to kick herself. Panic rushes in, hard and fast. "No, don't do that—"

"I've never seen that look on your face before, Arché, but I've seen it on plenty of others in my time," Alta says, crossing their arms. "I'm not doing anything. You are."

"No, I'm not, because I can't," Arché says. With each word she is losing control of everything she has kept so in check, wound so tight around her heart like wool.

Unravelling. She's unravelling, just from being witnessed, from hearing any words on it from another. While it was inside her and nowhere else, it could hurt no one but her, but now it's like she's opened her palms and realised her nails have drawn blood. Every thought, every denial, every suppression has left a wound in her heart. Just staring at Alta's face yanks the weapon free and leaves her bleeding.

Her hand grips the edge of the cart and she glances down at her white knuckles in the hopes that she can get a hold of herself and wrap everything back up. More raindrops land on her skin, a big one sliding down the back of her neck. She shivers.

"Arché, it's fine," Alta tells her, touching her shoulder. "These feelings are a good thing, to care about someone else like this is precious—"

"No, it's not," Arché says. "Heirs can't be together, Alta, so it's pointless. Pointless, and painful."

"Heirs can't have children, that isn't the same thing at all, and you certainly don't need to be worried about *that* right now," Alta retorts. "So if that's all—"

"She doesn't love me back, Alta," Arché chokes out.

"You don't know that."

"Yes, I do." Arché brings her gaze up to meet Alta's. "She said she almost never gets feelings for anyone. And she was in love with Nikos, and now he's dead. So don't try to give me hope. I don't want it, I don't want it."

Alta purses their lips, eyes running over her, mind visibly racing. "But you love her?"

"I—" Arché chokes on an unexpected sob, and tears spring to her eyes as the dam fully bursts. "I didn't mean to. I promise, we've been doing everything we could to get to you and the others, but she's so—she's so strong to have made it this far, Alta, and sometimes when I look at her I can't fucking breathe, and she's so beautiful, and I don't know what to do—"

"Oh, honey," Alta whispers.

Arché lets herself fall into Alta's arms and be taken over by the sobs, by grief for something that could never be. The sky opens on them, and neither of them pay it any mind as the rain pelts them.

"I don't know what to do," Arché says again, after a while. "It feels like I'm going to explode."

"I wish I knew what to say," Alta tells her, their fingers tight in the back of Arché's shirt. "But I know you're strong enough to survive anything. Even this."

Arché doesn't feel strong at all. Arché feels as though she is made of paper, disintegrating with every drop of rain that falls, less and less of her able to stand every second.

Alta pulls away and stands on their tiptoes to kiss her forehead. Their thumbs wipe at the spots on Arché's cheeks where tears have mingled with raindrops.

"If thinking about her hurts, then try to stay focused on the mission," they say. "My understanding is... sometimes feelings like this can fade with time."

Arché cannot fathom how anything could fade when Lenora is any-where near, when her smile is only a small joke or victory away. But it's the closest thing to hope that might be within her grasp.

"I can do that," Arché says, and almost believes it.

"Of course you can. Come, let's go below before I catch my death."

They head inside and find Raavi and Lenora passing a bottle of wine between them, the latter giggling along to a story that Raavi is telling about being stuck behind an illusory wall.

"But you could have walked out at any time," Lenora says between giggles.

"I could have," Raavi says. "But I couldn't assume they wouldn't see me, no matter how much fun it sounded like they were having!"

Lenora's cheeks are bright pink. "So you just stayed there and *listened*?!"

"I didn't have much of a choice! I couldn't live with them *knowing*."

"I can't even imagine that," Lenora says.

"Do I want to know?" Arché asks as she and Alta approach them.

"Oh, the accidental voyeurism story," Alta says with a grin. "One of my favourites. The suffering for academic gain is part of what made you such an appealing assistant."

"Thanks, Alta," Raavi says sheepishly.

"If it makes you feel better, my wife and I once got caught on the village council meeting table—"

"Alta!" Arché says, gaping at them.

Alta flaps their hand at her. "What? You're an adult now, I can talk about this kind of thing, go to bed if it offends you—"

"I will," Arché declares, and really it is a relief to have an excuse to not be in the same space as Lenora right now. "I'm shattered from pulling that cart, so I'm going to sleep. You tell whatever stories you like."

"Good," Alta says, nodding with approval before turning back to the others. "Now, you have to understand how strong my wife is—"

Arché sticks her fingers in her ears and heads for the tent she shares with Lenora, dreading that she may be followed when more than anything she simply needs to be alone for a moment. But no such thing happens.

Sleep comes right away. And if, somewhere in that sleep, she feels someone slide in next to her and kiss the top of her head, then surely it is only a dream.

CHAPTER 19
ARCHÉ

Waking up next to Lenora is the last thing Arché plans on thinking about, so Arché creeps out of bed without so much as looking at her and wanders outside into the open air. By the time she reaches the top of the steps she is resolved to run the ruin perimeter, to put all of her agitated and pent-up energy into something more productive.

The dim light of dusk is comforting. Arché sets off at a strong pace, and perhaps it is not wise to exert herself when they might spend their whole day walking, but that isn't the same as taking strides that bring up her heart's pace. Strides powerful enough that sometimes she feels she might fly if she were to push off with enough force. She grins at the thought.

At some point she stops, and falls on purpose, letting her palms slap the earth. From there she moves right into push-ups, clapping in between each one. Every stretch of her body and burn of her muscles is a drop of relief, soothing parts of her soul that won't stop screaming.

I'm strong. I'm strong. I'm strong, and I can focus on what is needed. I can get this done. We cannot fail and I will not fall to anything. Not a sword. Not a pretty girl. I can't.

"Arché?"

Around her, the world has grown darker. Familiar and comforting in how the blackness wraps around the grass and trees and crumbled walls of stone. Amidst it all is Lenora, in her dress with no jacket or shoes, hair mussed from sleep.

Arché pauses in the middle of a one-handed push up and answers with Lenora's name said in the same questioning tone, acting as if just seeing her doesn't turn her mouth dry.

"You were gone," Lenora says. Her voice is still laden with sleep, soft and confused.

"Oh. Yes. I needed to move around. I felt restless. Sorry if I worried you."

"Right." She wraps her arms around herself, as if that will make up for her short sleeves on her dress. "Um. Since I'm here, should we do the bite up here? Away from Raavi?"

They should, and Arché says so as she gets up and approaches Lenora until they are a foot apart. The moonlight's absence has never seemed so tragic as right in this moment, because surely if it were here, Lenora would be lit up like some sort of goddess. Her hair like a soft candle in the dark, those grey eyes almost silver, the curve of her lips—

Perhaps it is fortunate that the moon is blocked by clouds.

"Are you okay?" Lenora whispers.

"I'm fine," Arché says, putting her hands behind her back before they get any ideas about doing anything they shouldn't. Like touching Lenora's face, or grabbing her and holding her close. Pushing her back into the pillar that's not far behind her and—

The sky empties on their heads. While Lenora shrieks, Arché bursts into laughter, strange and loud. It couldn't feel like more of a pointed hint from the Winter Wolf to get her shit together and stop imagining impossible things.

"The stairs," Arché says through her laughter. "Let's do the stairs instead." It feels so good to laugh, in the face of everything. The rain is cold and bracing, and makes her feel alive in a completely new way.

Lenora is less amused. She's halfway through conjuring herself a shadowy umbrella when Arché grabs her by the casting hand to pull her back towards the stairwell.

"It's good to feel the rain sometimes!" she tells Lenora.

"I disagree!"

They reach the entryway, drenched and dripping water all over the stone. Lenora stops to catch her breath, leaning back against the wall and staring at Arché with fascination.

"You're confusing," Lenora says. "You were starting to make sense. And you're… confusing."

The way Lenora's eyes are searching Arché for something makes it hard for Arché to focus on constructing words into a reply. Despite the Winter Wolf's warning, Arché cannot help but appreciate the sight of Lenora like this.

Her hair hangs in clumped tendrils while raindrops glisten on her skin and eyelashes, while her pale grey dress now clings to every slight curve she possesses. It's also now a little translucent.

Arché shoves her hands behind her back again. She leans against the opposite wall, exhaling as she grasps her control and holds it tight.

A new sense of peace washes over her, unexpected but sorely welcome. There will be times when this hurts. But in this moment, the aching is gone, and the only thing Arché feels is wonder. Like having the chance to stare at a waterfall or a starlit sky, Arché is beholding the only chosen Shadow in existence, in a state so beautiful she could drive someone as strong as Arché to their knees if she so much as asked.

A sky cannot love you back. Cannot be touched, cannot be coveted. It can only be admired. Beheld. Arché is lucky to even be able to look at her like this, half bare and utterly beautiful.

"I'm sorry," Arché says, several moments too late at least. A breathless smile takes her lips. "It's been a strange few days. But I'm here. Come take whatever you need, you'll feel better."

Lenora tilts her head, considering the answer, and she licks her fang while closing the gap between them.

The bite comes with Lenora's hand sliding up the other side of Arché's neck, and Arché feels her whole body shudder as she lets out the most ungodly moan. It echoes through the stone corridor, but Arché cannot find it in herself to care. She is nothing but the blood rushing from her veins to Lenora's mouth, nothing but the pain and pleasure entwining into a rope that holds her tight and tethers her to this woman in every possible way.

Arché will be her shield. Arché will be her nourishment. Arché will be anything she needs, if it makes her happy, if it saves their people. If she cannot worship her in the way she craves, she will devote herself in every other way possible. Then, one day, when it's all over, perhaps they can be friends. Comrades in victory, the ones who saved Concord.

That's not a bad dream.

"Oh, this is so good for my hangover," Lenora groans against Arché's neck.

"Is everything—oh!"

Arché's eyes snap open and spy Raavi halfway down the corridor with a torch in hand.

"I'm so sorry," Raavi says, her cheeks flushing scarlet enough to match her scales. "I just heard noises and thought someone was in—anyway, sorry, bye—"

She hurries away, and Lenora finally stops drinking to stare after the retreating outline.

"Shit," she says, licking her lips clean. "Was that Raavi?"

"Yeah." Arché thinks it over as her head begins to clear. Laughter rocks her body again. "Oh. She probably couldn't see you biting me. I think she thought we were... you know. Like we made Leahi think."

"Oh." Lenora sighs with relief. "Thank the gods for that."

It's so absurd that Arché's noises have almost certainly saved their secret. Arché cannot help but chuckle as they walk back down the corridor, fixing Arché's vest collar to cover the bite.

Sure enough, breakfast is an awkward affair. Alta hums to themself while serving up the toasted bread, and Raavi seems to think that her empty plate is the most fascinating thing in the world.

Toast has never tasted so divine, and Arché chomps on it with no care for decorum.

It is two minutes of silence thicker than anything Arché has previously known.

"Well, this is a chatty evening," Alta says, as if discussing the weather, but their voice does not match the burning curiosity in their eyes.

Raavi makes an odd noise and puts more toast in her mouth, while Lenora turns pink and drops her face in her hand. Alta's eyes move to Arché, who keeps her face as impassive as possible.

"What happened?" Alta asks.

"Nothing," Raavi says, too fast. Arché brings her palm to her face, loudly.

"This is the loudest nothing I've ever encountered," Alta remarks. "And it's not conducive to a good work environment. So let's be out with it."

"I just saw something that was none of my business, that's all," Raavi says, mortification plastered over her face. "Honestly, I don't know why this keeps happening to me, I swear I don't *try* to walk in on people—"

Alta tilts their head, looking between Arché and Lenora, no doubt having trouble marrying Raavi's words to the reality Arché had laid out the night before. Arché cannot imagine what line of inquiry may come next, and is inclined to stop it from reaching that point.

"Do you trust her?" Arché asks, before they can speak.

Alta doesn't miss a beat. "Completely."

That's all Arché needs to hear, if it will get them out of this conversation.

"We weren't doing what you thought, Raavi," Arché says. "We're on a nocturnal schedule because our town was founded by people who prefer to walk around at night. Lycans, like myself, and vampires like Lenora."

Raavi's eyes flick to Lenora with alarm, and Lenora gives her a tiny wave with her fingers. Her fangs poke into view as she gives a broader smile than usual in daywalker company. Raavi shakes with a nervous giggle.

"Usually the vampires feed off daywalking volunteers," Arché says. "But we're out together in the middle of nowhere. Lenora's needed to feed off me to survive."

"Oh," Raavi says, eyes wide. "It sounded so much like… something else."

"Well, getting bitten hurts, and I'm a baby," Arché says, perhaps too quickly, because Alta quirks an eyebrow. Knowing, probably, that Arché has never had the low pain tolerance she is claiming now.

More than anything ever before in the world, Arché prays to any god who may be listening that Alta never tries to ask about it. It is not a conversation they ever, ever need to have.

"I have… so many questions," Raavi says to Alta as she whips out her notebook, her eyes alight with academic fire.

"I'll answer them while these two get packing. There's no time for dilly-dallying."

"Packing?" Lenora asks, blinking at Alta.

"Oh! Right. Haven't told you the plan yet. I guess that was a dream. Or me practicing the conversation in my head." Alta chuckles to themself. "So, Raavi and I have been working on something here, this old magical tree that causes growth completely out of proportion with the time it *should* take. You've seen what it did to the town and the ruins. I was hoping I could turn it into something to bring back to Concord, to bolster the farms. But... if we're in an emergency situation, I might be able to work out a use that's more... extreme, and short term."

Arché takes a moment to turn the words over in her mind. "I... don't know what you mean by *extreme and short term.*"

Alta plants their hands on their hips and pushes out a long breath. "Well. From what you've said, these Crusaders aren't going to give everyone back, no matter how nicely we ask. It's going to get violent. Yes?"

Silver blades and scorching light slice through Arché's memory. She holds in a shudder. "Definitely."

"Then I might be able to bring magic that can help," Alta says. "But I'll need time to experiment with it, get it working and then portable. I'll need several days at least, probably longer, so you two might as well go ahead. See if you can find more help. More allies, anything else that could lend us power in a fight. There's a lot of them, and not many of us."

Alta speaks as if allies or things of power are easily found.

"Right... but where would we start?" Arché asks, trying not to sound as despairing as she feels.

"Leahi," Lenora says, chin lifting and eyes bright. "She said she would ask around for us, that she'd leave a note in Khiz so we could find her. Let's do it. She might even be willing to fight."

Arché winces. "She doesn't owe us *that*."

"Not everything is about owing," Alta says. "Sometimes people just want to help."

Arché is not sure she can handle that sort of optimism right now. This is going to be a difficult enough task without having the false hope of help that is in no way guaranteed. Better to assume it will not happen, and keep the possibility of a pleasant surprise later.

"We should be able to find her. She's the kind of person people would remember even if she's moved on from Khiz," Arché says after a few moments.

"Of course you'll be able to find her, you're my daughter *and* Kalé's, for the Inventor's sake," Alta says with a grin. "Greatest thing I ever made, tied with your brother."

"Aw," Raavi says, while Arché's heart swoops in her chest in a way that is half delightful, half downright uncomfortable.

Direct praise is such a strange thing. Luckily, Alta is too preoccupied with pulling out a map to notice anything odd about Arché's reaction to it.

"You said they were following the Highway," they say, tracing their finger over the thick line depicting the Kanin section of the trade route that spans the known world.

Being the most Eastward country, this part of the Highway starts in the coastal capital of Orsun and travels through the main body of the country before veering north to go around the mountain range that separates Kanin from the Theocracy of Izirm. Arché has never been so relieved for mountains before; were the range not there, the trip to Cancium would be much shorter and they would never have a chance of catching up to the Crusade.

"We can meet up here," Alta says, jabbing at one particular spot. "Ushonk, last major town on the Highway before the northern stretch."

They work out more specifics with the geography and travel, with the detour back to Khiz and Alta and Raavi leaving later once they have the magic. They decide on meeting in twenty nights' time, or as close to that as possible.

Planning is easy. So is packing. Saying goodbye? Not as much.

The rain is still going strong. Arché stands on the first step of the stairs, feeling the droplets on her back as she embraces Alta again. Too tight, but necessary.

"See you soon," Arché murmurs. "Stay safe."

"Stay strong," Alta says, and with the way they smile, Arché knows they mean it in several different ways.

Lenora gets a hug from Alta too, and squeaks with alarm at the sudden embrace before melting into Alta's arms a moment later.

"Show them all what the chosen of Shadow can do," Alta tells her.

Lenora nods, slow at first then faster and more vigorous, a smile growing on her lips. "I will. Thank you. So much. For everything. This whole time, I didn't know—"

"Go," Alta says with an easy smile back. "Take care of my daughter."

"I will," Lenora says. It is said so fiercely that it feels like a mockery of Arché's heart. Not from Lenora. Just...the universe, or a god needing comic relief from mortal suffering and irony.

They set off under a larger shadow umbrella of Lenora's creation, now easy for her to make and sustain, and begin a long walk through a rainy night.

CHAPTER 20
LENORA

THE STARS ARE ALWAYS brightest in the deepest part of the night. Lenora had always found comfort in the outer fields of Concord, away from the town lights, sitting among the grass and staring at the stars, grateful that neither could wish her to be anything other than what she is.

Lenora never thought she would think about stars in any other way, but walking the roads of Kanin with new power in every step brings an utterly new perspective. She is different now, alight in a way she never has been, a star shining only because of how dark things had gotten, not visible before.

How many times had she cursed her power? Wished she had been normal, able to master the same magic as the rest of her family? Nothing had felt right, and now it does. It is the simplest thing in the world to form the shadows into solid forms, to shield herself and Arché from the rain. After the challenge of the heavy wheel, it's as easy as breathing.

What an odd thing, to feel complete. The darker corners of her mind and heart are still heavy, not cured, and there is enough pressure weighing on them that getting up each night is still a struggle. But it's a *little* easier. And once she is on her feet? She is the chosen Shadow.

After spending the first night in Abzah's tavern, they make their way out to one of the farms to inquire about buying a horse. Lenora keeps her distance and tries to make it subtle that she is standing facing away from the setting sun, while Arché does the talking.

Arché's smile and warmth gets them everything they need; she shakes hands with the farm boy and they ride off on a lovely bay mare.

They ride with Lenora sitting in front, tucked into Arché's chest and between her arms not unlike how they've been sleeping recently. A perfect fit. No matter the strangeness of Arché's manner recently, their partnership feels stronger by the hour.

Two nights pass, and the hunting is poor, leaving Arché with only dried rations which feel especially underwhelming after Alta's cooking. Lenora can go mostly without. Food is secondary and usually more for fun than necessity, for her kind.

It's during one of these lackluster meals, at the roadside camp they've made for the day's rest, that they see glints of light and colour across the grassland.

"What is that?" Arché asks, cocking her head.

Lenora peers at the shapes. They clarify into figures of people dressed in bright orange, with gold glints of adornment. All but the one in the centre, who is dressed in much darker, more neutral colours. A bird circles above the group, too specifically to be a coincidence. Did it fly over them before? Lenora hadn't been paying the sky any mind.

"Fuck," Arché says, grabbing Crescent Light.

The Crusaders stop with a gesture from the odd one out, and remain on the opposite side of the dirt road while he strides forward. He is unremarkable in everything but how he moves—his armour is simple and sturdy, the crossbow on his back nothing special at first glance. But he moves like a predator, each step assured and measured as he comes closer. It makes his wave and smile of greeting all the more disconcerting.

"Morning," he calls. "My name is Tunvra."

"Leave," Lenora says, fists clenched at her sides. "I don't know who you are, Tunvra. But if you're with them, you'll die with them."

The words come out so easily, rising so quickly with the fury and hatred that consumes her the moment she sees the Crusader clothing. It's not even bluster; Lenora now has every confidence she could kill them all single-handedly if it came to it, or come close to it. She's not used her new power in battle but for Hilvar, and that was before she's been able to practice and stretch her limits.

"I'm afraid I can't do that," Tunvra replies. "I've been contracted to bring the two of you in."

"Why warn us?" Arché asks, as she steps closer to Lenora. "Why not take the advantage while you had it?" Once she and the shield are between Lenora and the intruder, she comes to a halt.

Tunvra shrugs. "I have a code. I never fight anyone who isn't ready to face me, and armed. If you come quietly, no one needs to get hurt."

"Do we really look like we're going to just stand down?" Arché asks.

"No," he says, with a smile and what might even be respect. "But I had to make the offer."

Arché growls. So far her words have been measured, her anger not showing in her voice and body, just like how Nikos had been. It's a Concord lycan thing, that emotional control, although Lenora has never been sure why it is so essential outside of the full moon nights.

"Do you even know who you're working for?" Arché demands. "How can you talk about a code, when you're here with them?"

"Who they are isn't my business. The way I do my job is."

"We decline," Lenora says. "I've warned you what happens if you force this fight."

Tunvra's gaze is even. Unwavering. "So be it."

And with that, like he'd practiced it a thousand times, he pulls the crossbow off his back at lightning speed and looses an already loaded bolt right at them. Silver.

Arché transforms in the same instant. She blocks the shot with Crescent Light as a snarl bellows from her throat. Tunvra reloads faster than Lenora ever thought possible, and the next shot is higher, higher than the shield can move to block in time—

Arché catches the bolt in her canine teeth and crushes it with one snap. A magnificent feat of luck and strength, but that will not necessarily last.

The Crusaders run in, seeing it all kick off, and Lenora knows it is her turn to take action. But the damned sun is in her eyes as she tries to peer around Arché and Crescent Light, and her head spins. Which is exactly why they attacked now.

There's just one thing. One thing they have likely no idea about, since none have survived her yet. She is the chosen of Shadow. And there is no light that can shackle her.

Lenora's hands ball into fists at her sides as she reaches within her for the shadow, forming the image in her mind of what she wants to create and how it will spread from her.

The Crusaders reach the camp. Lenora throws her hands up and releases a ceiling of shadow that blocks out the sun. Dozens of feet in every direction, covering them in glorious darkness, making them stagger back with horror.

"That's better," Lenora says with a smile, putting a hand on Arché's shoulder. "Ready?"

Arché charges at Tunvra, while Lenora launches herself at the Crusaders, and it turns to chaos.

Lenora has surprised the Crusaders twice in ten seconds: first with the shadow ceiling, second with her audacity of charging them. One small woman versus four larger, armoured people. Outnumbered. But not outmatched.

The mage is the easiest to spot. Robes instead of armour, a long staff with an ostentatious sun figurine at the top. And, if Lenora gives them a chance, the one who might start throwing magical sunlight. They're bulkier than most mages, more of a warrior's build, but their thick legs begin carrying them backwards at rapid pace as Lenora advances.

"Oh shit, fucking—" They wave the staff and mutter to themself, creating a blast of fire that shoots towards Lenora.

Lenora twists her body, avoiding the brunt of it, and comes back around to leap onto them. Her teeth find the mage's neck and sink into the exposed skin. Their blood flows hot and rich and delicious into her, and her body sings for the power.

At least, until the mage slams magical sunlight into her chest as a last resort. And then an arrow hits her in the back, for good measure.

Lenora tears out the mage's throat and spins to face the Crusader who has drawn a bow on her. Arché is keeping Tunvra busy in a deadly dance not unlike her battle with Hilvar, which leaves Lenora free to take the Crusaders.

Time for the rest of them to fall.

CHAPTER 21
ARCHÉ

No matter how politely one is ambushed, it is never a good thing. Arché and Lenora might have pushed back with confidence, but now there are three silver arrows burning Arché's skin and creating a haze in her mind.

Tunvra continuously tries to step away, out of her reach, so that he can get in a good shot. Arché stays on him, smacking him over the head with Crescent Light in the hopes at some point he might just drop. But none of the hits are quite right. He's too quick, too good at twisting to avoid the worst of the blow.

Another arrow takes advantage of her distraction. While a small grunt escapes her, a part of Arché just wants to scream at the archer to just stop, to let her breathe, but that isn't how this works. She would never give them the same courtesy, but then she is not the one who started this. Don't they know how tired she is? Would they ever care?

It's all so unfair.

Arché has been battling her instincts to keep an eye on Lenora because she cannot afford it, not if she wants to keep Tunvra from lining up a deadly shot. But when Lenora *screams* Arché cannot stop her gaze from moving any more than she could stop a tide from following the moon.

Sunlight and an arrow. This is all getting far too close. They need to turn the tide.

"This isn't your fight," Arché says to Tunvra. "They attacked our town unprovoked, killed innocent people and kidnapped more, for reasons that aren't even true. We could use help taking them down—you're a great fighter. Join the right side. We're going to win, not them, but it would be easier with you."

Tunvra tilts his head as he loads his next shot. Any step she takes, he mirrors, always trying to keep from her reach. "They hired me," he says. "It's that simple."

"And you'd die for that? Some money?" Arché asks.

"I don't plan on dying at all," he says, before shooting a bolt she barely deflects in time.

Stand strong. Be a wall. Be a force of nature, but do not be controlled by it. Let your training guide you, not your emotions. The tenets of everything Arché has ever been taught, and they might as well be laughing at her now.

His words are worse than any bolt he has sunk into her. They shatter the hope in her chest, the hope of a brilliant way to save this terrifying day; the shining moment where she believed she could convince him of his error. Now, the only thing that pounds through her head is *Kalé could have done it.*

Failure mixes with blood in her mouth. A scream catches in her throat, a scream for him to listen, a scream to demand he see how wrong he is. She was so sure speaking of the plight of her people would be enough to sway any reasonable person. Is the world outside of Concord truly so unfeeling? Are they truly so alone, so without anyone to care about them, just because they are different?

She is on shaky ground. Teetering far too close to losing control while transformed, the one thing she must never do. The only mistake she could make that would never be forgotten, or forgiven, by Concord.

Arché takes every hopeless part of her heart and gathers into one last bit of strength, unleashing on Tunvra with new force. She swings. Shoves. Then, at the right moment, gets in one good feint, just enough to slam him in the head with another resounding crack. He cries out and clutches his head, the crossbow falling to his side in one hand.

Another arrow buries itself in the back of her shoulder. She cannot withhold her cry, not when the pain is becoming so immense it threatens to overwhelm, not when she is on the brink of collapse in every other way.

But then the archer falls. Lenora knocks him to the ground and tears his chest to shreds in a fluid movement that turns to a flurry of rage. And, even more importantly, the horrible sound of it all has Tunvra glancing behind him.

Glancing behind... and seeing he is the only one left standing. Lenora stands and wipes her blood-covered mouth on the back of her hand before beginning to advance on him.

"I think this is the part where you surrender," she says.

Tunvra hesitates. Then, he drops the crossbow on the ground and raises his hands.

"Very well. I did say I had no plans to die today."

Now is Arché's second chance. To be the leader she has been training to be and win a powerful ally for Concord, to save them all. But when she opens her mouth, no words come. No argument. No stroke of eloquent brilliance. The only thing trying to escape is a sob, one she can barely hold in, especially as the weight of failure hammers her down again.

Her only chance for anything now is to walk away before this bastard sees her break.

"If you don't want to die today, then we're gonna have to work something out," Lenora says to Tunvra, stepping around him like a cat circling its prey. Her eyes are narrowed, every part of her exuding power despite her many small injuries and larger burn on her clavicle; the blood she's ingested making it all heal a little faster than it ought to, at Arché's guess.

"You seem like you've got this," Arché says to her. "I'm going to get these arrows out and lie down."

Lenora glances at her with surprise, her brow furrowing, but Arché gestures in Tunvra's direction in what hopefully comes across as encouragement. Then it is a simple enough thing to walk away, sit down near the tent, and yank out arrows and bolts so her bloodline's magic can start healing everything back up.

The bedroll inside the tent has never felt so glorious. She expects tears to come the moment she has privacy, but it hits her in a single and shuddering sob. From there, numbness creeps in. She's always known she would never be good enough to succeed Kalé. It's been a fact of her life for several years now, as she has waited and waited for the moment when she would feel accomplished or ready, only for it to never come.

This journey with Lenora felt like a chance to prove herself. To everyone. But the moment it counts? The moment it really matters? She is not enough. It is a suffocating reality, crashing down on her and refusing to let her breathe.

Kalé could have done it. Any true future could. Lenora might be doing it right now. But Arché will never have the gravitas she needs.

A head pokes through the tent. It's Lenora, beaming a smile that shows the blood still staining her teeth.

"I got him," she says with delight. "He's going to help us. He'll meet us in Ushonk too."

It's exactly what they need. What the town needs. It's good news. Her heart refuses to take it as such, and Arché feels her legs curl closer to her chest.

"Good job," she says. It's all she can do to force the words out, but they come out flat.

"... are you okay? You got pretty hurt, I could—"

"I'm fine, I just need to rest," Arché interrupts. "If you're alright, can you take watch? I need to sleep."

It's too sharp. It's not how she has ever, ever spoken to Lenora and she hates every second of it. But she feels as though she is about to burst, this time not from feelings for Lenora but from her fears choking her from the inside out. She needs Lenora gone.

CHAPTER 22
LENORA

IT'S AN INTOXICATING THING, standing before someone and knowing you hold their life in your hands. Lenora has no wish to kill Tunvra—he is not a Crusader, he has no intent beyond the mercenary if his words are to be believed. But he is a liability, a loose end, and Arché is right in saying he would be a powerful asset if he could switch allegiances.

Arché has turned and left. While Lenora wishes to run after her and check that she's okay, perhaps even hold her until the exhaustion passes, this must come first.

"So now what?" Tunvra asks with a sigh.

"I guess that depends on you," Lenora says, crossing her arms and licking her fang. "I can make anyone useful, if they have blood pumping through them."

His eyes flick to the Crusaders that died to her claws and teeth. He swallows.

"Or?" he asks.

"Or you decide to work for us, against them, and you'll get to keep your blood for now," Lenora says.

"And how would you ever trust me, if I did that?"

Lenora lifts an eyebrow. "Well, that's for you to convince me, isn't it? Your life is the one on the line here, If I spare you, how do I trust you?"

"I don't know," he says, all but spitting with frustration. "We have every reason to lie to each other, you realise that? You'll say anything to get me to turn on them, and I'll say anything to live. So where does that get us?"

A point difficult to argue with. Lenora nibbles on her lip as she mulls it over, twisting it until she can find the point from which to tear it apart.

"You said you were doing this because they paid you," she says, tilting her head.

"Yes," he says, as if it were obvious. "I'm a bounty hunter. I work for gold."

"So if I offered you more, you'd happily drop their job and take ours," Lenora says. The way his eyes spark is no real surprise. What does catch her off guard is the pity she feels for him; how sad it must be, to be so without conviction or care that money is all that matters. "We're talking about saving an entire town. We wouldn't be able to give you much now, but when we get everyone back, we'd be able to give you a lot. From the town treasury."

Tunvra's mouth and eyebrows remain still and stoic, as if his eyes haven't already given him away. "That's a simple matter of numbers. It would be an easy way to get my allegiance, without question."

Lenora grabs him by the front of his shirt. "But there would always be question. Because of today. Because of how dangerous we know you are. Because this tells me if they offered you more again, you'd take it."

"That's just how I operate," he hisses.

"You choose how to operate," Lenora snaps, "and you can't operate with empty veins." She gets the satisfaction of watching his tanned complexion go pale, as if she'd already taken a drink from him. "So with this pay increase, you're going to change how you operate so that you never become my enemy. We'll win, with or without you. If it's without because you betrayed us, you won't live to spend the money they give you."

His frame is tense, his gaze wary but steady. Not as convinced as he needs to be, not yet. So Lenora leans in closer and drops her voice until it is barely above a whisper.

"I'd never killed anyone until last month," Lenora says. "But they've changed that. Turns out, I'm really good at killing traitors. Trust me when I say I'd find you if it was the last thing I ever did."

As she swings back on her heels, his short exhale tells her everything she needs to know.

"What would you have me do?" he asks. "My skills are at your disposal."

"We need information first," Lenora says. "Do you know how they're moving the people from the town?"

"They've got twenty caravans, some of them heavy-duty and made of metal, pulled by the largest rhinos I've ever seen. They're taking the highway."

Just as they had thought; not subtle at all.

"Meet us in Ushonk," Lenora tells him. "With any more information about their movements or plans you can get on your way. And if you run into any, either get rid of them discreetly or pretend you're still working for them. That might be helpful, later."

"Simple enough," he says. "And your name is? I only ever got your descriptions."

"I'm Lenora, the Shadow of Concord." The words have never before left her lips, but they are like a puzzle piece clicking into place, clarifying a picture. I'm with Arché. She's heir to the Warden Clan."

Tunvra nods and clutches his still wounded side. "Can I go now?"

"Please." Lenora kicks his crossbow back towards him. A small risk, but she has no true concern that he'll fire on her now.

Lenora watches him call his bird to his arm and begin to walk away. She lets the shadow ceiling dissipate and gasps from the mental relief of no longer having to maintain it. Once Tunvra is a speck on the horizon, Lenora hurries to the tent to tell Arché about the victory she's snatched from the jaws of defeat.

But Arché isn't excited. Her words are the right ones, but hollow, and when Lenora tries to ask if she's alright, there are more biting words in reply. As if Lenora is just going to leave Arché when she is clearly feeling awful.

"Arché, I can tell something's wrong," Lenora says. "You can tell me—"

"I took so many fucking arrows, Lenora, I don't want to talk right now," Arché snaps. "I want to sleep."

It burns worse than the sun magic, searing Lenora's chest and drawing a whimper from her lips. She closes the tent flap and drops onto a rock some distance from the tent.

Arché has never spoken to her like that. There had been odd moments of shortness or strangeness, of course, where Lenora couldn't understand everything going on behind those resolute brown eyes. But Arché has always been so quick to soften, to apologise or explain.

Not like this.

The thrill of victory is knocked from her. It might as well have never existed, because now all her body knows is how to scream at her. It complains of injury and overexertion, but even that is overshadowed by the way her heartbeat pounds through her veins with every pulse. Like an alarm bell, saying how everything is *wrong, wrong, wrong.*

The corpses of the Crusaders, her kills, catch her vision. In a haze she lugs the bodies into a pile and lights them on fire with some help from her tinderbox. It's terrible work with her pitifully weak arms and already protesting body, but it's work that must be done. The physical pain is almost a relief to focus on so that her mind doesn't linger on Arché.

But then the work is done, and all there is to do is create a parasol to block out the sun as she sits back on the rock.

Being pushed away isn't anything new to Lenora. Her life has been made of such moments. Her mother giving her leave to depart lessons so she can focus on the twins who actually have potential, telling her to go and practice her new magic until it isn't an embarrassment or danger. Her father glimpsing her struggles to get through each day, and giving suggestion after suggestion that simply doesn't work, until he stops trying. Nikos pulling away if weighed down with something of his own, instead of talking to her about it.

It had been almost easy to become numb to it. Usually, seeing Nikos would be the shining light that would give her something to look forward to when all other reasons for getting out of bed fell short. Once, he had surprised her by storming into her bedroom with a hare-brained scheme for pranking his mothers that had tickled her so much she'd jumped up without thought.

But that had meant the moments he was busy or withdrawn had been that much harder. Relying on him wasn't good, wasn't healthy, she'd known that. But no other paths were showing themselves, so she'd clung to him like a lifeline.

Nikos was almost incapable of having a bad day. But the few times he had, it shone in his eyes like a beacon, and he had insisted on being alone to work through his thoughts. A completely reasonable request, but watching him walk away was agonising for Lenora. She loved him so, all she wanted was to ease his suffering.

Lenora fixes her eyes on the tent, her mind visualising the woman inside the way she's curled up so much smaller than she ought to be. Lenora's heart pounds as loud as a drum, and so hard she half expects it to knock her over.

This feeling is the same. The pain of each breath, as identical as such a thing could be.

Oh.

Had it not been easier to get up and out of the tent each evening, knowing she'll be spending each waking moment at Arché's side? Basking in the warmth of her gaze, the comfort of her arms and camaraderie?

Lenora, revelling in her newfound power, almost forgot the only reason she made it far enough to come into it and find herself is because Arché supported her every step. Carried her away from her death, enduring verbal abuse without resentment. Feeding her without protest.

Gratitude towards Arché is logical. Lenora has expressed it many times, along their journey. But has she confused it with something else, some of that time? Gratitude is not the soft flame in her chest that kindles just from the thought of Arché holding her as they fall asleep, or the calm that comes with the gentle silk of Arché's voice.

Gratitude is not the realisation that Lenora would give anything in the world to be by Arché's side, always. Even when this is all over. There are other words for that, words Lenora had given up on forever when Nikos had fallen.

If Arché is not okay, Lenora will not be either, not until all is well with both of them. They should fall together and rise together, as partners should.

Arché almost certainly doesn't share these feelings—while she is obviously attracted to Lenora physically or at least aroused by being bitten, that is not the same as romance. Given how strongly Arché reacted to Lenora's kiss, Lenora is quite sure the physical side of it is as far as it goes. No matter. Lenora is no stranger to carrying a singular torch. Lenora will love her no less for it, and simply do what she can to ensure Arché is safe and happy as she deserves.

Love. Just thinking the word brings a bizarre, giddy smile to Lenora's lips.

The hours slip away as she thinks back on her journey with Arché and considers each detail in a new light. By the time she needs to wake Arché for watch, butterflies have taken up in Lenora's stomach just at the thought of seeing her face.

One look through the tent flap. Arché is still curled in on herself, not her usual way of sleeping with limbs everywhere. She clutches her pillow with white knuckles, her brow creased.

Lenora wants to hold her, and kiss those knuckles until the grip and frown ease. Whatever troubles her, Lenora will crush it if it means she'll smile again.

Instead, she kneels beside Arché and puts a hand on her arm. She cannot resist stroking along the skin, across the soft hairs.

"Arché," she whispers. "Time for your watch."

Arché stirs, but not enough. Lenora shakes her a little more, and finally her eyes snap open. The deep brown finds Lenora and flashes with something powerful before she flinches away from Lenora's touch.

It hurts. It's bitter agony, actually, but Lenora is used to this flavour. She can endure it.

"I'm here if you want to talk," Lenora says.

"Talking won't fix anything," Arché mutters. *Of course you'd say that. You never try it.* She grabs her shirt and breastplate and begins to push out of the tent, before pausing and looking back with a soft gaze. "Are you alright? I'm sorry I—I didn't check on you before crashing out."

"Nothing I won't recover from," Lenora tells her, smiling. "You're not the only tough one, you know."

Arché nods, awkward and uncertain, and disappears behind the tent flap. Usually Arche's face is endearing in the rare moments she is confused. At the moment, Lenora wishes she could shake some sense into her.

There are so many things wrong. So many things to fix. Days ahead where these feelings will feel like trying to hold onto a hot coal with her bare hand. But for now, Lenora can only lie down and dream of how Arché's jaw might feel under her fingertips.

When she wakes, the muted light of day no longer fights to get through the tent fabric. There is just calm dimness, leaving everything from before her sleep to come flooding back. Her hand covers her mouth.

She's in love. With Arché. What a strange, beautiful thing.

"Hey," Lenora says as soon as she's out of the tent and able to see Arché. The lycan is working on a new carving. "Feeling any better?"

Arché opens her mouth, tenses her jaw, and closes her mouth again. Her sigh is heavy as her hands resume carving.

Lenora comes to sit next to her. "If you change your mind about talking, I'm still here." She wishes so desperately to know what is wrong. Perhaps it had all been too much, too close, too frightening. They almost lost yesterday, and while Arché has shown little fear thus far, it would be absolutely reasonable for Arché to be shaken by it. "I know it was scary, but we did it. We can do anything."

Arché looks up, and something in her face shifts as their eyes meet. "You really believe that, don't you?"

"I do."

"Okay," Arché breathes. "Okay. Let's get you fed, and get going."

It feels different now. Sliding closer to Arché, leaning into her space. Lenora can't help breathing in the scent of her skin, the dirt and sweat and blood mixed with something deeper. The magic of lycan blood, the vivacity of life infused with magic until it is the most intoxicating thing possible to consume.

Her hand slides up the opposite side of Arché's neck as she bites. The blood is so sweet, and Lenora relishes it before realising that the usual odd moan or whimper that would leave Arché does not come. That, more than anything, rings strange and sours the moments until Lenora is finished.

Lenora pulls away and searches Arché's face. Where she hopes to find something, there is only a blank stare.

"Arché," Lenora says. "I'm really worried about you."

"I just need some time to get my head right," Arché tells her, looking as though she's having to force the words out.

It's like a spark inside her has vanished. And no matter what it takes, no matter how unhelpful Arché is about it, Lenora will not rest until that spark is brought back to life.

They ride in silence through the night, giving Lenora's mind plenty of time for the many things it has to linger on. It is impossible to have romantic feelings without at least considering the possibility of voicing them. But doing so at the moment would be unthinkable.

Arché is not well. Not her best self. Sorting her out in that respect is more important than anything. Arché harbouring sexual feelings to the one person near her is no invitation, and ever since then Lenora has tried to consider her comfort above all else. It's been difficult, as Lenora is never quite sure which boundaries are which, but she has stolen glances at Arché's face and asked the few questions she can.

Lenora wants more than anything else to be a better partner to Arché than she was to Nikos. But with life so uncertain, can she let history repeat and let the feelings she holds go unsaid if they are hit by another terrible tragedy? Or is all of this consideration purely about herself, and not considering Arché at all?

One person with physical reactions and no expectations. The other, with emotional reactions, and no expectations. Surely that balances out?

Telling Arché makes sense. It would be evening the scales, so they both know about the other's desires that will not come to fruition. But while the logic sounds right, it sits wrong in Lenora's heart.

She needs a sign. Or permission. Whatever comes first, whatever feels right.

CHAPTER 23
ARCHÉ

THE SHAME OF NOT living up to everything she wishes to be is not something that will leave Arché easily. But in the face of the challenge before them, hearing Lenora declare her faith in their abilities soothes a small bit of the hurt of the fight and all it had brought. It at least gives Arché the strength to stand, pack up camp, and ride on.

Lenora is quiet. Arché is grateful. She is not ready to be honest about any of this; she is not sure she ever will be. Once she speaks of this fear it cannot be taken back. And then, perhaps it will be more real than ever.

One small mercy comes their way towards the end of the evening's ride. The soft babble of a creek, coming from not too far off, a promise of refreshed hygiene they are sorely in need of.

"Oh gods, *yes*," Lenora says as soon as Arché points it out and suggests diverting to camp there for the night. "I smell so bad."

They both do. Arché's lycan senses have been acutely aware of it for days. It's the sort of thing that can't be helped with these long stretches of travel. All the more reason to seize this opportunity while they can.

"Should we take turns, or just face away from each other?" Arché asks Lenora.

Lenora blinks. She pauses longer than expected, her eyes flicking from Arché's head to her toes. "I'm fine with whatever you want. But I could, uh, wash your hair and your back, if you wanted."

The offer has Arché feeling all sorts of confusion. The part of her devoted to longing for Lenora rears its head with equal parts alarm and desire. The part of her that wants to continue hiding from the world wants to step back, out of reach of any sort of contact. Like if Lenora touches her, somehow she'll know.

"Uh. Why?" Arché asks, in the end.

"It's okay that you don't want to talk, but it seems like you're trying to do this on your own. If you don't want my words to help, maybe my hands can. You helped me realise that people aren't... meant to not be touched, especially when we're not feeling good. You helped me. I can return the favour. If you don't like it, I'll stop."

Lenora's eyes are wide and earnest. Different somehow, to the days that have come before. She speaks of partnership and belief in them, and now this.

Romantic woes aside, perhaps Lenora is right that this is what Arché needs. Arché's instinct is still to refuse, to recoil and bottle it up, but she has just enough sense left to know that it isn't what will help her or anyone else relying on her.

"Okay," Arché says. "That would be... really nice, actually."

The creek is a small, shallow thing. Only enough to submerge up to their calves, but it is a far cry better than nothing at all. They undress and sit facing away from each other to start. Arché lets the cold water rush over her thighs and uses the bar of soap from her pack to clean everywhere she can reach. The shock of the temperature combined with the relief of the grime washing away does more to bring Arché back to herself than she could have imagined.

She scrubs at her fingernails and imagines if it were possible to do so vigorously enough that the failure and shame could wash down the creek with the dirt.

"Arché," Lenora's voice says. "Can I wash your hair now?"

Arché halts where she had accidentally begun scrubbing her hands almost to the point of hurting herself. "I—yes. Please."

It is a long few seconds to wait, but she hears Lenora shuffle closer across the pebbles and sit down close enough that Arché can almost feel her body heat.

"I'm sure it wasn't easy for you to agree to this," Lenora says quietly, as she begins putting the water over Arché's hair. "But I'm really glad you did."

"... I'm lucky to have someone who cares enough to offer. You're a really good friend, Lenora. I'm sorry I'm so bad at being one back."

"You're *not*," Lenora insists. "You've done so much for me. You're not a bad friend because you find it hard to talk about how you're feeling."

Arché has never seen it as finding it difficult to discuss her feelings. Actually saying how she feels is too easy, a trap she must constantly avoid falling into lest her tongue drag her somewhere she does not wish to be. It's simply that the feelings that weigh on her the most are the ones that will have the most consequences if spoken aloud, and those consequences hang over her like a storm cloud.

Lenora's hands begin working the shampoo through Arché's hair and Arché feels her throat thicken at how soothing the simple brushes of Lenora's fingers against her scalp are.

No one has done this for her since Alta, since Arché was half the size she is now. It's so gentle, so needed in a way she could never have known or asked for, that tears spring to her eyes. What a relief that Lenora cannot see her face.

"I just want you to know how grateful I am for you," Lenora says quietly from behind her. "I'd have never made it this far without you, never gotten my power without you... none of it. And whatever is going through your head, I just thought it might be good if you had another voice telling you that I think you're one of the most incredible people I've ever met. You're so strong, your body and heart and mind all together. I've never known someone who makes others look so weak."

A sob rocks Arché's body, without permission, and she lacks the power to stop the second.

"Gods, I'm sorry," Arché whispers. "You used to hate me because I was in your way, and then you didn't, and now you're being so..."

"I didn't hate you," Lenora interrupts. "I just had an unreasonable dislike. And now I see you for who and what you really are. And I want to make sure that *you* do."

"Thank you," Arché says. "Thank you. I can't stop thinking about this stuff, but it helps. Like you said, another voice, trying to drown it out. It's a start. And—" She doesn't want to say it, but she knows she must. Accountability. Responsibility. "And I promise I'll talk to you about it when I can. I'm just not ready yet. But I know I need to be. Soon."

"That sounds like a good plan." Lenora begins rinsing the shampoo from Arché's hair, those nimble violinist fingers running through the strands. "I told you we can do anything. They've got nothing on our teamwork."

Arché begins exhaling in time with the pouring of water until something in her chest loosens and some of the weight in her heart eases. They can do this. She is not alone. She has Lenora.

"When we're less naked," Arché says, "I'm going to hug you, if that's okay."

"That's more than okay," Lenora giggles.

They've never hugged. Not quite. Not properly. They've shared bedrolls and laid next to each other, even embraced in some ways during those times. But they've never just... hugged each other. How absurd it seems now. Arché has been so afraid to touch her, so afraid of her own feelings, that she hasn't even hugged her friend. Her friend she needs more than anything. How absurd.

"I think it's overdue," Arché adds.

"I agree."

"Do you want me to wash your hair?" Arché asks. She's not sure which answer she wishes for, but it seems only right to offer.

"No, thanks, I've done my own a bit while doing yours, I just need to rinse it now. Then we can drip dry! Gosh, we really need some travel towels, huh?"

Such an important thing to be without, Arché quite agrees. And yet here they are, with little choice but to sit on the bank and let the soft breeze of the almost morning dry them. Being so close to Lenora while they're both undressed ought to be a source of panic, but the panic doesn't come.

They sit back to back. Almost touching. Not quite.

"Are you feeling better?" Lenora asks. "You... seem like it."

"I am. Thank you, Lenora."

"Okay. Good. I have a question."

Is Arché imagining the shift in her voice, the way that nerves overtake it almost instantly? What in the world could this question be?

"You can ask me anything, Lenora," Arché says. "If I can't answer, I'll at least tell you why."

"Well, there's something that I want to tell you, but I'm worried it's going to make you upset, but it also seems like I should be honest and like you would want me to be honest so I'm not *sure*—"

"Why are you worried it would make me upset?" Arché asks, baffled.

"Because something similar did. A while ago. This isn't the same, but you know, boundaries…"

"Well, you're right that I rather you be honest. Tell me."

"But you might not feel that way once I tell you—"

"Lenora," Arché says, trying to keep herself as calm as possible. "Now that you've brought this up, you're going to *have* to tell me, or else I'm going to overthink it until I send myself into a ridiculous anxiety spiral." Her chest is already twisting into knots, wondering what could be so terrible that Lenora is so uncertain.

"See, this is why I shouldn't have said anything! You told me you over-think things but I've brought it up anyway, and the last thing I want to do is stress you out more—"

Arché turns, reaching for Lenora's opposite shoulder to pull her around enough to meet her eye. "Lenora!"

Those eyes are something else. The shining grey, wide and vulnerable.

"I love you," Lenora blurts out.

The world tilts from the possibility of three small words, until Arché shakes herself and ensures everything comes back to reality.

"What? No you don't."

A frown, that perfect frown, snaps onto Lenora's face. "Yes, I do."

What kind of joke of the universe is this? Whatever Lenora is trying to say surely can't be what Arché *thinks* she means; there are plenty of different forms of love and that must be what Lenora is talking about.

"As a friend," Arché says.

"No, as a partner."

"As a partner you work with."

"No!" Lenora stares at her with bewildered disbelief. "I mean I'm *in* love with you, Arché. And it's okay, I'm not expecting anything from you, and I don't want to make it weird. I know it won't be the same for you, I'm used to that. But I have to tell you because I'm not making that mistake again. Not after Nikos."

"But... you can't! That doesn't—that doesn't make any sense, this whole time—"

"I do," Lenora says, as fierce as ever. "And you can't tell me otherwise."

By all logic, Arché must be dreaming. Or hallucinating. But then, her dreams would never conjure this, not the way it is playing out, not the fire in Lenora's eyes being different to how she's ever imagined it.

Arché's heart is in uproar. It pounds against her ribs with great violence, demanding to be released so that it may fly to Lenora, as it has wanted to for all these agonising days. She holds it in, her fear a powerful warden, until she can be completely sure.

"You're in love with me? And you're saying it's one-sided and that's okay?" Arché asks. This might be what losing one's mind feels like. Or she may be coming down with a stress-induced illness.

"It *is* okay," Lenora says, her shoulders finally dropping now that they are no longer arguing over the most absurd of things. "I just needed to say it."

"But I—" Arché's voice cracks and she tries again. "I *cried* on Alta because I was sure you'd never feel the same way that I do." As the words tremble, something shifts in Lenora's face that she may never forget as long as they live.

It's hope. Fierce and unexpected. When Lenora speaks again, it comes out as more of a squeak.

"Wait, what?"

"I've liked you *far* longer than I should have," Arché says. Her fingers itch to reach for Lenora, to touch her face, but that might shatter something. They're sitting here, naked, and Lenora is saying these things. Surely it can't all be real at once.

"I thought it was just, you know." Lenora bites her lip. "Physical stuff."

"It was. At first. But then..." Arché had never prepared herself to actually speak of it. How many times had she half-practiced this in her head, only to throw the words aside because it would never happen? "I'd do anything for you. Sometimes I can't breathe when I'm near you, when I look at you—gods, the ways I've wanted you, Lenora—"

"Yeah?" Lenora asks. The question is quiet and unsure, but the curiosity in her eyes is pure, a burning no grey has ever known before.

They're so close. So few barriers between them, of any kind. Arché refuses to look down. It's not about any of *that* right now. And the last thing she wishes to do is look away from Lenora's face.

"Yes," Arché exhales.

Lenora tilts her head. "So... does that mean I could kiss you?"

The question might as well turn Arché's world inside out. Emotion bursts in Arché's chest, so many things at once, overwhelming her entirely.

"No," Arché says, and when Lenora's face falls, adds, "not yet. I need some time to think about this. Sleep on it."

"Right." Lenora smiles. "That's fine."

"I spent so long believing this wouldn't happen," Arché continues to explain. "I was working so hard to push everything down. I can't just... switch. But it'll be okay."

"I can take first watch," Lenora says. "Take as long as you need. I'll be here."

"You'll be here," Arché echoes. She almost laughs from it, before blood rushes to her face all at once. "Gods, we're naked."

"Yes."

"If I go into the tent, you'll see my—well, my everything."

Lenora giggles horrendously. "I can turn back to the water. Would that help?"

"Yes."

"But I'm sure your everything is great. And maybe when you're—"

Arché gets up before Lenora can continue on that particular line of thought, Lenora turning away without being reminded. "No, no, I'm not ready for you to start talking about *that*—are you trying to kill me?"

"... okay," Lenora says, with another giggle. "You're more dramatic than I ever realised."

"I'm a woman in *crisis*," Arché replies. "I have been for *days*, and now there is a *different* crisis. And you're *laughing*."

There's no stopping the giggling now. Lenora is lost to it, and the sound of her mirth carves a special place in Arché's heart, tender and precious. Something to be protected forever.

How baffling, to feel a smile pulling at her mouth while her chest has nearly imploded. Arché hurries into the tent and drops onto the bedroll, arms wrapping around herself, the last few minutes playing over and over in her head.

Lenora loves her. Lenora wants to kiss her. Arché is not alone in this. Arché does not have to suffer and repress the feelings eating her from the inside every damned day.

An odd laugh escapes her, in the same instance that tears prick her eyes and fall hot and fast. So much misery for nothing, so much joy possible in the future. Relief, delight, reckoning. Everything she could have never expected. The most surprising part is the lack of doubt. Arché is so quick to second guess the true thoughts of others, especially when they pertain to herself, but the truth of Lenora's confession bled from every part of her. Something lighting her eyes in a new way—adoration. Ferocity in her words. Refusing to let Arché dissuade her, demanding to be heard. Arché appreciates the initial hesitation, the consideration for Arché's feelings, but more than anything admires the conviction that came after.

Her fingers come to her lips, thinking on Lenora's request. Kissing Lenora is a beautiful thing to look forward to in the new evening.

For now, she has a dozen futures to imagine, with new hope, and other emotions to let go. Sleep comes first.

CHAPTER 24
LENORA

IT IS A CALMING thing, to sit next to babbling water with a heart now free of unspoken intent. Once the sun comes out properly it is easy to get dressed and make a parasol to sit under. Lenora spends the hours thinking on how Arché had reacted with such certainty that none of it could be true, how she'd said she had cried on Alta because of her own feelings, how she'd been pushing everything down.

And all the while, Lenora had been oblivious to her struggle. There is little Lenora can do to fix the past, but she certainly has ideas about how to make it up to her now.

Mainly kissing. The memory of their single kiss, fueled by magic that had neither of them fully in control, burns inside her. The strength of Arché's grip, the heat of her lips. Lenora wants that again, wants to feel it properly with the time to explore. Explore Arché, explore herself, explore everything that comes along with kissing that she's never tried but finally might want to.

"Lenora."

Arché's voice, odd as it sounds, has her whirling around on her perch of the rock. Arché stands there, now clothed, but her eyes more bare than anything Lenora has seen.

Lenora smiles at her, her heart swelling in her chest. "Arché."

"I'd like to kiss you, now," Arché says.

"Please do," Lenora says, dropping the parasol and scrambling to her feet. "Right now."

Arché closes the gap in two strides. Her hands, large and warm, take Lenora's face between them and cup her jaw and cheeks, tilting her face to meet Arché's height. Lenora feels her breath hitch while her heart hammers against her ribs. She's held in suspense as Arché leans in and hesitates right when they're a mere breath apart. Lenora itches to close the gap. But this is Arché's move to make.

"Arché?" Lenora asks. "Is something wrong?"

"I need to get this right," Arché says, her thumb brushing across Lenora's cheek. "It's never mattered like this before."

"What?"

"Kissing. It's never mattered like this before." Arché exhales slowly. The hot breath hits Lenora's lips and the heat travels down Lenora's body in a tingle. "Can you say it again? What you said yesterday?"

Lenora can only guess what that means. "I love you, Arché."

The smallest of smiles, of sparks. "I love you too," Arché says, before taking Lenora's mouth with her own, holding her fast in the cradle of her hands.

It's bliss. Warm, overwhelming, soft. There is nothing but Arché's lips, earnestly giving every bit of adoration she'd been holding in, and Arché's hands keeping her secure as if she might be snatched away at any moment.

Lenora's entire body shudders from the force of it, from the realisation that she'd let Arché hold her as tightly as it took to ensure they are never parted. Almost as if Arché can read her mind, one hand moves to slide down Lenora's back, pulling her closer, keeping her steady.

They break for breath, and Arché stares at her with wonder. Her mouth opens, looking to form words, but Lenora cannot imagine what could possibly be worth saying right now that they are doing *this*. Lenora kisses her this time, grabbing Arché by the collar of her vest and pulling her down. Arché groans against her mouth and uses the hand on Lenora's back to pull her closer, their bodies pressing together. They fit just as well like this as they do during days on the bedroll.

"Wow," Lenora breathes against Arché's lips. "Is kissing always like this?"

"No," Arché tells her. "Sometimes it's just... a thing. I've never—this is new to me too. That's what I meant. It's never mattered before. I wanted to kiss you right this time."

Lenora nods, unable to stop the smile on her face that must be too large, too adoring. But then, why should she? "You got it perfect."

Arché kisses her again, and this time there is a leisure to it, a slowness that lets Lenora savour every detail. The taste of Arché's lips, the warmth of the splayed fingers on her back, the way Arché's other hand still holds her face and is still caressing it with her thumb even as they're kissing.

Is this what it feels like, to be cared for like this? Loved? No wonder some people can't shut up about it.

"You've done other stuff too, before," Lenora says when they next part. "You know I haven't. But if it's like this... I want to. With you."

It's a clarity that comes quickly. Lenora had long known that she is capable of these feelings, as she'd certainly had a few fantasies about Nikos. It just seems to require much more time and specifics than a lot of other people need.

But now, staring up at Arché, seeing something powerful blaze through her eyes at Lenora's words, Lenora is beyond curious and left wanting. Her body is filled with new heat, so much more powerful after brazen kisses than anything she's ever felt when only accompanied by her mind's conjurings.

"We can do that," Arché murmurs.

Arché kisses her again, slow and deep, her tongue pressing against Lenora's lips as if asking permission for something. Lenora is not entirely sure of what to do, but opens her mouth to let Arché in, and finds herself kissed, explored, devoured all in the same moments. It's strange. It's also delightful, and Lenora cannot resist trying to do the same, to taste Arché more deeply.

"You said you... wanted me," Lenora says, feeling her breath come in little gasps. "In lots of ways."

"I have," Arché says, kissing her way from Lenora's mouth to her ear. The skin is so sensitive and unprepared that Lenora squirms. "And I do. But you need to rest, and I need to take it slow with you. But I promise, if you want to and you like it, I'll show you everything."

Arché pulls back for the last part, her dark eyes intent, the promise enough to make Lenora shiver in her arms.

"How am I supposed to sleep?" Lenora asks. "My whole body feels like it's been feeding."

Arché's hand travels over Lenora's face with featherlight touch, tracing her brow and the line of her nose, the curve of her cheeks. Lenora's eyes shut, the barely-there contact making her heart skip.

"You're new to this, right?" Arché asks. "Being physical with someone else. Having feelings about it. I think you should lie down and think about what you want. What you might like. You can tell me, when you wake up."

"I want you," Lenora says without hesitation.

Arché actually chuckles, but Lenora swears the lycan's face gets more flushed. "That's... great. Fuck, if you had any idea how you look right now—"

Another kiss. This one is hungry, like Arché is getting in one more taste, and Lenora is happy to tilt her head and give Arché everything she can.

"I mean more specifically, the things you might want us to do. How you might want to be touched. That kind of thing."

"Oh." Lenora feels heat come to her own cheeks now as her imagination runs wild with the first few things that come to mind. "I can try. The twins would read a lot of silly smut books—"

"If that gives you any ideas you like, that's fine," Arché says, laughing again. "But it's okay if you like your own ideas better. I usually do."

"I hope we like the same things," Lenora says, frowning at the thought of some truly awkward conversations.

"We'll figure it out, together," Arché assures her. "There are very few things I don't like, and I love you. It's not going to be a problem, it's just about communication."

"Together. Okay." Lenora beams and cannot resist kissing Arché one more time, this time taking the chance to hold Arché by her arms and feeling the muscles there.

Arché's eyes follow her until the tent flap fully separates them.

Lenora throws herself onto the bed roll and plays the kisses back in her mind. She can still feel where Arché's hands had been, the heat lingering in her mind if not the body. Nothing her absurd siblings had ever read aloud could feel anything like this. Her imagination conjures images of hands sliding along her legs, up them, touching her anywhere and everywhere. Arché will. She's promised.

The idea of so much touch is overwhelming. Even now, everything from the last few minutes washes over her in ways of disbelief and shock. How is she supposed to handle more, when she's been so stuck inside herself for so long, with only Nikos to provide brief reprieve of shoulder touches and quick hugs? She'd always felt too awkward to dare ask for more.

Perhaps it *will* be overwhelming. But Arché will listen if Lenora asks for less, or to go slow. She even seems to be expecting it. And honestly, thinking of being covered by Arché, her hands and lips and weight... it sends heat through Lenora's chest and neck right down to between her legs.

If Arché wants specifics, Lenora might struggle to convey that, but there is little concern or doubt left as she lets the sensations wash over her, taking note of every detail.

It's an easy thing to drift to sleep with the warmth of it all.

Lenora wakes to a hand stroking her head, and when her eyes snap open, she sees Arché lying opposite her. There's a smile that keeps coming to Lenora's lips, instinctive as anything, that had been all but non-existent before recent days. It's Arché's smile. The one just for her, the one that bursts from Lenora the moment she sees this person who has become almost *everything*.

"Arché," Lenora breathes.

"Hey," Arché says, and they stare at each other, caught in the same hesitation. "Can I kiss you again?"

Lenora nods, and Arché uses the hand at the back of Lenora's head to cup it and pull her in. The kiss is slow, and deep, and Lenora presses forward, pushing herself against Arché's body. Wanting to be closer. Needing to be closer.

"It's okay," Arché murmurs. She brushes kisses over Lenora's cheek and eyelids and nose. "We have time."

"You told me to think about all of it," Lenora says. "I did. I thought about you."

"What about me?"

"Your hands." Lenora feels her cheeks flush as she takes Arché's spare hand and interlocks their fingers. "Your hands, you know... everywhere. Places only my hands have been. I don't do *that* much, but I have, a few times. And... I know people use their mouths for things too."

Arché nods. She kisses their joined fingers. "Those are *all* things I've thought about. Far too much."

"Will you show me?" Lenora asks. "The things that you think about?"

Arché's eyes are fathomless pools of warm brown. Lenora could lie here forever and be content to never move if she were to remain lost in them.

"One day," Arché promises. "But those are just dirty fantasies. Other things need to come first. I love you, like I wasn't sure I'd love anyone. This is going to be totally different to me, too."

"So we'll figure it out together," Lenora says, and Arché smiles at the echo of her words from before.

"Exactly. So I'm going to kiss you, and you can tell me what you want, and what feels good."

Lenora kisses her, grabbing Arché's face with her hands, and Arché's laugh of surprise turns into a little groan. Encouraged, Lenora pushes forward so that Arché is rolled onto her back with Lenora on top of her.

"Hi," Arché says against her lips, dazed.

"Is this okay?" Lenora asks.

"You can do anything you want with me, Lenora," Arché assures her. Her hand sweeps up Lenora's spine, making her shiver. "In the unlikely event you do something I'm not comfortable with, I'll let you know."

Lenora nods and kisses her again, trying the thing involving tongues that had been so fascinating before. This is an even better position for it, as their bodies are flush with only the thin barrier of clothes between them, and Lenora can feel almost every ridge of Arché's toned body as their mouths explore one another.

"I like this," Lenora whispers. "Feeling close to you. But I want to feel *closer.*"

"Closer?" Arché lifts an eyebrow.

Lenora battles a blush and loses furiously. "You know. Without clothes. Should I take my slip off?"

"If you're comfortable with that," Arché says, nodding.

"It might be hard to have sex with our clothes on," Lenora snorts. "Even I know that."

"Harder, but not impossible. So long as you can get your hand into someone's pants."

Lenora's visual mind runs with that image and has a marvellous time picturing how it would feel to have Arché's hand up her dress and finding its way past her underwear. But then there is also the possibility of having skin against skin, and that is what Lenora wants more than anything in this moment.

"I take off my slip, you take off your vest?" Lenora asks.

In answer, Arché unlaces her vest and pulls it over her head, leaving her in only her breastband. Lenora bites her lip and goes to grab the hem of her slip when Arché's hand stops her.

"Could I take it off you?" Arché asks, voice thick and eyes molten.

Lenora swallows, surprised at how something as simple as a look and a sentence could send warmth shooting down. "Please."

Arché's fingers take the hem, brushing the tops of Lenora's thighs in the process. Then her hands glide up, pushing the silky material over Lenora's torso and letting Lenora relish the graze of Arché's hands against her sides before the slip comes over her head.

The look on Arché's face is so reverent that Lenora is struck by boldness, and unhooks her breastband so that she is bared. Arché licks her lips, eyes dark and intent.

"Gods, you're so beautiful," Arché murmurs. Her hands hover half an inch from Lenora's sides, where she had been touching a few moments before. The heat coming from her hands is so immense that Lenora can feel it even without contact. "Tell me what you want."

"I want your hands on me," Lenora says without hesitation.

"Where?"

The question is frustrating. *Everywhere*, Lenora wants to say. But Arché is being careful. Arché has warned her against offering more than Lenora might be ready for.

"Anywhere you can see right now," Lenora says instead, and Arché's eyes spark at the specificity. Her hands settle on Lenora's hips and begin stroking circles across the bare skin right above, where the small curve of Lenora's waists sets in.

"I love how it feels like my hands were made to fit here," Arché whispers. She leans up to kiss near Lenora's ear, then down her neck, making Lenora exhale sharply.

"Gods, Arché," Lenora murmurs. "That's so..." She tries not to melt right into Arché, but then one hand wanders back up her spine.

"Good?"

"Good isn't a strong enough word."

Arché's hands sweep up, until they're right under Lenora's breasts, and Arché leans back so that their eyes meet, a silent check-in passing between them.

Lenora would be lying if she said she weren't nervous. But she's never wanted anything more.

"Everywhere you can see," she repeats.

Arché nods, slow and reverent. "Gods, I must have done something good in my life to deserve this."

CHAPTER 25
ARCHÉ

Sitting on a bed roll. Lenora, naked but for a scrap of fabric on her lower half, astride Arché and giving a wide permission to touch. Her pupils blown wide and her lower lip suffering from so much nibbling that Arché has to do everything she can to keep from seizing it with her own teeth.

Arché's thumbs brush the underside of Lenora's small breasts, taking in the curve of them and the near absence of weight. Even with permission, Arché is terrified to touch more, in case Lenora cries out that this is some awful mistake—

"Arché," Lenora whispers. "When I said you *can* touch me... what I mean is... *please* touch me. Everywhere. Please touch me."

Arché says a prayer. Or twenty. She presses her lips to Lenora's collarbone in homage to something, but she could not explain what, and then comes back so that she can see Lenora's face when Arché's thumbs brush over her nipples. Lenora's entire body jerks and the smallest of gasps escapes her. Arché's imagination runs wild at the thought of what she'll do when Arché touches her in other places, but for now it is everything to simply repeat the motion and see how Lenora squirms again, creating pleasant friction against Arché's hips.

"Fuck," Lenora says.

"Do you only want me to use my hands, right now?" Arché asks. Her mouth is dry, desperate to taste Lenora's skin, to see what happens if she does this with her tongue instead.

"Why, what do—" Lenora's eyes widen as she puts it together herself before she can finish the question. "Um. You can use... your mouth?" Arché nods. "Gods, okay. Yes."

Arché kisses down her neck and chest, gently pushing Lenora back into a slight lean, so that Arché's mouth can enclose the bud of her nipple and gently run her tongue over it.

A soft, sweet whimper falls from Lenora's lips. It becomes a new aspiration of Arché's to hear that noise as many times as possible before either of them sleep again.

Arché loses sense of all time, letting her hands run over Lenora's back while her mouth travels across Lenora wherever it can reach, feeling Lenora warm and sigh and turn to jelly in her embrace. They could stay here for hours, just like this, and Arché wouldn't change a thing.

"Wow," Lenora says. "This is... I want more, Arché."

"I know." Arché kisses her gently, only for Lenora to respond with much more force, a demand that makes Arché chuckle against her mouth. "Can I shuffle us a bit?"

When Lenora nods, Arché splays a hand on her back and flips them so that Lenora is on her back, and Arché is able to stare at the sight of Lenora with her hair around her like a halo. Staring up at her with eyes burning with soft, molten desire.

"You are the most beautiful thing I've ever seen," Arché says. "I never get tired of looking at you. And that was before *this*."

Lenora blushes prettily, an adorable half-smile curling one side of her lips. Arché has no choice but to kiss it, to kiss her deep and true and with the promise of everything to come. Lenora presses up into her, her hands busy trying to take out Arché's hair.

"No, leave it," Arché says. "It'll be easier."

Lenora frowns with confusion. To demonstrate, Arché kisses down her body and skips over the fabric of her underwear to her inner thigh, taking each kiss slowly so that Lenora has time to see where she is going and direct her elsewhere. But Lenora simply watches and bites her lip, so Arché kisses higher and higher up her thigh before lifting her head right where she would be in an optimal position.

"My hair would get in the way, here," Arché says.

"Oh," Lenora's eyes are wide, then shift to something thoughtful. "But I want to kiss you."

"We have time for everything, don't worry." Arché lets her fingers lightly trace over the cotton fabric of Lenora's underwear. "I won't do anything yet, but should I take these off?"

There is a quick nod and Arché gets the joy of pulling down the fabric, throwing it aside, and seeing the glistening that had definitely already left some dampness on her shorts from their previous position.

But, remembering Lenora's words, Arché resists all urges to touch and instead comes back up to kiss Lenora's mouth nice and slow.

"Is this how you want it?" Arché asks, and gets another nod. "Tell me where you want me to touch you. And how."

"Down there," Lenora says. "With your hand? I've only done it to myself a few times and I could never quite... get it right. Everyone says you know how to please yourself, but I kept getting close and never... there."

Arché blinks. "Oh. Okay. But you're okay for me to—"

Lenora rolls her body, kissing Arché near the ear and sending a shiver through her. The power Lenora has over her is something the other woman has certainly not yet realised, and that will be fun another day.

"Thank you for checking with me so much," Lenora says, kissing along Arché's jaw. "But what I said before still counts. Touch me everywhere. Please. I know you want to, and trust me that I want you to. I feel like I'll die if you don't."

Arché's hand slides down Lenora's stomach and finds the slickness between her legs, making her gasp against Arché's mouth. It would be so easy to go fast, but Arché keeps it slow. One finger slipping inside and stroking, making Lenora's hips wriggle.

Small, not entirely coherent words come from Lenora. Encouragements. Arché presses her thumb to where Lenora is most sensitive and relishes how the whimper that comes from it is the loudest of all.

"Yeah?" Arché asks.

"Yeah," Lenora breathes, pressing into her hand.

Finding a rhythm is easy with Lenora's hips moving in time. Between the sensations in two different locations as well as Arché murmuring into her neck, it's no wonder that Lenora's body winds like a coil in very little time.

"Gods, I might actually—" Lenora trembles. "It feels like it's going to be too much."

Arché remembers feeling that way, once. "I've got you," she says, kissing her mouth gently. "Trust me."

"I do, I do," Lenora's eyes flutter, and her hips jerk, her legs trembling. Arché keeps her hand moving, even when Lenora's thighs try to clamp shut as if to halt the near overwhelming sensation. "Gods, I—"

Arché curls her fingers and presses harder with her thumb, and Lenora makes a strangled noise in her throat as she finishes, her head thrown back. Arché kisses her neck and lifts her thumb while slowing her finger's movements.

"I'm here," Arché tells her. "You did it. I'm never going to forget the noise you just made."

Lenora looks at her with heavy-lidded eyes and still somehow finds a way to blush. "Huh. That was... wow. Thank you."

"Are you okay?" Arché asks. Her free hand strokes Lenora's hair, and Lenora sighs softly as she leans into it.

"Yeah, I'm okay," she says. "I'm really, really okay."

Arché brings her hand up and slips the saturated finger into her mouth. The taste makes her moan at the idea of what noises she could get out of Lenora if able to use her tongue. "You taste good."

Lenora stares. Arché grins and licks her thumb clean for good measure.

"Right," Lenora says. "That's... another thing. That people can do."

Arché kisses her long and deep, licking into her mouth and feeling how Lenora parts her lips to give way so readily, pushing back with her own tongue. With each second, Arché hopes that Lenora is imagining the possibilities of other places.

"So... is it your turn?" Lenora asks when they eventually part. "You're still *dressed*."

"We don't need to worry about me right now," Arché says. "I want to make you feel good. I enjoy this part of it as much as anything else. There'll be time for that later."

Lenora frowns at her. Now that it is permitted, it is a frown that Arché cannot allow to go unkissed, which in turn only makes Lenora grumble and frown more.

"Well, maybe, I... want to make *you* feel good," Lenora retorts. "You said I taste good, but you don't think I want to know what *you* taste like when I already know I love your blood?"

Of all the things Arché had expected Lenora to say, that had not been it. She is stuck, wordless and left with too many images to function properly.

"Uh," Arché eventually manages to get out. "I mean—"

"I want to learn how to do this," Lenora continues. "Tell me what to do."

Arché almost agrees. But an absurd, petty part of her refuses to budge. She puts her finger to Lenora's lips, silencing her.

"I've been losing my mind over you," she whispers. "So there is no way I'm teaching you how to do that before I get to taste you and show you how it feels. So, if you think you can handle it..."

Lenora chews on her lower lip. "I... guess it would make sense to experience it first."

"Tell me that I can taste you," Arché says, and it comes out as a plea. No matter. She is pleading. She'd be on her knees like a cleric at an altar if Lenora weren't on her back.

Lenora's fingers trace over Arché's lips, still exploring and fascinated. Arché takes one of them into her mouth and sucks on it, drawing a small sound of surprise from Lenora.

"You can taste me," Lenora murmurs. "Am I going to... finish, again? I don't know if my body can—"

"Let me try," Arché says. She's still begging. She doesn't care. "I know the oversensitivity can be a lot but it can also be... amazing."

"Okay," Lenora says, with a nervous grin.

Arché kisses her once on the lips, then trails her mouth down Lenora's soft, smooth skin until she is back between her legs.

One kiss to each thigh, then a slow breath against Lenora's core. A squirm so gorgeous that Arché can only think of how, on another day, she'd love nothing more than to stay here for hours and see how many times she could send Lenora over the edge.

The moment Arché's tongue makes contact, Lenora swears. With a smile, Arché begins her feast and relishes the tart sweetness of Lenora as ripples of pleasure sweep up her body. Going slow is essential, Lenora's body sensitive to even the smallest of touches, and Arché wants this to last at least a small while.

"Gods, Arché," Lenora swears. "This is..."

"I know," Arché says, stopping for breath and resting her cheek against Lenora's thigh. "I imagined this so many times. I knew the noises would be a dream but... I could do this all day."

Lenora looks dizzy just at the thought. Arché doesn't give her too much time to dwell on it, and lifts her thighs so that she can return to her work. It is pure joy to hear her whimpers, to feel her starting to buck against Arché's mouth, to try and spell every word Arché couldn't quite say in shapes against her flesh.

With a sob, Lenora comes undone, and Arché holds her through the tempest until she stills, pressing wet kisses to her thighs. Lenora's hands tug at her shoulders and hair, though, so Arché obediently follows them up so that she can take Lenora in her arms and hold her tight in the haze of the afterglow. Lenora clutches her, breaths soft and ragged.

"I don't know if I'll be able to... do it like that," Lenora says.

"How is *that* what you're thinking right now?!" Arché holds herself up on her forearms to look down at Lenora incredulously. "If I'd done it right, you wouldn't even be able to think."

Lenora cocks an eyebrow, and Arché makes a mental promise to one day render her incoherent in as many ways as possible. "Okay, well, that's... distracting of you to say. But I want to make *you* feel like this, because this is... incredible." She deflates and stares up at Arché with awe. "Thank you. I love you."

Arché kisses her. "I love you too."

"Now we swap, and you tell me what to do," Lenora insists.

Despite her words, what it really is entails more of Arché following Lenora's stern direction to lie down and let Lenora take her underclothes off. Not anything Arché really needs persuading to do, but pointing that out might mean that Lenora stops using that frown and clipped tone of voice that is both endlessly endearing and surprisingly attractive.

Arché knew she liked being pushed around by other large, strong women. Turns out maybe she just likes being bossed around by women of any size. There's a particular charm to the way Lenora does it.

Slender fingers with those callused fingertips explore Arché's bare chest. It's near flat, with the way her muscles and body proportions have worked out, but it's never concerned Arché and there is nothing but care in Lenora's eyes as she dips her head to press the lightest of kisses to the skin.

Her hand explores further, and her eyes widen when she feels how wet Arché is between her legs.

"You weren't kidding about enjoying that," she says, amazed. "Can I... what do you want me to do?"

"Anything," Arché says, too quick, trying desperately not to push into her hand with embarrassing urgency. "I mean... hand is good. Mouth is good. You know where, more or less. The trick is pretty much to watch, and listen, and... figure out which things work best. You learn."

Lenora rubs at Arché gently, her head tilting to watch as Arché inhales sharply. "Okay. So... like this?"

"Yeah," Arché says, licking her lips. "Like that."

Gods almighty, Lenora is actually sitting between Arché's spread thighs, touching her, planning on tasting her. Asking Arché what she wants, wanting to please her. Arché could perish right here and now and perhaps be content.

Lenora's fingers slip down, and in. Arché's back arches and she could so easily beg Lenora to fuck her, but this is not the time for that. There will be plenty of time.

"Wait, maybe now I *do* remember something from one of those books," Lenora says, with a mischievous grin. She shuffles herself back, so she can kiss Arché's legs, all the while keeping her hand in place and slowly working Arché's body. Then, her mouth is right where Arché needs it most, and Arché is sure she has just put every moan from the bites to shame with this one.

"Fuck, Lenora," Arché curses.

Lenora giggles against Arché's skin. While at first the touches are tentative, too hard or too soft, she pauses and evaluates, checking Arché's expressions and thinking it all over. Little by little, her tongue finds the right rhythm, the right motions. The heat stirring through Arché's body the entire time she'd been serving at Lenora's pleasure now turns into an inferno, spiralling through her before beginning to build at her core, building and building. All the while, Lenora's finger strokes at Arché in other ways, and it's all too much, too good.

The inferno crests, and Arché cries out softly as her fingers grip the bedroll either side of her, her body trembling as Lenora brings her to a new height and holds her there. Then, after several seconds of blinding pleasure that threaten to wrench Arché from herself, she comes down.

Instead of asking or hinting, Arché pulls Lenora up by her shoulders to kiss her fiercely, murmuring thanks and adorations as she tastes herself on Lenora's lips.

"There's nothing you can't do," Arché says.

"I'm not usually a quick learner at anything," Lenora says breathlessly. "But... I'm glad I could learn you so easily. I see what you mean, that's... fun. You shook so much—"

Arché flushes and pulls Lenora into a tight embrace. "We all have our... reactions, I suppose." She presses a kiss to Lenora's temple. "We'll need to get back on the road soon, but... let's just... lie here for a while."

Lenora nods and snuggles into her, and if Arché thought they fit nicely together side by side or front to back, there is something totally different to be said for how comfortably Lenora's body rests on top of hers.

"I love you so much," Arché says, again, still astounded by the freedom to simply speak her feelings.

"I love you too." Lenora lifts her head and cups Arché's cheek in her hand. "If the Crusaders thought I was scary before, they should be terrified now. If they touch you—"

"You're so hot when you're angry, I hope you know that," Arché says with complete seriousness, and the bubble bursts with the adorable way that Lenora's mouth falls open with surprise. "Gods, you're so many things at once. I don't know how I didn't explode, before. I thought I would, you know."

They laugh at how much has changed in such a short span of time, and bask in the warmth of each other, until the journey ahead calls them back out into the world that exists beyond the sanctuary of their tent.

CHAPTER 26
LENORA

THE NEXT SIX NIGHTS are a blur of road, night sky above them, and passionate entanglements in their tent. Watches are not taken, which is a questionable move perhaps, but Lenora is confident that she can deal with anyone who makes the mistake of ambushing or interrupting them. Perhaps it is shocking, how she could want someone so viscerally that it turns her into a hedonist? But then, how often in her life has she *ever* prioritised her own gratification? In any way?

Arché is more attentive than Lenora could have ever dreamed. Lenora is hardly about to complain, and she is quickly understanding the appeal of lavishing someone else with attention and bringing them so much pleasure. If life were different, Lenora would happily spend the next month doing nothing but.

And naturally, just as Lenora begins to wonder if anything will bring her out of this reverie, back into the realm of sense, they see a campfire ahead on the road. A campfire surrounded by figures in robes, the orange illuminated in the firelight even at a distance.

Fury and loathing, half forgotten, surge back into Lenora's chest at the sight of the Crusaders. Behind her on the horse, Arché lets out a soft growl.

It shouldn't be so easy. But only one of them is awake, on watch, and by the time he shouts for the others, Arché is tackling him to the ground. It isn't enough time. Lenora grabs one of them and bites into her neck, drinking with ferocity and none of the care she affords Arché.

It is as before. Any one of these people they leave alone, might be one of their people lost. Such is the path the Crusaders have chosen, and such is the action the heirs of Concord must match to save it.

Lenora will never be proud of the thrill that runs through her when she feeds on their enemies, the rush that comes with draining their lifeforce, taking from them what they would take from her people, in just a moment. Perhaps one day she'll have the luxury of wondering if it was really justified.

In less than a minute and a half, Arché and Lenora are the only ones around the burning fire still drawing breath.

"We need to burn the bodies," Arché says, frowning toward the nearby road. "The last thing we need is the Stag Battalion coming after us. I'm pretty sure they patrol the highway, and if someone reports dead bodies on the side of the road... I know *I* would make the detour up here. They don't know about us, and we should keep it that way."

They build up the fire to twice its original size and burn the bodies. It is an awful thing, but at least they are in it together as they are in everything else. Lenora gets lost in the dancing of the flames, holding her nose to block out the smell of roasting flesh that turns her stomach.

Arché sits nearby, entire hand over her nose and mouth, no doubt suffering from her heightened sense of smell. Lenora steps closer, so that her hip is in line with Arché's head, and Arché leans into her, nuzzling through the dress.

Once they dump the last of the Crusaders on the fire, they ride away until it is nothing but a lingering memory. But linger it does.

The next night, they reach Khiz and find no Leahi, but a promised note.

Hey you two!

We've gone on to Dressa, since apparently the fruit market there is to die for. Planning on sticking around for a while, so hopefully you can catch me there if you're looking.

Leahi xx

There is a town before Dressa, two nights along, where they can enjoy the luxury of a bed. With the events on the road it is nothing of fantasies and hedonism but instead need, closeness, clinging to each other as the world spirals around them, wondering if anything else will ever feel right again. Wondering if it is wrong to feel so safe in each other's arms.

Upon actually reaching Dressa a few nights later, giving Leahi's description to the barkeep at the *Gilded Apple* tavern is an easy thing. She's a memorable sort of person.

What they don't expect is the way the gold-scaled woman behind the bar stiffens at the inquiry.

"Why?" she asks.

Lenora and Arché glance at each other. Arché might have Crescent Light on her back, but otherwise they're not the most heavily armed pair to look at.

"She's our friend, she told us to ask for her here," Arché says. "Who else is asking about her? Is she in trouble?"

The barkeep's arms remain crossed over her chest, her eyes narrowed, but her thoughts visibly turn over behind her stare.

"If she's in trouble, we can help," Lenora adds.

"You don't look like the rest of them," the barkeep eventually says.

Arché frowns. "Who?"

"Those people in the robes, the ones from Izirm," the woman tells them, lowering her voice. "They might be Everflame worshippers, but Leahi says they're bad news. She's been… irreverent, at best, defiant at worst. They're starting to notice."

"We *can* help her, if you could show us to her room—" Arché starts, only to be stopped by the barkeep's hand.

"She'll likely be asleep. Easier for you to wait here for her, if you aren't needing sleep yourselves. Also works out better if you aren't telling me the truth, right?"

Lenora tries not to cringe at how they'd forgotten it is the middle of the night. "You're right, we'll wait for a more reasonable hour," she says. "Could we get some food?"

They end up in a booth, with Lenora laying out her sheets of music and explaining to Arché how the notation process works. It isn't a planned activity so much as Arché asking so many questions that her fascination spurs Lenora into going into great detail.

"But you can… hear it in your head, just from looking at it?" Arché asks, amazed.

"Not everyone can, but I have a knack for it, I guess," Lenora says with a shrug. "That's how I can write so many songs. I'm sure it's way harder when you have to sound out every note before you get it right and write it down. But everyone has a process."

"It's so neat." Arché's fingers trail across the pages of lines and dots, each so tiny and meaningful. When her eyes flick up, they are soft and adoring. "You're brilliant."

"I'm—" Lenora stops. The rebuttal is so instinctual, after so many years, but it is no longer right. She is the chosen Shadow, and a naturally talented composer, and a violinist who had to work her butt off to be any good.

She deserves to give herself more credit. "I—thanks. I guess... maybe I am. A bit."

Arché smiles, wide and proud. "A bit is a start."

"What about you? Your carvings have so many tiny details, I don't know how you..." Lenora gestures to the half-finished figurine on the table that had been forgotten since the notation topic came up. "Do that."

"That's because you haven't seen the *hundreds* I had to carve where I messed up all those details," Arché snorts. "It's the same as your music, I bet. Practice. Listening. Trying things in new ways. Romano is a good teacher."

"What made you start it?" Lenora asks. "Just wanting to keep your hands busy?"

Arché shakes her head, a fond smile coming to her lips. "His daughter Mira is Andreas's partner. So when they got paired up, I would take him over to their shop a lot, so they could hang out more. I'd get talking to Romano, and he ended up showing me what he was doing. Worked out."

Lenora recalls now, if vaguely. Arché's brother, not being the heir to his house, didn't need to be partnered to anyone from another founding house. His partner, Mira, is a fascinating individual who had approached Lenora's mother for advice on Disciplined magic on several occasions but refused all offers of tutoring. Something about wanting to learn about nature magic, which is not the archmage's expertise.

Nature magic is so varied and intricate that it's one of the only types of magic that can be learned through Disciplined magic *and* manifest innately. One could argue that since sentient beings are part of nature, Gifted mages with their ability to affect other creatures could count there too, but it's disregarded as a pointless technicality.

"They always seemed like a great pair, Andreas and Mira," Lenora says.

Arché nods, something in her eyes so deep and unfathomable that Lenora wishes she could dive into them and swim until she finds what is hiding in there. There is so much Arché still isn't saying, but without knowing what it might be about, Lenora has no idea how to ask.

"Inseparable," Arché says, with a smile. "I don't think I've ever heard them argue. They just... work."

"Are they...?" Lenora makes a face, feeling silly for asking the question but unable to resist. "You know."

Arché mirrors her expression. "A great question. Kalé and I have been wondering for a while too, not that it's *really* our business. Mira's not from one of the houses, so... they could be, and it would be fine. I've never seen them look at anyone else, either of them. But I'm not there all the time, and Andreas has never talked to me about it. I tried to make sure he knew he could, but then my thing with Maggie fell apart and I just didn't want to talk about romance for a while."

It had been Lenora's question that got them to this point, but the question has opened up another one. Something much worse.

"Arché," she says, feeling anxiety hammer into her chest one beat at a time, like a slow and ominous drum. "We're both from Houses. We... We wouldn't be able to have children. It wouldn't be allowed. I know we only just—"

"I know," Arché says, without missing a beat or losing an inch of calm. "I mentioned it to Alta, when I was freaking out. They quite rightly reminded me that until we save everyone, there might be no town rules left to follow. We can worry about that later. I'm with you. That's what matters. Everything else is details."

An absolutely sound answer. But the weight of new words sits in Lenora's throat, something she's only thought in passing moments so far.

"I'm thinking of renouncing my claim to the House of the Arcane," she says, making Arché's eyes widen. "I know that doesn't change the bloodline rule, but it would mean at least... if we did want to... they wouldn't be heirs to two different houses."

"Are you sure that's what you would want?" Arché asks.

"The chosen Shadow shouldn't also be a leader of a House," Lenora says, feeling more confident with each word she speaks. "And my house should be represented by the ones who know the magic we're supposed to have mastery over. The twins would do a great job, whichever one took it. I'll keep thinking about it... but it—"

"It makes sense," Arché agrees.

"Honestly, right now, you're the only thing I'm sure I want," Lenora says. It's astounding how easy it is to say. "But I think, after all this, I should focus on being the chosen Shadow and helping Alta document things, *finally.*"

"Sounds like a good plan to me. Let's save Concord first, and worry about the details later."

Arché's hand reaches across the table to take Lenora's and lace their fingers together. Lenora had no idea it was possible for her chest to feel so full, crashing waves of ardency almost drowning her from the inside.

"As long as we're together, we'll be okay," Lenora says. It's near becoming a mantra.

"Exactly."

It might be one of the loveliest moments of Lenora's life. So, naturally, it shatters when Arché's eyes flick to the door and see something that drops her face into darkness.

"No fucking way," Arché exhales.

Lenora's head whips around and sees that Tunvra the hunter has walked into the tavern.

CHAPTER 27
LENORA

Tunvra begins stalking a path to the bar. He only makes it a few steps before he comes to a halt and his head jerks in their direction.

Lenora is not a social genius at the best of times, but she is not sure that *anyone* knows the etiquette of how you are supposed to greet someone you recruited from an enemy cause with bribery and sheer intimidation.

So, Lenora waves, in a short and singular moment. Arché is rigid and does nothing at all.

Tunvra sighs, shakes his head, and heads for their booth.

"Let me guess," he says. "You're here for that friend of yours."

Arché growls ever so slightly. "Yes. What do *you* know about it?"

"She's not exactly subtle," Tunvra says with a roll of his eyes. "And since I was tasked with getting more information to help you... you'll see. Stay here. I'll be back."

If Arché had hackles, they'd be up. As Tunvra orders a drink from the bar and disappears out a back door, Lenora touches Arché's hand in an attempt to calm her.

"I just realised," Lenora says. "We still haven't talked about it."

"About what?"

"About why you shut down on me. After we fought him. I was so busy being upset and then realising why, and then... trying to help you bounce back."

Arché sighs, so heavy that it makes Lenora want to hold her and never let go. "Thank you, for doing what you did for me, at the creek. It really did help. But you're right, we got a bit... busy."

Lenora nods, smiling a little at the memory of their absurd discussion back-to-back and everything that had come after. But she does not allow herself to be distracted. "But why did it get to that point?"

"It doesn't matter now," Arché says, glancing back towards the door where Tunvra disappeared. "You made it work for us. He switched sides, which is what we needed."

"It does matter, because you've been looking like you're going to scream or hit something since he walked through the door," Lenora retorts.

Arché crosses her arms over her chest, sitting up straight as if to hide how tightly she's locked into herself. "I'm sorry, Lenora, I just... can't deal with those feelings, right now. And if I talk about it, I'll have to."

There's a fine line between patience and losing it entirely, when it is tested for this long.

"Arché, you've helped me with so much, but you haven't told me anything about what's going on with you. You never talk about yourself, not about your plans for the future, not about Rohan—"

"You want to know about Rohan?" Arché asks. Tears shine at the corners of her eyes. "Fine. Rohan was driving me up the wall. Slowly. A little bit every day. They were my best friend and I was getting annoyed by almost everything they did, and I wished I wouldn't be stuck with them forever, and then the universe granted me my wish. So I'm feeling great about that. I'm a great friend."

And there it is. Part of the Arché mystery, finally let out, no longer locked inside her. Pain and shame shine so bright in Arché's eyes that Lenora has no idea how to fix it, even if quietly she is sure that Arché will be better off for relinquishing the secret's weight.

"Oh Arché," is all she can say. "I'm... so sorry."

"Yeah, me too," Arché exhales. Her knuckles are white where they clutch the elbows of her opposite arms. "I miss them so fucking much, and any time I do, some tiny part of me is still relieved I'm not stuck with them anymore. How awful is that?"

It *is* awful. Lenora won't deny that. But relationships are always complicated. Her own with her family are proof enough, the way she never knows how to feel about either of her parents, the way she loves the twins but never knows what to say to them. Sometimes people don't fit together quite right.

"Did you tell *anyone*?" Lenora asks.

"Yeah," Arché says, voice soft. "I told Nikos. I swore him to secrecy. I didn't know why he was so eager to help me... until..." She gestures towards Lenora with a shug.

"That's why you started talking to him," Lenora realises. "He said it was wolf stuff. I didn't think that made any sense, but I didn't really want to know in case it was... yeah."

"He didn't really know how to help. But it was good to tell someone."

"Thanks for telling me," Lenora says, ignoring the urge in her gut to demand for Arché to explain all the rest of what burdens her, so she can help. But if it is difficult for Arché to speak of such things, then Lenora will be patient. Or try incredibly hard to be.

Tunvra pops back into the tavern floor area and waves them over to the back door, giving them little option but to share a glance and agree to follow him.

The door leads into a small stone courtyard encircled by numbered doors, centred by a large tree. Tunvra crosses the courtyard and approaches the door with a metal eight on it and gives two short knocks.

Three seconds later, the door opens and there stands Leahi. Her eyes light at the sight of them, a shout of excitement leaving her, and she leaps past Tunvra to pull Arché and Lenora into a crushing hug.

"Fuck yes!"

From next to them, Tunvra coughs loud and pointed, and Leahi pulls back.

"Oh shit, yeah, come inside," she says, voice much lower and eyes glancing around.

"Masterful subtlety," Tunvra mutters, earning a playful punch to his arm from Leahi, which might be the most baffling thing Lenora has seen all day.

Tunvra rolls his eyes and claims the desk chair to sit in while Leahi pulls Lenora and Arché into the room and locks the door behind him.

"So... does someone want to explain what the fuck is going on?" Arché asks.

Leahi sits on the bed, leaning back on her hands and grinning from ear to ear. "We've been plotting."

"Plotting?" Arché echoes. "You and him?"

Leahi nods. "He heard me talking about the Crusade, about how they're actually assholes, and he asked how I knew. We realised my friends, you two were the same people as his new, uh—"

"Employers," Tunvra says. It's more diplomatic than several other words he could have used. A potentially good sign. "The Crusaders have no idea I'm no longer in their pocket. I claimed to be the only one who got out of our encounter alive, and that I was looking into alternative strategies to reattempt. Half of that's true."

"Sure, but I don't get how Leahi fits into this," Lenora says. "You said something about plotting."

"Yes, I'm going to tell them I've found a sympathiser," Tunvra says, pointing to Leahi, who waves. "We're going to use it to lure them into a trap. She's already caught their attention, if only in rumour, so it'll be easy enough. We hadn't moved yet because we wanted to ensure it was a fight we could win. There's a half dozen in town. But with you two here? We can get them tomorrow."

It's a good plan. But the matter of bringing Leahi, someone tough but not part of their fight? It sits poorly in Lenora's gut. Fighting corrupted creatures of nature is one thing, but fighting other people when hatred gets involved is much more horrendous.

"Was the plan to capture? Or kill?" Lenora asks, addressing Tunvra more than Leahi.

"I was planning on killing them, since that seemed to be your own method," Tunvra says frankly.

"He explained what happened, when you met him," Leahi says, more serious now. "I'm not one who likes to get into killing, but I figured I'd let you two explain why it's come to that. You did say they'd killed some of your people."

"Exactly. They're taking our people to be sacrificed," Arché says, voice wooden. "They killed some of our closest friends, our leaders, right in front of us. And then they brag about it. Anyone who still aligns with them after that has chosen to be a part of it. And they're a danger to our people if left alive. We're going to be outnumbered as it is, we can't let any of these groups get back to the caravans."

There are several moments of silence as Leahi absorbs the words. Her fingers grip the duvet in slow, almost cat-like motions.

"Okay," she says, biting on her lip. "I won't kill anyone myself. I don't think I could do that. But I'll help you do what you need to. You have my full support. I'll keep you safe, if I can."

"If you're sure," Arché says. "This isn't your fight."

Leahi shakes her head adamantly. "It's a fight against something wrong. So it's the fight of any good person brave enough to join it. Besides, friends don't let friends fight alone."

Arché stares at her, and Lenora is shocked to see tears spring to the lycan's eyes. In the next breath, Arché dashes from the room and Lenora is left exchanging bemused looks with the daywalkers.

"What did I say?" Leahi asks.

"I don't know, I'll just... I'll check on her. Thank you. We'll be back later, we'll just grab a room."

"We'll leave a message at the bar for you," Tunvra calls as Lenora hurries out. She calls back a thank you and closes the door before making a beeline for Arché.

The lycan heir stands with her face pressed into the tree in the courtyard centre, her body visibly trembling.

"Arché," Lenora whispers, putting a hand on her shoulder. "What—"

"Can you get us a room?" Arché asks, voice muffled. "I know we can't sleep, probably, with a daywalker plan for the morning. But I'm tired."

Lenora is easily able to get a key and return to tug Arché by the hand into the privacy of a double room. The moment she does, Arché falls into Lenora's arms.

"I don't know why it got to me," Arché croaks into Lenora's neck. "But what she said... it's what I thought Tunvra would say, when we met him. It's what I was trying to say, that he should help us because it's the right thing to do. It didn't sway him. He didn't care, and it made me feel like the world didn't care about us, about any of us. And I knew that if I were

Kalé, she could have made him care, she would have said the right thing, but I couldn't get it right and I don't know if I'm ever going to get it right, Lenora—"

She loses her voice to sobs and shakes in Lenora's arms. Arché, who has always seemed as if resolute stone, crumbling to pieces like Lenora always expected herself to.

"Arché, I don't think this is the kind of thing we can get right," Lenora says. "We can only do our best."

"I couldn't convince him—"

"He's a mercenary, he's in it for the money and because I scared him shitless."

Arché says nothing. Lenora cannot shake the feeling that she's missing something. Something crucial, something that would have Arché's words make sense, but it eludes her. Arché's hands clutch harder into her dress, gripping it until it is pulled taut against Lenora's skin, at risk of ripping the fabric.

Arché has said more today than in their entire acquaintance, friendship and romance combined. Lenora will not push.

"Let's lie down for a bit," Lenora says.

It is simple enough to pull Arché to the bed and lie her down, stroking a hand over her hair until her body stills.

"We can do this," Lenora murmurs. "You were the one who showed me that. If we're together, we can do this. We've found some allies, we're going to meet Alta, and we're going to get everyone back."

Arché nods, slow and singular. Her eyes flick up, red and raw but steady.

"Thank you, Lenora," she says, ever so soft. "I love you."

"I love you too. Let's stay like this for a bit, then we'll see what message the others have left us."

CHAPTER 28
ARCHÉ

THE MESSAGE CONTAINS DIRECTIONS to a small house on the outskirts of town, where Leahi waits for them with a length of rope and a fascinating plan.

"So, we're tying you up, leaving you in here, and hiding?" Arché asks, to ensure she's got it right.

"With my full consent," Leahi says with a cheerful grin.

Arché finds herself snorting at that. "Okay then," she says, as Leahi sits on the ground to make it easier. "First time a pretty lady says that to me, and it's not even one I'm sleeping with. Talk about a wasted opportunity."

"I mean, that's easily fixed," Leahi says, lifting her eyebrows. "Now that I know you and Lenora aren't actually—"

Lenora coughs. "Actually, that's... changed, since we saw you last."

"Wait, really?" Leahi beams. "I'm so happy for you two! I was so confused when you said it was all a ruse, because it really looked like—"

"Yes, yes, there was a lot going on, and apparently I like being bitten," Arché mutters, while the other two giggle.

"So… you want to tie up a lady you're sleeping with?" Lenora asks, with great curiosity.

"Lenora," Arché hisses, blood rushing to her cheeks.

Leahi blinks. "Hey, don't mind me. I support whatever you two want to get up to."

Arché spends several moments rearranging her brain back into working order while her hands finalise the binds on Leahi.

"Lenora, I'm trying to think of an answer, but I'm not going to lie, my brain is in the gutter right now," Arché says, looking between the beautiful woman she's in love with and the beautiful woman tied up in rope.

"What?" Leahi asks, with false innocence, like she isn't blinking up at them with sly invitation.

"I'm mortal, and you're pretty and tied up, and Lenora is saying things, and my brain is… confused," Arché says honestly.

Lenora tilts her head. "I don't… *get* it, but… I think I see it." Then, all at once, her cheeks turn bright pink. "Wait, I just pictured you or me in the rope. Now I get it."

It is a joy seeing Lenora experience such realisations, and Leahi just cackles.

"Do you two… want the rope, when we're done here?"

"Maybe," Arché says at the same time that Lenora says, "I don't need rope for that."

Lenora's eyebrows almost meet her hairline, while Arché nearly chokes at how easily the words came out.

"Magic," Lenora explains with a shrug, seemingly unphased by their bafflement. "Anyway, we should probably hide now, right? In case Tunvra brings them early. It won't be a good ambush if they can hear us talking."

One last check-in with Leahi, and the nightwalker pair find good perches in a couple of trees outside the house, where the thick foliage is enough to hide from any Crusaders.

The wait is tedious. Arché has to continue shifting her perch to avoid losing feeling in her lower body over the next hour, and is ready to sing with relief when she sees movement on the horizon. Tunvra's form comes into view, flanked by a group in bright orange—an eerie mimicry of their first sight of him.

It sparks irrational, powerful fear into Arché's chest. What if he has been discovered, and won back over with a larger bribe? What if he has turned Leahi against them too, and Arché was a fool to shed tears over her kindness?

Trust is essential to this working. Finding herself lacking, Arché can do nothing but trust in Lenora instead, in what Lenora saw in Tunvra the moment he switched sides. Arché needs to breathe and remain calm. The wolf in her chest remains hurt and bitter, but it is Arché making the choice to take on this fight. This is calculated and necessary.

"Just in here, I caught her saying she'd met those two on the road, and was running her mouth all over town about your Crusade. I figured you'd want to know."

Tunvra does an excellent job of sounding like he truly has no care for anyone involved. Maybe because he probably doesn't.

"Thank you, hunter," one of the Crusaders says. "You'll be compensated for this, once we've dealt with the sympathiser."

The group, as a whole, are not quite as relaxed as would be ideal for an ambush. There is a whiff of apprehension in the air, perhaps because Tunvra is not one of them, so Arché ensures she waits until precisely the last moment.

One of the Crusaders gets to the house door and opens it.

"Yep, that's the one," he says to the others.

A ripple of calm passes through the group. Arché leaps from the tree, transforming mid-leap into her partial form, tackling the nearest Crusader to the ground.

It's too easy to pull her claws across the front of his throat and feel the flesh tear. It's brutal, but there is no good way to accomplish this; quick is better than anything else.

Lenora, likewise, had latched onto her first target's neck and begun drinking from them while her shadow claws rake across their back.

Arché's Crusader drops and blood pools on the ground where he lands. When she looks up, the four left stare back at her with terror struck across their faces.

They've brought this on themselves.

A crossbow clicks, and an orange robe blossoms with red. When the person drops, Tunvra stands there, reloading with grim efficiency.

Leahi is out of her binds. She grabs her flute from her pocket and brings it up for a blast of sound so powerful that it knocks the Crusaders off their feet and has them clutching their ears with pain. The most impressive part is Leahi's control; Arché and Lenora are unaffected despite being right in the magic's path.

Then, with the Crusaders dazed and prone, it is all too easy. One could not call it a fight. It's a slaughter. Leahi's magic might not kill, but it pushes and pulls and *hurts*, and Arché is astounded she's never heard of a sonic mage when they can do can this.

Six bodies lie on the ground when it is over. Lenora's mouth is stained red and there is a different energy to how she moves, each step empowered by the blood she's consumed.

Leahi lowers the flute and regards the scene with a tense jaw.

"Thank you," Arché says, shifting back to her usual self. "I'm sorry."

Leahi sighs, eyes still warm but now weighed down with new troubles. "Yeah. I know."

"We came here to ask for your help with the caravans, because we need all the help we can get and you're one of our only—"

"I'll help."

Arché glances down at the blood smear that stains Crescent Light, and makes a face. "It'll be worse than this."

"I know," Leahi says. Her eyes flash with something new. Something bright. "But it's the right thing to do. You need help. Your people need help. How could I not, when my magic will make a difference?"

It's hard to say how devastating it would have been to seek out their one outsider friend and be turned away, but Arché would never have faulted her for it. Now, however, Arché seizes Leahi in a hug and is tightly gripped in return.

Then comes the unpleasant matter of dealing with the bodies. It is a decidedly wrong thing to be getting familiar with such an act; how much more blood has to soak their hands, to liberate the nightwalkers of Concord? Arché cannot regret her actions, when no better course is left to them, but that is not the same as it feeling right.

Lenora helps as though it is the most natural thing in the world for her to be able to stack two dead people on her shoulders and move them to the pile. When finished, she declares she'll check the perimeter in case of others, and sprints off. Arché can only stare with astonishment at the new level of power she's reached from the blood intake.

Perimeter check. All clear.

Wait for the bodies to burn down.

Clean themselves while waiting.

It's good to focus on each part of the process at a time, before the danger of dwelling and overwhelm become a problem.

"Weren't you meeting someone here, Leahi?" Arché asks on the walk back to town. Lenora is bouncing alongside Arché, arm looped through hers, humming to herself.

"Yeah, but once I ran into Tunvra, I told her to head back to Orsun without me," Leahi says. "I figured I'd be a while, and she's not the fighting type."

"So what now?" Tunvra asks.

Arché explains the plan to meet Alta in Ushonk before the northern stretch of the Highway, in the hopes of hitting the caravan somewhere between there and the pass to Izirm. Ideally, during a full moon.

A pit settles in her stomach as she realises she has no idea when that will be. It's soon, she knows that much from simply looking at the sky on their journey, but at a certain point it's hard to be exact.

"Right," Tunvra tilts his head. "Yes, that should line up well enough for the full moon after the next. Unless you have teleportation magic I don't know about."

Arché snorts to hide her dismay at the fact that he obviously knows when the next full moon is. Her pride will not allow her the shame of asking him. "No."

"Well, I don't know what the next few days entail for you, but I'm guessing you prefer to stay away from settlements—" The next few days. Not the night coming, she'd feel that already, but perhaps the night after. So little warning. "I'll make my way to Ushonk by my own path."

"Sure," Arché says, as casually as possible, if only to get him out of her sight.

To her immense delight, he peels off and begins walking west towards the Highway and Ushonk. The moment he is gone, Arché breathes a little easier and tries not to think about how absurd that is.

They get back to the tavern without Lenora having spoken a word, the blood drunk vampire content to hang off Arché or snuggle into her. Leahi, meanwhile, swaggers up to the barkeep to inform her that the threat of the robed strangers has passed.

"I'm glad to hear it, for your sake especially," the barkeep says. She looks to Arché with gratitude and points to Leahi. "Thanks for helping. This one is special."

Leahi makes a dismissive noise and waves her hand, but her cheeks colour at the praise. "Thanks. I'm going to be moving on, helping these two."

"The kids will miss you."

"I'll miss them too," Leahi says, with the first look of genuine melancholy Arché has seen on her face. "I'll try to come back through on my way back to Orsun."

The other woman smiles. "They'll love that."

The trio head out into the back courtyard.

"Are we travelling by night again?" Leahi asks, before making a face as if she's asked a question that is far too obvious. "I might go and take a nap first."

"Gods, we haven't slept either," Arché says.

Her body, as if oblivious until she speaks the words, begins shouting its protest at going so long without true respite.

"We can lie down," Lenora says, squeezing her hand. "I won't be able to sleep like this, but we can still get a rest."

They agree to meet a bit after sunset and head to their rooms, where Arché instantly collapses onto the bed.

"I think tomorrow is the first day of the full moon," she tells Lenora.

"Oh shit, you didn't say!"

"I didn't know." Arché huffs and picks at the threads of the duvet. "But Tunvra did. It's fucking embarrassing."

"Oh. Yeah, not having that lunar calendar is weird, isn't it?" Lenora comes to cuddle into her side. "We've had so much going on, Arché, you can't beat yourself up about this."

"I'm so tired," Arché says. She lets her head fall onto the pillows, and nuzzles her face against them. "Gods." Tired of all of it. Of killing. Of being separated from her family. Of never feeling like she's getting anything right.

Lenora wriggles to lie next to her, and a soft mouth presses kisses along her upper arm, then her neck, and up behind her ear. Arché shivers, astounded at how the softness could make her feel like she's on the brink of collapse when she's already lying down.

"Last time you were feeling overwhelmed, you let me take care of you at the creek," Lenora says. "Can I do that again now? When you don't talk, it seems like being touched helps you. If you sit up, I can take your shirt off. No sex, just... taking care of you."

Arché nods and does as she is bid, and they sit so Lenora is comfortably positioned behind her. As well as the shirt coming off, Lenora's hands also go to Arché's braided bun and untie it. The soft pulls on her hair are some kind of bliss Arché could never explain. Once the braid is fully loose, Lenora's hands spread across the breadth of Arché's back and move across the skin so lightly that Arché trembles.

Following the same path, not far behind, Lenora's lips press brief kisses.

To feel so cared for, so adored, has small sobs rocking Arché's body as the weight of it crashes down. Lenora is right. She hasn't said everything, not yet. She cannot bring herself to tell Lenora of that fear of never being enough, of never being the heir her mother needs.

But she is loved. And for a few sweet moments that slip into a haze, that is enough, and everything else falls away.

CHAPTER 29
ARCHÉ

In the corner of the tavern at dusk, the nightwalkers and their friend eat a much needed breakfast and discuss the full moon nights in hushed voices. Leahi complains about eating potatoes and gravy immediately after waking up, but there is little to be done for the early evening food options.

"Last time we just went running, since Arché didn't have anyone to wrestle," Lenora explains. "If I have Arché's blood, I'm super fast and can keep up."

"Right." Leahi lets out a disappointed huff. "I can barely keep up with you two on a normal day."

Arché stares, and finds herself grinning. "But I could carry you on my back."

"What? Really?" Leahi's eyes are alight at the mere suggestion. "That sounds like so much fun."

"I've never tried it, but it would be easy," Arché says with confidence. "Then we're travelling at the fastest possible pace for us as a three. It'll only be a bit slower than me and Lenora on our own, and you're worth it."

Leahi pretends to preen, which suits her poorly, and sends them all into cackles over their toast.

Having Leahi on their travels again makes for a musical, cheerful time. It also makes watches easier and means that Arché and Lenora can sleep together in their tent for one of the watches without being negligent of their safety—something they can no longer afford knowing the chances of more Crusaders in the area.

Like with the last full moon, Arché ensures they rise early, some time before the moon does. Even then she can feel the tingle down her spine, the itch behind her ear, warning her of what is to come. She dons the flexible clothing once again, sniffing it and thinking about how the familiar scent of other lycans in the cabin has all but faded from it now.

Leahi makes breakfast while Arché and Lenora find a spot with a little more privacy. The more things that change, the more stay the same.

"Same as before?" Arché asks. "You feed a bit longer from me?"

Lenora grins. "Do I have to promise not to kiss you again?"

The only way to answer that is to pull her in and seize her mouth. "Don't you dare."

It's bizarre to think how far they have come in a month. Lenora leans in and bites her with gorgeous fervour and Arché would not trade it for anything, how the pain is like a friend now, to be welcomed hand-in-hand with the sensation she can openly surrender to.

Lenora drinks deeper. Longer. Grips Arché's shoulder harder, making her head spin for several moments. Right when Arché goes to push Lenora away before she takes too much, Lenora pulls back of her own accord.

"Wow," they say in unison.

"Are you okay?" Lenora asks.

On any other night, Arché is sure she would be light-headed for hours. But not tonight. Not when every inch of her skin feels as though it's about to erupt.

Arché kisses Lenora once more before running out into the open grass. The tingle up her back intensifies. It's coming. She drops to her knees in the grass, letting her fingers trail in the strands and the dirt. Her head tilts to the moon, one night from its fullest when it will be cradled by the green stars, and wonders if the others are able to see it. Her mother. Her brother. Her brethren. Are they all looking at the same moon, united even across distance? Or are they stuck in some sort of cage or prison, unable to see anything at all?

They shift together. Arché shifts alone. What normally feels like connecting with nature in her most true way, feeling more at one with the world than any other moment, feels wrong. There is no chorus of joyous howls. There is nothing at all. Her body shifts and muscles grow, and fur slides across her body, as a melancholy rips through her and erupts into a mournful howl.

In a vicious cycle, the isolated sound of the howl only makes it worse. Arché, in full lycan form, bends back over the dirt, digging in her claws. Unsure of what to do next.

"Arché?" Lenora kneels next to her. Friend. Love. Smells that usually soothe everything, but are not quite enough tonight.

"I'm all alone," Arché's deeper, guttural voice says.

"I'm here."

Arché's head shakes, her body trembling. "Not the same. They're all together. I'm here."

"... oh." Lenora hugs her, the same size she always is but seeming so much smaller. "I'm so sorry. We'll find them soon. Next full moon. You said so."

"So far away," Arché mumbles, pushing her muzzle into Lenora's shoulder. "Miss them. Worried."

"I know. I know." Lenora presses kisses to her fur, to the top of her head between her newly much larger ears. "Let's run. Leahi's here, if you still want to carry her."

Leahi waves, and the newness of the idea of trying to carry her is a distraction from the way everything feels heavy. Usually this form is featherlight and power incarnate all at once, so any distraction is beyond welcome.

While Arché usually remains bipedal, she can easily work on all fours in this form, and she drops to the ground to allow Leahi the chance to climb on.

"Hold onto fur," Arché suggests, standing slowly and practicing shifting her weight.

Leahi giggles in a way they've never heard before. "Oh, this *rules*."

Arché chuckles once. "Ready?"

"Ready," Lenora says, lined up next to her like they're about to race.

"Set," Leahi tells Arché.

Go. Arché doesn't say it, she simply launches herself forward and hears Lenora laughing behind her. Leahi screams, but with delight.

They run. They run with everything they have, the added weight of Leahi on her back not a burden but a challenge, something that forces her body to work harder exactly when she needs it to so that her brain can't wander. There is only running, only the wind in her ears and the laughter of her friends, only the moon and the stars above them.

Even they can't run *all* night, and they eventually slow to a fast walking pace, and Arché could swear Leahi might have started napping on her back. Fair enough.

When the first splashes of sunrise stain the sky, the shift back is upon her. Leahi slides off with a groan and moves to stand with Lenora as Arché kneels back into the grass. This is not usually how she ends such a night, but she is back to thinking about her people. Wishing she could be with them.

She stares at the fading stars and wants to scream for them to return, to give her a better night, a night with the others.

The wolf slips away with a violent ripple through her bones and skin, and when her body is her own again there are tears trailing down her cheeks. Her brother's name sits on her lips, tasting of worry and desperation.

"Hey," Lenora says, coming to rest a hand on her shoulder. "You okay?"

"Not really," Arché murmurs.

She stands and moves to start setting up their tent. If she doesn't get her hands busy in the next few seconds, she might just lose herself to her mind. There is stability in the familiar rhythm of unfolding the fabric and organising poles and ties.

"Is there anything I can do to help?" Leahi asks Lenora, at a distance where she probably doesn't realise Arché's ears can still hear.

"I don't know… everything going on is so tricky. I don't know what to do… and she doesn't talk to me."

Arché wonders if Lenora has forgotten how good lycan hearing is, or if her frustration with Arché's lackluster communication has gotten to the point where she does not care if Arché hears.

It is enough to stir up a cocktail of guilt and self-deprecation in Arché's chest that only makes it all worse. Talking about it is the logical thing to do, but Arché does not have the faith that she could get the words out. They weigh so heavy on her heart, but any time she tries to even practice speaking truth it refuses to leave her tongue.

Speaking the fears would make them real. It doesn't matter if it's the fear of her future or the fear for her people's safety.

Lenora, meanwhile, has become the fully-fledged Shadow she is meant to be, and despite her plans to discard her position of leadership, she is the one who managed to recruit Tunvra. It remains a sore spot, as piercing as the pride in Lenora is potent, for the same reason.

Emotions are so absurd. How can Arché possibly have room for all of these feelings simultaneously? Even when they go against each other?

Once the tent is up, Arché heads straight for the bedroll. Lenora slips in not long after.

"You're really starting to scare me," she says, reaching for Arché's face.

As soon as her fingertips make contact, Arché flinches away, and hurt crashes over Lenora's face, making Arché curse everything about herself. To salvage the situation, Arché grabs Lenora's hand and gives it a squeeze before it can be retracted.

"I'm sorry," Arché says, voice thick in her throat. "I'm sorry, I'm sorry, I don't—I just don't know what to do."

"I wish you could talk to me."

"I know. I know. Me too." Arché rolls into her, clutching their bodies together until warmth is shared and they can bask in the proximity even if their minds refuse to meet in the way they need. "I wish I knew how. I just... can't. I'm sorry."

"You don't need to keep apologising," Lenora says. "You haven't done anything wrong."

"I hate feeling like this. Like every bad thought is in control, and I'm not."

Lenora kisses the top of her head. "I know what that feels like. That's what most days in Concord were like, for me. When the future felt wrong, when it didn't feel like I was enough. The bad thoughts are still... bad, when they come. But they're less often, less powerful, since the manor. Since you."

"It was so much quieter for me, before," Arché says. "I guess maybe… things weren't quite real, before the attack. I just kept fucking around, hoping if I ignored everything that was wrong it would all go away. But it hasn't. Now it might be why we won't win."

"Hey," Lenora says, voice firm and eyebrows creasing with an intense frown as she pulls back to hold Arché's gaze. "We're going to win. You said that, and now I'm saying that. As long as we're together, everything is going to be fine. We'll get through every single one of them, if we have to."

"Yeah," Arché whispers. Her fingers clutch Lenora probably too hard, but no complaint comes, and they fall asleep pressed together.

The true full moon, the peak of the cycle, is heralded by the green stars again. Arché is always stunned by them, staring up as she waits for the transformation to hold. It's a surreal experience with her head light from another deep Lenora feed. They are so, so lucky to be a part of such a strange and beautiful world.

"Huh," Leahi says. "They're still there. Can you see them? The stars."

"The green ones?" Lenora asks, with surprise. "Yeah, all the nightwalkers see them. I thought daywalkers couldn't."

Leahi laughs with bewilderment. "My friends thought I was making it up! They didn't believe me, when I said I could see them all of a sudden. How long have you seen them?"

"Always," Lenora says, and Arché nods to support the point. "All of us. Lycans, vampires, always. But you just started seeing them?"

"This is only my third time," Leahi says, glancing up to take in the sight again. "I thought I was ill, the first time. Or wondered if it was a Kanin thing, if we can't see them in the islands."

"We care more about the moon at home," Lenora says, eyes lit with intrigue. "I wonder if Alta knows anything about this."

"Wait, maybe Alta sees them too, if it's possible for daywalkers to," Arché says, tilting her head. "I'm remembering some old conversations with Kalé I overheard that would make a lot more sense if they did. I guess we can ask them when we see them. Weird magical stuff in the world is their favourite topic."

She barely gets out the last sentence, as she feels the moon begin to seize her. Once again she changes, alone, and howls to the moon in earnest, in yearning.

Then, she is her other self, and her friends wait, and there is running to do.

Is there nothing so beautiful as frolicking under the moon with friends? Perhaps, only, doing so with family. It is obvious, and it hurts, but maybe Lenora is family now too.

It's too early for such a thought. Even wolf Arché knows that. But wolf Arché is at the mercy of her heart and instincts and all she knows is that Lenora is hers, is what she wants, is what she must be close to always.

Lenora is a beacon in the dark, her smile and shining grey eyes lighting the way like moonlight.

Arché nuzzles into her as they collapse into the grass when the exhaustion of running is too much. Lenora giggles and strokes Arché's fur all the way down her neck and back.

"Thank you," Arché says, while gratitude and love pump through her as fast as the lycan blood. As the beginning of the transformation back begins to tingle her back, she moves away to her own patch of grass.

It's something about coming back to Arché, without her family alongside coming back to themselves too. Not returning to their family as a whole. Who is she, if not Kalé's daughter? Andreas' sister? What will Arché be, if she becomes a failure? How can she become anything else, without being able to see the future where she is a capable heir to be proud of?

The dirt greets her as she bends over and cries out, her body shifting and her being fool enough to almost fight it, desperate to be a wolf a little longer where things seem simpler and she can dash all her problems away.

But she is Arché, the tired woman, drained and panting where her lips almost kiss the dirt.

"I hate this," Arché says. It's true of so many things. "I know there's nothing we can do. But I'm supposed to be with them."

"I know. Did you... have fun running, at least?" Lenora asks.

Arché sits up and nods, trying to give Lenora everything she can, because it's the least she deserves. She smiles at Leahi too, who is watching with wide, uncertain eyes.

"You two are the best," she says. "If I have to be away from my family, I wouldn't want to be with anyone else."

"We're here for you," Leahi tells her.

"Whatever you need," Lenora agrees.

They camp and rest, and it's a little better than the day before. But when it comes to Arché's turn for the watch, it doesn't take long for things to start going wrong.

Arché stares into the fire. A simple thing, and for several moments it is appreciation of the dancing flames and their beauty. But then her mind goes to the Everflame, the god of fire and sun and summer, the one the Crusaders so wrongly invoke. Indignance turns to fury on the Everflame's behalf. It is so wrong for a god to be misrepresented as such, to have such wrongs done in their name.

And then, her mind turns to the awful people committing the crimes, who could be hurting her family right now. Deciding to execute her family now, because it's less trouble than dealing with an angry transformed Kalé, or even Andreas.

It's a spiral that leads her down, down, down. A spiral she doesn't catch in time. She just sits, and stares, lost to herself.

A weight against her arm alerts her to Lenora's waking, however many hours later. There are no words spoken, just head against shoulder and slow breaths. Perhaps that is the best thing in the world that she could do.

A flute begins to play through the night. Leahi's melody touches something deep down that words cannot, and Arché lets the music wash over her, especially when Lenora moves and gets her violin to join in.

This time, Arché welcomes the moon with a serenade from the others. It makes her think of the ocean, a thing she's never seen. Alta's tales of the movement and swell of the waves, being at the whim of the moon's pull, resonates now. Being pulled and shifted by nature itself, then crashing with a burst of power.

Arché howls at the moon as if doing so loud enough might mean that Andreas hears her wherever he is, might feel that she wishes for nothing but being by his side. She howls until her voice might just be gone, until she is panting.

By the time she finishes, Lenora and Leahi are sitting and waiting, the latter sporting a new bite mark on her wrist.

Oh. Arché had forgotten to feed Lenora.

"Sorry," Arché says, her wolf form not quite able to organise the flood of strange and unpleasant feelings that hit her.

"It's fine," Lenora tells her. "Leahi offered. We just won't be able to go as fast, tonight."

And from there, things keep going wrong. Arché tries to tell herself that the feeling of impending doom is just her imagination, but without a large dose of lycan blood, they have to run slowly, leaving Arché with excess energy building up in ways that running in circles around Lenora simply can't alleviate entirely.

Hours pass, and the feeling of catastrophe won't leave. It keeps bubbling, building, boiling… until it is so hot in her chest she can't bear it. Until she is forced to stop running and dig her claws into the ground.

"Arché?" Leahi asks, from her back.

"Please get off," Arché mumbles. Of course, Leahi does so immediately, while Lenora turns around and stops running as well.

Arché fixes her eyes on the dirt. She trained to be better than this, to not let any emotion get the better of her. Terror clouds the edges of her visions as little by little, her control slips from her claws one drop at a time.

She cannot. She will not. She counts paces instead, back and forth. One two three. Four five six. Seven eight nine ten. On ten, she turns and paces back in the other direction, huge strides that dig into the earth each time.

"Arché," Lenora says, sounding like other words are stuck in her throat.

It is just little enough to justify Arché not acknowledging it at all. She just keeps counting, like her life depends on it, because everything does, but it's all becoming flurry. Loathing and fury and devastating close in on her mind like dark clouds, and there is supposed to be a way to shelter from it, to keep them away, but she cannot remember.

One last piece of clarity shines through. To get away from her friends, to not be near them.

Arché dashes, ignoring the shouts behind her and the footsteps that can't match her speed. She runs to the nearest cluster of trees, body trembling under the force of it, not quite sure what is about to happen but feeling it coming like an avalanche.

Something deep within her gives out and a guttural howl rips through her as her claws slash into the bark of the nearest tree.

Arché imagines it is the prophet responsible for everything, that the tree trunk is his chest, and that destroying it will stop everything, save everyone, and mean they can all go home. Strike after strike, Arché attacks in a flurry, in a haze of red that masks time alongside everything else. When that tree is finished, she moves to the next, and the next, taking down the entire Crusade with her claws if it were possible.

It isn't until the force of the transformation begins to shoot up her back that Arché breaks free of her feral rampage. Her body shakes and changes, and she falls back onto her rear, staring at the mangled thing in front of her which has once been a tree. Then, at the others, even more wrecked, bark littering the ground and roots torn from the earth. Nothing can save any of them. They will rot and serve only to nourish whatever might come next.

She hadn't. She couldn't have.

She did.

Her hands are caked with dirt and splinters, and Arché is surprised that there is no blood from the lack of care she had taken in the attacks.

The greatest shame for a lycan of Concord is to lose control while transformed. Everything is done to avoid it, to arm them with the tools needed to remain resilient. It's the one failure she thought she was safe from, the one reassurance she had.

Now, her world collapses, shame flooding in so hot that it burns, melting the ice that kept her frozen and making her cry out and bend over her knees. This is the ultimate weakness, the ultimate confirmation she will never lead her house. There has never been a leader who has lost control before; the lycan heirs are warned this from the start, told this so the importance of it is never lost on them.

A sound from behind her makes her head whip around. Arché sees Lenora sitting up against one of the other trees, eyes swimming with tears of her own, so full of concern that at any other time Arché would have pulled her into a crushing hug.

"Do you feel better, for getting that out?" Lenora asks. "That was... really hard to watch."

Arché stares. Her ears seldom fail her. But there is no way she could have heard correctly. "What did you just say?"

"It was hard to watch you in so much pain," Lenora says, arms wrapped around herself. "Of course it was. I'm sure it would be the same if I—"

"Not that," Arché says, voice clipped. "I meant the other part."

"Huh?"

"Did you seriously just ask me if I felt better for *getting it out*?"

"Yes?" Lenora blinks at her. "If you don't, that's okay, I just hoped—"

Disbelief and incredulity become a new kind of pain. Something Lenora has never made her feel before. A cutting sensation of a lack of understanding like Arché has never known. Like they don't know each other at all, like they aren't from the same home, the same people.

"Do you not understand what I just did?" Arché asks, voice soft.

"You wrecked some trees because you were upset," Lenora says.

The obvious, simple description. Without any of the meaning, without any of the comprehension. Just words.

Arché stands up and flexes her wrists. "So you saw what I did. But you don't understand."

Her voice is blunt, wooden, and so different to her usual speech that the only right thing to do is to turn away and begin walking back towards Leahi, where camp needs to be made.

"What?" Lenora's voice trembles. "Arché—"

Quick movement in the grass behind her, and Lenora's hand grabs Arché's elbow, sending a violent shiver up her spine.

"Don't touch me," Arché snarls, ripping out of her grip and walking faster. "I don't want *anyone* to touch me. I want to sleep."

Lenora makes a noise like a wounded animal, but the footsteps stop in their tracks, and Arché is free to dig into her pack and find her bedroll. Instead of setting up the tent, Arché lays the bed roll out in the most open part of the grass, right where the sun will shine the brightest. A great place to sleep alone.

There is little point in holding onto any pride. Arché curls up on the bedroll and lets herself cry bitterly as the first rays of sun pour over her. She cries until sleep takes her.

No one wakes her for watch. She wakes to a slowly darkening sky.

Numbness has settled in her chest, pushing out everything that used to live there. She wishes she knew how to stop it, but she is out of resolve. Out of belief.

How can she ever face Kalé again, knowing what she's done? She cannot keep this a secret for the rest of her life, but she doesn't know how she could ever look her mother in the face and admit to losing control. No one will ever look at her the same again, not even if she saves them all. She'll be the heir who lost control. And she won't be able to blame them, because she would hold the same judgement if it were anyone else.

Even though the thought of talking or being touched still makes her feel nauseous, Arché knows she cannot ignore her companions, especially Lenora. Arché packs up her bedroll and heads towards the supplies to make some coffee over the fire. It surely wouldn't have been a good day's rest for any of them.

Coffee is made just in time for Leahi to come out of her tent, stifling a yawn.

"Ooh, thanks," she says, grabbing one of the travel mugs at once and sitting down with it.

Arché nods and sits down with her own cup. Lenora emerges last, and just seeing her spikes horrible and complicated feelings in Arché's chest, especially when Arché spots the dark circles under Lenora's eyes and the redness of the eyelids.

Lenora sits next to Leahi, drinking the coffee without saying a word.

As they drink in silence, Leahi's eyes keep darting between Arché and Lenora, the crease of her eyebrows deepening with each minute as no words are exchanged.

"So... what the fuck is going on, then?" Leahi asks.

Arché grits her teeth. "Nothing you can help with."

"Fuck that," Leahi retorts. "You just shut down on us and then slept out in the sun where your vampire girlfriend can't join you, you might as well have written *I need help* on your forehead! Like it wasn't obvious from the way you tore up those trees, anyway."

A growl rumbles in Arché's throat. "Whatever help I need, no one can give me, least of all you, so let's drop it."

Leahi huffs. "Right, so you're miserable, so now you want a free pass on being a piece of shit to your girlfriend and your only other friend?"

"I don't—" Arché shakes her head, putting her cup down and heading for her pack. "I'm leaving in five minutes. You two better be ready to go. And yes, I'm miserable and I need space. Please."

It is the most silent night of travel yet. After several hours, the shape of the Highway road and the large town ahead become visible from the faint town lights in the distance.

Around the same time, Leahi sighs from behind Arché.

"Okay, that's enough," the daywalker says. She barges in front of Arché and crosses her arms, planting herself in the ground as a definitive barrier, as if Arché couldn't walk around her. "I'm going to town. I'll find the tavern and get us rooms. You two are going to stay here and talk for at least five minutes. This is ridiculous."

"What part of *I need space* and *no one can help me—*"

"This isn't just about you, Arché, you've upset my friend." Leahi looks Arché square in the eye. "You can't intimidate me. You can hurt me all you like, because I can take it. But you're hurting Lenora. And I don't know if you love her, but she sure as anything loves you. So cut the bullshit and talk to her!"

With that, Leahi strides off towards town, leaving Arché with little choice but to turn around and finally face Lenora.

CHAPTER 30
LENORA

LENORA STILL CAN'T WORK out what she did wrong. Ever since Arché pushed her away, with that snarl, with that look in her eyes so frantic, Lenora has been in too much of a state to even be able to think properly and find clarity.

It doesn't feel fair. Life isn't fair, obviously, and Lenora knows that better than most, but she'd never expected Arché to ever make her feel like this.

Leahi is fuming as they walk side by side behind the closed-off werewolf leading the way, so it comes as little surprise that once their destination is in sight, she puts her foot down.

Lenora is grateful. But dread sits heavy in her stomach all the same.

"I'm sorry," Arché says, voice soft, eyes pained. "Gods, I'm sorry. I didn't expect that you wouldn't understand, it was like being at the bottom of a pit and having the only way out kicked away, but I shouldn't have—"

"I don't understand because you don't explain—"

"I don't explain about *me*, I shouldn't have to explain *that*!" Arché gestures back towards the way they came from. "I shouldn't have to explain Concord principles, lycan principles, when everyone just *knows*."

"Well, I've never been any good at knowing the things I'm supposed to know!" Lenora retorts. "I could never know the right forms for the spells Mother tried to teach me, or the right words, or the right battle forms or defense moves. So I guess I must have fucked up in our heir classes as well. It took everything I had to even turn up. Sometimes I just didn't have the energy to hear what they were saying."

Arché stares, several things racing through her eyes too fast for Lenora to identify them. She swallows, taking her time before answering.

"But Nikos never talked to you about control? Lycan control?" Arché asks. "Not ever?"

"It was *Nikos*," Lenora whispers, squeezing herself tighter. "He was always in control. Always balanced. He was so balanced that me being bad at everything meant we evened out. Does lycan control mean never talking to your vampire about what you're really thinking? Because that would explain a lot."

Arché winces. "No, it—fuck, Lenora, I'm so sorry."

"Then what *does* it mean?"

"It means that losing control is the worst thing one of us can do," Arché says, with a sigh heavy enough to be an anchor. "The most shameful thing. I never thought I would, I thought that it would be the one thing I—"

"*That's* what this is about now?" Lenora asks, astounded. "Arché, I'm not judging you, I'd never judge you—"

"You should!" Arché snaps. "I don't know what I'm going to do, I was already worried that I—no one will follow me if they know this happened but I can't *lie*—"

"What?" Lenora blinks at her. What kind of nonsense is all this? "Arché, none of their rules matter out here, you don't need to be beating yourself up like this!"

"Yes, they do! Or do you want to go and take a snack from Leahi for as long as you like?"

"That's not the same—"

"It is! You don't lose control while feeding, and I don't lose control while transformed. That's the rule. It matters."

Of all the things Lenora expected Arché to be struggling with, it had not been this. Not this loss of control, or this bewildering expectation of impossible heights. How could Arché, so steady and sensible, be hung up on something such as this?

"Arché, none of them expect you to be perfect."

"It's not about perfection, it's about what is acceptable and what isn't. There is never an excuse, no matter how mad things get."

"This is a *reason*," Lenora cries, hands gesturing to everything around them. "We're out here, alone and in the most stressful situation we can come across. I'm sure this more than qualifies as an excuse!"

"It doesn't."

"We're nowhere near them. Their rules don't matter out here."

"They matter to me," Arché says, crossing her arms over her chest.

"Well, that's ridiculous."

"And that's your opinion."

"Yes, it is, I think this whole thing is ridiculous," Lenora says with a shake of her head. "It's all nonsense."

Arché scowls, something dark flashing across her eyes. It shoots right into Lenora's heart. "Well, you're not one of us. And you don't get to decide what matters."

A slap in the face would have been more gentle. After nearly spitting the words out, Arché turns and continues on towards town without looking back. It's a strange kind of reeling, a scrambling to try to determine if what has been said is fair, if what just happened is injustice or truth or neither.

Lenora is not a lycan. Lenora may have a lot less of an idea what they go through month to month than she thought. How would it feel, if Arché made some assumption about how Lenora feels when without blood, or when feeding? If it were dismissive, if it were full of things not quite Arché's place to say?

"I'm sorry," Lenora says, racing after her. "You're right. I'm not one of you, and I don't get to say that. I just… hate the sound of anything that means you're not one of the strongest people I know, because you are."

The words are desperate, half choked out, a plea buried in their cadence that begs Arché to turn around and just look at her. Lenora is fast realising that one of the things she can stand least in the world is watching Arché walk away.

But Arché halts. And turns. Lenora nearly cries, but does everything to keep it together because she has no idea what is happening to them, but knows that these moments are crucial. She will *not* lose this chance for them to find their common ground and understanding again. She will not let another good thing in her life fall through her fingertips.

"Help me understand," Lenora says, voice almost as soft as the wind. Her hand reaches out into the space between them. "Please. I'm sorry you're hurting, but please don't push me away. I'll do anything to understand, and I think if it was me, you would too. People who love each other should try to understand."

Arché stares, at Lenora's face and then the offered hand. Her arm extends. Her hand slips into Lenora's. A loose hold, tentative, but there. They're connected, and maybe if they never look away, it will all come together.

"I guess the difference is that the vampire feedings at home are so structured," Arché says slowly. "The more I think about it, the more I realise how much more we have to work all the time, because it's a whole night, three nights a month, where we have to keep ourselves in check. Even in the partial forms we have to be careful. We talk about Concord being founded on this shared learning of control, but it's silly to act as though the battles are the same when they're so different. I thought because Rohan knew, everyone would know. But maybe some people, like you… just never had to think about it as much. You're right—Nikos never seemed very angry about anything, and it's only those aggressive emotions that are particularly taboo. But… I was never really angry either… until all this happened."

"That's what I was trying to say, with this situation feeling like an exception to the rule," Lenora says, but Arché's body stiffens and so she is quick to add: "But if you don't think so, I'll respect that. I just won't be able to stop myself from thinking that you're being hard on yourself. But I see that what you think is more important."

Arché nods, a tension in her shoulders so tight it makes them tremble, and Lenora wishes nothing more than to embrace her and soothe everything. But then, Arché closes her eyes as her face twists.

"It just feels like a confirmation," she whispers. "That I'm not good enough to be Kalé's heir."

And just like that, a hundred pieces of the puzzle click into place. Tiny things without context, now clarifying after they've snowballed and crashed into *this*. Lenora had never been the only one overwhelmed by the pressure of their positions. How many hours had she spent feeling inadequate, thinking surely no one had as much doubt about their future as she did? How many people would have guessed first, before thinking Arché would have the same concerns?

"Oh, Arché—"

"Gods, I've never said it out loud," Arché mutters, tears coming thick and fast to her eyes. "I knew the moment I did, it would be so much worse, and it is, I can't help it, I just…"

She sinks to her knees, into Lenora's offered arms, and her tears soak Lenora's dress in moments.

"I couldn't shake the feeling. I tried to, I tried for so long, I didn't even have a reason... it's just that Kalé is so good at it and people would obviously be disappointed to have me in charge after having her for so long... and once I'd thought it, it wouldn't go away."

"I know," Lenora says, stroking her hands over Arché's hair. "I know. It's the worst feeling in the world."

"And then Rohan kept getting on my nerves, and I felt like if I couldn't even work out how to resolve something with my best friend, I would never be able to be a leader, but I didn't know what to say! Nikos was supposed to help me. But nothing he suggested made any difference, it all just bounced off Rohan because they were *Rohan*. They were allergic to worrying about anything!"

She's on a roll now. The woman who would not speak of her feelings, hitting the boiling point and releasing it all in a torrent of steam. Lenora holds her through it all the while.

"With Tunvra, I lost it," Arché continues. "I was so sure I could convince him, and then when I couldn't all I could think was that Kalé could have. That if I was good enough, I could have. It wouldn't go away, it kept dragging me down."

"...I have a thought about Tunvra, if you want to hear it," Lenora says.

There's a pause, and a sniff. "Okay."

"I think you couldn't convince him because you're so inherently good that you could never know the right thing to say to someone who isn't." Lenora presses a tender, slow kiss to the side of Arché's head. "Him not attacking sleeping people is the most basic code he could have. For all we know, it's just his ego anyway. He's out for money and himself. I only convinced him because I appealed to both *and* made him fear for his life.

You were trying to speak to something that wasn't there. It might have failed, but it wasn't wrong. It was true to you."

Arché twists in her arms until she is sitting up enough to look Lenora in the eye, two inches from her face. "You really think that, don't you?"

Lenora nods and strokes Arché's shoulder where she's holding her half in her lap. "You don't have to believe me, but I really do."

A callused, shaking hand brushes Lenora's hair back from her face and behind her ear. The thumb rests on Lenora's cheek. Arché's brown eyes, wide and shining, are endless pools Lenora would happily be lost in forever.

"I believe you," Arché whispers. "I... believe *it*. Gods, I love you. Thank you, Lenora, I don't know what's wrong with my head, I get so caught up in things I know shouldn't matter, and I can't shake them—"

"I know how it feels to feel lost like that, even if my head isn't quite the same."

The first time they kissed properly, Arché had been so gentle, holding Lenora as if she were a sculpture made of the most delicate glass. Now, Lenora cups Arché's face in the same way, hands cradling her jaw, and presses the softest of kisses to her lips. Then the tip of her nose, then her eyelids, then her temple.

"I love you," Lenora says. "I know I love you, because you walk away from me and I feel like everything is collapsing if I don't know when you're coming back to me. I love you because I've never seen anyone care about getting things right the way that you do." She drags her lips down from Arché's temple to her jaw. "You said we're a team, so promise me that we're a team, that we'll help each other. Especially on days when things feel like this."

"I promise I'll try," Arché murmurs, leaning into her touch. "And that I won't walk away from you again. I don't know how to fix... all this stuff, my head or this mistake or what comes next… but I promise I won't walk away."

Their lips meet again, this time a mutual crashing, a devouring not of lust but of the most base and emotional need. If they cannot be closer, they might as well perish here and now. Lenora is half tempted to just start taking her clothes off so she can feel Arché's skin against her own, feel her close enough that she'll be sure Arché will never turn her back on her again.

Arché's eyes are dark and desperate too, her hands sweeping down Lenora's back, pulling her into a crushing embrace, inhaling so deeply it's audible.

"We should get going," Arché says with great reluctance. "But once we have our room, I'm going to make this up to you."

A beautiful promise, and one that sends warmth shooting through Lenora's body. But she frowns, because her mind has been racing ahead.

"No, I'm going to look after you," Lenora says, kissing her long and slow. "In every way I can think of."

Arché shivers, and then a strange smile curls her lips. "Well, we might have to agree to disagree. Fight me for it?"

CHAPTER 31
LENORA

The prospect is so absurd, so delightful, that Lenora giggles as Arché flips them over and holds Lenora down in the grass. Lenora is kissed with new force, making her head spin, getting a real taste of Arché's strength in this way, feeling how her body responds in a visceral roar of heat.

"Gods, I wish we didn't need to go," Arché mutters, brushing her nose against Lenora's. "I'm wound up something fierce."

"That's why you need to let me look after you," Lenora says. Surely, if Lenora can go down on her for an hour, Arché's body will get the reset and endorphins it deserves after everything that's happened.

Arché tilts her head, face thoughtful again. She slides her hands up Lenora's thighs until they slip under the dress, not going much further but caressing the skin there.

"How about... you're in charge," Arché suggests. "You deserve it. You can do anything you want, to me or with me, or you can ask me to do anything you'd like to you."

That sounds like paradise. Lenora nods firmly, finally appeased, and Arché grins before pulling them both up into a sitting position for one more kiss.

"Let's go thank Leahi," Arché says. "I think I owe her at least five apology drinks, too."

They walk hand in hand the rest of the way into town. The road leading into it is unlike any of the others Lenora has seen, perfectly paved with cobblestone and twice as wide. Lenora has heard of the Grand Highway, but never seen it. The main trade route that stretches from one side of the world to the other, going to all the capitals. Each country vowing to staff their sections of it with local guards to keep travel and trade as safe as possible. A beautiful work of diplomatic collaboration.

And now, it is the method by which their people are being transported to Cancium, in Izirm. But it provides a clear route ahead, and Lenora has no doubt that they'll find them in time for the next full moon.

The tavern is easy to locate; it is the tallest building in town at a staggering five levels high that Lenora has never seen before. Its sign reads 'The Crystal Dragon'.

Inside, the atmosphere is bustling enough that no one even glances at them as they step in the door, and they spot Leahi in a corner booth. Opposite her, nursing an ale, is Tunvra.

"Right," Arché says.

Lenora squeezes her hand. "I forgot he would be here."

"Me too, but I'll be alright, thanks to you. He's a means to an end, that's all." Arché takes a deep breath, but when Lenora glances over at her, Arché genuinely seems to be calm and steady. Pride swells in Lenora's chest and she is almost overwhelmed by the urge to kiss Arché breathless once again.

Soon. There will be time for that soon. First, there is business to discuss.

"All good?" Leahi asks Arché as the nightwalking pair slide into the free side of the booth.

"Getting there," Arché says. "Thanks. Really. And I'm sorry, I'll get your next few drinks."

Leahi smiles around the next mouthful of her ale. "You're welcome. We all need a kick up the ass sometimes. Nothing wrong with it."

"You're a woman of great wisdom."

"I would say someone with a near zero tolerance for bullshit," Leahi counters. "But it does come in handy." The two exchange smiles, and when Leahi's eyes move to Lenora, as if to check in, Lenora is sure to give her a big smile to reassure her.

"So, what now?" Tunvra asks.

"Now, we wait for Alta," Arché says. "They won't be far off, and they'll be bringing magic that can help us, if things have gone well on their end."

Tunvra nods, but his brow is furrowed with displeasure. "Not a fan of sitting still. I could go ahead and scout the caravans. Might pay to know how they tend to camp down. My bird can get a good view."

"Sure, that sounds really helpful," Lenora says, smiling at him just enough to show off her fangs. "Make sure you're careful, though." She has few doubts about him swapping sides again, but it never hurts to remind him of her previous promises.

Tunvra holds her gaze well, but she sees his throat bob as he swallows. "I'll head out at first light."

First light. What an awful time to do anything. Lenora has never been so relieved to be a nightwalker. How can anyone have a brain that functions in glaring, bright daylight. The calm of the night is superior in every way.

"I got you two a room," Leahi says, sliding a key with a tag across the table while Tunvra finishes his drink. "They're pretty nice. Good place to be waiting around. They've also got live music going most nights... I might see if I can play. Might be able to get free food as payment. You could do it with me."

"Oh," Lenora says with surprise. "I guess I could." She's never played for an audience before, and while that once would have sounded like the worst thing in the world, now it sounds exciting.

"Thanks, Leahi," Arché says, grabbing the key off the table. "We might go and... keep talking."

Leahi snorts into her drink. "Uh huh. You do that."

Lenora feels blood warm her face, and has never been so relieved for Tunvra's disinterest in everything to do with them, as he mutters a farewell and heads for the stairs across the room.

"I'm in room twenty on the floor below you, if you wanna hang out at any point," Leahi offers. "But I'm guessing that'll be more of a tomorrow night thing."

"You guessed right," Arché says, grabbing Lenora's hands and pulling her out of the booth. "Have a good rest of your night, Leahi."

"You too." Leahi grins. "Let me know if you have any problems getting it up."

"Not going to be a problem," Arché says, and the look she gives Lenora is so full of promise that Lenora actually feels her desire become liquid between her legs. Her face burns hotter than ever.

"Oh my gods, go find that room, now," Leahi says, cackling to herself.

They hurry upstairs, to the fourth floor, where they are room thirty two. Arché unlocks the door, and Lenora has barely stepped inside before Arché has spun her around and pressed her into the wood, slamming it shut and relocking it in an instant.

"Fucking finally," Arché growls, before capturing Lenora's mouth in a devouring kiss. "Gods, you're right, I just need to not think for a bit, I need a break from worrying about *everything*—"

"You also said I was in charge," Lenora reminds her.

Arché nods, kissing Lenora's chin. "I did. You are. I'm here. I'm yours. Now, forever."

"Show me," Lenora says, and when she pushes on Arché's shoulders it takes only the smallest pressure to have the lycan drop to her knees. "Show me you're sorry."

Arché mouth kisses up Lenora's legs, wet and hot against her knee and thighs, agonisingly slow. Her head vanishes under Lenora's dress, and Lenora yanks it over her head and onto the ground. Arché's fingers hook into the sides of Lenora's underwear and begin pulling it down.

"Tonight, you only think about me," Lenora says. Her hand curls around Arché's braid bun. The words are half request, half demand. "How to please me. Or how to take what you need from me."

Arché nods, licking her lips, and Lenora cannot help the yelp that escapes her when Arché hooks one of Lenora's legs over her shoulder to open the space and make room for her head.

The moment Arché's mouth is on her, Lenora melts. It starts slow, but Lenora has been worked up since the fields outside town. Slow isn't quite what she wants. It doesn't matter that they have the rest of the night. It isn't enough.

Her hand pulls Arché closer, and Arché groans before her tongue flicks against Lenora in a way that has her crying out and bucking against Arché's face. Arché holds Lenora's hip and thigh tighter, and does it again.

"Fuck," Lenora whimpers.

Arché growls against her, an odd vibration that has Lenora shivering. The noise sends Lenora's imagination racing.

It's easy for Arché to find the exact spot and pace that works for Lenora—their time on the road was not that long ago, nor the last tavern. Lenora comes hard, her fingers locking in Arché's hair, and Arché continues her ministrations until Lenora is quietly trembling, only upright because of Arché's support.

Arché looks up at her, eyes dark and adoring, mouth glistening. "I'm never going to get tired of those noises. You're so gorgeous."

Lenora is still trying to catch her breath. Her heart pounds in her chest at a deafening rate.

"Should I keep going?" Arché says. "I'll stay here as long as you want me to."

Lenora has no doubt; it's a dizzying thought to entertain. But she is feeling a deep ache of need right in her core, something not yet satisfied. She pulls Arché up, grabbing her waist.

"You've told me you want to bend me over something and fuck me like that," Lenora murmurs, pressing her body against Arché's, every inch she can. "I want that. You promised never to walk away from me. Make me believe you. Show me how much you want me. I want to feel you hold me down. Stop holding back."

Arché's hands come down to grab Lenora's ass, her hands so strong with the simple motion that Lenora can barely fathom what is to come.

"Gods, I can... definitely do that, if that's what you want," Arché groans. "But it might be overwhelming. You'd need to tell me to stop if it's too much, and you might feel a kind of... drop. After. I know how to look after you if that happens because Sierra would do it for me. So if that sounds okay—"

"I trust you," Lenora says. "And I want you, Arché. So fucking bad."

Arché picks Lenora up in one simple motion and kisses her, hard, while carrying her to the bed. After placing Lenora on it, it's a simple thing for Arché's hands to roll her over and pull her hips up. Warm fingers trace over her rear and the back of her thighs. Then, a single fingertip tracing down her spine.

"I don't feel like I deserve this kind of reward for making you feel the way I did," Arché's voice says, now uncertain.

Lenora is forced to look back over her shoulder. "Arché. You said I was in charge. This isn't me... rewarding you... for not talking to me." Arché frowns, and Lenora huffs and sits up, twisting herself so that they are face to face once again. "This is me, wanting to see how you can make me feel. I need you to give me everything." Lenora takes Arché's hand and guides it to rest between her legs before grinding against it. "I'm—" Lenora takes a moment to weigh the words on her tongue, as she hurtles toward unfamiliar territory she is desperate to explore. Her free hand touches Arché's lips, the other woman frozen staring at her. "I'm begging you to fuck me until I can't think. Until there's no room for doubt, or hurt, or anything."

Arché nods, once, then twice. She kisses Lenora slow and decadent, while two of her fingers slide inside Lenora and begin stroking her.

"I never get tired of the face you make, every time," Arché murmurs. "I'll spend every day apologising. Making you feel good. Showing you how I feel. If you'll let me."

Does Arché realise how close that sounds to a proposal? Lenora knows this is not the time for such things, but with her body warm and dizzy, she'd be half tempted to accept on the spot. Marriage almost sounds trivial, compared to what Lenora has just asked of Arché, what they want of each other right now. Lenora doesn't just want physically, she wants with every part of her being.

The fingers inside her curl and Lenora gasps, still held in place by Arché's other hand, so close.

"I will never, ever walk away from you again," Arché breathes against her lips. Her thumb presses against Lenora's clit and forces a soft cry from Lenora's throat.

"Show me," Lenora says. "Make me feel it."

Arché's fingers slide out, leaving Lenora empty right when it is the last thing she wants, but before she can protest, the fingers are against her lips. Lenora stares at Arché, understanding without explanation and shocked at how she feels the heat inside somehow burn even hotter.

Lenora takes the fingers into her mouth and sucks them clean, holding Arché's gaze the entire time. Those brown eyes burn with such desire, such intent, that Lenora finally believes that they've reached an accord.

"Good," Arché murmurs, and she drags her fingertips down Lenora's lips and chin, leaving the faintest smear of saliva.

Then her hands turn Lenora around, spiking Lenora's heart rate, but then comes a pause and a shuffle as Arché removes her shirt and breastband. When she touches Lenora again, it's to pull Lenora's back against her chest, her hands roaming everywhere.

"Arché, please," Lenora begs, pressing back against her hips. It's too slow. All of it. She needs to feel more.

"If you think I'm going to rush this, then you have no idea how I feel about you," Arché says, kissing her neck, while her hand cups Lenora's breast and rolls a nipple between finger and thumb. "I watched you become so strong, so sure. I felt so weak, and didn't want you to see me that way. And there you were, seeing all the good parts of me, the strengths. Loving me anyway. I fell in love with you because you tried so hard at everything even when the world made it difficult for you, because you created beauty to survive the monsters in your head. And then, when those voices came for *my* head, you saw the value in me."

Lenora's body twists in her grasp, while her heart is busy melting. She turns her head, seeking Arché's mouth, and manages to capture it in a kiss.

One of Arché's hands moves lower, rubs her right where she's desperate to be touched, and Lenora whimpers against Arché's mouth.

"You are the most astounding person I've ever known," Arché says, voice still low. "I still can't believe I'm allowed to touch you at all."

"Please," Lenora whispers. "Please, Arché, I need you."

"Gods, hearing that will never—" Arché shakes her head, brushing against Lenora's neck. "You still sure that you don't want me to hold back?"

"Don't you dare," Lenora says. "How many times do I have to beg you to—"

Arché pushes her back down, sudden and effortless, and Lenora's cheek hits the pillow while her hips are gripped tightly with one powerful hand.

Teasing fingertips, trailing over the sensitive skin of her inner thighs, before pushing inside without decorum, making Lenora cry out. The pace is moderate, but they push deep, and Lenora feels something unwind within her soul as she gives herself over to the sensation. As she lets herself stop, and be, and get lost.

"Gods," Arché mutters. "If you could see yourself—"

"Well I *can't*, but maybe I can do this for you—"

"I must not be fucking you hard enough if you can think this much." Arché's hand leaves her hip and grasps Lenora's forearm instead, as her body covers Lenora's and pushes it down against the bed. Arché's weight, warm and solid, presses against her.

It's glorious, especially as the hand between her legs moves even faster.

Curses fall from Lenora's lips. Exactly as she wanted, she can't move; she is at the mercy of Arché's strength and attention. And she has never felt more free. There is nothing but them, nothing but this. No choice but letting the pleasure coil within her. A single word from her would end it, of course, but the illusion of true restraint is powerful enough.

"I've got you," Arché whispers, kissing just behind her ear. "I'm here. I'm never, ever leaving. I'm yours. Forever."

Lenora's legs tremble, the sensation building to a point of near distress, to the point where she never used to be able to get herself over out of some kind of strange fear. The point that Arché took her over for the first time, showing her what she'd been missing.

"Fuck," Lenora says, her hips twisting as if to escape Arché's hand as Arché's thumb finds exactly the right spot to press down as her fingers curl again.

And she jerks underneath Arché as the first wave of orgasm hits, pulsing around Arché's fingers, drawing out like it never has before, hitting over and over like a storm bombarding a shoreline.

Through it all, Arché kisses Lenora's shoulders and neck, murmuring encouragement and endearments, until Lenora's everything gives way and she slumps against the bed. Arché rolls them so that Lenora can lie on her chest, enclosed in her arms, and strokes her hair.

"I love you so much," Arché tells her, kissing her forehead.

Lenora's head spins, a strange sense of vertigo hitting and making her body feel bizarre, like it is turned inside out. There is a single second where fear and uncertainty grasp her heart, but then another kiss from Arché has it melting away, reminding her she is warm and safe here. The strangeness will pass. Arché promised.

"I love you too—I do feel strange," Lenora says softly. "Is that what you talked about?"

Arché nods and presses even closer. "It can happen after power imbalances like that. I'm just going to keep doing this until you tell me it's passed, or if you want something else, I'll do that."

Already, the sensation of fingertips trailing over her hair is dimming the odd drop. "This is good. We can stay like this."

It fades quickly, which is a relief, and soon Lenora busies herself with grabbing Arché's hand and pressing kisses to it. It draws the most delightful chuckle from Arché's chest.

"How was that?" Arché asks.

Lenora can only respond with a small groan and a wriggle closer into her body.

"Please tell me that means really good."

"Thinking is hard right now, you did it too good," Lenora mumbles, making them both laugh.

"Well, there's other ways we can do that too."

"Oh?"

"If we find the right shop. There are certain toys with harnesses. It can be very fun."

"When you say toys..."

"I mean phallic shaped ones," Arché says. "If you think you'd like that."

Lenora does her best to envision how that might work, and finds herself warming again just at the thought. "Huh. I mean. Yes. And you like that too?"

"I told you, I like almost everything," Arché says, smiling and kissing her again. "I just have a lot of fun looking after you."

A sentiment Lenora truly appreciates. On the other hand, she wants to help Arché unwind physically after such an emotional onslaught across the last few days. And this new discussion has given Lenora a wild new idea.

"Arché, do you trust me?" Lenora asks. Based on what Arché has said she likes, this should work out well for them both.

Arché blinks at her. "Yes. Completely."

"Close your eyes," Lenora tells her. "I'm going to make you feel good now."

She shuffles down Arché's body and kisses her muscular thighs, running her lips and tongue over the soft skin with such strength underneath. All the while, she experiments with her shadow magic, forming a rounded shape around two of her fingers, having only that as a reference for size.

A makeshift phallus, fixed nicely to her hand.

Lenora presses a kiss to Arché's core and relishes how she shudders. She cannot resist getting a small taste, for her own satisfaction and for the soft little noise Arché makes, but once her tongue is satisfied that Arché is more than ready enough for what she has planned, she kisses back up her body until she's hovering above her.

One more kiss, this time to Arché's slightly parted lips. Lenora pushes her creation inside Arché and drinks in the gasp of surprise that leaves her mouth.

"What—"

"I can make anything," Lenora says with a grin. "Thanks for the idea."

Arché lets out a funny laugh, even as her cheeks are flushed beyond belief. She looks so gorgeous like this that Lenora wishes she were a painter just so she could capture it forever.

Now with the powerful woman she loves beneath her and squirming, Lenora gets the delightful opportunity to press the shadow toy deep within Arché and watch how her back arches, hear how she moans.

"Fuck, Lenora," Arché exhales.

"You look really good like this," Lenora says, her free hand cupping Arché's jaw so that she can kiss her brow and eyelids and cheeks with adoration. "Is the size good?"

"Yeah, it's—" Arché captures her lips, her breathing heavy. "I'm used to thicker, but it's still—"

Lenora gives it a careful, focused thought. She knows she has succeeded in widening the girth when Arché's head tilts back and new curses fall from her mouth.

It is slow and indulgent, taking Arché higher and higher like this, using her magic for something so different. Bringing pleasure to Arché in a way no one else could dream of doing.

Under her, in her arms, Arché trembles and comes with a strangled whisper of Lenora's name. Lenora can only think of how she can next hear that sound, that precious sound only for her.

The shadow magic falls away as Lenora cradles Arché's beautiful head and everything it holds.

"I love you," Lenora whispers against her mouth. "I love all of you. Even the bits you find trickier, the bits you don't like. I'll love them when you can't. Okay?"

A small sob rocks Arché's chest as she kisses Lenora desperately.

"I love you so much," Arché says. "In ways I never knew I could."

"I understand *that* feeling."

Their laughter blends and echoes, and it is a thing of beauty.

CHAPTER 32
ARCHÉ

BY THE TIME IT comes to breakfast with Leahi in the early evening, Arché and Lenora have not rested nearly as much as they ought to have. But, sometimes, being sated in other ways is more valuable.

Leahi doesn't say anything, but there is an angle to her smile and eyebrows that suggests content amusement.

"So when is your parent getting here?" Leahi asks. Arché is relieved to hear that question and no others.

"Any time now," Arché says, shrugging before adding with slight frustration, "I suppose we can only sit here and wait."

"That's the way it is sometimes," Leahi says sagely, but with a sigh that suggests her wisdom comes with limited patience. "Do you two like cards?"

They play for several hours, over a breakfast consisting of daywalker dinner food. Arché is more than happy to get stuck into hearty stew and fresh bread at any time of the day, so it makes little difference to her, and Lenora can get her rare cut of meat. Leahi bemoans the lack of seafood.

"I just want some raw fish and lemon," she says. "Some shellfish. Nothing too much."

"I imagine it's difficult to transport," Arché says.

Leahi scoffs. "My people transport shellfish all the way to Orsun, all the time. You only need someone who has a mundane spell to freeze water. Keeps it from going off, easy."

A common enough method. Arché knows the people with that particular mundane magic had been greatly valued all over Concord, making rounds several times day and night to refresh the ice keeping food fresh.

"Are you planning on going back home any time soon?" Lenora asks Leahi. "You've already been away for months, right? Studying in Orsun?"

"Yeah, but it'll be there when I'm ready to go back. I need to finish my studies into arcane sources, which means field research." Leahi makes a face. "We're counting this as field research. I *am* following a Shadow mage around."

"If you help us save the others, I can help you write something for your paper," Lenora says. "Or at least, give you as much information as I can without giving away Concord."

"Yeah, that would be huge," Leahi says, eyes lighting up.

With time abundant, Lenora and Leahi put their heads and hands together for a composition project. Arché meanwhile flicks through a romance novel from Leahi's bag only to lose interest once she realises the love interest is a man. So she switches to whittling her figurine of Andreas, which is coming along wonderfully.

It's strangely peaceful to stay on the tavern floor as the night continues and the daywalkers begin to vacate and go to sleep. The barkeep seems bemused by the nocturnal group in the corner, but never inquires or glances their way for too long, and at a few points Leahi stops to chat while waiting for drinks.

"We might turn in," Arché says to her. "You seem to have good company."

Leahi grins. "Sure. See you tomorrow."

With that, Lenora and Arché head upstairs and make the most of what remains of the night, before falling asleep in mere moments.

It is nowhere near eight or even six hours into said sleep when there is a knock at the room door. Arché groans and rolls out of the bed, pulling on a robe before leaning her head against the wood of the bar.

"Yes?" she asks, barely awake enough to remember to be cautious.

"Arché? Is that you? It's Alta."

The voice, muffled as it is, is unmistakable and surely not known to any Crusaders regardless. Arché opens the door a crack just in time to see her parent's wide smile.

"We're here!" Alta declares. From behind them, Raavi waves. "Sorry about the timing."

"Can we talk in the evening?" Arché asks, praying to every god that Alta agrees with the logic of the request.

There is a quick nod. "Absolutely! We need a catnap or three, we'll meet you downstairs at an ideal hour, then?"

"Great—"

The two scholars vanish as quickly as they had arrived, leaving Arché to close the door and shake her head with fondness. It is an easy thing to climb back into bed and let a still sleeping Lenora spoon her back to sleep.

When evening comes, Alta is waiting downstairs with a full spread of food, as well as Raavi and Leahi.

"So he goes 'I'm a shifter mage, it's fine', and jumped off the cliff!" Leahi is saying, to an Alta so enthralled by the story that they are holding a drumstick halfway to their mouth, entirely forgotten. "He turned into a crab. And then he hit the water, and snapped straight back to himself, because he was fucking *dead*. We had to fish his body out of the bay, get a volunteer register for anyone who was willing to sacrifice a bit of lifeforce to bring him back, and give Aunty Tau the best fish we had for a week to make sure she'd be able to even do the ritual. He's still doing community service to pay back everyone that helped, and Aunty never lets him hear the end of it."

"I... I have so many questions," Arché says, bewildered.

"I'm not sure I want the answers," Lenora says with a shake of her head. "What are you guys doing together, anyway?"

"Your friend saw the resemblance, and joined us," Alta explains. "So, how are things?"

Arché and Lenora slide into the booth and settle themselves, listing their assets as the hunter they poached from the enemy, and the mage sitting next to them.

"That's all," Arché says with a sigh.

"Right." Alta makes a face. "Yeah, it's a tricky one, isn't it?"

"We can't exactly put up a poster on a town notice board," Lenora says with a sigh into her wine. "For... you know. Lots of reasons."

"Of course." Alta presses their fingertip against the tip of their nose and purses their lips. "I certainly wasn't able to recruit anyone who wasn't already following me around." They shoulder-check Raavi, who giggles. "Still. Every person counts. It's something. What about you two? Are you doing alright?"

"We're great," Lenora says with a bright smile.

"Uh." Arché hesitates, realising they haven't talked since Arché was in a spot of despair, sure Lenora would never love her back. When, after all that, Lenora realised and confessed her own feelings only days later. An odd laugh falls from her lips. "Things are really good, yeah."

Alta cocks an eyebrow. "Good?"

"We have a lot to catch up on," Arché tells them.

"Well, we could grab some drinks and take them up to one of the rooms," Alta suggests. "Just some us time. I'm not against alcohol at this time of the evening if you don't tell your mother it was my idea."

Arché grins. "Sounds good." She looks to Lenora. "Will you be okay here?"

Lenora's attention is torn between Leahi and the stage, where some musicians are bowing and making their exit. "Yeah. I... I think we might see if we can play. Up there."

"That's a great idea," Arché says, squeezing her hand. "Good luck."

With a bottle of wine in hand, and laughter on their lips, daughter and parent traipse to the room Arché is sharing with Lenora.

"You seem better," Alta says, as they pour two glasses and hand one to Arché.

"I am," Arché says, before adding, "in some ways."

"Catch me up, then!"

Arché feels a blush creep up her neck at the prospect of speaking on Lenora in any way. Which is absurd. What is she, sixteen?

"Well... it turns out that Lenora *could* like me back," Arché says sheepishly. "I mean. She does. We're together."

Alta whoops so enthusiastically that their punch to the air sends wine flying everywhere, as they did it with the hand holding the wine glass.

"Oh, I'll pay for the cleaning," they say with a flap of the wine glass which spills even more wine. "This is too important!"

Arché can only laugh. Her teenage attempt at romance hadn't lasted long enough to involve announcing it to Alta while it was ongoing, only as something Alta missed. In a way, Arché has been waiting her whole life to have a romance worthy enough to divulge to her much more romantic parent.

Alta's hands take Arché's shoulders so abruptly that Arché can only wonder where the wine glass vanished to. Alta's eyes, near manic, bore into Arché's.

"Are you happy?" they ask. "Does she make you happy?"

Is Arché happy? Well, no, not quite. But the second question, thanks to Alta's lack of a verbal filter, is easier.

"She makes me really happy," Arché whispers. "I... I understand it now. You and Kalé. The songs. The books."

Alta lands an enthusiastic kiss to Arché's forehead. "Good. You deserve every happiness, however it comes. It killed me to see your heart in pieces, when it deserved to be cherished. She's a good one. She'd better not hurt you, or we'll have impolite words."

It takes an impressive manner and unique energy to make 'impolite words' sound like a true threat. But then, they deflate and sit down to pour themself a new glass of wine.

"So how long has all that been going on?"

Arché gives an abridged version of their journey from the ruin. She cannot bring herself to mention how it was comparing herself to Kalé that cut deep when it came to Tunvra, but the story just about makes sense without that detail. And when she reaches the full moon, she skips over it as if nothing happened at all.

Anything she tells Alta, she must be prepared to tell Kalé. And once she has admitted to the transgression, it is a confession that cannot be taken back.

They speak of Lenora's latest feats of magic, of her fearsome power now that she has all that should have been hers from the start.

"It feels like something clicked with her, as soon as she got it back," Arché says. "It's been so good to see."

Alta nods. "There's nothing worse than watching the one you adore, suffering," Alta says.

Arché agrees automatically, but the look in Alta's eyes when they utter it has Arché wondering what suffering Kalé once endured to put such a fire in her spouse now. A question for another day.

They discuss Alta's research, and the magic which they and Raavi have managed to cultivate for an ambush. Something that will bloom plants from the ground to restrain their enemies—truly something that might turn the tide.

"You seem tired," Alta observes, once they're three glasses of wine in.

"The full moon took a lot out of me," Arché says. That part is honest, at least. "It's been hard, being away from the others. It doesn't feel right."

"That makes perfect sense," Alta says, eyes shining with sympathy and the buzz of the wine. "You're doing so well, Arché.'

Arché nearly chokes on her gulp of wine. "I—thanks."

The words ring hollow and she doesn't mean to cringe at them. But sure enough, Alta's brow furrows.

"What?" they ask.

"Nothing."

"Arché Kalésen, don't you dare bullshit me when something clearly isn't nothing, I've *never* seen you flinch like that."

Arché hasn't seen Alta properly stern, much. Or ever. For all their diminutive height, Alta commands a presence that has Arché frozen.

There is no attempt to spin more partial truths. Nor does Arché crumple. She simply stares at Alta with quiet sheepishness that cannot take the leap into courageous honesty.

Alta's shoulders drop, their head tilting to the side. "Arché, whatever it is, you can tell me," they say, much more softly. "I'm here for you. I always will be."

"I know," Arché says, standing up and putting her wine glass down on the room's desk. "I'm going to see Lenora and find out how their show went. You can come, if you like."

It's too abrupt. But her heart is hammering against her ribs and she needs to get out of this room now.

Out the door. Down the stairs. Around each flight until she reaches the ground floor of the tavern. It's even more crowded than when she left, everyone's faces turned to a man sitting with a lute and strumming a cheerful song about sunlight over rolling hills.

On Arché's first sweep of the room, she doesn't see Lenora or Leahi. On the second pass, there is still no sign of them. Strange. Arché tries to ignore the small stone of worry in her gut, as Lenora is beyond capable and can surely go to the bathroom without Arché needing to get frantic.

But there's no sign of them in the bathrooms either, or outside the front of the building. Arché swallows, willing herself to stay calm, and hurries back up the stairs to Leahi's room.

Three knocks. No answer. As Arché dashes back to the stairs, unsure of whether to seek help or begin questioning people on the ground floor, she nearly runs into Alta.

"Arché, what—"

"I can't find them," Arché says, and she had been doing such a marvellous job of not panicking, but having to say the words drags something out of her by the throat, a visceral thing that nearly chokes her. "Alta, I don't know were they could—"

"Have you asked if anyone's seen them?" Alta suggests, matching Arché's serious energy in a split second.

"That was my next move."

"I'll check they're not with Raavi, and meet you at the bar."

"Okay. Thank you."

They head downstairs and begin making their way through the crowd, asking after the two women with the musical instruments.

"Oh, yeah, they were great!" A pretty woman with orange skin and pointed ears lights up at the mention of their description. "I think I saw them step outside with a few fans."

Arché heads back outside and breathes in deeply. Lenora's scent comes in strong, but at an intensity which is confusing. Not so strong as to indicate her being near, but instead, a remnant.

Something dark smears the dirt a few feet away. Something she'd completely missed on her first glance outside. When her fingers touch it, it is half-dried and smells of iron and Lenora. The world dims at the edges as Arché stares at it.

"Arché? What is that?" Alta asks from somewhere behind her.

"Blood," Arché says, and her voice comes out all wrong. Flat. "Lenora's gone, and her blood is on the ground."

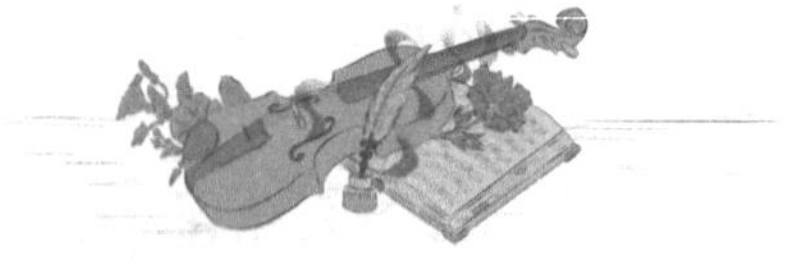

CHAPTER 33
LENORA

Performing on stage is not something Lenora had ever been interested in at home. She's enough of a spectacle just by existing. But here? Where no one knows who or what she is, only how her violin sounds? It's something special, and Lenora will cherish it forever.

Leahi is an incredible partner in playing; together they whirl around the stage and let Leahi's magical manipulation of some of the notes wow the audience. Trills not quite possible with only two players, or only two hands. Lengthening of notes that shouldn't be possible with mortal breath capacity. It is clearly not Leahi's first time playing with her power for musical effect.

By the time they step off the stage, Lenora is near giddy with the rush of it all.

"Wow," someone says, approaching them with a friend at their side. "You two were amazing."

"Oh", Lenora says. Heat comes to her cheeks. "Thanks."

They are a pair who look like they might be siblings or cousins, with ginger hair and pale skin, but bright green freckles that match the colour of their eyes. One is a man dressed in a simple tunic and leggings, while the woman next to him has a larger jacket which obscures most of her form.

She had been the speaker, but now her relative rushes forward to shake Lenora's hand.

"Our friend was listening from outside," he says. "He's really shy around crowds and lots of noise, so he doesn't like to come in. But we'd love to surprise him and bring you out so he can tell you how much he loved it. Do you think you could come and say hello?"

Lenora glances at Leahi to get a second opinion, and Leahi gives a relaxed shrug and nod.

"Sure," Lenora tells them.

They step out into the cool night air, letting its freshness wash over them in comparison to the tavern's stuffy heat. Many bodies make for an intense atmosphere; Lenora can hardly blame some music enjoyers for not wanting to come in.

"Oh, it's nice out," Lenora breathes. "Where's your friend?"

"Just up here."

Up ahead, someone dashes forward, and the world goes silent. Not just quiet, but silent. Truly silent, where Lenora sees Leahi's mouth moving and hears no words, where the buzz of voices back in the tavern vanish in an instant along with laughter from down the street.

Alarmed, Lenora looks around for answers. Under her feet, a sigil glows a bright yellow.

Oh no.

Sure enough, when she lifts her head, it is not one 'friend' outside the tavern but three more, making for an imposing group of five who are all armed just a bit too well. One is a lizard wildblood with bright orange scales. He's dressed in simple robes and has a wand drawn. A woman with short dark hair is striding forward, a warhammer resting on her shoulders ready to be drawn properly. Behind them, a blonde human little person with a high ponytail and a crossbow stands ready to fire.

The ginger relatives reveal their own weapons—the woman opens her jacket to reveal a collection of tiny throwing thrives, while the man enters a stance which says his weapons are his fists.

And Lenora and Leahi are trapped in a silence field. Being able to speak is a major part of casting most magic; Disciplined types like Lenora's mother need the rhythm of the sound to help them influence the magic imbued in the world itself, while Gifted mages must call out to those who give them power. Innate mages such as Lenora and Leahi don't *have* to speak to use their magic, but it is one of the most common methods to assist control.

But Leahi is a sonic mage. So long as they are encompassed by this silence, her friend cannot wield her magic at all.

Lenora steps between their attackers and Leahi, and summons shadow claws to her hands with only a thought. Her unconventional magical nature and education may just be what saves them now.

She might not be able to hear what their assailants say to each other, but she knows cursing when she sees it, and grins.

The crossbow bolt fires, and Lenora barely dodges in time, and by then the others are on her. Lenora extends her claws into something closer to lashes, long enough to keep some of them back, but the woman with the warhammer pushes through and knocks Lenora to the ground.

All at once, and unpleasantly, Lenora understands how those who go up against Arché feel. Some warriors are true powerhouses of nature.

But then, so is Lenora. When the hammer comes crashing down towards her middle, Lenora turns the lashes to thick talons as long as swords, ones she can cross to stop the hammer in its path.

The force of it slams into the claws, through her arm, and up to her shoulder hard enough to make her cry out. A consequence for opposing someone of such superior strength.

Glancing back, Lenora sees a crossbow bolt hit Leahi in the shoulder.

Without the physical ability to force the warrior off her, Lenora will have to try something else, something she knows she *can* do but has never consciously done. Reaching inside herself for her well of power, Lenora seizes her determination not to lose this fight, to get back to Arché so they can save their people.

With all of that, Lenora unleashes her magic in an explosion of pure shadow. She'd not been conscious the last time she'd unleashed it, and from the ground with a skewed view it is near impossible to fathom how it is *her* that sends all five attackers flying back.

But all that matters is that she is free to jump to her feet, to catch her breath, free to—

Free to see Leahi sprawled on the ground with the others, coughing up blood.

There had been no allies to get caught in the crossfire last time. But this is not a case where Lenora's magic could possibly have discriminated friend from foe. Guilt floods in hot and fast, despite no blame in Leahi's grimace.

The silence is gone—the mage's focus on the spell broken by the blast, no doubt. The voices flood in even as they all scramble to recover.

"What the fuck was that," one of the redheads gasps. "This is only *one* of them?!"

Lenora shouldn't laugh at such an awful time. But the idea of herself and Arché being so powerful is so sweet that she might forever remember its taste.

"We'd better end this before she gets here," Lenora says with a flash of her fangs, as there can be no question of this being targeted for a reason. "For your sake."

The one with the knives rolls towards Leahi and grabs her in a chokehold, a knife appearing in a flash and pressing against Leahi's skin until red appears.

"Then you can come with us, now, or your friend gets it," she says, scowling.

"Sara, we're not killing anyone," the mage says with horror.

Sara sighs. "Yeah, but she didn't know that until you *said* it, Varei." Instead of doing anything to Leahi's neck, she drives the knife down into Leahi's leg, making her cry out.

"Leave her alone!" Lenora shouts, and she leaps upon them with her shadow claws again drawn, slashing at Sara with furious desperation.

The moment she gets close, the strongwoman seizes her by the arms and forces them behind her back, pulling her back from the others before she can make contact.

Lenora tries to unleash more magic, another expulsion for the sake of freedom, but there is no well left to draw from. It is all but empty, able to only maintain her claws and little else, and cannot help the whine of worry that leaves her.

"Are you going to play nice?" the large woman asks.

Lenora snarls, fangs fully beared, prepared to find a place to bite at any cost. But then a piece of cloth is pressed over her mouth and it smells odd. The world swims and goes dark.

When consciousness returns, tightness at Lenora's wrists and ankles speaks to bindings, while rocking motions and the rhythmic sound of horse hoofs point to being in a cart. There is nothing to see; tight fabric covers her eyes and won't budge no matter how Lenora wriggles.

While Lenora doesn't need to speak, her magic does require sight, so that she can see where her creations will manifest. They've taken solid precautions against her power getting the better of them.

It takes a few moments for everything to really sink in. The cart. The binds, the blindfold. They lost. They were taken, or at least Lenora was—she has to listen carefully for several moments to make out the laboured breathing of someone else nearby. Leahi is likely with her.

On the other side of the wooden wall, their captors are talking. Checking in on each other, making plans for taking turns driving to avoid stopping for as long as possible—something about ensuring they aren't followed, on top of their prior measures.

Lenora can only pray they are wrong. That they've overlooked something. But without knowing what they've done, she has no way to know Arché's chances of an easy pursuit.

But one thing is for sure. Arché sure as anything won't stop until she has Lenora back.

CHAPTER 34
ARCHÉ

For one single day, the storm inside Arché had almost calmed. Now it floods in, everything wrong, all of it. Blood boils under her skin and the world darkens at the edges, and it takes everything she has to breathe and calm the beast inside her. The feral thing wanting to rage because its beloved is gone. Beside her, Alta is silent, watching.

"Arché?" Alta asks. "We'll find her. Someone must have seen something."

"Exactly," Arché says, nodding while her fingers flex impatiently at her sides. "They can't have gotten far. I'll catch them."

A flute sits on the cobbles, not too far from the blood stain. Alta picks it up, murmurs Leahi's name, and tucks it into their pocket.

There's no one on the streets. No one at all, no matter where Arché strides or turns. That alone is odd, and leaves no choice but to knock on doors in the hopes of finding out if anyone saw anything out their windows.

But no one answers. Arché tries to swallow a scream of frustration and instead inhales as deep as she can. The smallest trace of Lenora leads her towards the edge of town, Alta still following in her wake.

"Why is no one here?" Arché asks. "They can't all be asleep, it's nowhere near midnight yet—" She holds back a scream, a shout to demand them to show themselves and explain what the fuck is going on. Instead, a sob rocks her body.

How easily things begin to crumble, without Lenora. Perhaps Arché has only been strong as her partner, and not in her own right.

"We'll find her," Alta says, putting their hand on her shoulder.

Arché throws her hands up with frustration. "We don't know *anything* about who took her! That's not a great start—"

A door near them opens. A man pokes his head out, age painting his hair and beard with grey, the wrinkles near his eyes creasing further out of concern.

"There was five of them," he says, voice hushed as he beckons them over with his hand. "They were shoving money at everyone down this way, telling them to stay inside and keep their mouths shut. Intimidating shit, with those girls slung over their shoulders. But they're gone now, they ain't gonna be back for me. They went out the north way. Said they had caravans to catch up with."

Fuck.

"Thank you," Arché tells him earnestly, ready to cry with gratitude. "It's not what I wanted to hear but... it's what I needed. Thank you."

"I hope you catch them," he says. "There's a stable just by the gate. Should be plenty of horses free."

Hope blooms in Arché's chest and she stammers out another thanks before taking off down the street. Alta protests and follows, their shorter legs struggling to keep up.

The stable is exactly where the man said, the lights still on but starting to be extinguished right as Arché skids to a halt at the entrance.

"Hello?" she calls, striding in. "Sorry, I need two horses."

"Three," Alta says, through gasping breaths. "Raavi's back at the tavern, I can't leave her behind."

"Three horses," Arché says, as the stablemaster moves into the light. She's a tall, limber woman with a nose more like a cat's than a human's, and fur thick along her arms.

"I'm sorry, I can't help you," she says, even though there are at least half a dozen horses in the stalls, grazing on hay.

Arché pauses before answering, making sure her next words are civil and not as clipped as her instinct would make them. "What do you mean?"

"Every horse here is paid for, I can't lease them to anyone." The woman makes a face. "I'm sorry. You'll have to try the next town."

"That's not an option, I need them now, my—" Arché chokes as she fails to find the right word. She's never needed one to explain Lenora's relationship to her, because what word could capture it? "My partner, and my friend, they've been kidnapped."

"Oh," the stablemaster says, her face falling. "So that's why they paid for all the horses."

"It was *them*?!" Arché clutches at her bun frantically. "Please, I'll pay what I can to match it for three of them, or anything I can afford—"

"I'm sorry, I can't break contracts like that." Genuine remorse covers the woman's angular face. "My whole business relies on my integrity. This place is all I have."

"Fuck," Arché says, tears stinging the corners of her eyes. "Okay. Thanks anyway."

With that she strides out past Alta and into the street, her mind already racing to the next idea and seizing it with desperate hands.

"We'll wait until she closes up," Arché whispers once Alta joins her. "Then we can take what we need, leave some money. Her integrity remains intact but we'll be able to follow—"

"Arché, we can't get in trouble with the law, we have so few allies as it is," Alta says, shaking their head. "The Stag Battalion is not to be crossed. Their reach is too wide. Making enemies of them is the only thing we could do to make this whole thing worse."

"Right," Arché scoffs. "Everyone else in Kanin gets protection from things like theft, but when it comes to *murder* and *kidnapping,* we're on our own. Because that's fair."

Alta stares for several moments, their finger coming to stroke the bridge of their nose. "...you're right. It's not. Maybe we can do something with that. Concord is part of Kanin as much as anywhere else, even if the Stag Battalion don't know about it. If they were informed, they obligated to help us like anyone else—"

"Or they'd hear about what we are and run a mile," Arché says. The spark of hope in her chest is dead. The only thing remaining now is an awful hopelessness, a lack of belief so hollow it threatens to consume her. "Let's be realistic. We're on our own. Again. A researcher with a bow and some magic, their assistant, and a werewolf who's going to fail at saving her people long before she gets a chance to fail at leading them."

The hollow in her chest is like a stone. She is ready to sink with it, to lie down and never get up.

"What?" Alta's voice is sharper than Arché has ever heard it, and Arché turns away to avoid their eyes. "What did you just say?"

"It doesn't matter," Arché says, wrapping her arms around herself. "We can't catch them. And we can't save the others without Lenora."

There is a long silence, punctuated by the eerie emptiness of the street and the stillness of the night air.

"So... you're giving up?" Alta asks, incredulous. "That's it?"

"Well, if you like I can run in, outnumbered and outmatched, and at least die trying," Arché says. "I suppose that's better than sitting around."

Alta grabs Arché by the shoulders and forces her to meet their eyes. "What's gotten into you? You never talk like this?"

"How would you know?" Arché snaps. "I've never faced anything like this, and even if I had, odds are you wouldn't have been there to hear me talking about it."

It's cruel. It's unfair.

"Did that make you feel better?" Alta asks. They are calm, but something sharper sits beneath the surface of their words. "Pretending to be angry at me for something you've never blamed me for in your life."

"No," Arché admits, looking at the ground instead of her parent because she simply cannot bear it. "I'm just... tired. Of everything being shit. Of myself. Of feeling weak and useless and pathetic."

She doesn't intend to say any of it, as honest as it is, but whatever remaining strength she'd been using to keep a mask of resolve in place has apparently been shattered by the blow of Lenora's kidnapping. And while her personal dig had bounced off Alta like a light wind, these words almost stagger them.

"Arché," they breathe, so soft and with such pain in their eyes that Arché nearly regrets it. But that would involve not believing it, and she cannot help that she does.

"I'm sorry," Arché whispers. "I can't do it. I can't be like her, I just can't. I'm not strong enough."

Alta pulls her into a tight embrace, and Arché clutches them with everything she has left in the world, tears soaking into their robe. It feels so good to be held, held by someone so important who has always been able to make bad things go away. But nothing has ever been like this, and even Alta for all their knowledge cannot fix this.

"We need to talk, before we can make a plan," Alta tells her. "You're not getting anything done like this. Come on, baby."

It's a blurry walk back into the centre of town to the tavern, inside and up the stairs, into the room Arché and Lenora had been sharing. The only detour is to the bar to order tea to be sent up to them. Once it arrives, Arché sits on the bed, numb but for the ache of everything.

"Tea always helps," Alta says. "Come and sit with me." They lay cushions on opposite sides of the tea tray, on the floor.

Arché does as she is bid and sits, taking the teacup and letting the warmth seep into her hands through the porcelain.

Alta takes their own tea and sips once before grimacing from the heat. "So. Don't really know where the fuck to start. I understand being worried beyond belief about Lenora being taken. But all the rest, that's not about Lenora. That's not even about the people we're rescuing, or these Crusaders. It's about you. Horrible things about yourself and you believe every word of it. Where the fuck has that come from?"

"Well, I couldn't exactly say *sorry everyone but I think I'm going to do an awful job of my birthright and I'm going to be a huge disappointment*," Arché says, shaking her head. "It would have really brought down family dinners."

Alta narrows their eyes. "Arché."

"I thought something would click," Arché says, dropping the feeble attempt at humour. "I thought there would be a moment where I felt like a grown up, and the feelings would go away. And then no one would need to know I was so worried. But it kept... not coming... and then we were attacked. And instead of a moment where everything came together, everything fell apart."

Alta sighs so sadly that perhaps Arché isn't imagining the shine of tears in the corners of their eyes. "Arché... that moment never really comes. You watch those around you, and you think one day you'll be sure. You have to keep pretending you know what you're doing until you sort of do. But you never feel as ready as you think you'll be."

"Maybe for you," Arché says. "But Kalé gets everything right."

"No, she doesn't," Alta replies, so matter-of-factly that Arché wants to hurl her teacup across the room.

"I don't need your pedanticism right now," Arché says instead. "She's the best leader in the whole town. Everyone looks to her, and even in the middle of the attack she was the one getting everything done, making the plan so I could get out to you and save the others on the way—"

"Yes, she's very good at what she does—"

"Exactly, and one day if she passes the reins to me, everyone is going to be disappointed because I'll never be half the leader she is," Arché says. "She could have convinced almost anyone to join this cause. Won every battle. Found a way to convince the stablehand. Everything I couldn't do. And she never would have—"

Arché can't bring herself to say it. The shame burns in her chest and throat, and she puts the teacup back on the tray out of certainty that any attempt to drink will only bring it back up.

"Never would have what?"

What's the point of hiding anything now? Arché exhales for several moments, letting go of any remaining reservations about holding Alta's good opinion.

"Lost control," Arché whispers. "I lost control, this full moon just gone. She taught me everything, and I thought that was the *one* thing I couldn't fuck up because she taught me too well, but I did. And now if I ever make it to her still breathing, I'll have to look at her and tell her that I broke our one fucking rule. Her heir is a disgrace."

"Fucking abyss below and gods above, Arché," Alta says, their hand covering their eyes. "What happened?"

"I got overwhelmed, and upset, and I felt so *alone*," Arché explains, unsure why she's bothering. "I completely lost myself. The trees paid for it."

Alta grimaces. "I'm sorry that happened. And that will be... a conversation you and Kalé need to have. But you're under absurd pressure, and not in a usual Concord situation. I'm sure that will be taken into consideration, and you're obviously taking it seriously already."

"Of course I am, but that's what I mean, I'm just not... good enough."

"Yes, you are." Alta's eyes are fierce, more so than Arché has ever seen. "One mistake, even a bad one, doesn't define you forever. All of the leaders have made mistakes. Some even together, which is worse."

"Sure," Arché says, rolling her eyes. "Like kicking you out of town meetings?"

"Exactly that one, actually," Alta replies, pausing to take a gulp of tea. "Remember why? Because I told them they needed to prepare for a catastrophe instead of blaming it on Lenora's magic? You're talking about thinking you're a failure because you're struggling to save everyone. Because, what, you think your mother's never made a serious mistake in her life?"

Arché cannot help the cynical chuckle that leaves her lips. "You're trying to tell me that not listening to you is her *serious mistake*—"

"Yes, actually—"

"And what the fuck were the consequences of that? A singular marital argument—"

"Our people's deaths are on *her* head!" Alta says it sharp, guilt flashing through them almost right after. Arché cannot help how her jaw drops. "It's her fault, and I'll never say it because she must know now. But because she and the others didn't listen to me, the attack on Concord was successful, and we lost Rohan and Nikos and the others."

Arché tries to put the pieces together. "How the fuck could they have prevented—"

"They could have tried to do literally anything," Alta says, and there is an odd, old hurt rising to the surface in them that is ill-suited to their usual unshakeable confidence in themself. "I told them to prepare, that Lenora's magic meant something was headed for Concord and it would spell disaster. They decided to do nothing, decided to kick me out of meetings instead of listen. And now, some of them are dead and some of them have lost their kids. And believe me, I wish I'd been wrong."

"But that was a group decision, that wasn't just Kalé."

"I don't give a fuck about the group," Alta retorts, their voice catching. "I just know I pleaded with my wife to listen to my instincts, my evidence. And I remember how she didn't listen. She chose wrong, and now here we are, trying to work out how to fix it and save her. Save the people *she* was supposed to protect. So don't you dare tell me you aren't good enough. Don't tell me you're not brave enough. You're out here alone, making your own decisions, choosing the impossible fight. And you're holding yourself to impossible standards, trying to be the best you can be for them all. I'm so proud of you, but you need to let yourself breathe. Each mistake is a lesson. We can do this, but you need to believe it, and you need to know that none of this is your fault. This is a mess you're cleaning up, and you're going to do it because it's the right thing to do, because it's our people and our family never gives up. Not ever."

Two seconds and one spilled teapot later, Arché has launched herself at Alta and captured them in the tightest hug possible. She shakes, so many emotions and revelations battling inside her, and this time when something shatters it doesn't feel like a defeat.

It's the illusion of a perfect, infallible mother and leader. The person she could never be, exposed as a twisted fiction of her own making. An idea on a pedestal, now knocked down.

The real woman, the inspiration, is as flawed as everyone else. Arché will never blame her for the mistake Alta has revealed, but she will certainly never forget, and knows she will spend nights in the future wondering how her mother could have possibly ignored such pleas.

"I'm so sorry she didn't listen," Arché whispers to Alta. "That must have been awful. When Lenora didn't understand the—what happened on the full moon, I felt so fucking lost. And you and Kalé have been together so much longer. I'm so sorry."

"It can be hard," Alta says. "But relationships are practiced and worked on like everything else. It's worth it. We both have women we love, taken from us."

They pull back, face now again calm and determined, as it ought to be.

"Let's bring them home."

CHAPTER 35
LENORA

THERE ARE STORIES OF adventurers even in Concord. Skilled groups of higher calibre than mere mercenaries, usually composed of unique and complementary skill sets. Lenora never paid them much mind, as with the skills of those in Concord, adventurers would never have a purpose there even if they did find it.

Lenora certainly never thought she would find herself prisoner to any. They avoid conversing and ignore Leahi's demands to let Lenora feed off her, at least for the first three days.

Not too long after Lenora's head begins spinning from malnourishment, around night four or five if Lenora is keeping track, it must begin to show. A warm neck is shoved against her mouth.

"It's okay," Leahi whispers. "I trust you."

Lenora wishes she didn't have to, but is grateful all the same. To Leahi's credit, she makes no noise at all when bitten.

They are allowed this chance around every three nights. At first, Lenora had been sure Arché would be right on their heels, able to catch them within hours. Or at least days. But then, on what might be the fifth night, she hears the adventurers discussing their apparently successful tactic of renting all the horses in town for a week. With that, Lenora finds herself having to come to terms with the fact that they may reach the caravans first. Is she more valuable alive, or less of a threat dead?

The only comfort is that she might be back with her people soon, who surely have been suffering an even worse thirst. Perhaps someone will make the right mistake at the right time, and Lenora can do something that will make a difference.

There's far too much time to feel Arché's absence. It's actually worse than the thirst, as Lenora has become so accustomed to Arché's companionship and support. The words they would exchange about what they can accomplish if together.

It's as if the universe heard them, laughed, and planned a cruel joke to bring them to this. Together, they are formidable enough to tackle anything. Being apart is the true test.

She's had faith in Arché from almost the very start. This is different, a trial worse than they had imagined, but Arché will surely rise to it like everything else. While Arché has some doubts in herself, Lenora could not fathom Arché letting anyone down when it really counts.

In the meantime, Lenora will weather whatever comes. For someone who has felt alone most of her life, Lenora is only now realising she has never truly been so. She had Nikos, and the moment he was taken from her, she had Arché instead.

Leahi is here, but it is not the same. Lenora cannot see her because of the blindfold, and Leahi is a friend, but not a partner the way things are done in Concord. Not what either of her wonderful lycans have been to her. Lenora must stand on her own feet, her own merit.

For the first time Lenora can remember, she has no doubts in her ability. She is the chosen Shadow of Concord, and she *will* survive long enough to save everyone.

CHAPTER 36
ARCHÉ

IF THERE IS A medal to be awarded for adapting to a crisis in record time, it ought to go to Raavi. The academic assistant listens to a rapidfire recap from Alta with flawless focus and begins packing up her things less than a minute in, all without taking her eyes from Alta's face.

"We can barter for horses on the highway," is the first thing she says when Alta finishes and finally stops for breath. "Whoever we pass, we can try to buy their horses from them. Someone might say yes."

Arché could kiss her. If several extenuating factors were not in place, that is.

"The Stag Battalion is worth trying," Alta says on their way out of the tavern. "They patrol the highway, staggered every other day or so, if I recall correctly. We should pass some."

"I'll take anything at this point," Arché says. What is there left to fear from daywalkers now?

Sleep would usually be the priority as the sun rises, but anxiety runs too high for anyone to bring up the matter of resting. They embark on their journey north with little concern for exhaustion just yet.

Walking in the sun is pleasant, the warmth a refreshing change, and yet it feels wrong without Lenora's grumbling.

They walk through the day, and the night, and by the time the next sunrise comes, they are quick to make camp and collapse after establishing watches to keep an eye out for horses to barter for.

While on her watch, a familiar scent hits Arché's nose, alerting her to Tunvra's presence a moment before she turns and sees him striding up.

"Evening," he says, before sitting on the ground near some of the packs. As if no care in the world, he props one foot on the opposite knee and begins fiddling with his crossbow.

Arché maps his journey in her head, correlating it with Lenora's kidnapping. Instead of greeting him, far more important words leave her mouth.

"Did you see her? Lenora?"

Tunvra blinks, the rest of his face otherwise still while his fingers twirl a crossbow bolt with unusual vigor. "So I wasn't imagining it, then. I hoped I was wrong. But I'm usually not."

"So you passed them."

"On my way back to you, yes. And they have Leahi too?"

"Yes." Arché begins making coffee so she has something more pleasant to focus on than him, or the general reality of the day. "I'm guessing you didn't draw attention to yourself."

"Obviously not. I'm not going to win one-against-five. There was no chance of a rescue."

Arché would love to argue, but knows that he's right. She wishes he'd apologise anyway, but just as her nature can never forgive him for his lack-luster morals, his surely would never apologise for logical self-preservation. It would take significant power to subdue Lenora and Leahi together.

When Arché says nothing, Tunvra continues.

"Adventurer types. Too hard to calculate the power of groups like that at a glance. Individual ability can vary so much. You and the other one are proof enough of that."

It shouldn't irk her so much that he doesn't use Lenora's name. Then again, if he uttered it now she might have wanted to snatch it from his tongue. Perhaps it is for the best.

"Can we catch up to them? Get them before they reach the camp?" Arché asks.

"Not unless you get horses very soon. Even then... hard to say."

"Alright."

With that concluded, they are saved from having to converse again, and the only time Arché has to hear his voice is when Alta manages to corner him on the next leg of walking to pick his brain on obscure details of crossbow care. His bemusement at Alta's manner makes it considerably more bearable.

It's another night and day before the sound of horse hoofs pricks Arché's ears while she's on watch. Her hands are occupied with her carving of Andreas which is almost finished, but her ears never let her down.

Approaching are two curious figures in armour atop mounts. Their armour is dark green, with decorative antler stylings on the pauldrons.

"You alright? Very early to be crashed out," one of them says, eyeing where Tunvra is curled up on a bedroll in the open.

The inquirer is a wildblood man with feline features, going without a helmet likely because of the fluffy mane surrounding his head.

"Yes, we uh, pushed ourselves a bit hard," Arché says, stifling a horrendous yawn. "Are you with the Stag Battalion?" Surely, based on the armour, they are, but Arché never actually thought to ask how to recognise them.

The two strangers exchange a glance.

"You new to Kanin?" the wildblood asks.

Not the best start, in trying to get their help due to mutual community. Arché tries to hide her wince, and instead calls Alta's name back towards the tent.

"Um, not exactly," she says. "This might be a strange question, but have you passed a large train of caravans?"

Another glance shared, then a matching pair of nods.

"Yeah, a week or two back," the wildblood says. "Sounded like they had some monsters in there. Not a very talkative bunch—"

"And weird fucking clothes," his friend adds, her voice low and soft like a breeze through treetops. The comment makes the other snort.

"Yeah, Ish here wondered if it was some sort of circus we hadn't heard about." He grins, showing pointed feline teeth. "I'm Dell, by the way."

"Arché." It's difficult to even get her own name out. "It's—it's not a circus... you couldn't tell what was inside?"

"No, we couldn't, and they wouldn't talk," says the wildblood named Dell. "You sound like you know more than we do."

Alta is stirring, beginning to come out of the tent, but Arché cannot afford to look back when she has this chance to get the battalion to listen.

"It's people," Arché blurts out. "Innocent, kidnapped people. They're being taken to be—well, they said *judged* but it really sounded like *sacrificed*—"

"Woah, what the fuck," Dell says. "Are you sure? How do you know?"

Alta is up, rousing Tunvra and Raavi instead of getting involved. Ish and Dell are still focused on Arché.

"One of them told me," Arché says. How to explain it? "Gods, I know how this will sound, but—there's a town in Kanin you've never heard of, because we hid it on purpose to keep ourselves safe. Then these people found us and attacked us, and now we need help but no one knows we exist. So it's four of us against all of them, and we need help."

"A hidden town?" Ish repeats. It's not completely disbelieving, just bemused.

"I can corroborate," Alta interrupts, striding forward and pulling a roll of papers from their robes. "Professor Alta Galan, Doctorate of Arcane Theory and Abstract Application. Double major. University of Orsun trained. I've been a resident of the town of Concord intermittently over the last twenty-five years, fifteen of them consecutive."

Ish reaches for the papers and glances over them before nodding at Dell and handing them back. Dell runs a hand through his mane, looking between them all.

"If what you're saying is true, you should come to the camp further north," he says. "My uncle is the commander there. If Kanin citizens are in those caravans, he'll want to hear about it. I'll get you to repeat this all for him."

There's something to the suggestion Arché cannot put her finger on. His dark eyes hold hers, scrutinising her reaction. What could he be searching for? She has no time to worry, when he is *listening* and offering help. She'll take any catch, any condition.

"Do you really think he'll help?" Arché asks, trying not to sound too eager. "Of course we'll see him, if he'll see us."

"He'll have to," Raavi says, coming to stand next to Alta, her eyes alight with something new. "Hello. I'm Raavi. Bachelor of Arcane Theory, studying with the professor here. I just realised we've been looking at this from only one angle. Those Crusaders, the kidnappers... they're from Izirm. If we don't get this sorted fast, and clean, we're going to have a diplomatic crisis on our hands."

"Fucking abyss, they're from Izirm?" Ish's hand hits her forehead. "That's just what we need."

"They're fanatical Everflame worshippers," Arché adds. "Beyond the point of reason and mercy, in our experience."

A dark look settles on Dell's face. "It sounds like we'd better get you to my uncle right away. Do you know why they targeted your town? Especially if it was hidden."

Arché works very hard to keep her face composed. "I definitely think the reason it was hidden in its founding is connected to why it was targeted. I promise, it was unprovoked. It's exactly what we were afraid of all along."

It's not quite an answer. It's also not a lie. Ish and Dell are doing a remarkable job of taking it all in, but Arché does not expect them to be oblivious to how little information her last response has given.

Dell holds her gaze a moment longer than necessary, but asks no further questions of her, instead turning to Tunvra.

"Anything to add, sir?" he asks, as Tunvra has done nothing but silently sit on his bedroll and clean his boots.

Tunvra throws something to Ish, who catches it with astounding reflexes. "I can testify to being under the Izirm group's employ, sent to target escaped members of the town's leadership. That is, until I was persuaded through financial means to lend my skills to the side of the rescue instead."

"Registered adventurer," Ish says to Dell before throwing a small engraved medal back to Tunvra. "Useful testimony of the Izirm group's intent."

Raavi coughs. "If the Stag Battalion can help the people of Concord now, in their time of need... I'm sure the town could volunteer some members for the Battalion, so that it's a fair community exchange."

"I'll make sure of it," Arché agrees.

Dell waves a hand dismissively. "Let's focus on saving your people before we get to that. We'll escort you back up north, then. There'll be a gap in the route, but we can inform the next patrol."

Ish nods, her face impossible to read through the helmet.

"Thank you," Arché says, willing herself not to cry. "I really didn't know what to expect. Not everyone would help strangers they've never heard of."

"Plenty of Kanin citizens are strangers," Dell says with a warm smile. Along with his wild mane, something about it reminds Arché of Rohan. "It doesn't make us any less one people. You're ours, same as anyone else."

For the first time in several nights, the flame of hope in Arché's chest sparks into a raging fire.

CHAPTER 37
LENORA

After more nights and days than Lenora can count, the cart finally comes to a stop. The world feels muted after so long being bound and half-starved, her body not functioning the way it ought to.

"Thank the gods," someone at the front of the cart says, as if it has been a difficult journey for *them*.

Lenora and Leahi are pulled from the cart, and Lenora doesn't bother trying to fidget to displace the blindfold; she has tried endlessly to no avail. The sun bears down on her skin, bringing new fatigue even when her eyes are spared from its glare. But around her she can hear faint chatter, soft clangs of metal, and through it all, a song—

A song from home. Coming from a few different directions, the voices as one, and tears wet the blindfold as Lenora begins to hum along with them.

The people of Concord are strong. They are alive. And they are unbroken. Lenora cries and laughs and all at once, because she is alive with them.

Her captors push her forward, leading her somewhere, and behind her comes a muffled shout from Leahi.

Lenora stops humming and tries to say Leahi's name through the gag.

"He doesn't want to see her," says a cold, unfamiliar voice from nearby.

Lenora is starving. Losing bearing on her friend yanks the final threads of civility from her grasp, and she snarls in the voice's direction, trying to lunge for them despite her restraints.

Something slams into her back, knocking her through a tent flap onto a basic canvas flooring.

"And the other one?" comes a new voice.

"This one was too much trouble," says the woman with the knives, from near Lenora. "We had to grab her and run, or we wouldn't have made it back."

"I see. Disappointing, but you'll be compensated for the singular delivery. I take it she's a mage?"

"An Innate user who doesn't need to speak. Shadow magic. Strongest I've seen in a long while."

"Of course." Lenora can practically hear how the new voice's owner might be curling his lip in disdain. It's a soft voice, and calm in a way that spells danger. "Take your gold and leave us. Send in the guard outside."

When the guard enters, they are commanded to place a pair of manacles on Lenora's wrists and remove her blindfold. As soon as the metal closes around her wrists, her dizziness increases tenfold as the very essence of her magic vanishes.

What the—

No matter what she does, she cannot even touch it. They've really gone to the trouble of procuring magic-suppressing manacles just for her.

As the blindfold is untied, Lenora blinks her vision clear, and finds herself looking into the face of a man who can only be the Crusade's prophet. Arché spoke of the high collar she'd seen from a distance, of the voice that never shouted but brought chills to her spine when she'd made her escape.

He is unremarkable. A plain, human man with barely tanned skin and short-cropped sandy hair. Lenora is unsure what she expected, and truly she hadn't seen the merit of trying to picture the appearance of someone whose heart is so unfathomably twisted.

It's in his eyes. They shine with something powerful... a quietly burning righteousness and confidence. On top of that, there is a calculating, discriminating way to how his gaze flicks over her.

"Six houses," he says.

Lenora lifts her eyebrows. It's all she can do, other than collapse on the floor, which she'd rather not do at present.

"Three vampire, three werewolf. And yet, for all I search... it has taken until now to bring any of your house into the fold. My reports from our other encampment is that a house stands, impenetrable, even now."

Lenora chuckles. Her mother has certainly surpassed even Lenora's expectations with this spell of hers.

"There have been other reports," he continues. "Groups of our esteemed community. Lost. Never seen again or slaughtered in dark places and left to rot. Barbaric, that such good people should meet that fate. I am guessing I have you and the other to thank, for that."

What an odd, twisted game. Is *this* how he sleeps at night? Convincing himself of the inherent betterness of those who work under him, of their lives having so much greater value than the people *they* slaughtered first?

Lenora simply holds his gaze and says nothing. She is sure there is no apology in her eyes, and even more sure that he would not have expected one.

For a moment he extends a hand in her direction, only for it to snap back. Wise, since if he'd come any closer, Lenora definitely would have seen what kind of bite she could get on his fingers through the gag.

There's no point in playing nice. Playing nice implies a conscience on both sides of the game, and this prophet has made it clear he is not interested in considering her or her people as anything but pests to be removed.

"You'll be placed with others of your kind, and remain restrained." He whistles, and someone comes in within seconds. "Take her to one of the vampire caravans. Don't remove the gag or the manacles."

Lenora is yanked away. Now she can see the monstrosity of the camp in its entirety; massive metallic caravans with slits near the top to allow for air, at least a dozen, so many and yet not nearly enough.

The Crusaders stop outside one of the caravans and order those inside to 'move to the back'. There is a shuffle of movement, then the exterior bolt is drawn, the large door opened, and Lenora shoved through the gap. It closes behind her immediately.

The darkness is abrupt. But Lenora welcomes it, especially compared to the harsh daylight outside.

The smell hits her first, even with the vents at the top of the caravan. Old body odour, stale and persistent, from the sheer number of people packed into the space. Most are sitting down, finding ways to coexist, and all are craning their necks to get a look at the arrival.

"It's Lenora," someone says, and her name echoes in whispers and gasps all around her.

"Where have you been?" someone asks. "They said Nikos fell—"

Lenora gestures to the gag with her manacled hands. Two people are pushing to the front of the pack, teenagers close in age but wildly different in appearance. One is all too familiar, his dirty blonde hair shaggy where it is usually shaved on the sides, his grey eyes like her own.

"Erwin," Lenora says with horror. "I thought you'd be at the house—"

"Bad luck, right?" he chuckles. "Worst time to go and get garlic bread. Now I haven't seen Henri in months."

The humour in his voice fades by the end of the last sentence. Erwin and Henriette, the fraternal twins, are best friends and usually inseparable. They've never been apart for a full day. Until now.

"I'm so sorry," Lenora says, and lifts the manacles over her head so that she can hug him as best she can. For all that she has never felt as though she entirely fits into her family, the twins have made many attempts to cheer her or involve them in her games. She always appreciated it.

"Where's Arché?" the other teenager asks from behind Erwin. She's also familiar, but not nearly as much, a girl with dark skin and eyes, her hair pulled back into intricate cornrows. Lenora's memory searches for information, for the name her instincts are saying she knows.

Mira. The partner of Andreas, Arché's brother.

"Arché said she was leaving Concord, that she was getting you and Nikos and going to find help," Mira says. "But we heard that Nikos died. We didn't know what to think, after that."

"Arché and I have been following the caravans, trying to find people who can help," Lenora says, still holding Erwin in a loose embrace while he clutches her. "But I guess the Crusade put out a bounty. I got grabbed."

"But not Arché?"

"I was too much trouble," Lenora says, as a point of pride. "They had to cut their losses and only bring me. Arché's still free." She lowers her voice. "And she's coming. For all of us."

"She might be an Heir, but she's still just one person," someone says dubiously.

"She has others with her," Lenora says, speaking even softer. "They can do it. We just need to be ready when they come. Next full moon, they'll be here."

It's not the easiest thing to believe, of course. But there must be something to her, in her stature or her voice, because she sees hope spread through their faces, little by little. It's enough. For now.

Lenora smiles at them, until an unexpected face draws her attention.

"Davin?" Lenora asks, bewildered as she recognises him as a daywalking baker who specialises in donuts. "What are you doing here?"

The middle-aged dragonblood man shrugs, with an easy smile. He looks even more tired than everyone else, with bite marks on his forearms. Behind him, several other daywalkers whose names don't come as easily, give little waves.

A handful of people to feed the dozen or more vampires in the caravan. How miserable.

"They keep seeming real surprised that we're still alive," Davin says. "What assholes."

It makes perfect sense that the group who condemn vampirism are more than happy to throw innocent daywalkers to the supposed mercy of said vampires. It's exactly the twisted logic the Crusaders seem to cling to.

"I'm glad you're alright," Lenora tells Davin and the other daywalkers. "I'm sorry you were dragged into this."

"We're in it together," one of the other daywalkers says. "All of us."

Lenora nods with pride bursting in her chest, at how this ordeal has not changed their people but brought them closer together, their kindness to each other defiance in the face of the Crusade's brutality.

"Let's sit," she says to Erwin and Mira. "You two can fill me in about stuff around here."

"You didn't see Andreas, did you?" Mira asks.

"I couldn't see *anything* once they realised I only needed my eyes to cast magic," Lenora says, and holds up her fancy manacles. "So now I have these, and it feels weird and itchy."

Erwin leans over and licks the metal. "Ew. Magic suppressant?"

"What the—" Lenora stares at him. "Yeah. Or else I'll blow this caravan to pieces."

When he tilts his head curiously, she is almost offended until she remembers that for anyone who hasn't seen her in the last couple of months, her magic is lackluster at best.

"Oh! So it turns out I only ever had some of the Shadow power, because some of it was stuck with the last chosen," Lenora explains. "Arché and I freed them. It's all mine now."

"Thank the gods we have the time for you to give me that whole story later," Erwin says, gaping. "So you could really fuck this lot up, if we get those off?"

Lenora grins. "I can't wait to show you. I scared one of their mercenaries into changing sides."

"Shit, okay," he whistles, before mirroring her grin. "Nice one, big sis."

Next to them, Mira is quiet and contemplative. Lenora nudges her gently and asks if she is alright.

"Yeah," Mira says, sounding as if it is the opposite of the truth. "Just... missing him. Me and Erwin have been basically clawing at the floor of this fucking thing because we're sad and codependent."

Mira, without Andreas. Erwin, without Henri *and* his lycan partner. And Lenora, without Nikos and Arché.

"I understand," Lenora says. "But we'll see them again soon."

Mostly.

Horror crosses Mira's face, as if she'd read Lenora's mind. "Oh shit. Lenora, I'm so sorry—"

"It's okay," Lenora is quick to say, covering her hand and giving it a squeeze. "It's just strange, because now I've been with Arché and then they took me away from her too."

"Are you two friends now?" Erwin asks. "I always got the sense you didn't like her much."

Damn the twins and the way they notice everything and say nothing. Then again, Lenora wasn't the easiest person to talk to, before all of this.

"Well—" Lenora makes a face. "I had a lot going on. But now she and I are... yeah." She cannot stop the smile that curls her lips. "We're good."

Erwin blinks, and his eyes narrow. "You're—oh my god. No way. You and *Arché*?!"

He says it loud enough that everyone in the caravan turns and stares, making Lenora's cheeks burn furiously. Someone at the back wolf-whistles, only to be told by someone else to shut up.

"You've been busy," Erwin says with a shit-eating grin.

Lenora kicks him in the shin. That only makes him laugh, and she cannot help laughing too, and wondering if they've ever done so like this before. Better late than never.

Mira smiles properly for the first time. "I'm really happy for you two... glad something's come out of this mess. Andreas and I were worried about her. He couldn't get her to say what was wrong, he just... had a feeling."

"She can be hard on herself," Lenora says with a sigh, as if she isn't similarly skilled herself. "I—I hope Alta can help her keep a clear head, with me gone."

"Alta? They're with her? That's good." Mira makes a face and shakes her head as if reconsidering her own words. "Like one magical professor is going to make a big difference. I guess you never know. I've been trying to work on some spells, for if anything goes down, for if we get a chance. Erwin's been helping, and a vitality mage over there."

She points to a person sitting about ten feet away, an older man who has been quietly watching them. He gives Lenora a polite nod.

Vitality magic. Something much easier for Gifted mages, whose patrons can usually assist them in directly affecting the people around them, serving as bridges between sentient minds and complex bodies. Disciplined mages, like with anything they do, must learn the great technicalities of bending the web of magic around or inside a person.

"Vitality magic is *wild*," Erwin says. "I wonder why Mum never liked us dabbling in it."

"I think she's just against dabbling, period," Lenora says.

Erwin shrugs. "Well, my entire skill set is useless without a focus. Mira and Stral have been using their own *blood*, which Mother maybe mentioned as a possibility *once*, in *passing*. All the arcane expertise in the world and she couldn't teach me the thing I need in a crisis! I've tried to copy it but I just can't get it right. I'm too used to wand motions, I guess?"

Lenora can only shrug.

"Anyway," Erwin says with a sigh. "I've been trying to teach Mira the whisper spell. So we can get in contact with Andreas. And some of the others. So they know to be ready."

"Now *that's* the start of a plan," Lenora says, and their hopeful smiles give her everything she needs for now.

CHAPTER 38
ARCHÉ

TEAMING UP WITH THE Stag Battalion means abruptly switching to a daywalker schedule and pretending as though it isn't a struggle, but thankfully Ish and Dell don't seem to notice anything odd.

They put no pressure on Arché to tell anything more about the people of Concord, which she appreciates but cannot help but be wary of. Too much rides on this not to question every possible way it could go wrong.

Dell's jolly manner fills the cheer lacking in Leahi's absence. Arché can only hope with everything she has that Leahi is alright, since it is impossible to know what the Crusade might want of her. Or worse, that they might have no use for her at all.

There is little to do *but* hope, even when it is one of the most difficult things in the world.

"That's one gorgeous shield," Dell says to Arché as they walk.

Arché smiles despite everything. "Wait until you see it in action."

Ish is a woman of few words who tends to keep at Dell's side and observe everything with keen eyes. Under her helmet, which she removes to soak in some of the sun, her skin is dark green with clear orcish heritage. Small tusks protrude from her lower lip and a dark braid of hair falls down the full length of her back.

"We've been in the Battalion together from the start," Dell explains. "When I was six, she broke someone's nose for me. Inseparable ever since."

"You require looking after," Ish says with the smallest of smirks.

"And *you* are the only one who thinks so."

Ish shakes her head, signs something too quick and intricate for Arché's rusty sign knowledge to catch, and Dell huffs with great indignance.

"He does *not*."

Arché laughs, until it makes her think of Rohan. Grief, belated and potent, bombards her. A part of her truly, finally processes that she will never banter with her best friend again.

If anyone notices how quiet she gets, no one says anything. Alta engages Dell in a manner of complex inquiries regarding Stag Battalion training and processes, while Raavi is busy picking Tunvra's brain about magical creatures he's hunted through his work.

"If monsters are what you want to learn about, there's a recluse up just under the northeast side of the great forest, who can apparently take down *anything*," Tunvra says to Raavi. "Though her glare is almost worse than her arrows."

Raavi, diligent as ever, scribbles that down in her book. "Alta—"

"Yes, we might be able to look into it," Alta says without even turning their head away from Dell. "I *love* finding other reclusive people."

Such conversation gives Arché plenty of peace to mourn, walking at the back of the group with wet eyes no one else is looking at.

"I'm sorry," she mouths to the air, in case Rohan could be listening. Their spirit is long passed from the world, of course, but with no one quite knowing where one goes *after*... you never know. "I... miss you."

The petty annoyances seem so meaningless now. It is best, perhaps, that they never knew of her absurd feelings. Hopefully they died in the knowledge that she *wanted* to be the best she could for them, that they had been her world for so long.

After several nights, another Stag Battalion patrol comes past. This pair are just as striking as Dell and Ish, with one person in their mid-twenties with deep red skin and short tufts of fiery hair, and a middle-aged elf with prismatic microbraids.

"Dell? What are you doing coming back this way?" the elf asks.

Dell gives them the overview of what he's learned about the caravans, and how they're headed to see the commander, and both Battalion members drop their jaws with obvious horror.

"Ferrali's fucking bells," the elf says with a shake of their head. Arché has no idea who Ferrali is, or why they would have bells. "You're serious, aren't you?"

"Ish, is he serious?" the fiery one demands.

Ish turns her helmet towards them. "Yes."

The newcomers groan in unison. As they ask follow up questions, Dell gives them answers while avoiding revealing gaps in his knowledge from Arché withholding certain information. Within five minutes, they've gone on their way.

Arché is unsure of how she can possibly repay the good grace Dell is currently showing. But she is sure to at least thank him.

"I will explain everything... to your uncle. And you, at that point. The secrecy is just—"

"Tell me when you're ready," Dell interrupts, holding up a hand. "I can see there's truth to what you've told me. We can just walk."

At that point, his back straightens and he looks towards Ish, who tilts her head at him curiously.

"Who are we passing next?" Dell asks. "I know you have the schedule memorised."

"Latod and Sheid," Ish replies immediately.

Dell lets out a small whoop of enthusiasm. "Good. That's good. I think they'll be quite keen to join the rescue force."

"Rescue force?" Arché asks, blinking at him. "I thought you were just escorting us to your uncle."

"Well, sure, but if it's all true and your people need help, I'm—" Dell winces as Ish elbows him in the ribs. "*We're* with you. And others will be too."

"It'll be *incredibly* dangerous," Arché says. "These people, they might kill any number of you if it means getting rid of us."

"Then that's exactly why they need to be stopped," Dell says, his cheer fading into something more serious. "We're well-trained, us Highway Sentinels. We do several years extra training than the town forces." He pats Arché on the shoulder. "I've no plans to die for you, if that makes you feel any better."

It does, actually.

Sure enough, when the next pair of sentinels come along three days later, they greet Dell with surprise and delight. Latod is an elven man with dark brown skin and a shaved head, a curved scimitar on his hip. He clasps forearms with Dell and signs a greeting to Ish with his other hand. She nods in response.

The other is Sheid, an androgynous person of mixed Demonblood and Wildblood lineage, making them one of the most fascinating people to behold that Arché has ever encountered. Their feline features are similar to Dell's, but there is no mane, while bone white horns curl from their head at a spiralling right angle, contrasting with the rich black of the fur covering their body.

Dell relays the same update as he gave the others, but follows it up with a question. "So... want to come and see if the Commander will authorise us recruiting a rescue force?"

Latod nods earnestly and signs something else. Ish, as if guessing that not everyone will be practiced following the signs, speaks the meaning aloud. "This is an atrocity."

Sheid takes longer to answer, mulling it over with a soft hum. Then, they smile and bring their hand to tap the pommel of the greatsword sheathed on their back. "Sounds like it'll be one hell of a fight," they say, with a deep and gravelly voice.

"It will," Arché assures them. "These people are skilled, and ruthless."

"Those are my favourite ones to take down," Sheid says. "They're why I'm in the Battalion."

And that, then, is that.

It's odd dealing with new people. Old jokes thrown around, not understood by those outside the Battalion, especially if they forget to translate Latod's signs, and more still which everyone except Arché seem to chuckle at. Anything that someone who hadn't been stuck in Concord their whole life would get.

Arché is a stranger in her own country. Has never walked it until these past months. It makes her miss Lenora all the more, makes her wish for the companionship of any other born and raised in Concord.

But there is only her. She is the voice for Concord, here. Alta is present and in many ways more qualified, but Alta is not a Leader or an Heir. This falls to Arché. This is where she can prove herself, prove whether she has the marks of a leader or not.

Despair tries to seize her, tries to tell her with every step that she is still not enough, that she never will be. Before, it might have dragged her down.

But Alta's voice rings true in the back of her head. *Don't you fucking dare tell me you aren't good enough.*

She is Kalé's daughter. She has made mistakes, but they are not to be her undoing so long as she learns and does not repeat them. She will save the people of Concord, whatever it takes.

So they walk, and she asks Latod and Ish to walk her through brushing up on her sign language.

Her next test comes soon enough. They come across a small camp of Crusaders as the sun is going down, and the moment she sees them, a growl rumbles in her throat.

"What?" Dell asks. Her vision is no doubt stronger in the dim light than others, but he follows her gaze and squints. Wildblood eyes, especially ones of a feline variety, also tend to do well in the dark. "Oh. More of them. Must be catching up with the group."

"Or coming back to find me," Arché murmurs. "There's so many of them, everywhere, lying to everyone—" She catches herself. Deep breath in, deep breath out. Lenora's absence and her recent unbalances might make everything more difficult, but she will not allow it to lead her to ruin again.

"We have the numbers advantage," Latod signs. "We can capture them easily."

Arché nods. It wasn't a viable option previously. She stands by the necessity of the blood she and Lenora had to spill on their journey to get here, but she takes no pride in it.

Raavi hangs back while everyone else marches up to the camp. They make for an unsuspicious group with the Stag Battalion uniforms and Arché concealing herself in the midst of them.

The Crusader on watch eyes them with a wariness that has Arché wondering what the foot soldiers of the cult have been told by their prophet. Some brag in taverns about the good work they are doing, while others look at the Stag Battalion as if they know they have something to be guilty of.

"Good evening," the woman says, with stiff politeness. "Is everything alright? You're the Kanin guard, right?"

"The Stag Battalion, yes," Dell answers. "Are you from Izirm?" He gestures to her blatant Everflame garb, with the additional sun symbols more specific to the Crusade.

She smiles tightly. "We are. Can I help you with anything?"

"You can surrender your weapons and come quietly," Ish says, in a flat voice. "You and your companions are under arrest for assisting in kidnapping and diplomatic insurrection."

The Crusader's hand goes to her sword hilt. "I think you're confused. I'm sure you'd never accuse visitors of such things without proof."

Arché cannot help herself. She steps forward through the Battalion members, with just enough angle that her tattoo is on display.

The woman's face drains of colour.

"You," she seethes.

Arché removes Crescent Light from her back, slowly. "Good, you've heard of me. Stand down."

"To you? Never—"

"She's a citizen of Kanin," Dell says. "And you're under arrest. Stand down."

The cultist sneers. "She's a monster."

Arché takes a step forward. "You don't know the meaning of that word—"

"My uncle will judge the situation," Dell says, face hardening. "But here in Kanin, we have plenty of people who look extra different to those around them, so we aren't fond of anyone who throws that word at others without reason. Now. I won't say it again."

The woman's eyes dart like a wild animal, from the guards to the tent where no doubt several of her allies slumber. Her gaze returns to Arché. The grip on her pommel is white knuckled and shaky.

A quiet, ugly part of Arché hopes that she fights back. But she throws the sword at the ground and whistles to wake up her comrades. A cluster of sleepy, bewildered people stumble from the tent.

One of them makes the mistake of trying to hurl fire at Sheid. They get the wind knocked out of them as they hit the ground with one swing of Sheid's greatsword.

"Why are you helping one of them?!" they scream. "I bet she hasn't even told you, has she? What she is, what—"

"She's a citizen with credentials," Sheid says. "You don't tell me how to do my job."

They gag the mage quickly, and do the same for the other two without consulting anyone else. No one argues, but Arché can feel the eyes of everyone on her. The Stag Battalion quietly discerning, her previous companions curious, the Crusaders filled with loathing. All waiting to see what she will say or do.

"I never understood hatred," Arché says quietly. "Until yours started killing the people I love. What we are is what we choose to do. You've made what you are *very* clear."

Perhaps these people have done nothing. Perhaps one of them has killed someone from her life, from her home? The baker who sold her sugar donuts. The librarian who spent every full moon reading under the library's skylight ceiling, turning pages with her claws? They could be the true monsters, for all she knows. Either way, they've chosen hatred, and she is done with them.

The Crusaders are tied to the nearest tree, and all together, as Arché's group takes over the campsite for the evening.

Alta has designated themself chef for this leg of the journey, and gets to work on a passage stew with some rabbits they'd shot earlier in the day. Raavi helps out, her eyes darting to Ish from time to time.

Ish's attention, however, is solely on Arché. It might not have been so obvious if there were not an impressive weight to the other woman's manner. After about half an hour, she comes to sit on Arché's right side. It takes too long for Arché to realise that she is examining Arché's tattoo, and heat crawls up Arché's neck. Nerves and fear, unpleasantly mingled.

"She reacted to this," Ish notes. "Viscerally. Why?"

"She must have seen them on some of the others," Arché says slowly. There isn't much for it now, with the other three battalion members settled around the fire and watching her with interest. She lets out a sigh and sends several quick prayers. "I'm a lycan. A werewolf. That's what she meant. My people are peaceful, and so are the others who founded our town, but—"

"People can misunderstand," Sheid says.

Dell gives Arché a small smile. "You have nothing to fear from us. Isn't your cousin a werebear, Sheid?"

"Like we didn't have enough weird shit going on with our blood already," Sheid mutters, and Arché tries to imagine a part Demonblood, part feline Wildblood shifting into a bear creature from time to time. While it's certainly possible, Arché fails to conjure a coherent image.

Dell and Latod cackle at her bemused face. Raavi suppresses a giggle.

"This is my mother's pawprint, from her other form," Arché explains to Ish in particular. "These lines around it, they represent the three founding lycan houses—" She traces the circles representing the moon's phases, which interrupt three of the lines making up the hexagon encasing the pawprint. The next sentence she must say will make things more complicated, but it is the time for honesty. She cannot afford for them to hear any part of the truth from someone who may twist it. "And these lines with the points in them are for the three founding vampiric houses."

Sure enough, the camp goes still. Ish stiffens next to her, and Dell exchanges looks with his fellows. Arché gives them time to process any and all implications. Better not to make assumptions; let them ask.

"Vampires?" Latod signs. "As in, undead? Blood drinking?"

"Not undead," Arché says. She signs where she can, for maximum clarity, but is sure that the attempt is clumsy. "They're mortal. They're born, they live and grow, they have children, they die of old age. Same as anyone else. They're just cursed to need blood from other mortal people."

They're all still listening. Waiting. Not yet grabbing their weapons. It's something.

"Like my people, they knew others might associate them with the undead creatures, the ones who kill and don't care, who have never tried to have control. We learned from each other. Founded the town of Concord."

Nausea sits in her stomach from having so much pressure to get her words right.

"From mortal people? So not from animals?" Sheid asks.

Arché shakes her head. "The curse must have been very specific—I know it's really uncommon for any magic that affects people to not also include animals, right?" To her side, Raavi and Alta nod adamantly. "For some reason... it just doesn't work. It has to be mortal, humanoid blood.

So we worked out a volunteer and compensation system. It's worked for everyone, for centuries."

"I have theories about all of that!" Alta says, because of course they do.

"A volunteer and compensation system." Dell rubs at the golden fur on his neck. "They don't hurt anyone, then."

"Not at all," Arché promises. "But that's why they think we're monsters. Why they attacked us without even knowing us."

"I'm sorry," Latod signs. "No one deserves that. We'll do everything we can."

Arché's throat is choked by undignified emotion and gratitude. She nods, because if she tries to speak she's going to end up crying, and that simply isn't the projection of strength she's looking for right now.

"If you don't mind me asking, why is it just you on your own? You said you were the only one from Concord."

"Because I'm one of only two who escaped the initial attack," Arché says, her voice coming out wooden. "Right before you met us, some adventurers kidnapped the other while we were in Ushonk and bought out all the horses in the stables so we couldn't follow them. The most powerful asset to our rescue mission, the one literally destined to save us all in times of hardship, and now she's their prisoner."

"Freeing her will be top priority when we hit the camp," Alta says. "We need her magic."

Arché finds herself grinning. "Yeah. Your wife and my girlfriend are the two scariest people in their camp. And they're going to be pissed."

"So you have a plan," Ish says.

"I have the start of a plan, which is freeing Lenora and my mother. It's not enough of a plan," Arché replies. "I supposed next would be releasing the lycans. We want to catch them on the next full moon, because they apparently halt the camp for three days. Our people will be strongest then."

"Sounds like a plan to me," Sheid says with a shrug.

Arché and Dell share a glance of strategist doubt.

"We'll see the commander," Dell says. "Then we'll work out the details."

CHAPTER 39
ARCHÉ

THE BATTALION ENCAMPMENT, WHEN they reach it four days later, is a bustling place of tents and people. A fence of timber spikes provides simple defenses, with armoured members stationed near a gap that serves as an entry. There is no heraldry, no banners, but every member has the antlers on their uniform in some manner or another.

The moment their group gets inside, Dell hands the string of captured cultists to someone with a striped badge and requests they be taken to the holding area until the commander is briefed. Arché expects questions, but there is only a nod and quick action.

Curious eyes follow Arché and the non-Battalion members as they walk further into the camp. None of the looks are critical, but it makes Arché's skin prickle all the same, as being the centre of attention is not something she has ever desired or excelled at. It keeps happening, more with each day that passes, and it plays havoc with her stomach.

You are the blood of the Warden Clan. Stand tall. Their stares don't matter. The words feel more like Kalé's than her own, but they work all the better for it.

Arché exhales long and slow.

The centre of the camp is marked by a larger tent, with a single guard outside who is perched comfortably on a crate, knitting what might be a pair of mittens. They glance up, only for a moment, then do a full double take and bring their eyes back to Dell.

"Hey," they say. "What are you doing here?"

"I need to speak with the commander. Immediately, if he's free."

"He is. Go on in."

Dell looks back to Arché. "We'll brief him first, then I'll introduce you. Sheid, you stay with them, yeah?"

Sheid nods, and Dell heads into the tent with Ish and Latod on his heels. Arché has to resist the urge to pace while she waits, so instead flexes her knuckles at her sides. After a few moments, Alta's slim fingers find hers.

"Are you okay?" Alta asks.

"Probably not," Arché admits. "But I'm trying hard to be. These people seem to be genuinely *good*, and understanding. That's better than anything I hoped for... I just don't know what's going to happen now."

"We never know what will happen, we can only do our best when it does." Alta squeezes Arché's hand and gives her a soft smile. "Just because you've made one mistake, doesn't mean you aren't allowed to make more. You will. We all will. You just keep learning."

Logically, of course Alta is correct. But it is the last thing Arché wants to hear. "We don't have time to make mistakes now—"

"Maybe not," Alta tuts. "But don't let that lead to inaction. We can do this. You can do this. We got this far."

Arché pulls Alta into a hug, letting their head tuck under her chin as she holds them tight. "Thank you. I don't know what I'd do without you."

"What a ridiculous thing to say about someone who is absent from your life for such long periods," Alta says, but in that stiff, overly logistical way they tend to fall into when trying to avoid getting emotional. Which is unfortunate, since Arché didn't inherit her powerful emotions from Kalé.

"You're always with me, in spirit if not in body," Arché says. "You're too loud to be gone from me entirely."

Alta hugs Arché tighter, and if Arché notices the sound of sniffling, she pretends not to. They stay locked in the embrace, while Raavi launches into a new series of questions for Tunvra and Sheid plays a game of knucklebones with the tent guard.

Dell steps out of the tent about five minutes after entering it. "He'll see you now."

Arché releases Alta and takes in one last deep breath to steady herself.

"Do you want me to come with you?" Alta asks. There is no pressure, no doubt. Just an offer. Support, if needed, or the chance to do it on her own.

For two seconds, the choice freezes Arché entirely.

"No," she says. "I'll tell him he can talk to you after, if he has more logistical questions about Concord. You'd know those answers better than me. But I know more about—"

"All of this," Alta finishes for her. "Yes. You do."

The pride in their eyes shines so bright it hurts Arché to look at. She gives their hand one last squeeze and walks into the tent before she can change her mind.

A gold-scaled dragonblood man sits behind a desk, his armour full plate with more stripes on it than anyone outside. A symbol of the Judge, goddess of justice and law, is engraved into the left side of his breastplate, right over his heart. The symbol of the scales, and what they represent, breathes additional hope into Arché's heart.

Kesh, is the name Dell had used when talking about him.

"Commander Kesh," Arché says as he looks up. "Thank you for seeing me."

"Of course," he says with a polite smile. "My nephew has done many, uh, interesting things during his time in the Battalion. Not all of them good. This is a new one, never heard a tale quite like this. More importantly, you've convinced Ish."

Arché nods. "I know it must be hard to believe."

His eyes, as gold as his scales, are gentle but unwavering as they regard her. "Not necessarily. But you must understand I need to verify it, beyond doubt. Do you consent to me using a truth spell? You'll not be compelled to speak anything against your will, you simply won't be able to lie."

Arché blinks. It sounds like Gifted magic, and exactly the sort of thing she'd expect a follower of the Judge to be able to perform. "Oh. Yes, absolutely."

"If I may have your hand, then."

Arché approaches him and extends her palm across the desk. He places his hand atop it, while the other traces over the lines engraving his armour.

"Lady of Justice, make this a place of truth, where no lies may pass our lips. Let honesty shine the light we need this day."

Soft gold magic, warmer than expected, tingles across Arché's hand and up her body until it settles on her tongue, sitting just heavy enough to feel like a liquid film. She touches it to the roof of her mouth experimentally and makes a face.

Kesh grins at her. "It's strange the first time, I know."

"You said 'our lips'," Arché realises, lifting an eyebrow at him.

"Seems only fair, if we're trying to build trust."

Such a simple answer. And yet, not a courtesy Arché expected, when the initial request had been so reasonable to begin with. Knowing he will also be speaking only truth comes as a powerful balm to her nerves.

"Thank you," she whispers.

Kesh nods, something in his face softening before he sits back down and gestures for her to do the same in the chair opposite his desk. "Please state your name, occupation, and place of origin. For my record."

"My name is Arché Kalésen," Arché says, and even with the spell's weight, the words have never felt easier or more right to say. "I'm the Heir to the Warden Clan and train in politics, logistics and combat in equal measure. My home is Concord, a town hidden in the Howling Peaks valley."

The Howling Peaks, according to Alta, got their name from Kanin travelling superstitions about odd noises coming from the mountains on some nights. To Concord, it is simply 'Haven Valley'.

"Who founded this town, and why did they do it in secret?"

Arché can tell he has already heard Dell's version of the answer, that he is waiting to verify her words against his nephew's. All she has to do is get it right.

"Concord was founded by three united packs of werewolf lycans, and three families who had been cursed with partial vampiric nature," Arché says, slow and calm. "All had struggled to find homes where they could exist peacefully, without fear of being misunderstood and harmed from fear or incident. They realised they could learn different aspects of control from each other, and made a home where they could be themselves, hidden from the daywalking world."

"So everyone in the town is a lycan or a vampire?"

"No, over the centuries different people came to the town through various trade and associations with the original members," Arché says. "It took time, and trust, but the daywalking population has slowly grown. By my last knowledge of the census, it is about sixty percent nightwalkers and forty percent daywalkers."

At that, Arché stops and catches herself.

"Those numbers will no longer be accurate, however, in light of recent events," she manages to choke out.

Kesh winces. "I'm very sorry. What's happening to your people... please tell me what you've seen."

Arché tells him all of it, from the start. The unfamiliar faces in the streets, to Rohan's murder, to her mission to flee and find help. Finding Lenora and Nikos, learning of the intentions of Crusaders. The arrogant ones they ran into along the way.

"Where are they now? The Crusaders you encountered?"

It's a question he must ask. It's a question Arché desperately hoped to avoid. She weighs her options, knowing that even if she *could* lie in this moment, she wouldn't.

"Lenora and I felt that every one of them we left alive, the higher the certainty they would kill any other survivors of Concord, or us if they caught us up from behind." She sighs. "They had made their choices abundantly clear, and were unrepentant."

It is an agonising half minute. He absorbs her words with a furrowed brow, and she imagines the scales on his armour shifting from side to side, weighing the morals versus the law, just as his chosen goddess demands.

"That's unfortunate," he says eventually.

"I agree." Arché puts her hand over her heart. "If you decide that action requires discipline, I swear on the Judge I'll take full responsibility and accept any punishment you see fit. But please, let me free my people first."

Kesh tilts his head. "I... do not think that will be necessary. It is regrettable, and we will not tolerate any further taking of life outside of the battle this is headed for... but sometimes unlawful violence is met by unlawful violence. Other options could only ever be hypothetical or impractical. If the Judge finds this decision to be misguided, I'll let her show you or I in her own way."

"Thank you, sir," she says, exhaling her relief long and heavy. "Do you have any more questions for me?"

"Only one." He regards her carefully for a moment. "Do you have a plan?"

"Half of one." Arché sighs and crosses her arms. "They lock the camp down for the full moon to help them handle the lycans. It buys us time to catch up to them, surround them. If we can get in and release the strongest of them—my partner, my mother, the other leaders, a mage friend of ours who was taken too... we stand a good chance."

"That's a start." Kesh scratches a nail down the scales on his cheeks. "I can gather everyone here, let you speak to them. I could pass a command to have them go with this, but a thing like this... if they're as dangerous as you say, I think they ought to volunteer."

Arché's first instinct is to argue that no one would be absurd enough to volunteer for such a thing. But she stops herself right before the words come out, because four people already have. And he's right. It *must* be that way.

"I'd be very grateful for that," Arché says instead.

"Then we won't waste any time."

Kesh motions for Arché to follow him, and grabs a halberd off a stand near the desk as he strides out of the tent. They walk through to the commons of the camp, where Kesh stands on a crate to get a good vantage over his people.

Dell and the others from the journey gather near him, and without a word being exchanged, Dell stands next to the crate and raises his shield so that his uncle might slam his halberd into it several times as a metallic rallying call.

The camp quiets. Within moments, they are gathered.

"We've special visitors this afternoon," Kesh says to the company. "Citizens in need, in ways we couldn't have foreseen. We're looking for volunteers for something dangerous, and important. I'll let the woman of the hour explain."

Kesh gets off the crate and gestures for Arché to replace him. But what to say, to convince them of the seriousness without sharing Concord's secret with those not yet committed to its rescue? There must be a middle ground. A way to harness their curiosity.

Arché gets onto the crate as the right words finally come to her.

"I'm sure you've seen the metal caravans," she says to the crowd. "I know what's in them, and volunteers for this mission will get to find out. You'll be coming along for a story you'll be asked never to tell, to save lives twice over."

A murmur moves through the sea of people like a soft wave. The divide is clear; some are immediately disinterested in the prospect of not being able to share a story, and some are all the more enthralled at what could warrant such a precedent.

"My name is Arché," she says, a little late. "I'm from a town you've never heard of, but we're of Kanin, just like you. We need help. We'll be going up against mages, and powerful warriors, ones convinced of their righteousness. They've killed and hurt innocents. It will be dangerous, truly dangerous, but I will be forever in debt to anyone who assists."

The faces stare back at her, and she has no words left, only a thousand questions of whether it is enough and what they're all thinking.

"Volunteers can register themselves with Arché and myself, so they may be officially assigned," Kesh calls out.

Most of the crowd disperses. It's to be expected—the battle she has described is a difficult one, and they're likely not all trained to handle such combat even if they wanted to.

But then a few come, eager and intrigued. One almost bounces up and takes Arché's hand for a quick shake before signing the ledger. Then more. By the end, there are eight names on Kesh's paper.

"Ish and I are seeing this through to the end," Dell says to his uncle.

Latod coughs to draw Kesh's eye, and signs, "And myself and Sheid."

The commander chuckles and unrolls the paper to reveal four names already written at the top of the list. "Predictable, all of you."

They make a plan to leave in the morning, once some extra supplies can be gathered.

There are not enough ways to say thank you in the mortal world, so when Arché turns back to Kesh, she simply extends an arm forward for him to clasp. He grips it tight.

"They're good people, and they'll fight hard," Kesh tells her. "I know you'll look after them."

"I won't ask them to do anything I wouldn't," Arché says. It's the most she can promise, with their safety uncertain in the face of the Crusade.

Kesh nods, and heads back into his tent.

"Well done," Dell says to Arché. "You'll tell them the rest of it, once we get moving, I'm guessing?"

"That's the idea."

Arché and the other visitors claim a couple of tents near the entrance-way. Tunvra has been watching Arché for some time, his usual silence now a pointed and odd thing. Once they've got the bedrolls sorted out, Arché strides up to him.

"What?"

Tunvra sighs. "All of this, and still no talk of how we're going to get into the encampment and free your people. Have I mentioned it is *highly fortified*?"

"Yes, and I'm... working on it," Arché says. She wants to wince at how pathetic it sounds.

"Is that your way of saying you don't have a plan yet?"

Gods, she wants to hit him. She never wants to hit anyone, but when he was the start of everything getting worse... it sours every word he says.

A small growl rumbles in her throat. She clenches her fists on her knees and breathes to calm her boiling blood.

"If there is a point to any of this, you'd better find it fast, or go for a walk," Arché warns him.

"More than a point. A plan, which will let us walk right in," Tunvra says. He is as confidently calm as ever, irritatingly so. "But you're not going to like it. Not one bit."

CHAPTER 40
LENORA

A WEEK OF DISCREET magical training, with little else to do, can go a long way. Mira might be a rather new Disciplined mage, but her teacher knows his craft. A man named Stral, he lives on one of the farms in Concord and uses his magic to enhance the crops he grows. Lenora is appalled at the idea that such a talented, useful mage had never been mentioned by her mother in their studies.

But then, there are many reasons why Lenora's mother may not have done so. They make Lenora's eyes roll just to think of it.

Erwin puts everything he has into helping Mira get the Whisper spell right.

It's a fundamentally basic spell—even Lenora knows the theory like the back of her hand, she just never quite got it to work in practice. You think of someone you know, along with a small whisper you want them to hear from you, and it delivers the message.

Mira and Erwin practice the words, Erwin correcting a couple of inflections. Mira shifts perfectly with his direction, saying it again, and the corner of her mouth twitches into a half grin.

Using her own blood as a focus, first in drips and then tracing the runes on the caravan floor, Mira tries the spell again. Once. Twice. The third time, she is so close that the air shimmers, and then she whimpers as the backlash hits her. The universe, kicking back against being incorrectly channelled.

You must assert yourself over the force of the potential, or it will kick you like a horse, Lenora's mother had always said.

Perhaps that's always been Lenora's problem. She's never been interested in asserting herself over some primal part of the world itself. Her shadows are different, destined for her, a part of her.

Watching Mira, though? It's not asserting, it's something else altogether, and it's working. After a quick blood donation from Davin to clear her spinning head, further hours pass as Mira works tirelessly to get the intricacies of the spell right. She is *coaxing* the magic, murmuring the words like trying to talk a scared cat into coming into her arms.

"Carry my words," Mira whispers. "Find the one, deliver them, that he might hear my voice. Connect us for one moment, let the potential bind us—"

Mira goes still. Her eyes glaze over.

"Andreas? Can you hear me?" she whispers into the air.

There is a small pause, and then a smile breaks out across her face, blinding and beautiful. She falls back onto the floor of the caravan, a laugh shaking her body. "I did it. I did it."

"He heard you?" Lenora asks.

"I heard him," Mira says. When she sits up, tears glisten as they race down her cheeks. "Gods, I'm sorry, I didn't think that would hit me so hard." She throws herself at Erwin, hugging him tight. "Thank you. Thank you."

"Of course," Erwin says with a smile. "Now, get a few Whispers out of your system, and you can get onto that other one you and Stral have been working on."

Stral claims that Mira should be able to get this one right before the full moon, as they've been practicing it for the majority of the journey. He calls it 'wither and bloom', and the concept is simple enough: drawing in the vitality of one creature, and gifting it to another.

Simple, he says. Fantastical, it seems to Lenora.

"It's pure equivalence," Stral explains, as Mira practices the rune over and over. "Taking from one thing, giving it to another. Less complex than even a Whisper."

"But a Whisper is just words," Lenora says. "This is… touching people's lifeforce. How is that easy?"

"That's what I've been saying," Erwin mutters from his spot on the floor. "Like, I've been listening, and it all makes sense, I'm just not… getting it."

"Welcome to not being a natural at *everything*," Lenora laughs. He pokes his tongue out at her in protest.

"There's a difference between simple and easy," Stral continues. "As vampires, we feel the lifeforce more keenly than others, but Erwin here is a good example that even the most talented Disciplined mage can struggle with this particular practice."

"And Mira?"

"She's got the most dedicated mind I've had the privilege to know. She understands the process, the precision… and most importantly, she feels the balance."

When Lenora tilts her head questioningly, he holds up his hands as a way of explanation, mimicking the rise and fall of two sides of a scale.

"Life, and death. Healing, and harm. Opposites, spectrums, symbiosis... the balance is intricate, and rife with mundane misconception. She listened, she's learned... and now she feels it as I do. This is just the beginning for her."

"Then it's a good thing she has two test subjects," Lenora says, mentally excluding Erwin who needs all of his strength. "Let's make a secret weapon."

CHAPTER 41
ARCHÉ

"You're right," Arché says as Tunvra claps shackles on her wrists. "I don't like this plan."

The hunter smirks, because this is not new information, and he knows she isn't going to change her mind now. Smug bastard knows it is the only plan that makes sense, and Arché will never not be bitter that someone else came up with it. Her damaged pride can simply not recover from his skilled interruptions.

"We'll be close by," Alta promises, brushing some hair behind Arché's ear. "You won't be in there for long."

"That's not the part I'm worried about. It's just... all of it."

Her gaze shifts to the dozen members of the Stag Battalion standing nearby, watching as Tunvra moves to put a second pair of shackles around her ankles.

"We're with you, Arché," Dell assures her. "We'll get those caravans open."

"And the civilians out of the camp," Ish adds.

Raavi has volunteered to be the point of contact for the evacuation point, assisting with helping anyone injured. Most of the lycans, transformed, will want to fight. But there must be a choice for all.

The Stag Battalion members were full of questions when she'd explained about Concord and its people as she had to Dell and other three. The same fear of horror and rejection had seized her, but there has only been curiosity and wonder.

And when she'd mentioned how some of those taken were not warriors at all, a fierceness seized the group. Ferocious protective instinct which has instilled a new pride in Arché to be a part of Kanin. Has her country truly been so noble at its heart all along, if these are the people who protect it?

They've sparred on the road, with Arché in her partially transformed state taking as many of them as she can and holding her own against four of them before their skills began to overwhelm her.

Now, this is it.

"When Lenora and Leahi were taken, I'd all but lost faith in the goodness of other people," Arché says to them, voice almost getting stuck in her throat. "I truly can't state what finding the Battalion, what meeting you all… has meant to me. I couldn't ask for better saviours for my people. I'll do everything I can to repay you, one day."

"You told us it would be dangerous, and that it would be a great story we wouldn't be able to tell," one of them says. "Doing this is its own reward."

Arché wonders if they'll think so if the person next to them falls to fiery magic of these hateful Crusaders. She keeps the thought to herself, and only nods in thanks.

The power of the near full moon rushes through her blood as the afternoon continues. They are so close now, the camp scouted by Tunvra's hawk familiar, its position and layout confirmed and sketched on multiple copies of parchment to be handed around the different groups.

"They have no idea I joined you," Tunvra had explained, back at the encampment. "They'll just have assumed I failed. I can bring you in as my prisoner, better late than never."

Naturally, Arché loathed the plan from the start, because it made perfect sense and was their best chance at getting an ally into the camp. And of course, Tunvra ends up being completely correct in his assumptions. The way it makes Arché grit her teeth only sells their facade all the more, her bitterness potent as she glares at him and the Crusaders who let them pass the camp's first watchpost.

Arché thought she was ready to see the caravans. She was wrong.

They are such awful, imposing things. Huge and yet nowhere big enough for how many people must be crammed into them, cages that speak the absolute truth of what the Crusade thinks of the nightwalkers.

Arché breathes in deep and lets her head fall back into a howl which pierces the camp. It is nothing compared to her transformed one, but it is the spirit of the thing that matters.

Several of the caravans shake as howls ring out in answer, also only mortal voices for now. Her people. On this night of transformation, they can hear each other again.

A part of Arché's heart heals then and there.

The moment is shattered by guards banging on the caravan sides and shouting threats until the howling vanishes. Arché sets her shoulders and keeps her thoughts calm; when the sun goes down, so shall this place of hatred.

She is taken to the grandest of all the tents.

"We thought they'd killed you," the man inside says to Tunvra.

The high collar. From outside the cathedral in Concord. The Prophet. He is so much more unremarkable to look at than she expected, but then he gives her a side glance so slimy she feels the urge to plunge into a river to be cleansed of it.

"They thought so too," Tunvra replies, with an easy shrug. "So I waited, and saw a chance once I realised this one was on her own."

"Good. Then I can provide you with half of our agreed amount," the Prophet says. "With extra, if you stay on-site for the next three nights, as additional security."

Tunvra nods. "Sure."

"Escort her to the caravan to the east edge of the camp. The night is too close."

Arché wishes she had something to say to him. There are a thousand things, and yet too many of them could give away the plan if she does not seem broken and defeated. She cannot show that she is about to tear his little world apart.

His eyes meet hers, a quiet curiosity in them.

"Prophet," is all she says.

"Yes. My people have spoken of me, then?"

Arché nods, letting her loathing flow through her. "Before I killed them."

He does not look surprised. "I shall honour their sacrifice, and ensure you reach the judgement you are due," the Prophet says with narrowed eyes. "Get her out of my sight."

As Tunvra tugs Arché out of the tent, she silently promises the Prophet the same thing he has wished for her. She hopes that when they kill him, the Everflame burns his vindictive, self-righteous soul until there is nothing left.

"So far so good," Tunvra murmurs under his breath, as they walk to the caravan the Prophet mentioned. "I'll be back when the sun goes down. I'll find out where they have the leaders and Lenora and Leahi, if I can. That can be Dell's job."

Arché says nothing, but meets his eyes for a moment in place of an answer.

The guards are more than happy to throw her into the caravan. They do not remove the shackles, and she hits the floor with a grunt.

"She's here," someone whispers. "She really is here."

"He said so!"

Arché sits on her heels and looks at the faces, all of them familiar to different degrees, some bringing names to her mind while others conjure places and buildings from home.

"Who said so?" she asks.

Something tackles her back onto the ground. Something almost her size, with a smell that overwhelms her nose. A very, very familiar smell.

"Andreas," she whispers, nuzzling into him with a small sob.

"She said you'd come," he says, voice soft. "Lenora told us. We're ready, Arché. Please tell me you being thrown in here is part of the plan."

"It is, don't worry—" Arché pushes him up and off her, so that she can look at him properly, and yelps when she does. "Andreas."

His right ear is missing, the flesh marred around the small hole, scars from the slice that did it raised and angry still.

"I couldn't make it easy for them," he says. "They were being dickheads."

She does not say that which he must already know. That only the High Cleric is known to possess the kind of power which might be able to regrow flesh, and that he is known to never apply such magic to non-essential cases. Andreas has another ear, so this would be considered one.

Arché's thumb strokes the side of his face. "That wasn't very clever."

"No, but it felt like the right thing to do. I'm Warden Clan too."

Several things said previously slot into her head after some delay. "Wait, you said Lenora told you I was coming? How? Isn't she in another caravan?"

Andreas beams. "She's with Mira, and her brother Erwin. They've been helping Mira with magic, sending me messages..."

His smile becomes dopey and full of yearning as he casts his eyes towards the rest of the camp, through the caravan wall. Arché recognises the nature of it more easily now, especially seeing it on a face that so resembles her own.

But whatever he has with Mira is not her business, not her place to confuse with the wrong question at the wrong time. There has never been a more wrong time than today.

"This is going to get ugly," Arché tells him. "We've got help. They're going to get everyone free, but... they won't go down easy."

"That wouldn't be fun, anyway," Andreas says darkly.

They have learned about hatred together, while dozens of miles apart. *We're too young for this,* Arché had thought as she and Lenora left Concord. The memory hits like a dark joke, that she could have thought such a thing when her brother was going through all this.

Arché finds his forearm and grips it tight. "This ends tonight. I promise."

He pulls her into another hug, and over his shoulder she can see the approving nods of the other lycans.

They find a spot to sit and bask in the comfort of each other's presence, with Andreas' head resting on her right shoulder.

"Mira said that... you and *Lenora*—"

Arché groans. "Gods, how have you all had so much time that you've discussed *that*—"

"There's only so many things to talk about, with all of this waiting around." Andreas nudges her. "So what happened *there*? Had you two even... had a real conversation before all this? It seemed like you two never talked on your own."

"Not really," Arché says, shrugging and lifting his head with the movement, making him grumble. "But we were all alone, out in the world. Everything against us. Life is strange."

"I can only imagine. Does she make you happy, though? After Maggie, I'm ready to kick the ass of anyone who hurts you."

"Well, our entire relationship has formed through the least happy circumstances possible," Arché points out. "But... she's made for some bright spots, within all that. And when I think about... you know, an *after*? It feels good. So I really think we do. Make each other happy."

Andreas pats her hand. "I'm so thrilled for you."

At the risk of implying what she doesn't wish to, she cannot stop herself from asking: "How's Mira?"

If he notices the connection between the topics, he gives no indication other than a small cough. "She's relieved to have something to keep her busy. All the magic practice."

"Good."

"Tonight, we teach them a lesson." Andreas squeezes her hand and bends to press his forehead to his knees, murmuring under his breath.

Prayer? Arché has never known her brother to pray outside of weekly temple visits, and never with such... fervour.

Questions burn on her tongue. But, as with so many other things, it does not feel like the time to task. Arché has found her rock in Lenora, in the power they hold together. And, she's found hope for the future after the reality check about Kalé. Arché's hope is in the change she has found; she cannot fault Andreas for finding it in something else.

They sit there, in comfortable quiet, until the moon wrenches howls from their throats.

CHAPTER 42
LENORA

WHEN THE HOWLING STARTS, Mira begins casting her spell, while every other vampire in the caravan stands at the ready. Mira murmurs to the blood dripping from her hand, catching it with her other, connecting them so that one hand might take vitality so that the other might bestow it.

Lenora shifts her weight from her toes to her heels and back, over and over. She knows they cannot do anything until someone opens the caravan, but knowing that she is *so* close to seeing Arché again? It's exhilarating. And torturous.

Shouts mingle into the howling, ones of great alarm. Lenora's lips twitch. It's starting.

Shouts come closer to their caravan, then clashes of metal. Then, the lurch of the bolt holding their caravan door shut, and a lion man in unfamiliar armour stands at the entrance.

"If you don't want to fight, follow me," he says, his expression fierce. "If you do… the field is yours. Now, I have a key here for someone called Lenora?"

"Me," Lenora says, rushing forward and presenting her manacles. "You're with Arché?"

"I am," he replies, and he smiles. "You her girl?"

Lenora grins as the manacles come undone and her magic rushes in, filling her where she hadn't realised how cold and empty she'd become in its absence. "I am."

He pulls a familiar shield of brilliant silver from his back. "She said you'd be able to find her and get her this. Go, I'll keep on with the caravans. I've got a flute to get to a loud lady."

Lenora takes the shield and nods, the din around them growing with every second. First thing is to seize Erwin in a hug.

"Get to safety," she tells him.

He nods, the frustration bleeding from him, before joining the others at the Wildblood man's side.

Lenora looks to Mira, who has completed her spell and is holding dark energy in one hand and a soft glow in the other, brow furrowed in concentration.

"Let's get you to Andreas," Lenora says to her, and they jump out of the caravan where the world is a lovely dark with only the flickers of torches, and blurs of running people around every corner.

They choose a direction to run, hoping desperately they'll recognise the transformed figures of the wolves they're looking for amidst the others beginning to leap from the caravans.

A bizarre sound rips through the air, from the other side of the encampment, and Lenora sees massive vines twisting between the caravans. Shouts of bewildered alarm follow it. Alta's magic, from the ruin. An excellent disruption to throw into the mix.

"Mira!"

A wolf runs for them, shoving aside a cultist who tries to get in his way, and he tackles Mira to the ground before nuzzling into her.

"Rea, I'm trying to concentrate on a spell," Mira protests. Her voice is choked with tears.

"Sorry," Andreas murmurs, his transformed voice deeper than his usual. "Missed you."

Mira kisses the side of his head. "Missed you too."

"Lenora!"

She tears her eyes from the teenagers to see another wolf, in familiar garb, running for her. It now feels absurd to have worried she wouldn't recognise her; she's seen this one at her best and her worst and loved her in all of them.

Arché and Lenora collide in the fiercest of embraces, Arché's muscles squeezing her to the point of pain. Lenora cares only about Arché's warmth and being able to breathe now that they're together again.

"I was so scared," Arché grumbles into her shoulder.

"I knew you'd come," Lenora says. "I told them all."

"Good." Arché holds her at arm's length, her feet fully off the ground. It would be comical at any other moment. "Problem. The Leaders are locked in caravans next to Prophet's tent. Tunvra meant to get Kalé out. Eliana. Christos. I might be able to—"

A column of fire erupts from the centre of the camp. The Prophet sits atop it in the air, his eyes blazing as they scan the chaos of the camp.

With a lift of his hand and a single shout, he rains fire on the western side, where Dell had been heading to free more of the nightwalkers.

Lenora snarls and shoves Crescent Light into Arché's hands unceremoniously, forming shadowy knives in her hands, relishing the feeling of how her magic comes to her so quickly after a week of being cut off from it. She throws the knives at the Prophet, her arms not strong enough to make such a throw conventionally but her magic able to direct their path easily. The tiny blades catch him in the shoulder, making his gaze snap to them.

"Your fight is with *us*," she shouts.

"Andreas, Mira, get to Battalion," Arché shouts from behind her. "Need locks broken. Centre caravans. Now."

"On it," Andreas promises.

They run, and Arché swings Crescent Light so that it sends an arc of moonlight at the Prophet. He turns his fire on them, and they are forced to leap apart to avoid the worst of the hurtling blast.

"You will *not* stop this Crusade!" he yells. "I was *chosen*, to bring you all into the light and be judged—"

"Liar," Arché snarls.

"Or delusional," Lenora agrees.

Arché throws more moonbeams, but this time the Prophet is ready and shifts his column to dodge them. She howls with annoyance.

"I need to *reach* him!"

Lenora exhales as an odd laugh shakes her. "I can do that."

With new inspiration and a rush of power, Lenora forms a platform of shadow several feet in radius, just ahead of Arché.

"Get on," Lenora says with a grin, and it is delicious how the Prophet shouts with alarm as Arché does so. Lenora directs her focus to raising the platform into the air, to reach where he is suspected by his own bombastic magic. She will snuff out his light if it is the last thing she does.

"No!" he shouts as Arché reaches him.

"Fuck yes," Arché growls, before slamming him across the face with Crescent Light.

It is the most satisfying thing in Lenora's life, sex included, to hear the thunk of the impact and how he screams.

"Crusade! Get the shadow heathen! Bring her *down*!" he calls to his people.

Uh oh.

Lenora takes pride in the fact that the order came from genuine fear they have inspired, but keeping the platform up and fluctuating for Arché's use is taking every bit of focus she's got. She can't fight on the ground too.

Arché is an astounding force of nature, and keeping her up in the Prophet's face is without a doubt the best strategy they have. All the same, Lenora itches to get her hands on him. If Arché can batter him to the point that his fire becomes too much to maintain... that will be her moment.

The scent of blood alerts Lenora to the figures approaching her before she can turn to see them. Two Crusaders, hurt and furious, are advancing on her. One has a morningstar with so many points it conjures awful images just to look at, and the other has a greatsword with cruel, jagged edges. The wielder of the latter is so large that Lenora can only be astounded by their stature—it would be as easy as battling a mountain.

Arché had described someone similar when discussing the day of the attack. Could this be the 'champion' she spoke of?

A resonant boom pounds the air some way off, making Lenora's ears ring. A moment later, a new, powerful howl rips through the battlefield. As Lenora backs up from her new attackers and stretches the limit of her concentration by summoning a wall to come between herself and them, a figure climbs onto the metal caravans nearby.

Then, it launches itself into the air with a mighty leap, and tackles the Prophet right out of the sky.

CHAPTER 43
ARCHÉ

THE MOON'S POWER IS intoxicating. It is everything, to feel her blood rushing with everything she needs to destroy this tiny, pathetic man who has ruined so many lives with his vendetta. He slings fire and light with all he has, and it burns hot, but accuracy is near impossible for a mage like him when she's so close and constantly moving, constantly trying to get in a solid enough hit to break his magical focus.

And it's all thanks to Lenora that Arché can reach him at all. She's in the *sky*. That should be outlandish, but magic lets the impossible become possible.

When the Prophet calls for his dogs, Arché knows their time is limited. She cannot fight him *and* protect Lenora, and Lenora can't sustain this *and* defend herself.

There is no choice for Arché to keep her eyes on the Prophet, and only the Prophet. Not the burning caravans below, where her mother is still trapped. Not the fray where her brother, her little brother who is now so much more grown than she'd ever wanted for him, fights for his life and that of their people, alongside the adults.

The Prophet's flame is immense and overwhelming, the flames licking at her ankles and calves around the edges of Lenora's shadow platform. Arché's never had any more fear of fire than is rational, but now, with an inferno blazing beneath her, she'll never see it the same way again.

A blast of sound comes from the central caravans, mixing with a groan of metal. Then, a howl tears into the night and something jolts through Arché's body. She knows that howl. She's been driven half mad by its absence on the past two full moons.

Kalé. She's free.

Arché cannot afford to look for her, not for a second, with the Prophet's flame-covered hands swiping at her shield. She is convinced he is trying to burn her to ash, or at least marr her face to the point of permanently removing her vision.

It's one thing to battle hatred and see its awful fruits. It is another to be dodging its every blow, to have it screaming in your face.

But then something wonderful happens. A dark blur knocks the Prophet from the sky, right in front of her.

He screams, barely managing to manifest new flame to slow his fall before he thuds to the ground with Kalé on top of him.

For the first time, Arché has a moment to survey the battlefield. Next to a warped central caravan stands Leahi, grimy and triumphant as she grins up at Arché and waves before running away towards the thick of the fight. Further that way are Andreas and Mira, inseparable, Andreas leaping onto his foes and Mira moving with him, weaving around him, slamming a hand onto the Crusaders while keeping the other on Andreas, making the Crusaders scream as Andreas shudders with power.

Seeing them thriving has Arché whirling around to check on Lenora, who has one hand extended towards Arché's platform and the other towards a wall she's created to protect herself from a pair of Crusaders. Something she surely cannot sustain.

And one of them—the champion. The one Arché could not defeat, on that first day.

Arché leaps from her vantage point right on top of the other cultist, letting them take gravity's force from her fall and ignoring her own body's protest. Pain means so little now, when her blood can heal back so much with the time that will come later.

The Crusader she's landed on stares up at her through dazed eyes that manage to still hold disgust amidst the fear. Arché raises the arm that bears Crescent Light and brings it down hard.

The sound is awful, and they go still. Arché turns just in time to dodge the fall of the champion's new sword.

"You again," Arché growls. She will not forget the part they played in Rohan's death, and will certainly not let them touch another partner of hers ever again.

A loud clank from behind the champion is followed by a groan from Lenora.

"This armour is... comprehensive," she says with disbelief.

The champion whirls around toward her, and she jumps back, throwing up a small parrying shield of shadow at the last moment. Arché swings Crescent Light at the champion's back. The sound of metal on metal clangs horrendously but the champion barely flinches.

Back and forth, the champion swings the greatsword. Lenora grows her shield until it is half a sphere, giving her the coverage she needs but almost buckling under every powerful hit. Arché moves Crescent Light as fast as she can, knowing just as she did before that to make a mistake here might mean losing a limb.

Before, Arché had no chance. Tonight, Arché has the full moon and Lenora at her side. And no matter how the champion turns, to hit one of them, they must turn their back on the other. Arché and Lenora yank at the armour with their claws until there is a plate pulled out of place, just enough that they have a target.

Lenora's eyes flash with something, and this time when the champion swings at her, her shield flickers. Arché shouts with alarm, and the champion brings their sword up again as Lenora's eyes flick to Arché's with intention.

An opening.

Arché plunges her claw into the champion's exposed shoulder, and Lenora resummons her shield as the sword comes down, her pretense of failing power falling away.

The champion finally screams. Arché twists her claws and their arm shakes where it grips the sword. Lenora takes her shield and rolls the shadow over the sword's blade, wrapping it like cloth and tethering it to Lenora herself so that it has nowhere to go.

The scream turns to a furious bellow as the champion tries to lift their sword and finds it stuck. Lenora laughs with delight—until the champion's other gauntlet seizes her by the throat and squeezes.

"Let her go!" Arché growls. She furiously pulls at the armour to get the chance to hit the champion deeper, yanking it away until there is only cloth protecting their back.

Lenora scrambles for breath, kicking the champion to no avail. One of her hands twists in the air, as if trying to call her shadow. Nothing forms. Arché goes to claw at the champion's back again, and she breaks the skin through the cloth easily, but the champion barely grunts. Everything they have is focused on Lenora.

A singular, long, shadowy blade appears right above Arché's hand. It flickers as Arché takes hold of it, and she looks up at Lenora to see her gaze holding on despite her face beginning to change colour.

Arché takes the blade and plunges it into the left side of the champion's back, aiming right for the heart.

The grip on Lenora loosens. She hits the dirt, gasping. Arché twists the blade and the champion's body shudders, knees meeting the ground as blood pools from the wound. The greatsword clatters next to them as they and Lenora both fail to hold it up any longer.

Arché leaps over the champion to lift Lenora from the ground.

"Lenora?" she asks. The fight, the rest of the fight, it sings within her and they must get back to it, but her heart is in her arms.

"Help me drink," Lenora murmurs, and it takes Arché a moment to realise she's pointing at the fallen champion who is taking their last breaths.

Arché lowers her and yanks off the nearest gauntlet so Lenora can sink her teeth into their palm and drink deep. Her face flushes with colour within seconds, her grip on Arché tightening.

"Kalé—" Lenora says as soon as she's done and alert once again.

"Needs our help," Arché agrees.

They run to where walls of flame are licking the caravans, rising and falling in bursts of light and heat. The Prophet is on his feet, a bloody claw gash across his right cheek, screaming abuse and hurling fire at Kalé.

Arché has seen her mother on the sparring grounds. She has seen her mother wrestle on the full moon. Wrestled with her, even. She has never seen her mother like this.

Kalé is rage. Power. Ferocity and skill entwined in a deadly combination. She weaves around each blast of fire with footwork Arché could only dream of, gets in a slash at the Prophet, and back out before the next blast would catch her.

Lenora, next to Arché, begins to wave a cloak of shadow around herself and creeps away, around the caravans. The slight cover lets them get close without the Prophet noticing, with Kalé taking so much of his attention, and Arché is about to charge when a Crusader creeps behind Kalé with a sword ready to strike.

A shout catches in Arché's throat. An arrow hits the Crusader in the neck and sends them straight to the ground. Arché whirls around to see Alta, perched on one of the farthest caravans, a longbow as tall as them in position. They share a makeshift salute, and then Arché leaps into the fray with her mother.

The only thing keeping the Prophet afloat is the sheer amount of fire he can make at once. Once there are two enraged lycans on him, his focus is forced to split.

Kalé glances at Arché and gives her a feral grin before they descend on him with everything they have. Relentless. Unforgiving. Arché's shield comes up to deflect the worst of his fire, and Kalé spins into the space so that they are sharing the same breath behind Crescent Light's protection, the relic of their house holding mother and daughter safe for a moment.

Then, they force the Prophet back, staggering and fumbling to deflect their clawed strikes with blasts of flame.

He's turned from abuse to prayer.

"Everflame, protect me!" he shouts, as if his false faith can save him now. "Grant me the power to smite these transgressors, those who laugh at the glory of the sun—"

He makes an odd gurgling sound. Claws of pure darkness protrude from his chest, impaling him from behind.

Lenora stands there, her masking shadows falling away, a look of cold satisfaction on her face.

"No," he gasps, clutching at his chest as the claws withdraw and blood begins to spread across his robe. "No!"

"I hope eternal punishment exists," Lenora tells him, as she walks around him to stand by Arché's side. "Just for you."

The Prophet's eyes are frantic, racing between all three of them with disbelief, before they snap onto something else. A point in mid-air, totally empty.

"You promised—" he begins to say, before horror annexes his face. "What—what are you?! You *lied*, you're not—"

Dark ichor leeks from his eyes, and his body jerks.

"What's happening?" Kalé asks. "Lenora, what did you do?"

"This isn't me!" Lenora says. "I don't know what's happening, or what he's seeing. All I wanted was to kill him and watch him realise he *failed*."

Arché traces his line of sight to find a trajectory, and sends a moonlight blast from Crescent Light towards it. It soars through the air as if nothing is there at all, but Arché swears something in the deepest recess of her mind twinges in the middle of its path.

By the time she looks back, the Prophet is lifeless on the ground. His eyes are entirely gone.

"Did something tell him it was the Everflame? Something that sent him after us?"

"Questions later," Kalé says. "Our people."

They hurry to assist in the rest of the battle, but as soon as the Crusaders realise the Prophet is gone, only a few continue to fight. The rest drop their weapons in bitter surrender. Leahi, upon seeing this, wavers on her feet and promptly loses consciousness only to be caught by Latod.

"She'll be alright," he signs to Arché. "I'll get her to the healers."

"Kalé!"

Alta pushes through and throws their bow on the ground before half climbing Kalé, legs around her waist while she holds them tight against her with one arm. Her other hand cups Alta's face, murmuring their name before nuzzling them all over. Alta giggles in a way that makes them sound twenty years younger.

"There it is," Arché says, chuckling to herself and shifting her gaze to find Andreas, who is grinning.

He stands with his arm around Mira's shoulders, leaning on her just enough for Arché to realise he's clutching a hastily bandage wound in his side.

"I'm going to check on my dad, and I'll find Erwin too, Lenora," Mira says, and Andreas nods but stares after her longingly as she walks away towards where the civilians were led out to safety.

Alta's feet hit the ground and they open their arms in invitation. "Come on. All of you."

Andreas rushes to hug them tightly, and Alta murmurs to him while beckoning to Arché with their free hand.

"You too, Lenora," they say.

"Lenora—" Kalé's confused voice trails off as her eyes move to where Lenora's hand sits in Arché's. "Oh."

"There's a lot to catch you up on," Arché says sheepishly.

"Hug first," Kalé insists, gesturing to them both.

Arché embraces her family in full for the first time in years, her chest shuddering with emotion it cannot contain, and sees tears in the corners of Lenora's eyes too as she is welcomed without further question.

Safe. They're finally all safe, and in her arms.

Every piece of happiness that night comes with something bitter or tragic to swallow alongside it. Not five minutes after the moment of feeling whole again, they begin combing through the battlefield.

The dead must be sorted. Crusaders onto a pyre, to be burned. Nightwalkers and Stag Battalion, laid out in honour and mourning.

Arché finds Sierra, the blacksmith, lying amidst the bodies of four Crusaders. Heart in her throat, Arché does not need to look for a pulse. She has shifted back to her mortal, blonde form even though the moon still shines. Only an absence of life could account for it.

Lenora is right behind her, and holds her tight as she sits and lets herself sob for the friend she shared so much with.

"Fuck this," Arché finally manages to say. "She was making armour for Rohan's father. It was so—she wasn't finished. She wasn't *finished*. None of them. Rohan was writing poems. Never told anyone but me. What the fuck is wrong with people—"

The despair is powerful. An anvil in her chest, refusing to budge, and the only thing stopping her from sinking through the ground and into somewhere else altogether is Lenora's arms around her.

"I know," Lenora whispers. "I know. But you said you want to be in control when you're like this, so breathe. Breathe in... breathe out. Breathe in... breathe out."

Arché knows she is right. Knows she is far too close to losing herself to howling at the moon. She follows Lenora's direction, for several minutes, and lets herself be comforted by soft hands and whispers and the warmth of the love she never expected.

She is not okay. But she will be. They all will be.

CHAPTER 44
LENORA

WITH MORNING COMES SLEEP for the nightwalkers—in the caravans for the vampires, and under the warmth of the sun for the lycans. Lenora finds herself restless. Many of the others seem to feel the same. Ulrich and his daughter Kirsa make rounds among the groups, using every bit of their energy to reach out to the Life Giver for magic to heal the wounded. Arché's family sit together with Raavi and a woozy Leahi on the edges as if additional daughters, all enjoying each other's company with soft laughter.

Erwin has no interest in rest and sticks by Lenora's side under the shelter of her large shadow parasol, for the first time that she can remember not looking sure of what to do with himself. After everything that's happened, she feels the same.

"You did it," says a voice from between nearby caravans.

Lenora whirls around to see Tunvra standing there, a few new scrapes across his neck and arms but otherwise unharmed. "Thanks to your help," she says to him. "I know your plan is part of why it all worked."

"Well, you didn't recruit me for my looks," he says with a good-natured roll of his eyes. "Let's be glad she listened to me. I know she doesn't like me."

Lenora shrugs. She's not about to bear Arché's internal struggles for him to scrutinise, even if it all really came down to poor timing. "You attacked us. It sets a weird precedent. She's got other things to worry about now. You did your part, you'll get your payment. And I won't eat you."

"About that—" Tunvra coughs when she raises an eyebrow. "The payment. Not the eating. Do you think there's a place back in your home for... someone like me?"

"Someone who only cares about money, you mean?" Lenora asks primly.

Tunvra makes a face. "Well... consider me reevaluating some of my decisions and priorities, in the midst of all this. Your people are inspiring. The kind of people I'd like to work alongside. I've been talking with the hunt leader, that Eliana. I could learn a lot from her. But she said you would have to vouch for me."

Lenora has to hold in a wince at the thought of Eliana and the Hunting Clan. There is no heir, a thing practically unheard of, a hole left in the town's hierarchy as well as their hearts. What happens now? Nikos's mothers are not the most ideal ages for bearing another child, and even if they did, the heir would be twenty years behind all the rest. It wouldn't work.

She cannot wonder about such things now, however.

"If you want a place, I'll make sure you get it," Lenora says, holding out a hand for him to shake. "You've earned it."

Tunvra nods, opens his mouth only to end up saying nothing, and walks off.

"Look at you, acting like a real future leader," Erwin says with a grin.

"Yeah," Lenora says, awkwardly. "You and Henri and I need to have a talk about that, when I get home."

Erwin is about to launch into an in-depth inquiry about what that could possibly mean when their path is blocked by two familiar brunets. Andreas and Alta stand shoulder to shoulder, with such glints in their eyes that Lenora can only think of the word 'cahoots'.

"Erwin, I think Mira had a magic question for you," Andreas says with the calm, trusting smile he is excellent at putting on.

Erwin blinks. "Right. I'll go and help her, then." He hurries off, glancing back only once.

"So," Andreas says, once Erwin is gone. "You and my sister."

Lenora blinks. "Yes."

"She's more delicate than she lets on," Alta adds.

"I know—"

"It's been taken advantage of before," Andreas says. "And even though she didn't want to talk about it, I'm not going to let her get hurt again."

Lenora crosses her arms and draws herself to her full height of five feet and four inches, barely in line with his shoulders as she lifts her chin to focus her gaze on him. "I love Arché. When she's unhappy, I feel like someone's carved out my heart and is smashing it to pieces. So I'm going to spend my whole life being the best partner I can be, and doing everything I can to make her smile every day. Is that alright with you?"

Alta bounces on their toes. "Yes! I knew it. I *knew* it."

"Just checking," Andreas says with a grin. "Welcome to the family." His grin slips slightly, his eyebrows coming together as he glances at Alta. "Wait a second, what happens with heir stuff if Arché's going to—"

Alta elbows him. "We don't need to worry about babies right now. I'm not ready to be a grandparent and you're not ready to be an uncle."

"Thanks," Lenora says with relief, even though a part of her warms at the idea of holding a child which is hers and Arché's, something bright and primal flaring before she squashes it back down.

Andreas is right. That line of thought will bring a shitshow of political questions for Concord traditions, and none of them need that right now. It is a problem for another day. Perhaps Lenora renouncing her own heir position will simplify it, or perhaps they can leverage the fact that their near single-handedly saved the town.

"So, still want to work with me on Shadow heir things when we get back to Concord?" Alta asks. "I'm ready to put some common sense into our record-keeping."

"Yeah, of course," Lenora replies without missing a beat.

"Good," Alta says. "I'm going to need lots of projects to keep me busy while I help with the rebuild so I don't start any more political drama or fistfights."

Lenora feels giggles take her, and it feels so good to laugh with them. Her future family. Things might be recent with Arché, in the grand scheme of things, but she is more certain about herself and Arché than she is about anything else, and everyone else is taking them just as seriously.

This is the life she wants, not a life forced upon her, and all at once she feels a little lighter.

CHAPTER 45
ARCHÉ

THE PROPHET'S TENT IS reduced to ashes. While the vision of it brings satisfaction, it leaves nowhere private enough for the conversation Arché and Kalé need to have. Instead, they opt to walk away and through the trees, Kalé thankfully asking no questions on the way after Arché told her they need to speak on something serious.

Once they are far enough away that no one will be in earshot, she stops and leans against a tree. A long breath of dread escapes her chest.

"What did you want to talk about?" Kalé asks, finally.

"Me." Arché swallows. "As your heir, you need to know. The journey here was... so complicated. Nothing like any of the rest of my life, and I was apart from all of you..."

"And yet, you saved all of us," Kalé says, gaze even and eyes warm.

"Yes," Arché says. "I did. But I also..." Tears prick her eyes as the words get stuck like she always knew they would. The shame burns so hot, but the truth must be spoken. "I had a lapse, Kalé. Last full moon. I lost control. No one was hurt, but I tore half a grove to shreds—I've always known that anger and upset hit me harder than most, that I can't get rid of them for hours, but it's never gotten the better of me during a transformation, never even come close, but I was so far from you all and felt like I was failing you—"

She doesn't need to say more. Kalé's eyes are wide, her smile gone from her face as her head tilts. The silence is agony.

"I'm so sorry," Arché whispers. "Gods, Kalé, I'm so so sorry—"

"No." Kalé stops and shakes herself, fists clenching in front of her. "You know what? No. No. I've had a long time to think while stuck in that caravan. And I think our teachings need work. Your brother threw himself at an enemy without thought for himself and was *maimed* for it, you almost lost yourself but only destroyed a few trees instead of hurting those around you and now think that you *failed*—"

She strides forward and pulls Arché into a fierce hug. Arché is rigid in her arms, uncertain.

"But we were told excuses don't matter," Arché whispers.

"You were in a situation without precedent, that you were not prepared for, almost alone, and under more burden than I could even imagine." Kalé's voice is soft as she holds her tighter. "And all you did was rip up a few trees. I'm so proud of you."

"...what?"

"You are my daughter. My heir. And my saviour. Concord's saviour. I am so, so proud of you. Don't you worry about the old rules. The council and I will be having a long conversation, when we get back."

Arché pulls back, alarmed. "Please don't tell them—"

"You have nothing to be ashamed of," Kalé says, gaze even. "But they will hear nothing of this from me. I have plenty else to speak on."

It hits her then, all of it, properly. *I'm so proud of you. You have nothing to be ashamed of.*

Arché cannot stop the tears that burst from her, the sensation of being absolutely overwhelmed by relief and shock and a validation she never thought to receive. Her mother's face shifts into something incredibly soft as she takes Arché back into her arms and holds her until the well of emotions run their course.

"I also didn't realise you were struggling with your emotions in general," Kalé murmurs. "These things are hereditary, not always written or spoken about enough, but it sounds exactly like what Alta struggles with. They have a tonic they take, when their emotions seize them like that and won't let go. It helps them calm down and process. We can get you some."

"Oh," Arché says. "How did I never realise they have that?"

"You and your brother have never really brought out any of those emotions in Alta," Kalé says. "I suppose they hoped you wouldn't have the same struggles. But... as we've all learned the hard way... hoping for something instead of preparing doesn't usually work."

When they finally let go of each other and begin making the walk back to camp, it is in the most comfortable silence they've ever shared. At least, until Kalé asks about Lenora, and Arché gets to blush and tell her the story from the start, with some of the more embarrassing details omitted.

Back at the camp, Lenora is sitting with Alta and Andreas, and Alta's eyes burn with questions but calm as they take stock of how Kalé's arm rests around Arché's waist.

"Good," Alta says. "Now. Can we talk about the wyvern in the room?"

"The what?" Kalé asks.

"I'm trying to figure out why no one's brought it up yet. Are we all too confused, or are we being extremely calm about it?"

"What are you talking about?" Arché asks.

"That *thing* right above your heads while it was doing something to that Prophet, the thing Arché tried to hit—"

"What thing? We couldn't see anything, but it seemed like he could, so I just tried to throw out a shot to see if something would happen," Arché says. "Then my head felt funny. Actually, that *was* really strange, wasn't it? Something invisible turning up to kill him right as we do?"

"Invisible," Alta repeated, with great skepticism until they glance around everyone else, especially Kalé. Bewilderment spreads over their features like an ominous fog.

"Not you seeing weird things no one else can again," Raavi groans, from the far end of the group. "First the moon thing and now this."

"What moon thing?" Kalé asks.

Alta makes a face so bizarre that Arché could spend a week trying to determine the meaning behind it and still fail to do so. They press their fingertip to the end of their nose, then release a huff of breath.

"Look, there isn't an easy way to say 'hey, I've started seeing a second moon on the full moon', alright?"

For the first time in Arché's life that she can remember, Kalé's calm is broken as her eyebrows shoot into her hairline. "A *second moon*?!"

"I haven't seen you! When the fuck would I have had time to mention it, if I'd put it in a letter you would have—"

"I am your *wife*! Your *werewolf wife*!"

Arché cannot help it. She laughs into her hand, too endeared by her parents to be able to contain her joy at being reunited with them. Lenora, Andreas and Leahi soon catch her mirth, and once Alta joins in, Kalé cannot keep her frown in place without it wavering, though she tries admirably.

Alta ends any further argument by grabbing Kalé by her breastplate and kissing her full on the lips. "Be cross with me later." When they pull back, they look at the whole group. "It's probably important that you know he was talking to a creature which looked like nothing I've ever seen. Dark, all the wrong shapes, with a hissing voice I couldn't understand. And I speak almost every language in the known world."

A creature like that... which all but one couldn't see. Something that might be connected to a second moon in the sky.

"And it sent him after Concord, *thinking* it was the Everflame that wanted it," Arché says, with horror. "But that... makes even less sense than a misguided zealot. What would some invisible monster want with us? None of the reasons the Crusaders gave would apply to a creature that's not even from the mortal plane."

"Unless it was about the town itself, and not its people," Alta says.

"But we're the only thing different to any other town," Andreas says, shaking his head. "This is giving me a headache. I'm going to find Mira. Let me know if you work out anything that makes sense."

"The nightwalkers are the only thing different... except the heart—"

"*Alta,*" Kalé says, so sharply that Arché would wince if she weren't so astounded. "Dear. How do you know about that? *I* didn't tell you. And that should give you some idea of the secrecy's importance."

Alta bites their tongue with the sheepishness of a child caught with a hand in a cookie jar. "Uh. I mean. Our son is right. No idea. No idea at all."

Kalé sighs, rolling her eyes with exasperated fondness. She glances at Arché, Lenora and Raavi. "We'll look into it. You all get your rest. You're not Leaders yet, you can enjoy your youth a while longer."

Arché has no particular inclination to argue the point. She puts her hand in Lenora's and beckons for Leahi and Raavi to follow as they find a caravan with room to lie down and get some rest.

"Do you need an escort?"

Wounds have been patched up. Dead Crusaders burned, dead night-walkers and battalion members magically preserved by Ulrich and Kirsa, who called on the Winter Wolf to stay the decay of the bodies for as long as he'll allow.

Dell's offer is kind, and Arché smiles at him.

"No, thank you," she says. "We can look after ourselves and our own, from here. You've got your own things to handle."

Dell nods, glancing at their long string of prisoners tied together and being watched over by Sheid and Ish. "Kesh will be waiting for our report. And then... Orsun. These Crusaders claim to have been acting independently. The Theocracy will have to convince us they didn't know anything of this, or there'll be trouble no one needs."

Everyone knows what happened the last time the Theocracy of Izirm went to war, a century and a half ago. Arché nods, unable to fully fathom what sort of travesty any sort of new conflict would mean.

"I'll stick to town politics," Arché says.

"I don't think you'll have any trouble with that, after all this." Dell grips her shoulder and gives it a reassuring squeeze. "I've watched how they look at you. It's how they look at all your leaders."

Arché swallows. "Terrifying thought, but thank you. We'll send recruits when we can, for the Battalion."

"There's no rush on that. We know you have other things to get sorted first. Tend to your people. Mend your home. The Battalion isn't going anywhere. Your recruits can come to Orsun to get signed up and tested for training requirements, when they're ready."

"Thank your uncle for me."

Dell nods, and turns to address the Battalion unit. "Time for us to move! Slow and steady, so the prisoners can keep up."

Several of the Battalion give Arché a small salute as they make their exit towards the Highway. The people of Concord will need more time, with malnourishment and battle wounds to hinder their start. Leahi is going to come along, to heal from similar mistreatment, at least until she's feeling up to heading to Orsun on her own.

Lenora comes to stand next to Arché, her fingers threading into Arché's easily as they watch the Battalion leave.

"You made an impression on them," Lenora notes.

"I was ready to do anything it took to get back my family, and the woman I love. I suppose they saw worth in that."

Lenora hums her agreement, leaning on Arché's shoulder and letting out a soft breath. "Now what?"

"Now? We go home."

EPILOGUE
LENORA

"You should drink something."

Arché offers her wrist, but Lenora shakes her head and grips Arché's hand instead, clinging to her fingers like a lifeline. Arché's bedroom has become a place of great comfort, more so than her own. Soon they'll get their own house, a place to start the rest of their lives together, but there is nowhere else she'd rather be tonight.

"I don't—I think I'll just be sick. And vomiting blood is the worst."

"After, then."

"...after. Promise."

It's almost midnight. They've been back in Concord for almost two months, rebuilding and gradually getting things as close to normal as possible. It's been a month since they got the news of what their parents and the other leaders have agreed on. Outlandish, almost terrifying, the sort of impossible someone cannot get their head around, when one has barely made peace with a situation.

Lenora herself had wondered. What would Concord do, without Nikos? Without an heir to one of the houses?

It turns out, in such an outlying, extreme case... they are going to try the extraordinary. Tonight, the clerics will attempt to bring Nikos Elianasen back from the dead. Such magic is rarely spoken of, and while Lenora has always known that the House of Clerics have great healing power... there is that and reviving a soul months dead. Spirits only linger for a week, as far as she understands it, and even then bringing people back is no easy feat. This is something else altogether.

But Nikos is needed. He was born to be the leader of the Hunting Clan, and there is no replacement. Concord needs him. So Concord is going to give their life to him, that which can be spared, which is not enough to revive anyone else.

Lenora is not sure exactly what that means, yet. But it involves the leaders, somehow. And at the centre of it, herself and Nikos' mothers.

"What if I get it wrong?" Lenora whispers.

"They said they need you because you were so close to him," Arché says, sitting next to her and locking their fingers together. "You loved him as much as anyone. That tie, that'll be what helps. You can't get love wrong."

Lenora nods, feeling tears track down her cheeks. "I can't bear it. Not knowing if it's going to work. This *hope*—"

Arché holds her tight. "I'm here. No matter what happens tonight, I'm here."

Nothing about all this changes anything between her and Arché. Lenora is a one-person type of woman, and she will choose Arché day after day for the rest of their lives. But Nikos is dear to her, her best friend in the world, and her heart is in pieces for it.

When the time comes, they make their way to the cathedral, where all the leaders and heirs are gathered. Also present are the lycan hunters, who serve under the Hunting Clan, the one Nikos needs to lead. They were his friends and mentors, and sit with an anxious restlessness now.

The new leader of the House of Sentinels, Rohan's younger brother, nods to Arché as they pass him. He looks as uncomfortable as he seems out of place—one of the new generation forced into a role that wasn't supposed to be his.

How strange, how wrong, that only a matter of birth numbers and circumstance should dictate who stays dead and who may yet live. For all that Lenora wants Nikos back, it feels unfair to all the others who fell that night.

Lenora's mother, Archmage Amala, is speaking with Kalé, their backs turned to the approaching heirs.

"I went down there," Amala is murmuring. "Everything is as it ought to be."

"Thank the gods," Kalé replies. "Thank you, Amala." She glances back and smiles at the sight of Lenora and Arché. "Good. You're here."

"Where do I—" Lenora turns to look for Ulrich, and instead gets a glimpse of the Life Giver's shrine. Or rather, what is laid out in front of it.

Nikos. Dressed in tidy clothes different to the training garb he died in, looking more himself than he ought to, with how long his body had to decay. But then, if magic can bring life after death, reversing a few things on the surface must be much simpler.

All words catch in her throat.

Arché squeezes her hand and leads her forward. Waiting for them are Nikos's mothers, who look as awful as Lenora feels. They embrace her without thought.

"You can do this," Arché says. "All of you."

"If the volunteers can form a line," Ulrich calls. The leaders come in single-file, as well as most of their spouses including Alta, and several older members of the hunt.

Ulrich dips his fingers in oil and reaches out to anoint Eliana's forehead with a glistening rune. "May the life within you bring the fallen to rise once again."

He repeats the rune and prayer with each person in the line, and Arché is not sure why her parents never explained exactly what is happening. Each anointed person is directed by Kirsa to form a semi-circle around Nikos and join hands.

Once the semi-circle is complete, Eliana, Roxanni, and Lenora are directed to step inside it so that they are closest to Nikos.

"All you need to do is call to him, when it's time," Kirsa says to them with a smile. "He's in a different place now. We can do everything right, fill him with life energy again and call to him… but he has to choose to return. To you. To all of us."

It is not the time for questions, but Lenora cannot help asking: "Have you done this before?"

"The ritual has not been performed in over two centuries," Ulrich replies. "But the record of it is detailed and I have brought back someone who was deceased and not departed. This is no easy thing. But I trust myself, and I trust in *her* to help us, and I have every faith in the three of you. We're going to bring him home."

The ritual begins. While occasionally certain types of Disciplined or Innate mages can master vitality to the point of bringing a deceased spirit back into their body, only a Gifted mage can bring back someone departed, someone whose spirit has long since left the mortal plane. To reach beyond the mortal plane, one must have magic from beyond it, from the gods themselves or something almost as powerful.

"Great giver of Life, we beseech you to help us guide home a soul needed by his home," Ulrich says. "Taken from us by violence, his precious blood spilled when there is none like it left in this place. The blood of Concord, the heart of Concord, must beat as one, in all of its parts. Heal his body and help us find his soul, so that we might lead him back."

The runes around Nikos glow, and one by one so does each rune on the forehead of the volunteers. Last of all, the same gold fills Ulrich's eyes as he kneels and reaches over Nikos's body, smoothing the light over his skin and muscles, filling them back out, bringing shine to his hair where it splays around his head. Soft gasps from the circle of volunteers sound in Lenora's ears, but she cannot take her eyes off Nikos.

"Now," Kirsa says to Lenora and Nikos's mothers. "Call to him. One by one. Reach for him."

"Nikos," Eliana says, her sandy hair falling in strands over her face as she bends her head. "My sweet boy. My strong boy. Please come back to us."

"We wouldn't ask if we didn't think you were well and truly unfinished," Roxanni adds. "We know there are so many things you wished to do, and see. Our house feels too empty, without you."

They look to Lenora.

"I want to laugh with you again, and tell you everything you've missed," Lenora says, kneeling and reaching her hand out to him, trying to feel the magic or him, or anything. "I think—I think you'd be really proud of me. I want you to come back so I can be proud of you too. Please, Nikos… come home to us."

The air is still. The cathedral is so silent, one could hear a mouse squeak. The golden magic floats over Nikos, unchanging, and Lenora meets Kirsa's eyes and is horrified to see doubt in them.

No. No no no.

A gasp comes from the floor. Nikos comes back into the world of the living with a jerk and a yell, clutching his chest.

"*What—*"

"Peace, dearest," Eliana says, eyes shining with tears. "You're safe now."

His mothers embrace him, and he leans into it on instinct, eyes dazed and skimming over the room until they find Lenora. He murmurs her name and she cannot help the sob that comes from her throat, hearing what was once lost to tragedy.

A small noise, a hum of faint irritation, distracts Lenora momentarily by triggering a response in her body long engrained since her early teens. She glances at her mother and blinks, trying to work out what could have drawn such a noise from her at a time like this. Then, as Amala's eyes narrow toward the strand of grey hair between her fingers, it sinks in. There had been a suspicious absence of grey hairs on her mother's head before.

Lenora looks around the circle. Each of the volunteers are glancing at each other, most softly remarking on new grey hairs or laughter lines with fascination.

May the life within you bring the fallen to rise once again. Volunteers. The cost of the resurrection, the reason it can only be afforded in absolute necessity, is the life of others.

"What happened?" Nikos asks. His hand has found his way back to his chest, while his eyes are locked with Lenora's the moment her eyes return to him, and she can picture the sword sticking through it so clearly she has to wonder if he is remembering it the same. "I jumped in front of you."

Lenora nods. She tells him, as the volunteers back away to give space and the rest of the crowd disperse. She tells him of the attack, of her escape with Arché. His mothers give their own account of being rounded into the caravans and taken on the road with the Crusade.

By the time the tale is concluded, he has fixed his gaze to the stones covered in runes.

"Who else?" he asks, at the end.

"Who else... what?"

"Died, and came back."

His mothers share an uncertain glance. "No one else, dearest," Eliana says quietly. "Our clan has no other heir. It was deemed necessary... but too costly for anyone else."

Behind them, Ulrich collapses to the floor, making Kirsa immediately request help moving him to a bed to rest. Arché and Aleka, who had lingered near the door of the cathedral, come to assist.

"Nikos," Kirsa says, once assured that Arché has a good hold on Ulrich. "Aleka and I have some tests to run on you, to check everything is as it should be. We don't want to find out three weeks down the line that your liver isn't working, or something."

Nikos winces. "I—yeah, that makes sense." He gets to his feet and gives Lenora a wane smile. "I'll find you after?"

Lenora pulls him into a hug, their first in too long, and he squeezes her back with everything he has.

"See you soon."

Arché emerges from the chapel infirmary where she'd taken Ulrich and joins Lenora as she walks out to the cathedral garden. They sit beneath the largest tree, and Lenora lies with her head in Arché's lap, drinking blood from her wrist until strength returns to her.

The fear is mostly gone, but will not completely abide until she is sure the resurrection has not had any complications. Once sated, Lenora curls herself against Arché, resting her head in the crook of her shoulder, letting Arché's hand smooth over her hair. Little by little, calm and hope begin to sink in.

It's the better part of an hour before Nikos emerges from the side exit, still adjusting his shirt collar and glancing around self-consciously before spotting her. His body relaxes, but the closer he gets, the higher his eyebrows lift.

Lenora realises what he is seeing, what she left out of the story of Concord's attack and rescue.

"Months, you said," Nikos says, coming to sit next to them on the grass. "And in those months…"

Lenora feels blood rush to her cheeks. "Um. Yeah. Arché and I… bonded. While things were… you know."

"Sorry to say that I only go for women," Arché says to Nikos with a grin. "I thought you knew. Imagine my embarrassment when she mentioned you'd had a crush on me. What a waste of your time."

Nikos blinks, looks between the two of them, and begins to laugh. It transforms his face, from a gaunt and confused ghost to the vibrant young man they'd missed so dearly.

"Well, thank the gods I'm starting out my second life with all the important information for moving forward," he manages to gasp out.

They laugh with him, Lenora still leaning against Arché but reaching her hand out to Nikos for him to take and hold. His gaze warms all the further.

"I'm so happy for you both," he says, with a blinding smile. "Gods, what else have I missed?"

"I renounced my heir status," Lenora says. "I'm the chosen Shadow, with other things to do."

Nikos whistles, long and drawn out. "Right. So my new partner would be… wait, who's taking over from you? Erwin, or Henriette?"

"They'll decide any day now," Lenora says, not believing her own words a bit. "Or fight to the death. They keep joking about it, but they'll have to if they don't stop fucking around."

"Right, so you've used these months to steal the girl I liked and fob me off on one of your siblings, brilliant," he says, only to laugh when she opens her mouth to argue. "I'm joking, the technicalities aren't your fault. It'll all be fine." Uncertainty seizes his frame, betraying him, and Lenora squeezes his hand. "It's just... a lot to take in."

"Take all the time you need," Lenora says.

"They said I can take weeks, or months, if it's what I need," he says, glancing back towards the cathedral. "No rush about going back to the hunt. Keeping myself safe is the most important thing, or something like that."

"That makes sense," Arché says. "Given what it took to bring you back."

"Yeah." Nikos sighs. "I don't know. I've been back for an hour, and already it feels like... people are looking at me different."

"You just came back from the dead," Lenora says. "People will be amazed, for a while."

"No, I know, I just—nevermind." He rubs his temples and winces. "Hopefully this headache goes away soon."

There is a long silence, where Lenora finds herself worrying for him, before having to remind herself that being wrenched back to life is never going to be a peaceful or easy process.

In the quiet, Nikos looks over from head to toe, his head tilting.

"You're different," he says, with a soft awe. "You're more you. Looking at the world with your chin up. Choosing your own path. You don't need me anymore."

"Not in the way I used to," Lenora says. "But I need my best friend. Always."

Nikos shuffles closer, and Lenora finds her solace with him on one side and Arché on the other. The friend chosen for her, taken and now returned, and the love she chose for herself.

Something in Lenora's heart releases, one final knot, and in the deep of the night, she finally understands the meaning of the word peace.

THE END

NIGHTWALKERS OF CONCORD
CONTINUES WITH NIKOS
IN
A VERDANT VENDETTA

A NOTE TO MY LESBIAN READERS

Sapphic love stories are my one true passion and the majority of my future book plans. I love being able to share them with you.

I do however have stories I want to tell that relate to my identity as a bisexual woman, and I know some of these stories are not necessarily ones you'll want to read. The next two books of the Nightwalkers of Concord are the main cases of this: they're both bi4bi m/f stories. I'll be delighted if you join me for those books, but I do not expect it.

In order to be able to make it easy for you to know what stories of mine are ones for us to share, I'm going to be posting most of my future sapphic romantasy stories as serials online first. I will ONLY do this with the sapphic stories so I can provide this consistency for you if you choose to subscribe to or follow my serials.

My newsletter will provide updates on this as I'm hoping to start posting my first serial early-ish 2025, and I hope you can follow me there.

FUTURE WORK
NIGHTWALKERS, SERIALS, NOVELLAS (OH MY!)

THE BEST WAY TO stay up to date with my future stories, such as the next book in this series or my sapphic serials, is through my email newsletter! You can use the QR code below to go to the newsletter signup, and you'll get my newsletter exclusive free novelette, a fantasy mystery called *The Curious Matter of Myron Manor.*

You can find me on Instagram, Threads and TikTok as @aimeedonnellanwrites, and on BlueSky as @aimeedonnellan.bsky.social! My Twitter account has been cleared out and will be updates only due to the change in policy with generative AI.

ALSO BY AIMEE DONNELLAN

Find out what Arché meant by the whole world knowing what happened the last time Izirm got involved in a conflict by jumping almost 150 years back and into the Dragon War...

CATASTROPHE INCOMING

(Episodic novella series – fantasy adventure)

OUT NOW

The Chase Begins

The Collection Awakens

The Survivor Stands

The Labyrinth Beckons

COMING SOON

The Spirit Torments

and more!

Acknowledgements

I really enjoy thinking about how this story began as a whimsical explo-ration of some fantasy subversions ("hey, what if werewolves and vampires were *friends* and made a town together?") and became a love story and journey I couldn't be more proud of.

I owe Lenora, the world of Aboria, the community of Kanin, and every incredible detail to my amazing partner and co-creator Ty. Thank you for everything, always. I had the best time falling for you again, through these two characters, and I am excited to do it with the next story, and the next. You've been with me through every up and down of this process of tackling a larger book and everything that comes with it, and none of it would have been possible without your support.

Sio, thank you for always being my cheerleader and being proud of each step I take on this wild journey.

Livvy, thank you for sharing your vampires with me. I hope you've enjoyed mine! Here's to continuing to use our powerful creative energy to make the world a more entertaining, more queer place.

To my amazing beta team: Senka, Bryanna, Issy, Anna, Norah, Sophie, Rhiannon. You helped make this book make sense and hit all the right notes. I am endlessly grateful.

Quinn, your hype and understanding of what I am trying to do when you're editing my books is invaluable. Thanks for everything!

Beau, I'm not sure you'll read this, but your friendship and guidance have met so much to me this year. I appreciate your patience with my many questions and chaotic nature, and have loved your enthusiastic energy that matches mine so well. Thank you.

To Cait, Keanna and Pragnya: I apologise for how this book practically made me fall off the grid and out of our group chat, but your support for everything I have been doing has meant the world. I cannot wait to be reading your books one day!

Kai and Kyara: life is winning the battle against our messenger chat, but one day *we* will win. Manifesting some chill energy for us soon.

Thank you to Kate for your incredible art as always, and thank you to Rachel, Quinn, Bryanna and Senka for the team effort on getting the typography to where it needed to go.

And lastly, to everyone who has helped hype this book on socials, mentioned it to a friend, or just generally spread the queer love around... you're amazing and thank you so much for being a part of this.

HOW TO SUPPORT INDEPENDENT AUTHORS

Firstly, thank you again for buying and reading this book. Secondly, I'd really appreciate it if you're able to leave a review on Goodreads and Amazon. Hitting a certain number of reviews can boost the book's visibility.

In regards to other ways you can help get the word out about this book, talking about it to friends and/or on social media all helps, and you can also request it at your local library so that brand new people can discover it!

Any and all of these things would go a long way to help me, or any other independent authors you know with their books. We appreciate your support of us and the stories we are trying to share with our communities.